MW00716178

Edward Henry Bickersteth

Yesterday, To-Day, and for Ever

Edward Henry Bickersteth

Yesterday, To-Day, and for Ever

Reprint of the original, first published in 1871.

1st Edition 2022 | ISBN: 978-3-36812-669-8

Verlag (Publisher): Outlook Verlag GmbH, Zeilweg 44, 60439 Frankfurt, Deutschland
Vertretungsberechtigt (Authorized to represent): E. Roepke, Zeilweg 44, 60439 Frankfurt, Deutschland
Druck (Print): Books on Demand GmbH, In de Tarpen 42, 22848 Norderstedt, Deutschland

OPINIONS OF THE BRITISH PRESS.

"We feel assured that the reader will feel grateful to us for having made him acquainted with the most simple, the richest, and the most perfect sacred poem which recent days have produced. Less pompous and pretentious, more tender and more powerful, with greater sweetness and Christian modesty than Montgomery; less lugubrious and heavy than Graeme; and less labored, sententious, and didactic than Pollok, Mr. Bickersteth leads us by the hand like his own guide Oriel." — *Morning Advertiser*, January 1, 1867.

"This is a remarkable poem, and one likely to attract a great deal of attention. While antique in form, it is modern in spirit, and is animated by an enthusiasm which carries the reader along without any sense of weariness. . . . . In no English poem have we met with so perfect an imagination of what the intermediate state might be. . . . . As a poetical vision the picture is perfect. . . . . The ninth, tenth, and eleventh books are, to our minds, the best, opening up fresh ground, and containing the highest flights of imagination." — *The Imperial Review*, January 19, 1867.

"The epic narrative begins with an account of the creation of angels and men: here he treads the same ground as Milton, treating the subject differently and with great power. . . . . Mr. Bickersteth, like Shelley, is most at home in celestial scenery. . . . . The last four books are to our mind the best. Their subjects are more untrodden, and they are full of bold imagination. As materialized theology in its most poetical form, we must give them the highest praise. . . . . It is a poem worth reading, worthy of attentive study; full of noble thoughts, beautiful diction, and high imagination; and, more than all, penetrated with a spirit of holiness which cannot fail to purify and sanctify the mind of the reader." — *The Standard* and *The Morning Herald*, January 25, 1867

"If any poem is destined to endure in the companionship of Milton's hitherto matchless epic, we believe it will be ' *Yesterday, Today, and For Ever.*' " — *The Globe*, February 4, 1867.

"The poem opens very naturally, describing the narrator's death. . . . . The actual divorce of soul and body is conceived and expressed with masterly effect. . . . . In the second book there are some portions of extreme beauty. . . . . The meeting of the soul and the Lord is, we think, admirably pictured, the deep reverential awe on the one side, the condescending love on the other. . . . . We think the character of Lucifer very graphically drawn. First of created beings, to him the Son intrusts the vice-regency of earth; and the subtle questionings and uncertain sophistry by which his mind fluctuating is overpowered and led away from its allegiance to a fancied independence are sketched with a skilful hand. . . . . Mr. Bickersteth's work is not a crude effusion. He tells us that it has been elaborated in his mind through many years; and we will say that his labor has not been in vain. He has produced a poem which we believe will be largely read, which will dwell in the memory of those who read it, and which will leave often, we doubt not, holy thoughts in the hearts of those who have followed him from the deathbed of weakness on to the endless life of power in the joyful mansions of our Father's house." — *Christian Observer*, May, 1867.

"The whole first book, 'The Seer's death and descent to Hades,' is really of high merit. . . . . The same strain of felicitous description prevails in the second book, 'The Paradise of the Blessed Dead.' The descriptions of the Seer's meeting with his lost babes and with the glorified from among his own flock are very beautiful." — *The Contemporary Review*, June, 1867.

YESTERDAY, TO-DAY,

AND FOR EVER:

A Poem, in Twelve Books,

BY

ℛℯⅴ. EDWARD HENRY BICKERSTETH, M.A.,

*Incumbent of Christ Church, Hampstead, and
Chaplain to the Bishop of Ripon.*

NEW YORK:

ROBERT CARTER & BROTHERS,

580 BROADWAY.

1871.

CAMBRIDGE:
PRESS OF JOHN WILSON AND SON.

PREFACE.

THE design of the following Poem has been laid up in my heart for more than twenty years. Other claims, however, prevented me from seriously undertaking the work until little more than two years ago. But then the deep conviction that those solemn events, to which the latter books of my poem relate, were already beginning to cast their prophetic lights and shadows on the world, constrained me to make the attempt. If it may please God to awaken any minds to deeper thought on things unseen and eternal, by this humble effort to combine some of the pictorial teaching supplied by His most holy Word, it will be the answer to many prayers.

E. H. B.

HAMPSTEAD, LONDON,
September, 1866.

Note to the Second Edition.

I have taken advantage of a second edition to introduce, at the suggestion of a friend, a few lines (Book ix. 490—495, and Book xi. 262—288), and also to make a few verbal alterations and corrections.

August, 1867.

Note to the Third Edition.

The author cannot allow a third, and now stereotyped, edition of this Poem to issue from the press without expressing his very grateful sense of the acceptance which this work has found in England and America. Assurances of the deep interest, which the thoughts suggested in these pages have kindled or confirmed in many hearts, have reached him from aged pilgrims at whose feet he would gladly sit and learn, from laborers who are bearing the burden and heat of the day, and from many sufferers and mourners in homes of sorrow and bereavement. The reaping has already far exceeded any toil of the Sower, who can only pray that He, whose prerogative it is to multiply the seed sown, may graciously water it with the dew of His blessing.

January, 1869.

CONTENTS.

YESTERDAY, TO-DAY, AND

FOR EVER.

—◆—

Book First.

THE SEER'S DEATH, AND DESCENT TO HADES.

THE last day of my earthly pilgrimage
Was closing; and the end was peace: for, as
The sunset glory on the hills grew pale,
The burning fever left me — I was free
From pain — albeit my strength was ebbing fast.
And quickly' as dreams, though not confusedly,
The landscapes of my life before me rose,
From the first breath of dewy morn to that
Its sultry afternoon.   Nor seem'd my past,
As often heretofore in retrospect,   10
A fragmentary discontinuous whole,
But one and indivisible, — a brief
Short journey, only steepest at the last.

Seven nights agone the message came for me.
The midnight chimes had struck: the echoes sank
Far in the distance, and the air grew still, —
A strange oppressive stillness. In the woods
The leaves were motionless, and on the grass
Unwavering the moonlight shadows slept,
And I was communing with solitude,   20
And listening to the silence; when I thought
A voice, as of an angel, spake to me,
" Thy time is come, prepare to meet thy God."
'Twas gently spoken, yet a sudden chill
Struck to my heart; for I was scarcely more
Than midway on life's pathway, nor had thought
For long years to lay down my pilgrim's staff,
Unless the Bridegroom's voice were heard in heaven.
And was I now already summon'd home?
I ask'd, and half incredulously gazed   30
Upon the crystal of that starlit sky,
Until again within my spirit's depths
I seem'd to hear that subtle spiritual voice,
" Seven days, and thou shalt enter into rest."
And then I knew it was no idle dream,
I felt that One was standing by me, whom
I saw not, and with trembling lips replied,
" Thou calledst me, O Lord, and here am I."

    That night I spent in prayer. The lamp that hung
Suspended in my chamber slowly paled   40
And flicker'd in its socket. But my soul
Was lit up with a clearer purer light,

The daybreak of a near eternity,
Which cast its penetrating beams across
The isthmus of my life, and fringed with gold
The mists of childhood, and reveal'd beyond
The outline of the everlasting hills.
'Twas more than half a jubilee of years
Since first I knelt a suppliant at the throne
Of mercy, and bewail'd my sins, and heard   50
The voice of absolution, " Go in peace: "
And daily since that birth-time of my soul
Had I found shelter at the feet of Christ.
But in the glory of that light, aware
Of the immediate presence of my God,
I saw myself, as I had never seen,
Polluted and undone: and, clothed in shame,
Awestruck, like Peter, cried aloud, " Depart
From me, who am a sinful man, O Lord."
But, as I raised my eye to read His will,   60
I saw, as never hitherto, the cross
Irradiated with celestial light,
And love divine, unutterable, pour'd
Around the form of Him who hung thereon.
I gazed entranced, enraptured; and anew
l wash'd the dark stains of my travelling dress
White in the fountain of His blood; and then,
Methought, He laid His hand upon my head,
And whisper'd, " Go in peace, and sin no more."
And the words seem'd to linger in the air,   70
Whether an angel caught them up or not
I know not, but they seem'd to float around me,

" Sin no more, weary pilgrim, sin no more,
No more at all for ever, sin no more."

And thus long hours of peace and prayer and praise
Pass'd noiselessly, as gliding slumber; though
That night was more to me than years of life,
If life be measured, its true gauge, by love.
I feasted upon love ; I drank, I breathed
Nothing but love. But when the morning came   80
I knew no more what pass'd around me: earth
Sank from my view, and yet I was not free
To climb the heavens. As when the aeronaut,
Borne sunward on his too adventurous car,
At length emerging from the seas of mist
(Which circumfused long while about his path
Clung darkling, but now roll in lucid waves
Of clouds beneath him), hovers there a while,
A stranger in that crystal atmosphere,
Exiled from earth, and yet not wing'd for heaven: 90
So in my fever dreams I seem'd to hang
On the far confines of the world of sense.
Unconscious of the lapse of day or night,
If lonely or in loved society ;
But conscious of my spirit's fellowship
With the Eternal Spirit. God was there:
I knew it: I was with Him. And meanwhile
His angel gently loosen'd all the cords
Of my frail tabernacle, and the tent
Flutter'd to every breeze.   100

Six days I lay
In that strange borderland, so she, who watch'd
Unwearied as an angel day and night
Beside my pillow, told me when I woke
From the fruition of celestial love
To drink in, like a thirsty traveller,
The sweetness of her human love once more:—
Never so sweet as now. They sin who deem
There can be discord betwixt love and love.
Six days had pass'd; and now the morning sun
Bore through the open casement all the glow   110
Of summer; more than six days out of seven
Since that strange midnight summons:—so I knew
My hours were number'd, and that I should see
No other sunrise on this weary world;
And gently said, intolerant of suspense,
" My wife, my darling, I am going home;
God wills it, darling, — going home to night."
Sorely I fear'd the first shock of my words
Upon the tenderest of human hearts,
A wife's, a mother's heart. But softly laying   120
Her hand upon my burning brow, she said,
" I know it all, beloved husband. God
Hath spoken to me also, and hath given
These brief hours to my wrestling prayers. Enough,
To-morrow and all after-life for tears,
To-day and all eternity for love."

And leaning then her ear close to my lips,
Her soft cheek touching mine, we spoke or thought

(A broken word was clue to many thoughts)
Of things long past, and holy memories, 130
That glow'd in sunlight through the mist of years,
Or cast their solemn shadow o'er the hills ;
Those anniversaries, that sanctify
So many Sabbaths in a pilgrim's life :
The day that interlink'd her heart with mine,
Our ramble through a laurel greenery,
My soul full charged with its own feelings, nor
Well able to restrain their passionate flow
Into the waveless mirror of her love ;
Not able long. The intervening years 140
Of tried affection and of hope deferr'd ;
And then the plucking of the tree of life,
With its ambrosial fruitage and fresh flowers,
Upon our bridal day. We took and ate
And lived — God's smile upon us. Then our home,
All fragrant with parental thoughtfulness,
Close nestling by the village church, my charge :
Say rather ours : our lambs, our flock, our fold,
For I was shepherd, and she shepherdess,
And we, as one, were married to one spouse. 150
Indissoluble bond ! names, faces, hearts
Came back upon us fresh as yesterday :
The precious seed not seldom sown with tears,
The golden grain that ripen'd here and there,
A wave-sheaf of our husbandry. And link'd
With all the memories of pastoral life
The birth-days of our children, those dear ties
That bound us ever closer each to each.

Us to our people, them and us to God.
Nor births alone: for twice the gates of pearl   160
Had open'd on their musical hinges, while
The angels ministrant had ta'en each time
A little tender ewe-lamb from our arms,
To nurture it, so Jesus will'd, in heaven.
And then we spoke of other blessed dead,
Akin to us by blood, akin by grace,
And friends, and fellow-travellers, whose names
Sprang to our eager lips spontaneously:
Their forms that hour were present as when last
We wrung their hands upon the shore of time.   170
And ever the horizon grew more clear
And wider as we gazed.   Our little life
Was interwoven with the universe
Of God's eternal counsels.   We were part
Of the whole family in heaven and earth ;
The many were in heaven, the few on earth ;
Part of the mighty host whose foremost ranks
Long since had cross'd the river, and had pitch'd
Their tents upon the everlasting hills.
How shrunken Jordan seem'd.   180

                         The day wore fast.
My wife look'd up.   I saw her anxious eye
Measuring the shadows more aslant, and read
Her thought, and whisper'd, " Call them to us."   Soon
Our children cluster'd round my bed.   Dear hearts, —
The eldest only in the bloom of spring,
The next in earliest prime of youth, the rest

In order opening like forest flowers,
A wreath of girls with brothers intertwined,
Down to the rosebud in the nurse's arms.
They were but learners in the infant school   190
Of sorrow, and were scarcely able yet
To spell its simplest signs.   But when they caught
The meaning of their mother's words, and knew
That I was going to leave them, one low sob
Broke from them, like the sighing of the wind
That frets the bosom of a silver lake
Before a tempest.   Each on the other look'd ;
And every lip trembled ; and tears, hot tears,
Gush'd forth, and quickly would have drench'd all eyes.
But fearing their most innocent distress   200
Would, like an irresistible tide, break down
The barrier of their mother's holy calm,
I raised my head upon the pillow, saying,

" Weep not, my children, that your father's work
Is over, and his travelling days are done.
For I am going to our happy home,
Jerusalem the golden, of which we
On Sabbath evenings have so often sung,
And wish'd the weary interval away
That lay betwixt us and its pearly gates.   210
You must not weep for me.   Nor for yourselves,
Nor for your mother grieve too bitterly.
The Father of the fatherless will be
Your Father and your God.   You know who says,
' I will not leave you orphans.'   He will send

The Blessed Comforter to comfort you,
And soon will come and take you to Himself,
That where He is there you may also be
In glory.   And the time I know is short.
The Bridegroom cometh quickly.   Let your loins   220
Be girded, and your lamps be trimm'd alway.
Methinks your earthly sojourn will be closed,
Not like your father's with the sleep of death,
But by the archangel's clarion.   Be it so :
Or be it that ye walk the pilgrim's course
To life's far bourn, the God of Israel
Will shield you, and will give you bread to eat
And raiment to put on, until you reach
Your Father's house in peace.

                           " Come here, my child,
My firstborn, who hast ever been to me   230
Thy mother's image, doubly blessed thus ;
Subdue thy grief that thou may'st solace hers,
And with a daughter's heavenly art reflect
Her former brightness on a widow's heart :
I leave it thee thy charge.   And thou, my boy,
Son, brother, father, pastor thou must be,
And with a thoughtfulness beyond thy years
Enfold thy mother in thy filial love,
As the leaves cluster round a shaken rose ;
And shade thy sisters and thy brothers, as   240
A granite wall the flowers.   Thy hour is come
To take the banner of the cross : it was
Thy sainted grandsire's once, and fearlessly

2

He bore it in the thickest fight, and then
Entrusted it to my unequal hands.
Now it is thine. I leave it thee to guard
And part from only with thy parting breath.

"Come near to me, my children. Let the hand
That traced the cross upon your infant brow,
Rest on your heads once more: come hither, nurse, 250
Upon my babe, my tenderest blossom first,
God bless him: and the others, dear, dear lambs,
On each and all a father's blessing abide.
And Thou, Great Shepherd of the flock, look down
In mercy from Thy throne of heavenly grace
On those whom Thou hast given me. From Thy hand
I first received them, and to Thee again,
Thee only, I resign them. Let not one
Be wanting in the day Thou countest up
The jewels in Thy diadem of saints.   260
I ask not for the glories of the world,
I ask not freedom from its weariness
Of daily toil: but, O Lord Jesu Christ,
Let Thy omnipotent prayer prevail for them,
And keep them from the evil. In the hour
Of trial, when the subtle tempter's voice
Sounds like a seraph's, and no human friend
Is nigh, let my words live before Thee then,
And hide my lambs beneath Thy shadowing wings,
And keep them as the apple of Thine eye: 270
My prayers are ended, if Thy will be done
In them and by them: till at last we meet

Within the mansions of our Father's house,
A circle never to be sunder'd more,
No broken link, a family in heaven."

And now the sun had sunk behind the hills;
The twilight deepen'd; and the stars peep'd forth
Betwixt the drapery of silver clouds.
And the nurse understood the sign I gave,
And led the younger children from my room;   280
And what with weeping and with weariness
It was not long before they slept. The rest
Silently praying lean'd against the foot
Of my low couch. Never a word they spoke,
But look'd their inexpressible love, till thoughts
Of luminous stars, and large and loving eyes,
Were strangely blended in a dream that came
Enamell'd with rich pictures of my life,
And floated like a golden mist away.

The time-piece striking nine recall'd me; for   290
I felt the involuntary thrill it sent
Through my wife's heart, as kneeling by my side
She clung: and almost unawares my lips
Repeated words she loved in other days
Though long forgotten — "All thine own on earth,
Beloved, and in glory all thine own."
They open'd a deep fountain; and her tears
Fell quick as rain upon my hand, — hot tears
On a cold hand, — so sluggishly my blood
Crept now. And I said, " Let the children read   300

Some of God's words." All others would have jarr'd
That night, but His are tender in their strength,
And in their very tenderness are strong.
And straightway, like a chime of evening bells
Melodiously o'er broken waters borne,
They read in a low voice most musical
Some fragments of the book of life.

                               The first
Chose words she loved from David's pastoral, —
" The Lord my Shepherd is; I shall not want:
He leads me in green pastures, and beside   310
Still waters; and restores my soul to tread
For His name's sake the paths of righteousness.
Yea, though I walk the shadowy vale of death,
I fear not; Thou art with me; and Thy crook
It comforts me. My table is prepared
In presence of my enemies: my head
Thou, Lord, anointest; and my cup o'erflows.
Goodness and mercy shall attend my steps,
And in Thy house I shall for ever dwell."

    She ceased; and then another from the Psalm   320
Of him, who call'd his son " a stranger here,"
Read, " Thou, O Lord, hast been our dwelling-place
From age to age, the everlasting Thou,"
Until he linger'd on the children's prayer,
" O satisfy us early with Thy love
That we may live rejoicing all our days."

Methinks, they hardly caught my low amen,
For almost without pause a gentle girl,
With a voice tremulous for tears not shed,
Repeated, for she knew them, the dear words   330
Of Jesus on the night He was betray'd,
" Let not your heart be troubled ; ye believe
In God . . ." nor ceased till she had pleaded all
The eloquence of His High-priestly prayer.

And then my son began, " Now is Christ risen,
The first-fruits of the dead who sleep in Him."
The words burnt brightly' as beacon fires at night,
Till as he utter'd " This corruptible
Must put on incorruption, and this mortal
Its immortality ; " and ask'd in tones   340
Where faith with feeling wrestled and prevail'd,
" Where is thy sting, O Death ! and where, O Grave,
Thy victory ? " we heard, but heeded not,
The warning that another hour had pass'd,
For our responsive hearts were echoing " Thanks
To God who giveth us the victory ! "
And now for the last time the manna fell
Around my pilgrim tent. My eldest child
Turned with true instinct to our home, and read
The vision of the new Jerusalem,   350
The Bridal city, built of crystal gold
And bright with jewels, whether real types
Or rather typical realities.
And, as she read, we often paused and spoke,
Though but as children speak, of things unseen ;

Until the closing words, " His servants there
Shall serve Him ; they shall see His face; His name
Writ in their forehead. And they need no sun
Or moon to shine upon them, for the Lord
Doth lighten them with uncreated light,   360
And they shall reign for ever and for ever."

Then there was silence : and my children knelt
Around my bed — our latest family prayer.
Listen — it is eleven striking. Then
I whisper'd to my wife, " The time is short ;
I hear the Spirit and the Bride say, ' Come,'
And Jesus answering, ' I come quickly.' Listen."
And as she wiped the death-dews from my brow,
She falter'd, " He is very near," and I
Could only faintly say, " Amen, amen."   370
And then my power of utterance was gone :
I beckon'd and was speechless: I was more
Than ankle deep in Jordan's icy stream.
My children stood upon its utmost verge,
Gazing imploringly, persuasively,
While the words, " Dear, dear father," now and then
Would drop, like dew, from their unconscious lips.
My gentle wife, with love stronger than death,
Was leaning over those cold gliding waves.
I heard them speaking, but could make no sign;   380
I saw them weeping, but could shed no tear ;
I felt their touch upon my flickering pulse,
Their breath upon my cheek, but I could give
No answering pressure to the fond hands press'd

In mine.   So rapidly the river-bed
Shelved downward, I had pass'd or almost pass'd
Beyond the interchange of loving signs
Into the very world of love itself.
The waters were about my knees; they wash'd
My loins; and still they deepen'd.   Unawares   390
I saw, I listen'd — who is He who speaks? —
A Presence and a Voice.   That Presence moved
Beside me like a cloud of glory; and
That Voice was like a silver trumpet, saying,
" Be of good comfort.   It is I.   Fear not."
And whether now the waters were less deep
Or I was borne upon invisible arms,
I know not; but methought my mortal robes
Now only brush'd the smoothly gliding stream,
And like the edges of a sunset cloud   400
The beatific land before me lay.
One long last look behind me: gradually
The figures faded on the shore of time,
And, as the passing bell of midnight struck,
One sob, one effort, and my spirit was free.

They err who tell us, that the spirit unclothed,
And from its mortal tabernacle loosed,
Has neither lineament of countenance,
Nor limit of ethereal mould, nor form
Of spiritual substance.   The Eternal Word,   410
Before He hung upon the Virgin's breasts,
Was wont to manifest Himself to men,
In visible similitude defined:

And, when on Calvary He gave up the ghost,
In that emancipated Spirit went forth,
And preach'd glad tidings to the souls below.
The angels are but spirits, a flame of fire,
And subtle as the viewless winds of heaven;
Yet are they each to the other visible,
And beautiful with those original forms   420
That crown'd the morn of their nativity.
Each has his several beauty. It is true
The changes that diversify their state,
Wrought with the speed of wishes at their will
And pleasure who are pleased as pleases God,
Are many as are the leaves and bloom and fruit
That shed new lustre on the orange groves
And vineyards of the south : but still remains
Their angel ideality the same,
As we confuse not orange-trees and vines.   430
And so the spirit inbreathed in human flesh,
By death divested of its mortal robes,
Retains its individual character,
Ay, and the very mould of its sojourn
Within this earthly tabernacle. Face
Answers to face, and limb to limb ; nor lacks
The saint immediate investiture
With saintly' apparel. Only then the mind
Which struggles here beneath this fleshly veil,
As the pure fire in a half polish'd gem —   440
Ruby or amethyst or diamond —
Imprison'd, when the veil is rent in twain,
Beams as with solar radiance forth, and sheds

Its glow o'er every motion, every look:
That which is born of spirit is spirit, and seems
All ear, all eye, all feeling, and all heart; —
A crystal shrine of life.

            And I was now
A spirit, new born into a spiritual world.
Half dreaming, half awake, I lay awhile
In an Elysium of repose: as glides   450
A vessel long beset with boisterous winds
Into some tranquil port, and all is still,
Except the liquid ripple round the keel:
So in a trance I lay. But gradually,
As wakes an infant from its rosy sleep
To find its mother keeping by its side
Enamour'd vigil, dreaming I awoke,
And slowly then bethought me whence I came
And what I was, and ask'd instinctively
" Where am I ? " And a gentle voice, in tones   460
More musically soft than those the wind
Elicits from Æolian harp or lute,
Made answer, " Brother, thou art by my side,
By me thy guardian angel, who have watch'd
Thy footsteps from the wicket gate of life,
And now am here to tend thy pathway home."
I turn'd to see who spake, and being turn'd
I saw two overshadowing wings that veil'd
The unknown speaker. Slowly they disclosed
A form of light which seem'd to rest on them,   470
So, to compare the things of earth and heaven,

As rests the body of the bird, which men
Call for delight the bird of Paradise,
Upon its waving feathers poised in air,
Feathers, or rather clouds of golden down,
With streamers thrown luxuriantly out
In all the wantonness of winged wealth.
Not otherwise behind that angel waved
His pinions tremulous with starry light,
Then droop'd close folded to his radiant side: 480
But, folded or diffuse, with equal ease
Buoyant he floated on the obedient air.
The very sight was melody; such grace
Flow'd in his lightest motion. Save his wings
The form was human in the spring of youth:
I guess'd a warrior by the fiery sword
Girt to his thigh; and yet his flowing robes,
White as if woven of the beams that fall
On the untrodden snows, bespoke a priest;
And his mysterious crown, a king: but when   490
Smiling he look'd on me, so much of love —
Pure, holy, unimaginable love —
In that one glance his spirit pour'd into mine;
Nor warrior then, nor priest, nor king he seem'd,
But only brother.

     And again he spoke,
"Before yon hills have caught the Eastern glow
Will they expect us at heaven's golden gates.
The road is long; but swifter than the beams
Of morning is the angelical convoy

Sent for thy escort home. Myself thy guide :   500
And with me other two, who on their hands
Shall bear thee as they bore blest Lazarus
Into his father's bosom, ready stand,
Waiting our summons. But, so pleases thee,
Ere we set forth, rise, brother, and look round
Upon the battle-field where thou hast fought
The fight of faith."

                 Immediately I rose,
My spiritual essence to my faintest will
Subservient, as is flame to wind, and gazed,
Myself invisible, around. O sight   510
Surpassing utterance, when the mists, that veil'd
That borderland of heaven and earth and hell,
Dispersed, or rather when my eyes became
Used to the mysteries of things unseen!
My dwelling had been situate beside
The myriads of a vast metropolis :
But now astonish'd I beheld, and lo!
There were more spirits than men, more habitants
Of the thin air than of the solid ground :
The firmament was quick with life. As when   520
The prophet's servant look'd from Dothan forth
On Syria's thronging multitudes, and saw,
His eyes being open'd at Elisha's prayer,
Chariots of fire by fiery horses drawn,
The squadrons of the sky around the seer
Encamping. Thus in numbers numberless
The hosts of darkness and of light appear'd

Thronging the air. They were not ranged for fight,
But mingled host with host, angels with men.
Nor was it easy to discern the lost   530
From the elect. There were no horned fiends
As some have fabled, no gaunt skeletons
Of naked horror; but the fallen wore,
Even as the holy angels, robes of light;
Nor did their ruin otherwise appear
Than in dark passions, envy, and pride, and hate,
Which like a brand upon their brow obscured
The lustre of angelic loveliness.
It was not open battle, might with might
Contesting; but uninterrupted war   540
Of heavenly faithfulness and hellish craft.
By every saint a holy watcher stood;
By some a company of blessed spirits;
Each had their ministry assign'd. And oft
From some superior chief the watchword pass'd,
Or warnings came of stratagems foreseen,
Or tidings from the court of glory sped
From lip to lip more quickly than the thoughts
Which men decipher from electric signs.
Far off their armor gleam'd. On the other hand 550
The spirits of darkness freely intermix'd
With all; innumerable legions arm'd;
And, baffled oft, to their respective lords
The thrones and principalities of hell
Repairing, better learn'd their cursed lore
To win or storm the ramparts of the heart
Except to treachery impregnable.

Around some dwellings, thick as locust-swarms,
I saw them cluster. Flush'd with wine there pass'd
A young man through the solitary streets —   560
Not solitary to angelic eyes —
Home to his father's house : a dark spirit waved
A fascinating spell before his face :
And straightway to those tents of wickedness
He bent his easy steps ; and, as he cross'd
The threshold through the crowd invisible,
I heard their fiendish laugh of triumph. Soon
Another, on the call of charity,
With haste that dimly-lighted pavement trod ;
And him the spirits malign assay'd to draw   570
With the same sorcery : but an angel stoop'd
And interposed his buckler, and the youth
Went on unscathed, though mindless of his peril.
A lonely garret drew my eye ; for thence
A flood of roseate brilliance stream'd afar,
Such brilliance as a spirit alone may see :
There on a bed of straw a sufferer lay
Feeble, but strong in faith ; and by her side
Two of heaven's noblest principalities
Kept watch : and to my look of marvel, why   580
Such high pre-eminence was hers, my guide
Made answer, " She is one whom Jesus loves."
But now another sight attracted me :
'Twas but a children's orphanage ; but there,
Say, is it Jacob's ladder once again
Planted upon the earth ? Such forms of light
Were passing to and fro continually,
So frequent was the intercourse with heaven

It boots not further to declare what things
I saw that hour; but wheresoe'er I look'd   590
Methought there was an earnestness and awe
Presaging coming crisis.   As I gazed,
Questions innumerable to my lips
Rose as live waters to a fountain's brim.
But I was mute with wonder; and my guide,
Responding to my quick unspoken thoughts,
Said, " Brother, I will tell thee all ere long;
But now one more permitted glance of love
Upon thy earthly home, and we must then
Assay our long precipitate descent."   600

I follow'd where he led.   Is it my home,
My widow'd, desolate, and orphan'd home?
O hush! o'er every child an angel bent,
Nor was the nurse the only one who watch'd
The cradle of my sleeping babe.   My wife
Had stolen to our silent chamber back,
And knelt in tears beside my lifeless clay :
And o'er her stood a seraph, watching her
With wondrous tenderness and love and grief.
"And is it true," I ask'd — my words were quick   610
And irrepressible for eager thought, —
" Hath it been ever granted those who have pass'd
The river, to appear and show themselves,
Unchanged in form, in heart unchangeable,
To loved ones they have left behind ? "   " 'Tis true
It hath been so," gently my guardian said,
" But only by His sovereign will and word

Who holds the keys of Hades and of **Death,**
And opens, as He wills, the mortal eye
To see the mysteries of things unseen.   620
There are who fondly call upon the dead
To hear them, and imagine they receive
Some dark response in symbols or in sounds :
But either in their minds their own prayers raise
Distemper'd phantasies, or spirits unblest,
Perceiving that the bond of fealty
Is broken with the One and Only God,
Assume the very lineaments and voice
Of those invoked, and answering them allure
Their worshippers to ruin.   Yet sometimes   630
The veil is lifted by His high behest
Who separates eternity from time,
And spirits have spoken unto men, and then
Their eye is open, and their ear attent.
Blest seers, blest auditors : but higher still
And holier is the pure beatitude
On those who have not seen and yet believe ;
. And such is hers who kneels before thee : **hers,**
As thine was, is the victory of faith.
Leave her to God.   Our journey summons us."   640
" Enough, enough," I answer'd, "All is well ;
I would not pluck one jewel from her crown :
Arise, let us be going."   And at my words
The spirit who watch'd beside her look'd on me
A look of tender gratitude, and waved
His hand in token of a short farewell.

And I was now aware of two who stood
Beside me, courier angels, wing'd for speed :
Twin brothers they appear'd, so like their mien,
So like their garments dipt in rainbow hues ;   650
They bent on me the beauty of their smile,
And singing as they took my hand in theirs,
" Home, brother, home," unclosed their wings of light :
And we, my guardian leading us the way,
Set forth upon the road to Paradise.

Smooth, easy, swifter than the winds of heaven
Our flight was.   In the twinkling of an eye
We brush'd the mantle of a silver cloud
That floated in mid sky.   Like flames of fire
We mounted upward, for awhile within   660
The limits of the mighty shadow cast
From the earth's solid globe athwart the heavens.
But soon, emerging from its gloom, we saw
The sun unclouded, but its disc reduced
To half its former radiance, — faint its warmth,
Feeble its light, and lessening every league.
But when I saw that we had left the earth
Beneath us, and were ever soaring higher,
I turn'd me to my radiant guide and said,
" O blessed angel, wherefore calledst thou   670
The road to Paradise a long descent
Precipitate?   Upward our pathway leads,
Ascending, not descending : and the earth
Already lies a planet at our feet."

And he, benignly smiling, answer'd me,
" Call me, I pray thee, Oriel, such my name —
One little beam from God's great orb of light.
Ascension and descension, height and depth,
Are here not measured by a line through space
Drawn vertical or perpendicular　　　　　　680
From any spot on the revolving earth : —
Of which let it suffice thee to reflect
Thy highest hitherto hath ever been
The lowest to the other hemisphere.
Not so our zenith and our nadir lie.
But height with us is where the Eternal God,
Though omnipresent in the universe,
Reveals the lustre of His throne supreme,
Through clouds of glory in the heaven of heavens :
And depth is the remotest opposite.　　　　690
We are descending now : for Hades lies
More distant from the everlasting throne
Than central earth.　Fear not ; for He who sits
High throned above all height pre-eminent,
Not only stoop'd from thence to Bethlehem,
But dying, descended lower than the earth,
And captive led captivity, His prey,
In those vast realms beneath.　Descending first,
Soon He ascended far above the heavens,
And with His presence fills the universe.　　700
His pathway, brother, must be thine.　Nor think
That Paradise, though situate in the deep
Which lieth under, is not real heaven :
Heaven is where Jesus is, and He is there.

3

Even as in those mysterious temple courts
Built on mount Zion, figures of the true,
There was the outer court, the holy place,
The Holiest of Holies, and yet all
Were but one house, One Father's house of prayer;
So is it in the heaven of heavens.   And now   710
The veil is rent for ever, and He walks
Who bears thy name engraven on His heart
Before the throne of mercy, and amid
The golden candlesticks, and where the souls
Beneath the altar cry ' How long, O Lord ?'
Fear not ; there thou shalt see Him as He is,
There clasp His sacred feet, and rest beneath
The beaming sunlight of His countenance,
And follow where He leads through fairer fields
Than Eden, by the gushing springs of life   720
Fresh water'd.   He makes heaven : and every part
Of His great temple with His glory shines."

So spake he ; and I hung upon his lips
Entranced, whose words were sweeter to my taste
Than droppings of the honey dew.   But now
I was aware the pathway that we clomb
No longer was a solitary track,
Rather a mighty highway of the heavens :
For other travellers, angels they seem'd,
Were passing to and fro unweariedly,   730
On manifold behests commission'd.   Some
Swept by us, swift as lightning, on their road

From Paradise to earth: and other some
Journeying the way we went, in groups of light,
Bore in their hands, like my angelic guard,
A weary pilgrim to his home of rest.
Others, and they were many, had each in charge
A sleeping infant folded to his bosom,
And ever and anon would stoop and gaze
Upon it with unutterable love.   740
Of some the flight was slow: but when I look'd,
The spirit they carried was in chains, and all
His stricken lineaments bespoke despair.
And still the path became more throng'd, and shone
With living meteors, so as to compare
·The things of sight and faith, at midnight when
A rose-blush as of morning seems to steal
Across the northern firmament, with jets
Of ardent flame and undulating light
Incessant.   On our right hand and our left   750
The stars sang Hallelujah, as we pass'd
Now in the splendor of some nearer orb,
Whether a satellite or blazing sun,
And now within the twilight interval
That lay betwixt their vast domains.   But I,
Solicitous regarding those whose look
Of woe once seen was ineffaceable,
Ask'd, " Holy Oriel, are those prisoners,
Whose slower course we pass continually,
Angelic, or lost spirits of human birth?   760
And wherefore are they on this road with us? "

And he replied, his words were grave but calm,
" They are the disembodied souls of men
Who lived and died in sin.   Lightly they spent
In Godless mirth or prayerless toil unblest
Their brief inestimable day of proof,
Till the last golden sands ran out : and now
Their hour is come, and they are on the road
To that profound abysmal deep, wherein
The rich man lifted up his anguish'd eyes —   770
Eyes never to be closed in sleep again :
Nor marvel that one track their footsteps leads
And ours.   Remember he of whom I spake,
Himself in torments, though far off, beheld
The holy Lazarus, and call'd aloud —
A bootless prayer — on Abraham for aid.
And when that desperate monarch, Saul of old,
Impenitent, besought of Endor's witch
The knowledge that insulted Heaven refused,
The prophet's spirit, which rose at God's behest,   780
Baffling the arts of sorcery, replied,
' To-morrow thou and thine shall be with me.'
All die, for all have sinn'd.   Their mother earth
Has but one sepulchre for all.   And here
One Hades, by us call'd the under-world,
Receives the spirits of the damn'd and blest :
One world, but widely sunder'd by a gulf
Inevitably fixed, impassable,
Which severs to the left hand and the right
The prison-house of woe and Paradise.   790
Before us now it lies."

                                   I look'd, and lo
Before us lay a sphere girdled with clouds,
And glorious with illimitable lights
And shadows mingling. Momently it grew
Dilated, as with undiminish'd speed
We outstripp'd lightnings in our homeward path,
Until in vain I toil'd to mark the line
Of its horizon. Boundless it appear'd
As space itself, a nether sea of mist
Unfathomable, shoreless, infinite.   800
Thither our pathway led. But as we near'd
Its extreme confines, I beheld what seem'd
A defile in those mountainous clouds, a chasm
Whence issued floods of radiance, pure white light,
And rainbow tints, roseate, and gold, and blue,
Unparallel'd on earth: though he who sees
The virgin snows upon the Alps suffused
With blushes underneath the first salute
Of morning, sees a shadow of this light.
This was the gorgeous avenue which led   810
Straight to the gates of bliss — a pass to which
The grandest and the most sublime on earth,
From Caubul to the sunny plains of Ind,
Were but a miner's arch. The massive sides,
Massive they seem'd, of this ravine were built
Of clouds which ever hung there undispersed,
And caught on every vaporous fold and skirt
The glory of the sportive rays that stream'd
Forth from the happy Paradise beyond
Innumerable. But before we pass'd   820

Under that radiant canopy, I saw
Another road far stretching on our left
Into the outer darkness, vast and void,
And from its depths methought I faintly heard
The sighings of despair. Time was not now
For mute surprise or question. On we flew,
As shoots a vessel laden with the wealth
Of Ceylon's isle, or Araby the blest,
Right onward, every sailyard bent with wind,
Into her long'd-for port. And now the air   830
Grew tremulous with heavenly melody.
Far off at first it seem'd and indistinct,
As swells and sinks the multitudinous roar
Of ocean : but ere long the waves of sound
Roll'd on articulate, and then I knew
The voice of harpers harping on their harps.
And lo, upon the extreme verge of cloud,
As once at Eden's portals there appear'd
A company of angels clothed in light,
Thronging the path or in the amber air   840
Suspense. And in the twinkling of an eye
We were among them, and they cluster'd round
And waved their wings, and struck their harps again
For gladness : every look was tenderness,
And every word was musical with joy.

" Welcome to heaven, dear brother, welcome home .
Welcome to thy inheritance of light !
Welcome for ever to thy Master's joy !
Thy work is done, thy pilgrimage is past;

Thy guardian angel's vigil is fulfill'd; 850
Thy parents wait thee in the bowers of bliss;
Thy infant babes have woven wreaths for thee;
Thy brethren who have enter'd into rest
Long for thy coming; and the angel choirs
Are ready with their symphonies of praise.
Nor shall thy voice be mute: a golden harp
For thee is hanging on the trees of life;
And sweetly shall its chords for ever ring,
Responsive to thy touch of ecstasy,
With Hallelujahs to thy Lord and ours." 860

So sang they; and that vast defile of clouds
Re-echoed with the impulses of song
And music, and the atmosphere serene
Throbb'd with innumerable greetings. Sounds,
Such as no mortal ear hath ever heard,
Save those who watch'd their flocks at Bethlehem,
Ravish'd my soul, and sights surpassing words,
Till, ear and eye fulfill'd with pure delight,
I turn'd me to my angel guide, and said
Unconsciously, " 'Twere good to sojourn here ! " 870
But he, in tones of buoyant hope, replied,
" Brother, thou shalt see greater things than these."

END OF THE FIRST BOOK.

Book Second.

THE PARADISE OF THE BLESSED DEAD.

ON, through that mountainous defile of clouds,
My guardian and his winged ministers
Bore me with smooth undeviating flight,
And speed unslacken'd : round about us play'd
Our retinue of angels, carolling
And harping as they flew : the while an hour
Pass'd peradventure of terrestrial time,
Measuring in space leagues almost measureless,
Though travellers along that blissful road
Wish'd it were longer.   But at last aware   10
Of brighter radiance circumfused, I look'd
Far in the gleaming distance, and behold,
Barring our onward course were gates of pearl,
Translucent pearl, through which the glory' of heaven
Came softened in a thousand tender hues —
Distinguishable Iris, chrysolite,
Sapphire, and emerald, and sardius,
And peerless hyacinthine amethyst.
The deep foundations of those gates were sunk

Lower than thought may fathom, and their top   20
Appear'd to touch the empyrean's arch ;
But at the echo of the harpers' song
Back with melodious sound they softly flew,
As if themselves instinct with sympathies
Of welcome, and disclosed the scenes of bliss
That lay beyond them bathed in amber light.

Here first upon the threshold of those gates
My heavenly escort paused.   Here first I trod
A pavement of transparent gold, and gazed
Upon that luminous ravine, which brought   30
Us hither, in admiring marvel.   Such
A cincture, to compare great things with small,
Of waters and of vaporous clouds composed
Some hold the golden ring which circulates
Round Saturn's orb : or such, as others tell,
The lucid atmosphere enveloping
The central sun, whose solid globe opaque
Is only visible through rents which show
As spots to the inhabitants of earth.
But what might be the mantle, which enwrapt   40
The unseen world of spirits, I ask'd not.   Clouds
Were none before us.   Through the gates of pearl
We pass'd, and on a terraced platform stood,
Which overlook'd the realms of Paradise,
And gazed awhile, like Moses from the rocks
Of Pisgah on the promised land.   O, scene
Surpassing words !   Beneath us lay outstretch'd
A garden far more large than if the earth,

From pole to pole, from sunrise to sunset,
Bloom'd with the countless roses of Cashmere;   50
And yet not larger to the dark abyss
That couch'd beneath it and beyond, than was
Blest Eden to the whole primeval world.
And this, like Adam's sinless nursery,
Was planted by the hand of God Himself,
And water'd with the rivulets of life,
And shaded with innumerable trees,
Fragrant and flowering and hung with fruit —
Trees beautiful to view and good for food.
All here was good.   Nor were there wanting hills   60
With valleys interspersed, and placid lakes,
And plains, and forests, as of cedars, fit
For holy intercourse of friend with friend,
And opening glades between.   The distant seem'd
Near as we looked upon it : whether this
Were due to that crystalline atmosphere
Purged from all film, or rather that the eyes
Of spirits and angels in themselves excel
The virtues of those lenses wherewith men
Have arm'd their ineffective vision, as   70
A microscope and telescope in one.
For a brief space we gazed enamour'd.   Then
Cleaving with ease the light elastic air,
By love's strong magnet drawn, we sloped our flight,
As slopes a meteor with its train of gold
Across the summer firmament, nor stay'd
Till in a wooded vale beside a stream
We lighted — we and our angelic choir.

We lighted ; and my guardian with a smile
Of gladness, which no thought of self obscured, 80
Turn'd to me, saying, " Brother, this is home :
This is thy Saviour's rest, and this is thine,
Until the archangel's trumpet sound in heaven ;
Here thou with Jesus art, Jesus with thee ;
Go forth and meet thy Lord. Beneath this shade
Meantime we tarry for thee, while alone
Thou seest Him whom thou hast loved unseen :
That is an incommunicable joy
With which no other hearts, angels or men,
Can intermeddle. By yon grassy bank 90
Follow where leads thee on thy way this stream
Of flowing crystal ; such is His command :
And here will we await thy blest return."

So they retired a little space aside,
Under the grateful shadow of those trees
Rich with ambrosial fruit : and ere my lips
Could utter thanks I found myself alone —
Alone, and on my way to meet my God.
The solitude was sweet. So many scenes
Of glory and unprecedented joy 100
Had crowded on my vision, that I long'd
To gather and compose my thoughts awhile
In meditation. Such an interval
Of brief but blissful solitude the bride,
Left lonely on her bridal evening, feels
To still the beating of a heart that beats
Too high with virgin bashfulness and hope,

Ere she receives her spouse.   And, as I trod
Those banks enamell'd with the freshest flowers,
Soothed with the gliding music which that stream   110
Made ever, brokenly at intervals,
Communing with myself, I thought aloud.

" And am I, then, in heaven ?   Is this the land
To which my yearning heart so often turn'd
Desirous ?   This the Paradise of saints ?
And is it I myself who speak ?   The same
Who wander'd in the desert far astray,
Till the Good Shepherd found me perishing,
And drew me to Himself with cords of love ?
Has He now brought me to His heavenly fold,   12()
Which sin can never touch nor sorrow cloud,
Me who have water'd with my frequent tears
The thorny wilderness, and struggled on
Footsore and weary — me, the wayward one ?
And shall I never wander from Him more,
And never grieve His brooding Spirit again ?
O, joy ineffable !   But am I now
About to meet Him, see Him face to face
Who made me, and who knows me what I am,
Of all His saints unworthiest of His love?   12()
Why beats this heart so tremulously ?   Why
Do thoughts within me rise ?   Is it not He
Who bought me with His blood ?   Hath He not led
Me on my journey hither step by step ?
Came He not to me at the hour of death,
And whisper'd that my sins were all forgiven,

And now hath sent His angels to convoy
My spirit safely home, and welcome me
With songs of Hallelujah?   What is love,
If this indissoluble bond that links   140
Me and my Lord for ever be not love?
His costly, precious, infinite, divine:
Mine human, limited, and mean, and poor,
And yet His inward Spirit whispers, true.
For what were all this gorgeous Paradise,
The music of these waters, and these bowers
Fragrant with fruitage, what were all to me,
And tenfold all, twice measured, without Him?
Without Him heaven were but a desert rude;
With Him, a desert heaven.   And art Thou here,   150
Jesu, my Lord, my life, my light, my all?
When wilt Thou come to me, or bid me come
To Thee, that I may see Thee as Thou art,
And love Thee even as Thou lovest me?"

And as I spake I heard a gentle Voice
Calling me by my name.   So Adam heard
And conscience-stricken Eve the voice of God
Walking abroad through Eden in the cool
Of sunset.   But with other thoughts to theirs
I turn'd to see who called me; and lo, One   160
Wearing a form of human tenderness
Approach'd.   Human He was, but love divine
Breathed in His blessed countenance, a love
Which drew me onwards irresistibly
Persuasive: whether now He veil'd His beams

More closely than the hour His brightness shone
Around the prophet by Ulai's banks,
And in the solitary Patmos smote
Prostrate to earth the Apocalyptic seer;
Or whether the Omnipotent Spirit of God   170
Strengthens enfranchised spirits to sustain
More of His glory.   I drew near to Him,
And He to me.   O beatific sight!
O vision with which nothing can compare!
The angel ministrant who brought me hither
Was exquisite in beauty, and my heart
Clave to his heart: the choristers of light,
Who sang around our pathway, none who saw
Could choose but love for very loveliness.
But this was diverse from all other sights: 180
Not living only, it infused new life;
Not beautiful alone, it beautified;
Nor only glorious, for it glorified.
For a brief space methought I look'd on Him,
And He on me.   O blessed look! how brief
I know not, but eternity itself
Will never from my soul erase the lines
Of that serene transfiguring aspect.
For a brief space I stood, by Him upheld,
Gazing, and then in adoration fell   190
And clasp'd His sacred feet, while holy tears,
Such tears as disembodied spirits may weep,
Flow'd from my eyes.   But bending over me,
As bends a mother o'er her waking babe,
He raised me tenderly, saying, "My child."

And I, like Thomas on that sacred eve,
Could only answer Him, " My Lord, my God."
And then He drew me closer, and Himself
With His own hand, His pierced hand of love,
Wiped the still falling tear-drops from my face,   200
And told me I was His and He was mine,
And how my Father loved me and He loved.

That hour for brevity a moment seemed ;
For benediction, ages.   But at last
Calmly He said, " The night is almost spent ;
The morning is at hand.   Fearless meanwhile
Rest thou in peace.   Oriel, thy guardian spirit,
Shall lead thee to those bowers felicitous,
Where now thy parents and thy babes await
My kingdom with the other Blessed Dead."   210

So saying, by the hand He led me forth,
Lowly in heart as when He stoop'd and led
The blind man of Bethsaida aside),
And brought me to the spot where Oriel stay'd
Expectant with those courier seraphim
And all that choir of angels.   Reverent
They rose, and knelt in worship at His feet ;
And there was silence till again His voice
Breathed new delight ineffable in all.

" Soldier and servant of the Lord, well done !   220
My faithful Oriel, well hast thou discharged
Thy long and arduous ministry of love

'Twixt earth and heaven, now for six thousand years :
And not least faithful proved in guarding this
Thy youngest brother from the hosts of hell
Confederate to destroy My child in vain.
And ye, My winged ministers of light,
Well have ye brought him hither. And, ye choirs
Celestial, I have heard well-pleased your songs
And notes of welcome. For a little while   330
Abide ye in these happy fields, for soon
A mightier triumph shall awake your harps.
And, Oriel, be it thine to take thy ward
Where wait his coming those he loved on earth :
And, when fulfill'd with their society
And all the present bliss of Paradise,
Lead him apart, and patiently disclose
That which thou knowest of eternity's
To-day and yesterday. The morrow dawns.
Make him partaker of thy thoughts, whom thou   240
Hast brought to share thy glory. And meanwhile
Receive from Me this token of thy trust."

He said, and from His bosom pluck'd what seem'd
A gem of fire, a globe of liquid light,
As Venus in her prime shines on the earth,
And placed it in my guardian's starry crown :
An amaranthine diadem, enwove
With many jewels, now at last complete.
New love beat in all hearts, new joy, new praise :
And in a moment we were there alone ;   250
Yet not alone, I felt that He was there,

Invisible, but personally there;
Spirit with spirit: I with Him, and He
With me.　Such virtue Omnipresence hath,
Which only hides its glory in itself,
That it may manifest itself anew
In forms of unknown beauty, light with cloud,
Voices with silence, movement with repose
Combining in eternal interchange.

And through an open glade we took our way,　　　260
And many an avenue of forest trees, —
Such forests Paradise alone may rear, —
And on through many a deep ravine, which slept
Beneath the guardianship of shadowing hills,
Gliding as easily as glides a train
Of golden mist amid Norwegian pines;
Or as a parting smile of evening, shed
By the proud king of day, ere he retires
Within the crimson curtains of the West,
Breaks over the cloud-mantled Pyrenees,　　　270
Till their peaks glow like opal, and the lakes
Catching the transitory radiance gleam
Like liquid pearl: so smoothly without sound
Of footfall on the printless flowers we pass'd.

The track was long, soliciting our stay;
The time was briefer than my words.　And lo,
A valley open'd on our sudden gaze
Pre-eminently beautiful and bright
'Mid that bright world of beauty.　But straightway

4

Or ever I could utter words of praise,   280
Voices familiar as my mother tongue
Fell on me; and an infant cherub sprang,
As springs a sunbeam to the heart of flowers,
Into my arms, and murmur'd audibly,
" Father, dear father; " and another clasp'd
My knees, and falter'd the same name of power.
One look sufficed to tell me they were mine,
My babes, my blossoms, my long parted ones;
The same in feature and in form as when
I bent above their dying pillow last,   290
Only the spirit now disenrobed of flesh,
And beaming with the likeness of their Lord.

The one who nestled in my breast had seen
All of earth's year except the winter's snows.
Spring, summer, autumn, like sweet dreams, had smiled
On her.   Eva — or *living* — was her name;
A bud of life folded in leaves and love;
The dewy morning star of summer days;
The golden lamp of happy fire-side hours;
The little ewe-lamb nestling by our side;   300
The dove whose cooing echoed in our hearts;
The sweetest chord upon our harp of praise:
The quiet spring, the rivulet of joy;
The pearl among His gifts who gave us all;
On whom not we alone, but all who look'd,
Gazing would breathe the involuntary words,
" God bless thee, Eva — God be bless'd for thee."
Alas, clouds gather'd quickly, and the storm

Fell without warning on our tender bud,
Scattering its leaflets; and the star was drench'd 310
In tears; the lamp burnt dimly; unawares
The little lamb was faint; the weary dove
Cower'd its young head beneath its drooping wing;
The chord was loosen'd on our harp; the fount
Was troubled, and the rill ran nearly dry;
And in our souls we heard our Father, saying,
" Will ye return the gift?" The Voice was low —
The answer lower still — " Thy will be done."
And now, where we had often pictured her,
I saw her one of the beatified; 320
Eva, our blossom, ours for ever now,
Unfolding in the atmosphere of love:
The star that set upon our earthly home
Had risen in glory, and in purer skies
Was shining; and the lamp we sorely miss'd,
Shed its soft radiance in a better home;
Our lamb was pasturing in heavenly meads;
Our dove had settled on the trees of life;
Another chord was ringing with delight,
Another spring of rapture was unseal'd, 330
In Paradise; our treasure was with God;
The gift in the great Giver's strong right hand;
And none who look'd on her could choose but say,
" Eva, sweet angel, God be bless'd for thee."

But, were it possible, more beauteous seem'd
The cherub child who clung about my knees —
A different beauty, hers. Sweet Constance, she

Had trodd'n a longer, rougher pathway home,
And not unset with thorns, — long for a babe,
Two winters and three summers was her life —   340
Rough only for a babe ; but every step
Ta'en by her little bleeding feet had left
Its tracery upon her spirit now
In tender lines of love, and peace, and praise.
Yet both were only infants ; babes of light
In God's great household : heaven with all its joys
Had perfected, not changed, their infancy :
The younger, with the fearless gaze of one
Who never knew the shadow of a cloud,
Sparkling as sparkles a pure diamond :   350
The elder, with a child's deep confidence,
Which trusts you with illimitable trust,
And with one look summons and wins your heart.

A babe in glory is a babe for ever.
Perfect as spirits, and able to pour forth
Their glad heart in the tongues which angels use,
These nurslings gather'd in God's nursery
For ever grow in loveliness and love,
(Growth is the law of all intelligence)
Yet cannot pass the limit which defines   360
Their being. They have never fought the fight,
Nor borne the heat and burden of the day,
Nor stagger'd underneath the weary cross ;
Conceived in sin, they sinn'd not ; though they died,
They never shudder'd with the fear of death :
These things they know not and can never know.

Yet fallen children of a fallen race,
And early to transgression, like the rest,
Sure victims, they were bought with Jesus' blood,
And cleansed by Jesus' Spirit, and redeem'd   370
By His Omnipotent arm from death and hell:
A link betwixt mankind and angelhood:
As born of woman, sharers with all saints
In that great ransom paid upon the cross:
In purity and inexperience
Of guilt akin to angels. Infancy
Is one thing, manhood one. And babes, though part
Of the true archetypal house of God
Built on the heavenly Zion, are not now,
Nor will be ever, massive rocks rough-hewn,   380
Or ponderous corner-stones, or fluted shafts
Of columns, or far-shadowing pinnacles;
But rather as the delicate lily-work
By Hiram wrought for Solomon of old,
Enwreathed upon the brazen chapiters,
Or flowers of lilies round the molten sea.
Innumerable flowers thus bloom and blush
In heaven. Nor reckon God's designs in them
Frustrate, or shorn of full accomplishment:
The lily is as perfect as the oak;   390
The myrtle is as fragrant as the palm;
And Sharon's roses are as beautiful
As Lebanon's majestic cedar crown.

And when I saw my little lambs unchanged,
And heard them fondly call me by my name,

" Then is the bond of parent and of child
Indissoluble," I exclaim'd, and drew
Them closer to my heart and wept for joy.

But other voices of familiar love,
And other forms of light reminded me   400
By the deep yearnings of my soul, I was
Myself not only' a father but a child;
Nor child alone, but brother, pastor, friend.
How often had I long'd in dreams o' the night,
Or meditative solitude, to see
The beaming sunshine of my father's smile,
Which ever seem'd to me a reflex joy
Cast from God's smile; or haply oftener yet
My mother's face of fond solicitude, —
Solicitous for all except herself.   410
They were before me now.   Nor they alone:
Betwixt them leant a slender seraph form,
My sister's spirit, who with frailest bark
Year after year had stemm'd the wildest sea,
Pain, conflict, cloud. and utter weariness,
Till the last billow, almost unawares,
On its rough bosom bore her into rest.
And can this be that wave-tost voyager,
This she?   Radiant with beauty and with bloom,
As if the past had written on her brow   420
Its transcript in those shades of pensive grace
And breathing sympathy, wherein remain'd
Nothing of sadness, all of saintliness.
She stood and look'd on me a moment, saying,

" My brother, it is he ! " and on my neck
She fell; nor arms alone were interlock'd
In that embrace.　And then the pent up thoughts
Of many years flow'd from our eager lips,
As waters from a secret spring unseal'd.

　　I was no stranger in a strange land there:　　430
But rather as one who travel-worn and weary,
Weary of wandering through many climes,
At length returning homeward, eyes far off
The white cliffs of his fatherland, and ere
The laboring ship touches its sacred soil
Leaps on the pier, while round him crowding press
Children and kith and friends, who in a breath
Ask of his welfare, and with joyous tongues
Pour all their love into his thirsty ear.
Such welcome home was mine; such questionings　440
Of things that had befallen me since last
We met, and of my pathway thitherwards,
And of the dear ones I had left behind : —
Words with embraces interspersed.　And then,
Taking my hands exultingly in theirs,
And singing for delight, they led me on
Adown that heavenly valley: and the joy
Of Oriel, who resign'd me to their charge
Awhile, and with his radiant retinue
Hung on our footsteps, was fulfill'd in mine.　　450
Straight towards a river bank they bent their steps,
Shaded by trees of life, whose pendent boughs,
Fann'd by soft gales, and laden with fresh fruit,

Dipp'd in the living waters. Every step
Some fondly loved familiar face was seen,
Whom I had known in pilgrim days, unchanged,
And yet all bright with one similitude:
One Lord had look'd on them.

So pass'd we on,

And lo, a group of the beatified
Advanced to meet us, on whose lips methought,   460
Hush'd to a whisper for delight, I heard
The strange salute of father. In amaze
I ask'd what meant such gratulation there?
And one for many answer'd, " From thy mouth
We heard of Jesus' love, and thine the hand
That led us to His feet." It was enough:
For all the parent and the pastor woke
Within me; all the holy memories
Of bygone days flow'd in a refluent tide
Over my soul once more. Some I had known   470
From rosy dawn of childhood, and had watch'd
Their hearts like buds beneath a cottage wall
Unfolding to the sunshine of God's love.
Some I had shepherded, yea many, who
With all the throbbing impulses of youth,
Gave me the inviolable confidence
Of their young life. And some in after years
Had pour'd the burden of a wounded spirit,
Suffering and sunken, into mine; and we
Had wept together, and together sought   480
The sinner's only Friend, nor sought in vain.

And others, dying, heard me read of him
Who on the cross for mercy cried to Christ;
Heard, and themselves believed. All these I knew;
And quickly' as light their story flash'd on me.
But in that group of filial spirits there came
Many I knew not — part of that great store
Of unsuspected treasure heaven conceals:
And they too pour'd on me beatitudes.
Nor, what I chiefly noted, seem'd my heart   490
Surcharged, or freighted overmuch, with love.
Affections with affections jarr'd not. All
Was music. As through some cathedral aisles
An organ of a thousand pipes pours forth
Its rich and multitudinous harmonies,
While the rapt organist touches at will
Its various stops, hautboy, and trump, and flute,
The clarion with the dulciana smooths,
And chastens with the plaintive tremulant
The diapason's thunder-roll: so love   500
Without confusion blended there with love,
Symphoniously distinct: and I embraced
Each one with all my heart, and all as each.

But now arrived upon that river bank
Whose lucid waves were shaded by the trees
Of life, along its marge in loose array
We wander'd, saints and angels, hand in hand,
The children dancing in their innocent glee,
And showering roses round our steps. But soon,
Hard by a wooded precipice, whence fell   510

The living waters with melodious fall
In numberless cascades from rock to rock
Exultant, like a rain of diamonds,
Through gates of woven myrtle' and vine we pass'd,
And enter'd what they call'd their bower of bliss,
One of the countless bowers of Paradise.
Or rather it might seem a sylvan shrine
For worship; so precipitous the trees,
Trees loftier than those giant pines which cast
Their shade athwart Peruvian forests, shot   520
Right upward towards the crystal firmament,
And wove aloft branches and leaves and fruit
In arches intricate, a fretted roof,
Through which the light cool'd and empurpled came,
Leaving beneath wide clearance, carpeted
With moss of amaranth and delicate ferns.
On these the spirits elect straightway reclined,
And I with them: while Oriel over me
Leant gazing with such pure perfect delight
As guardian angels only know. And then   530
My children placed within my hands the wreaths
Which they had woven of unfading flowers
Against my coming: these my mother took
And set upon my brow, smiling, and said,
"Thy crown of glory other hands than mine,
And in an hour of holier victory,
Shall give thee."

          And at Oriel's signal came
My father, bearing in his hand a harp

Of simplest form but manifold in tones
Of musical modulations without end,　　　540
And gave it to me, saying, "Take it, my son;
It is heaven's workmanship, and made for thee."
I took it, nothing loath; and, though on earth
In lute or harp my skill was nothing, then
Immediately I felt the tremulous strings
Responsive to my every thought, as when
The wind in sportive or in pensive mood
Wakens Æolian music.　Strung it was
And pitch'd in most mysterious unison
With my heart's sympathies; for when I laid　　　550
My fingers on its airy chords, straightway
My very soul gush'd forth in melody,
The harp and harper vibrating in tune:
While words, like echoes of an old refrain
That heard in childhood haunts our riper years,
Broke in heaven's music from my lips — " To Him
Who loved us, and hath wash'd us from our sins
In His own blood, and made us unto God
And to the Father kings and priests, to Him
Be glory and dominion, power and praise　　　560
For ever and for evermore.　Amen."
And all the ransom'd spirits rejoicingly
Answer'd, " For evermore, Amen."　And all
The choir of angels struck their golden lyres,
Prolonging the sweet melody, until
On every face a brighter radiance fell,
And He, whose presence in the bowers of bliss
Is Omnipresent, secretly reveal'd

Himself to each, diffusing fragrance round
And joy unutterable; as when the wind   570
Moves clouds of incense from an altar flame,
And sheds a momentary roseate light
On priests and worshippers and temple walls.

The gleam o' the Divine glory pass'd: and then
My children brought me fruitage they had pluck'd
From off the trees of life, and water drawn
From living springs, and ruddy juice of grapes
More large and luscious than the fruit which grew
On Eshcol's sunny vines.   Nor deem it strange
That bodiless spirits partake of meat and drink.   580
Are not the angels spirits? and ate they not
At Mamre, by the tent of Abraham,
Press'd by his courteous hospitality?
And when the manna fell for forty years
Around the watchfires of that pilgrim host,
Was it not angel's food — the corn of heaven?
The Increate alone is self-sustain'd,
Life in Himself possessing, and all other
His creatures, from the burning seraphim
That sing around His everlasting throne,   590
Even to the moth which floating in the light
Wings in an hour its little life away,
Feed on the bounty of a Father's love,
Who opens wide His hand and satisfies
All living things with life-sustaining food.
And so we bless'd the Ever Blessed One,
And ate and drank with such pure appetite,

As gives not pain but pleasure to the feasts
Of angels.   Nor was lacking there the joy
Of innocent laughter (they who weep on earth   600
Shall laugh in heaven) and all the genial glow
Of brotherly endearment, heart to heart
And eye to eye, after long severance,
Meeting for ever in our Father's house.
Sweet and refreshing interlude.

                              But soon
To graver converse turn'd we : and they ask'd,
With keen expectancy, what last I knew
Of the great warfare waged by saints on earth?
What lights of morning in the golden East
Streak'd the horizon? what the tidings sent   610
From heathen shores and from Emmanuel's land?
What victories the cross had last achieved
Over the paling crescent? whether still
The doom'd embattlements of Babylon
Stood in apparent might? and if the Bride
Sustain'd her weary vigil, as of old,
From watch to watch repeating "Till He come?"
They ask'd : I answer'd, marvelling to find
How thin a veil parted the blessed Church
Triumphant, and that militant on earth ;   620
And how the wrestlers, racers, combatants,
Wrestled and ran and fought, encompass'd round
So closely by a cloud of witnesses.

     Farther I may not linger to relate

The infinite delights of that first tryst
With those, who earlier than myself had won
Their rest, and tasted of the fruit of life.
It might be many days of earthly time,
Which pass'd in glory without weariness
Or measure. But at length our hearts were fill'd, 630
Even to the overflowing brim of joy,
Each with the other's love; and forth we pass'd,
In groups or singly, on our several paths
Of rest or service: service there is rest,
Rest, service: for the Paradise of saints,
Like Eden with its toilless husbandry,
Has many plants to tend, and flowers to twine,
And fruit-trees in the garden of the soul,
That ask the culture of celestial skill.
Some wander'd amid vines, and flowery meads, 640
And from the grateful lips of angels learn'd
More virtues than he knew who spake of trees
From cedars to the hyssop on the wall.
Some perfected their skill in dance and song,
With lyre or lute accompanied, and made
Those woods and valleys vocal with sweet sounds,
Sweeter than those which from a thousand birds
Fill Vallombrosa's vale in spring-time. Here
It was perpetual spring. Some clomb with ease,
Swift as the winds, the everlasting hills, 650
And from their summit bathed in light survey'd
The glorious landscape. Some in silence mused:
Heaven has its calm unbroken solitudes
For prayer and lonely meditation meet.

And some in clusters, walking or recline,
Heard from an elder saint or guardian spirit
The awful story of the past, or bent
Over the mystic chart of prophecy,
Brother to brother saying, " It is done.
The day-spring is at hand."   660

                    Me Oriel led
From bower to bower, from peopled glen to glen,
From saintly company to company,
And show'd me of the mysteries that fill
That world of spirits, that nether Paradise,
That suburb of the New Jerusalem,
That Beautiful gate of heaven, that vestibule
Where the saints wait their bright apparelling
Of glory 'neath the veil now rent which hangs
Betwixt the Holy and Most Holy Place.
Children of light, through fields of light we pass'd 670
Unchallenged, not ungreeted with the smiles
Of welcomes without number.   And I mark'd
How largely the redeem'd though free to range
Within the limits almost limitless
Of those celestial regions, group'd themselves,
They and their guardian spirits, with other saints,
Their fellow-pilgrims on the earth.   It was
No rigid severance; for many walk'd,
As we were walking, to and fro abroad
Throughout those blissful mansions : but enough   680
Of chosen and endear'd companionship
To mark the character of centuries

And generations, as concentric rings
Of increase chronicle the growth of trees;
Or as the strata of the rocks record,
Not without many an intercepting vein,
The onward march of ages. Oriel read
My wonder, though unspoken, and replied:
" Remember that the same Omniscient Love
Design'd this temple built of living stones,   690
Wherein Himself to dwell for evermore,
As hung the firmament with globes of light,
And group'd them, as it pleased Him best, in groups
Of suns and planets, and in spiral coils
Of stars innumerable, and decreed
Amid this maze of constellations each
Should minister to each, and by one law
Of gravitation be for ever link'd.
So by the vast necessity of love,
Necessity with equal freedom poised,   700
Saints cling to saints, angels to angels cleave,
And men and angels in One Father's house
Are all as brethren. Not that love can be
Without the chosen specialties of love,
The nearest to the nearest most akin.
But none are strangers here, none sojourners:
And as the cloudless ages glide away,
New fountains of delight to us, to all,
Will open in the fellowship of hearts,
Unfathom'd by us yet. Nor time will fail;   710
For an eternity to come is ours
With humble contemplation to adore

The counsels of a past eternity.
But mark who next seem waiting our advance
In yonder vale."

           Straightway I look'd, and lo,
We were among the parents of that age
In which my life was cast — my father's peers —
Some of them standard-bearers in God's host,
Who, when their mortal course was finish'd, left
Large space, and in the front ranks, as they fell,   720
Till comrades pressing onward fill'd the chasm:
And others walking in the lowliest paths
Of earth, now comrades with the high'st in heaven.
The first who greeted me by name was one
Whom I had known long since, an aged saint,
Dwelling all lonely in her little room,
On scantiest means subsisting and content,
But with a queenly heart, wide as the world,
And loving all for His sake who is love:
Hers now was meet society.   And then   730
Saluted me the venerable man
Whose writings first waken'd my dying soul
To deathless life — one of those secret bonds
Which interlink the family of God.
But here I must not register the names
Of these, and spirits of every clime and tongue,
Who throng'd this region clothed in dazzling white.
For through them, bent on traversing the fields
Of Paradise, onward to other ranks
Of that illimitable host we pass'd,   740

5

Their fathers and their fathers' fathers, men
Whose lamps burn'd brightly once in earthly gloom,
And now themselves shone forth as stars in heaven,
Illuminating with eternal light
The brightness of that filmless firmament.

So pass'd we on from saintly band to band
Among those vales resting from all their toil,
In multitudes more countless than the tribes
Of Israel when from Dan to Beersheba
Flocking to Zion's sacred hill they kept   750
The feast of tabernacles, seven days
Of song and gladness.   In their midst I saw
Some who appear'd more radiant than the rest,
And ask'd what meant their bright pre-eminence
In glory.   Oriel answer'd, "These are they
Of whom the Church on earth so often sings;
Some of the martyrs' noble army : these
For Christ gave up their bodies to be burn'd,
Or bow'd their necks beneath the murderous sword;
Or, though their names appear not on the scroll   760
Of martyrologists, laid down their life,
No less a martyrdom in Jesus' eyes,
For His dear brethren's sake — watching the couch
Of loathsome sickness or of slow decay;
Or binding up the ravages which men,
Marring God's image, deal on fellow-men;
Or visiting the captive in his cell;
Or struggling with a burden not their own
Until their very life-springs wore away.   770
These too are martyrs, brother."

As he spake,
The high supremacy of sacrifice,
The majesty of service filled my soul
With thoughts too deep for words.

And not a few
I saw there of the goodly fellowship
Of prophets, the ambassadors who stood
Age after age amid the scoffing world,
And lifted up the standard of the cross,
Unmoved, undaunted. Nor, as some have deem'd,
Form'd they an order to themselves of saints,
But mingling moved, like shepherds through their
        flocks,   780
Amid their fellow-saints, wielding the sway
By them, by all, felt rather than confess'd,
Of grateful and predominating love.
There is predominance in heaven, and grades
Of lower and superior sanctities ;
All are not equal there ; for brotherhood
And freedom both abhor equality,
The very badge of serfdom ; only there
It is the true nobility of worth,
The aristocracy of gentleness,   790
The power of goodness and of doing good.

And when I look'd upon those blessed saints,
Those perfect spirits, albeit the lowest there
Was greater than the greatest upon earth,
For all were clothed in sinless purity,

At once I knew the principalities
And virtues and subordinate degrees
Amongst them.   And when Oriel told their names,
A deep chord vibrated within my heart,
And past things lived again.   And then I saw   800
That many first were last, and last were first —
Not all, not most, but many.   There were those
Once foremost in the foremost ranks, not now
Distinguishable from their peers in light:
And some, aforetime hidden and unknown,
Now shone in lustrous dignity sublime.
But one and all were circled with a cloud
Of infant spirits, pure mirthful innocents,
Like sunbeams glancing to and fro, like birds
Warbling their song of praise.   The elder saints   810
Seem'd to my eyes a countless multitude ;
But these cherubic babes outnumber'd them,
As the dark pine-trees of Siberia's wilds,
Unfell'd immeasurable forests, yield
In numbers to the ferns and summer flowers
Which grow beneath their shadowing boughs, and
          fringe
Their gnarled roots with beauty.   Heaven methinks —
So awful is eternal life, so vast
Its lights and shadows — heaven itself would seem
Too solemn and severe without its choirs   820
Of infants revelling in innocence,
Who never knew a touch of sinful grief,
But live in joy, and joy because they live.
So hath God will'd.   So will'd the Son of God

What time He took the children in His arms,
Laying His hands on them and blessing them,
And saying, " Suffer them to come to Me,
Forbid them not, for of such babes as these
And sucklings is My kingdom in the heavens."
But time and space would fail me to narrate   830
All I beheld in that great under-world ;
The golden grain of threescore centuries
Reap'd from a thousand harvest-fields and stored
In heaven.   Backward from age to age we traced
The course of time along those wastes of gloom,
When darkness brooded o'er the Church of God,
A darkness amid which the lurid flames
Of persecution blazed, and witnesses,
A mystic time and times and half a time,
In ashes and in sackcloth prophesied,   840
Now clothed in dazzling light : and with them those
Who underneath the skirts of Antichrist
Bewilder'd clung to Christ, and led by Him,
In cell or cloister groped their way to heaven :
Not one was wanting there.

                              And there we saw
The children of the Gospel's holier dawn,
Austin, and Chrysostom, and Cyprian,
And Irenæus, and blest Polycarp,
Names representing many not unlike
In love and labor, fellow-travellers   850
On earth, now fellow-citizens in heaven.
And there was holy Antipas, and there

The protomartyr Stephen; and the band
Whom Jesus chose, the Apostolic Twelve,
As heralds of His love to all the world.
Peter and John were walking, as of old
They used to walk along the silver sand
Wash'd by the waters of Gennesaret,
In closest converse; and beside them he
Of all men likest Christ, whose cross he preach'd   860
Unwearied from Jerusalem to Rome,
Burning with fire or melting into tears,
As God's Spirit moved upon his human spirit —
The myriad-minded lion-hearted Paul:
Amid heaven's peers peerless triumvirate.
Yet as we pass'd they bent a beaming smile
On me the humblest and the last arrived
Of all their brotherhood, so full of love
It seem'd to promise feasts of intercourse
In after ages.   And not far from them,   870
Half hidden by a branching tree of life,
Type of herself, the blessed Mary sate,
In calm humility musing alone
Upon those mysteries of grace, which seem'd
Vaster in length and breadth and depth and height,
The measureless dimensions of God's love,
As still the Bridal of the Church drew near.
Hard by, Elizabeth and Zachary,
Anna the prophetess, and Simeon stood,
Engraven on whose countenance I traced   880
The light of summer suns and mellow tints
Of autumn, not the wintry frosts of age.

And with them he who in the wilderness
Was the voice heralding the Word, the star
That hid itself within the golden beams
Of the uprisen Sun of Righteousness.

Nor was there any chasm betwixt the saints
Who wrought before and after. They were one, —
One building, and one body, and one bride.

I saw the wise sons of Betirah there,   890
Hillel who loosed, and Shammai who bound,
And Rabban, Hillel's son, and Jonathan;
And near them those great worthies, who deserved
So nobly of their noble fatherland,
The dauntless and heroic Maccabees;
And there the mother of those tortured sons,
Who in their dying suffer'd sevenfold death,
Yet flinch'd not: round her clustering they stood
A retinue of everlasting praise;
She was not childless now. Esther was there,   900
More lovely than upon that golden eve
When she her royal captor captive led;
And saintly Daniel, and the three who walk'd
Unsinged and scatheless in the fiery flame;
And all the holy seers from Malachi
To Samuel; there the rapt Ezekiel,
And plaintive Jeremy, and he whose lips
A seraph touch'd with a live coal of fire.
And there the kingly Hezekiah moved
Among the thrones of heaven; and David's son   910

Was there; and David the beloved himself,
Touching a sweeter harp than that he struck
Upon the grassy slopes of Bethlehem.
And there I saw the captains of God's hosts,
Samson and Jephthah, not without his child,
Who for her country and her father's vow
A virgin lived and died; and Gideon;
And Deborah the warrior prophetess;
And him who led his people Israel
Through Jordan's smitten waves, the son of Nun; 920
And, of the elder saints haply the first,
Moses the man of God, who, looking down
On all the royalties of Egypt, sought
A nobler sceptre and a name inscribed,
Not in the hieroglyphic scrolls of men,
But in God's book of life. And there were all
The pilgrim fathers in the better land
They long'd for; Joseph and the patriarchs,
The princely Israel, and that child of prayer,
The meditative son of Abraham,   930
And Abraham himself, the friend of God;
And Noah and his children, who by faith
Condemn'd the faithless world; and those who pray'd
In time's first dawn the matins of the Church,
Seated around our primal ancestors,
The father and the mother of mankind,
Who through the Son of Man, the woman's Seed,
Had won in heaven a nobler Paradise
Than Eden, forfeited and lost by sin.

Long while I gazed in silent awe ; for these   940
Were only some familiar names and few
Among ten thousand times ten thousand saints,
All diversely felicitous, and each
On each reflecting gladness.   But at last
The fire of love and admiration burn'd
So hot within me, that I spake and said,
" O blessed Oriel, can the highest heavens
Surpass the glory of this Paradise ?
If only all I loved were present now,
Here, here methinks I could for ever dwell.   950
What beauty can excel these radiant forms ?
What do they lack of excellence or grace ?
Are they not swifter than the viewless winds ?
Are they not pure as is the light itself ?
Say, are there brighter robes in heaven, or harps
Of tenderer music ?   Or have they who walk
The golden streets and fill with songs of praise
The mansions of the New Jerusalem,
More open vision of the Lord their God,
And in Him more divine beatitude ? "   960

Smiling, my guardian answer'd, " It is sweet
Be sure for me, who hither led thy steps,
To hear thy words of rapturous delight
In this fair world of purity and peace,
And in these blessed spirits who here throng
Heaven's portals, waiting their investiture
With resurrection glory.   Yes, the Bride
Is almost ready for her bridal robes :

The heavenly temple is almost complete.
How different from that hour, for I was here,   970
When the first saint, disrobed of mortal flesh,
The martyr'd Abel, trod these fields, and we
His angel brothers sought, and not in vain,
To gladden his else solitary rest.
Since then six thousand years have pass'd : and now
The countless multitudes of God's elect,
The festal throng and church of the firstborn,
Are well nigh gather'd home.   Yet think not this
The crown and final summit of their joy.
They are not perfect here, whose bodies sleep   980
And moulder crumbling in the silent tomb,
Death's trophies ; for the union, flesh and spirit,
In one compacted, was the fruit mature
Of God's eternal counsels, when He breathed
Into the moulded clay the breath of life,
And man became a living soul : and when
The dust returns unto its kindred dust,
And the lone spirit to God, this strange divorce
Is the permitted reign, gloomy though brief,
Of the dread king of terrors.   Here unclothed   990
Of their own natural apparelling,
Man's proper garb, their puissance is weak
To that of angels who were form'd by God
Pure spirits.   Nor is this Paradise of saints,
Albeit large and glorious, more than one
Of many mansions in our Father's house,
Wherein His children, by their birthright free
Of His whole universe, and citizens

Of the celestial city, wait the hour
Which shall for ever consummate their bliss.   1000
But see who yonder walk."

                              I look'd, and, lo,
Two diverse from the rest appear'd.   Their form
Was that of men, and yet not mortal men ;
Their likeness spiritual, yet not spirits alone ;
So pure the texture of that robe they wore,
The light translucent through transfigured flesh,
As onyx stones, or ruby flashing fire.

" Who are these," I exclaim'd, " these royal priests ?
Are they Elias, and that saint who walk'd
With God and was not ? "

                              " Rightly hast thou judged,"
Uriel made answer ; " and their presence here   [1010
Is pledge and earnest to the Blessed Dead
Of that great resurrection day, whose dawn
Already gilds the Easter of the world :
They with the saints who rose when Jesus rose
Are wave-sheafs of the harvest.   But of these
And other mysteries in earth and heaven
Conversing, on the range of yonder hills,
Whose summits bound these beatific fields,
And look far off into the waste beyond,   1020
If such thy pleasure, let us wait the end."

END OF THE SECOND BOOK.

Book Third.

THE PRISON OF THE LOST.

C ᴏᴍᴇ, Thou Eternal Spirit, who on the face
Of the abysmal waters, when the earth
Was without form and void, brooding didst move,
Silent Omnipotence, unseen but felt,
The while beneath Thy penetrating power
Light at the voice of God brake forth, a faint
Far tremor in the sunless starless gloom,
Creation's twilight, nor didst cease Thy work,
Till looking forth upon the vast expanse,
By mountains, rivers, lakes, and placid seas   10
Diversified, on that first sabbath's eve,
Infinite Goodness said that all was good :
·Come Thou, and brood over the deep unknown
Which bounds the known in me, nor suffer clouds,
Born of unfathomable mysteries,
To cast their shade athwart heaven's blessed light,

While, led by Thee, I speak of other worlds
Than those fair fields I lately walk'd, and tell
What from the' utmost precincts of Paradise
I and my angel guardian saw and heard   20
.Of outer darkness and Tartarean night.
Come; for Thou dwellest in the highest heavens,
Thyself inhabiting eternity,
Alone, Supreme, beyond all time and space,
Yet deignest in the contrite heart to' abide
As in Thy chosen temple; Spirit of Truth,
Who, in Thy Pentecostal might, from heaven
Descending as a mighty rushing wind,
Didst rest upon Thy suppliant saints of old
In likeness as of cloven tongues of fire,   80
A crown of lambent and innocuous flame;
Purge Thou mine eyes from film, my heart from fear;
Inspire, illumine, fortify my soul;
Breathe, O Thou Breath Divine, on my emprise;
Touch my fain lips, strengthen my feeble hands:
Nor let my footstep unawares intrude
On counsels Thou art pleased to veil from man,
Nor where Thy lamp shines dimly press too far
Adventurous, nor in coward disbelief
Shrink back appall'd where Thou dost lead the way. 40

As sweeps a breeze from off the spicy plains
Of Florence to the lonely Apennines,
Its passage only mark'd by rustling leaves
In the thick olive-groves, and stronger waves
Of light upon the mountain rivulets,

So from that peopled glen, where last we saw
The parents of mankind, Oriel and I
Along those plains and smiling valleys pass'd,
And up a forest-clad ravine that scarr'd
The bastions of those everlasting hills, 50
Heaven's boundary, and, emerging, found ourselves
On a vast table-land, leagues upon leagues
In breadth, which traversed, led our rapid course
To other hills hidden before from view :
These scaled, we landed on a second plain
Sublime, engirdled by yet distant peaks,
The triple wall and battlements of heaven.
Harder than adamant these rocks, yet seem'd
Of such original substance, as those beds
Of ice which with the flow of centuries 60
Creep along Alpine glens : rocks, half opaque,
Half lucid, where the piercing light was lost
In depths impervious of intensest green :
Ramparts far loftier than those giant hills,
With rhododendrons clad, and crown'd with snows,
The ancient Himalays. But, light as air,
We clomb that uttermost of Paradise ;
A path no vulture's eye hath ever seen,
A height no eagle's wing hath ever soar'd,
And standing on its extreme ridge, look'd down, 70
Lone sentinels. Strange promontory ours :
Behind us lay the radiant fields of bliss ;
But who, unblanch'd with terror, may describe
The scene before us ? Not in terraces
Or tiers of hills, mountains on mountains built,

Yielding access, though arduous, but a sheer
Precipitate descent, a horrid chasm,
Few paces off from where we stood, there yawn'd
Right at our feet: down, ever down, a depth
Equal the height of those eternal hills, 80
And how much lower no created eye
Might fathom: for a sea of clouds midway
Surged up and sank, and sinking, surged again,
Not vaporous mists alone, but sulphur smoke,
Mingled with sparkles, and with lurid flames,
Earth, air, fire, water, formless, shapeless, waste,
A chaos of all elements disturb'd,
Fused and confused, which seem'd a billowing tide,
Hither and thither sway'd, storm-tost, suspense,
Betwixt that awful cliff of Paradise 90
Rolling, and the far distant shore beyond.

Was it a shore beyond? At first it seem'd
Darkness alone, the absence of all light,
Blackness of darkness. But the while I gazed
Astonied, and mine eye more used became
To bear the dazzling terror of that gloom,
Dim lineaments before me slowly stretch'd,
And distances receding without end
Into the utter void; the realm of night,
A land of darkness and of gloominess, 100
Dark mountains, and yet darker vales between,
And waveless depths profound, darkest of all;
A world o'ershadow'd with the pall of death,
The sepulchre of life. But whence it came

Those outlines were not wholly' invisible,
I knew not. Loom'd there such a sullen glow
As fire suppress'd, not quench'd, emits : or such
Faint earthlight as our planet casts reflex
On the dull surface of the crescent moon ;
Or likest that sad mockery of day   110
He sees who, standing near as dread permits,
Beside a stream of burning lava, views
The blasted landscape in the dead of night.

Awe-struck I gazed ; but for relief ere long
Turn'd to the happy fields of light, which lay
Behind us, nurturing my soul awhile
With their pure joys. Then first I ask'd myself
What made that heavenly Eden luminous
With glory, and look'd up instinctively
On the blue crystal of the firmament,   120
Blue only from intensity of clear,
As if expecting there some orb of light ;
But there no lamp appear'd, no sun, no moon,
No star far glimmering in the azure vault ;
And yet the islands in the southern seas,
Basking in light when rains have clear'd the sky,
Were never bathed in radiance pure as this :
And Oriel saw my wonder and replied :

" Brother, remember Paradise is heaven,
Heaven's portal, and the portal of God's house   130
Needs not the shining of created light ;
For He, the Light of Light, is ever there,

And, where He is, darkness can ne'er exist;
Such virtue His eternal Presence sheds
Throughout the courts where He abides well pleased,
Rejoicing in the beauty' of holiness.
Far otherwise those realms of utter night,
Which lie beyond the mighty gulf thou seest,
Are darken'd with the shadow of His wrath.
That which is glory here is darkness there;   140
As when the fiery cloudy pillar stood,
A shield betwixt the hosts of Israel
And baffled Egypt's chariots. Nor can those
Who fain would pass from us to yonder world
On thoughts of pity' intent, or hence to us,
Traverse with foot or wing yon chasm profound :
Not for the interval, — for as thou seest
The landscapes of those desolate regions lie
Within our range, and listening we might catch
(So subtle here the waves of light and sound)   150
Far off its cries and voices ; and as spirits
Ourselves, with speed of lightnings, to and fro
Go and return ; but that a spiritual law,
Akin to that magnetic force which binds
The mortal habitants of earth to earth,
Has laid its viewless interdict between,
And bound the sons of darkness and of light
Each to their proper home. There is no path
From hell to heaven, from heaven to hell direct.
But haply thou remember'st, ere we touch'd   160
The outer confines of this world of spirits,
A roadway wrapt in clouds and gloom which stretch'd

6

Far to the left of our celestial course,
A roadway with funereal blackness hung
As ours with bridal light, and resonant
With sighings of despair, as ours with songs
Of triumph. To the gates of hell it leads,
Meet access for meet bourn, and down its track
The angels, the executors of wrath,
Bear in their hands lost men and rebel spirits,   170
Consigning them to their awarded prison
Of darkness, till the judgment trumpet sounds."

"And hast thou ever trodden that dread path,
And enter'd those eternal gates, and seen
The secrets of that penal world?" I ask'd,
And my voice falter'd as I spake.

                                "Yes, thrice,"
Oriel replied with calm unfaltering lip,
And with his words his countenance benign
Grew more and more severely beautiful,
The beauty of triumphant holiness,   180
The calm severity of burning love:
"Thrice in my ministry of saints hath God
Ordain'd me to fulfil His missions there;
And, brother, His behests are always good;
Pure goodness without stain of evil, light
Without the shadow of a shade of dark.
The earliest that I trod that awful road,
It was my charge, with other spirits elect,
A legion arm'd of warrior seraphim,

To bear in chains to their dark prison-house   190
Those angels who forsook their high estate
Through alien and unnatural lust. Of this
Thou shalt learn more hereafter. But the first
Of disembodied human souls I bore
To his own place in yonder realms of wrath
Was one I fondly loved, of noble birth,
Of high and generous bearing, who, alas,
Like some brave vessel cast on shifting sands,
Made shipwreck of his faith and sank to ruin.

"In brief, the story of his life was this:—   200
Three centuries and more had pass'd away
Since Jesus' birth in Bethlehem ; and he,
Of whom I tell thee, was a chieftain, born
Of Christian mother, but of heathen sire.
This was the bitter fountain of a stream
Of bitterness. For when in evil hour
His mother gave her heart to one who loved
The gods she loathed, and loathed the cross she loved—
She married immortality to death,
Faith to distrust, and hope to dark despair: 210
Discordant wedlock, whence discordant fruit.
Fondly she dream'd by ceaseless prayers to win
Her spouse to Christ. Vain hope ! her broken troth
Hung like a leaden weight on every prayer :
And he, a haughty consular of Rome,
Scorn'd her low creed, himself incredulous,
Yet loved the lovely votary. And when
The sweet pledge of their bridal joy was given.

And she would dedicate their child to God,
With equal scorn he yielded to her tears   220
A thing indifferent. In a lonely cave
Amid a group of trembling fugitives, —
For hatred then pursued the Christian name, —
An aged priest baptized him Theodore.
God's gift, his mother whisper'd. And thenceforth
She pour'd upon him, him her only child,
The priceless treasures of a mother's heart.
I was his chosen guardian. No light watch,
No easy vigil ; for his home, unlike
The moated fortress of a faithful house,   230
Was ever open to the spirits malign.
But not an arrow reach'd him. From himself,
And not from hellish fraud or violence,
His ruin. O mysterious web of life ;
Its warp of faith, its woof of unbelief;
The mother teaching prayers the father mock'd !
And yet her spell was earliest on her child,
And strongest. And the fearless Theodore
Was call'd by other men, and call'd himself,
A Christian. Love, emotion, gratitude,   240
All that was tenderest in a tender heart,
All most heroic in a hero's soul,
Pleaded on Christ's behalf. And oft I hoped,
Hoped against hope, that his was real faith,
A graft, a germ, a blossom — hoped till I
Could hope no longer, for I never saw
That warrior (he was train'd to arms) prostrate
A broken suppliant at the throne of love.

"The hour drew on that tried him.　Constantine,
The first of Christian emperors, was now　　　250
Marching with lion springs from land to land
Triumphant.　Him to meet in mortal fight
Maxentius hurried. vowing to his gods
That, if they crown'd his eagles, he would crush
The cross throughout the universe of Rome.
And Theodore, won by his mother's prayers,
Was with the faithful army; when it chanced,
In sack of a beleaguer'd city, he saved
A Grecian maiden and her sire from death:
Her name Irene, his Iconocles:　　　　　　260
Among the princes he a prince, of all
Fair women she the fairest of her race,
Not only for her symmetry of form,
But for the music and the love which breathed
In every motion and in every word.
Yet both were worshippers at Phœbus' shrine,
Fast-bound in midnight-dark idolatry.
And, when the enamour'd Theodore besought
His daughter of her sire, Iconocles
Made answer, ' Never shall my child be his　　270
Who kneels before a malefactor's cross.
Thy choice Irene, or the Crucified.'
And she by oath affirm'd her father's word.

"Then was there tempest in the swelling heart
Of Theodore: truth struggled and untruth
In terrible collision.　For an hour
He paced before his tent irresolute;

Now cleaving to his mother's faith, alas,
More hers than his; and now by passionate gusts
Driven from his anchorage, a helmless bark. 280
Conscience was quick; and God's Spirit strove with him.
'Twas mine to ward the powers of darkness off;
And singly with himself the awful fight
Was foughten, and, oh woe! for ever woe!
Was lost. And he said, 'Adam chose to die,
Not circumvented, not deceived like Eve,
But braving death itself for her dear sake.
So will I die. I cannot leave that spirit
Angelic in a human form enshrined.
She must be mine for ever. Life were death 290
Without her.' And straight entering, where she lean'd
Upon her father, as white jasmine leans
On a dark pine, slowly, resolvedly,
As measuring every word with fate, he said,
'Irene, if the choice be endless woe,
For thy sake I renounce my mother's faith:
I cannot, will not leave thee. I am thine.'

"And through the dusky twilight that same eve
The three forsook the tents of Constantine
And join'd Maxentius' host. And without pause, 300
Amid his early friends, Iconocles
Unto the marriage altar proudly led
The offering who had won so great a foe:
Small space was there for hymeneal pomp:
A soldier's spousal 'mid the clash of arms.

"That very night Great Constantine beheld
The fiery cross upon the sky, and read
The signal, IN HOC VINCES. And the morn,
Strange portent, saw far floating o'er his ranks
The labarum emblazon'd with the cross. 310
The armies rush'd to battle. Theodore
Rose from his nuptial couch, a desperate man;
No thought of penitence, none of retreat;
But in his eye a wild disastrous fire,
Sign of the fiercer flame he nursed within.
Lost, ruin'd, hopeless, and as glad to' escape
The tempest raging in his heart, he strode
Impetuously into the thickest fight,
And prodigies of valor wrought that day,
Felling beneath his fratricidal blade 320
Whole ranks, his comrades and his brethren late,
Brethren in faith and arms. But as he stamp'd
Upon the fallen in defiant pride,
And now as madden'd or inspired by hell
Pour'd blasphemies upon the Holy Name
His mother taught his infant lip to lisp
In blessings, even as he spake the words,
An unknown arrow, not unfledged with prayer,
Transpierced his eye and brain. Sudden he fell:
One short sharp cry; one strong convulsive throe; 330
And in a moment his unhappy spirit
Was from its quivering tabernacle loosed.

"Oh awful passage! from the din and roar
Of battle, from the trampling of horse-hoofs,

The roll of chariots, and the measured tread
Of thousands, from the brazen trumpet's blare
Drowning the shouts of victors, and the cries
Of wounded, agonizing, dying men,
From the worst dissonance of earth and time, —
The soul, in an eye's twinkling, brought to face   340
The calm deep silence of eternity.

" As stunn'd, the disembodied spirit awhile
Fix'd upon things unseen a vacant gaze :
But quickly' awaking from that dreadful swoon
To worse reality, he cried, the first
If not the strongest passion of his life
Surviving all the earthquake shock of death,
' Mother, where art thou, mother? where am I?'
And not till then emerging on his view
I spake and said, ' Lost spirit, it is not mine   350
To aggravate thy utter wretchedness
By words of idle grief or vain rebuke,
But to convey thee to that viewless world
Where thou must wait thy sentence from the lips
Of infinite, supreme, eternal Truth.
But thus far only, to anticipate
Resistance ; — to resist were futile here :
Almighty Power hath given thee to my charge,
And thou wert strengthless in my grasp. Our road
Lies yonder. Lost one, rise and come with me.'   360
So saying I laid my hand upon his hand,
And through his nerveless spirit he felt the touch
Of might superior to his own, and shrank

Appall'd, but soon remembering my words,
Yielded, and went with me the way I trod,
In tearless silence and in mute despair.

" It is not thus with all when first they wake
To consciousness of ruin.   Some straightway
Will wring their hands in agony, and weep,
And pour their lamentations forth in words,   870
And wail for bitter anguish.   Others strive
With proud reluctancies and vain despite
Against their dark inevitable doom.
Others, palsied with terror, shivering stand.
Others curse their creation.   Theodore
Was diverse from such men on earth, and now
Was diverse.   As I spake, at one fell glance
He seem'd to measure the abyss profound
Before him, and by terrible resolve,
Alas, too late submissive, to accept   380
The everlasting punishment of sin.

" At first our pathway was the same as that
Which led thee homeward, brother.   Through the
   heaven
Which wraps the earth in its cerulean robe,
And through the starry firmament, until
The sun which lightens the terrestrial globe
Paled like a distant lamp, slowly we pass'd ;
Slowly, — I had no heart for speed, nor was
The King's commission urgent.   He delights
In mercy, and His embassies of grace   390

Have never found seraphic wings too swift:
But judgment is His strange and dreadful work.
And, as with measured step we trod adown
That highway through the heavens precipitate,
My hopeless captive gazed a long last gaze
Upon the fading sun and passing stars
As signs which he should never more behold:
And drawn from out his bosom's depths at last
A groan brake from him, and he sobb'd aloud —
' My mother, oh my mother, from thy love　　　　400
I learn'd to love those silent orbs of light,
God's watchers thou didst call them, as they peer'd
Evening by evening on my infant sleep,
And mingled with my every boyish dream:
Are they now shining on thy misery?
Who, now that I am gone, will wipe thine eyes?
Who, mother, bind thy bruised and broken heart?
Broken, by whom? by me, thy nestling babe,
Thy darling child, thy pride in arms; by me,
Thy wretched, renegade, apostate son.'　　　　410

" So mourn'd he, and I answer'd, ' Theodore,
Thou hast enough to bear of things that are,
Without this load of unsubstantial grief.
Thy mother knew not thine apostasy,
Nor otherwise will deem of thee than slain
One of the Christian host, the little while
Weeping she sojourns in the vale of tears.
Such fear she never harbor'd, and the cloud
Of mercy veils thy ruin from her eye,

Until the awful shades of time are seen   420
In the clear noon-day of eternity.
Thus far it is permitted thee to know.'

" My words were only the bare utterance
Of truth, but never will this heart forget
The impress of the look he cast on me.
He had not wept before ; but now a tear
Hung on his trembling lids, through which he look'd
Such gratitude as utter hopelessness
May render, like the Grecian fire that burns
Far under the deep waves, a look which said,   430
I thank thee as the damn'd alone can thank :
Lost as I am, hell will not be such hell,
The while my mother thinks of me in heaven.'

" Again in speechless silence we moved on,
Until that billowy sea of mists and clouds
Which wraps the world of spirits appear'd in sight ;
And to our nearer step the avenue
Celestial open'd its translucent road,
Emitting floods of glory ; and there distinct,
Hovering upon its golden skirts, we saw   440
A group of angels waiting to receive
An aged pilgrim home, and heard far off
Their jubilant acclamations.   Ours, alas !
Another path.   Far to the left it led,
Gloomy as night.   And as we turn'd aside
From those fair portals, piteously I mark'd
The longing, lingering, almost loving look

Which my unhappy captive cast behind,
As if heaven's sights and sounds, once seen and heard,
Might haply prove a gracious memory   450
Amid the cries of everlasting woe
And discords without end.

                   " But now the light
Was fading: shadows into shadows gloom'd
More awful; and obscurity itself
Became more inexpressibly obscure,
More solid, as the interposing clouds
High overhead, beneath us, and beyond,
Built up impervious ramparts every way
Except the desolate ravine we trod.
Night reign'd sole monarch here, and spread around 460
Palpable darkness, darkness unrelieved
Save by the radiance of my form, a faint
And feeble torch in that ungenial air,
But yet enough to show the massive sides
Of fogs impenetrable.   Never yet
Saw I such darkness: for, when last I march'd
This dreadful road, I came accompanied
By a whole legion arm'd of spirits elect,
Whose light, each on the other, blaze on blaze,
Reflected, and turn'd midnight into noon.   470
But now I was alone — the Lord of Hosts
Makes all His servants lean on His sole arm —
Alone, my clinging captive and myself:
Though in the distance more than once methought
I heard the rushing of cherubic wings,
And, like a glimmering meteor, caught the flash

Of some good angel's transitory flight.
Haply the whole ravine equals in length,
Nor more than equals, that resplendent track
By which my courier angels bore thee on　　　480
To sound of lyres, and lutes, and welcome songs,
Up to the pearly gates of Paradise ;
But here our flight was difficult and slow,
And seven times seven appear'd the weary length
Of that interminable road.　At last
A dull and ruddy glow tinctured the gloom :
Not light, but something which made black itself
Not viewless.　As to one standing aloof,
When Etna or Vesuvius pour their wrath
In giant folds of smoke voluminous,　　　490
A gloaming, from the fiery crater cast,
Paints from below the dark impending mass ;
So to our eyes the steep descent became
Not all invisible, its cloudy walls
And wide abysses cavernous betwixt
Of horrid emptiness.　But on we moved,
And swerved not to the right hand or the left,
For now, far off, fronting our path profound,
Before us rose the iron gates of hell.

"We paused ; for lo, before these dreadful doors　500
Waved what appear'd a fiery sword, or swords
Innumerable, haply not unlike
That flaming falchion, which at Eden's gate
Revolving every way, flame within flame,
Guarded the tree of life.　Only these blades

Were vast as are the rays a setting sun,
Hidden itself, will sometimes proudly cast
Up to heaven's vault athwart a thunder cloud.
But straight, as if they knew my mission, these
Parted to right and left, and oped a way   510
High overarch'd with fire, through which we pass'd
Unscathed: and of themselves, dreadful to see,
The adamantine doors of hell recoil'd
Back, slowly back, with ponderous noise, — as when
An Alpine avalanche moves from its ridge
And with one crash of ruin overwhelms
A valley's life, — and with their harsh recoil
Disclosed the secrets of that world of woe.

" Brother, come stand with me upon the edge
Of this far-looking cliff, which overhangs   520
The gulf betwixt that cursed land and ours
Impassable.   Not otherwise that day,
Nor seen in other than yon dusky glow,
The infernal realms, when we had pass'd the gates,
Beneath us lay outstretch'd.   Hills, valleys, plains,
All mantled in disastrous twilight, couch'd
Under our feet.   But then it was no hour
For marvel or for mute astonishment.
Straight from the threshold of those gates sublime
Through the oppressive sultry atmosphere   530
I guided our slant flight, until midway
Upon a barren mountain's steep ascent,
(Yonder it rises girt with lesser hills,)
Where a vast glen was ramparted with rocks,
Alighting I relax'd my captive's hand.

"And then and there upon that guilty man
The Eye of everlasting righteousness
Open'd. God look'd upon him. Through and through
His naked spirit, searching its darken'd depths,
Pass'd like a flame of fire, that Dreadful Eye,   540
Pass'd and repass'd, and passing still abode
Upon him; till the very air he breathed
Seem'd to his sense one universal flame
Of wrath, eternal wrath, the wrath to come.
And yet the glory of that majesty,
That burning brightness, shone not then full orb'd,
But veil'd in part; for disembodied souls,
Dismantled of their proper robe of flesh,
Could neither suffer nor sustain the weight
Of that unclouded Holiness Divine,   550
Which in the age of ages will subdue
All foes beneath the footstool of His throne.
So half eclipsed it shone: and a low wail
Ere long brake from those miserable lips —
'O God, and is this hell? and must this last
For ever? would I never had been born!
Why was I born? I did not choose my birth.
O Thou, who didst create me, uncreate,
I pray thee. By Thine own omnipotence
Quench Thou this feeble spark of life in me.   560
Why should I longer live? I never more
Can serve Thee: that Thy justice interdicts.
I am no adversary worthy Thee.
Can power be magnified on strengthlessness?
Put forth Thy might but once, and crush a worm,

For love, for hate unequal both.   O Christ,
I kneel, I fall a suppliant at Thy throne.
I ask not pardon.   Grace, I know, is past:
Redemption cannot cross those iron gates.
But art not Thou the Son of God?   Thyself   570
God over all, supreme for evermore?
And are not all things possible with God?
O God, destroy me.   Grant this latest boon
Thy wretched ruin'd child will ever ask,
And suffer me to be no more at all.'

   " And then at last I spoke, ' Is this thy hope,
Unhappy one, this aimless bootless prayer?
Thou cravest what Omnipotence can do:
Know that Omnipotence can but perform
The counsels which Omniscient Love decrees.   580
And therefore vainly dost thou now invoke
Almighty power to thwart All-seeing Love.
It cannot be.   Discord can never dwell
Within the bosom of eternal Peace,
Nor darkness stain that uncreated Light.
What then remains for thee?   To flee were vain,
And would but bring thee adamantine bonds ;
And fresh rebellion here at once incur
Immediate instantaneous punishment.
Free service, which is heaven's perennial joy,   590
Guilt, said'st thou truly, interdicts.   What then?
Passive submission is the only way
Left thee to serve thy Maker.   Hades knows
No other law.   The judgment is beyond.

Meanwhile this valley is thy prison assign'd;
And not in utter solitariness,
For other souls, who like thyself have sinn'd,
Some known to thee on earth and some unknown,
Here wait their sentence, whose companionship
Will mitigate or aggravate thy woe,   600
As thou submittest to the flame that burns
The sin in thee with fire unquenchable,
Or vainly chafest against its scorching ray:
This yet is in thy choice.   Haply at times
This valley will be trodden by the feet
Of angels on the embassies of God:
But at rare intervals, for many and vast
Are the dark fields of punishment, and few
The ministrations of the sons of light
In this the land of overshadowing death.   610
And here there is no sentinel but God;
His Eye alone is jailer; and His Hand
The only executioner of wrath.
And now I leave thee: let my words abide
With thee, lest added torment scourge thy soul:
Passive submission is the law of hell.'

"But, even as I turn'd to leave him, slowly
He raised his eyes, bow'd hitherto beneath
The intolerable Eye of Holiness,
Which rested on him evermore.   And lo!   620
Far off, beyond this intervening chasm,
Through an embrasure in heaven's triple wall,
Where mountains distant mountains intersect.

7

He caught a glimpse, permitted him by God,
Of some sequester'd spot in Paradise.
It riveted his gaze : it fill'd his soul
With longing : and unconsciously he cried,
' Am I asleep ? there is no slumber here.
Is it a dream ? there are no dreams in hell.
I see, I see far off the fields of bliss ;   630
And there are figures moving to and fro :
I see them by the liquid fountains walking,
And resting underneath the trees of life.
There I may never walk, there never rest :
But oh, for one small ministry of love !
Oh, for one leaf of those delicious groves
To soothe the scars of my eternal pain !
Oh, for one drop of those pure rivulets
To cool, not slake, my agonizing thirst ! '

" I could not leave him thus, vainly consumed   640
By idle phantasies of hope, to which
The fabled pangs of Tantalus were ease,
And in mere pity answer'd, ' Theodore,
Those whom thou seest are reaping now the seed
They sow'd on earth, and thou must do the same.
Time is the seed-plot for eternity ;
Eternity the harvest-field of time.
Thy lot is fixed, and theirs.   Nor can the foot
Of disembodied spirit, nor angel wing,
Transgress the deep inexorable gulf   650
Betwixt the worlds of darkness and of light.'

" Still gazed he on, and gazing still replied,
' There is no hope for me ; but art not thou
Returning to thy ministry on earth ?
Would it were not so ! would that thou couldst stay
For ever here, whose light ethereal form
And heavenly essence suffer no eclipse
From hell's dark murky atmosphere ! At first
Sorely I fear'd thy dreadful touch of power,
Before I knew thee good ; but now I see   660
That in the hands of goodness power is love,
And crave thy longer presence. That is vain :
I know that thou must leave me. Thou canst do
No more for me. But is there not a hope
For one I briefly passionately loved —
Irene ? surely she is mine, for whom,
Fool, fool, I barter'd immortality.
Angel, I would not she should perish too.
Go to her straight, I pray thee. Lay thy hand
Upon her, as on him who linger'd once   670
When wrath o'ershadow'd Sodom. Force belief.
Tell her, in mercy tell her, where I am —
What suffering — what must suffer evermore :
It may be, she will turn and live. And if,
Whene'er my mother's pilgrimage is pass'd,
And she, entering the gates of bliss, shall search
Through every field of yonder Paradise
To find her only son, and search in vain,
If then thou wilt but try and comfort her —
What way I know not, but thou know'st — and should
Her restless eye intuitively glance   [680

Towards this valley, instantly divert
Its gaze else whither, thou wilt have done all
I ask for, and far more than I deserve.'

"I answer'd, 'Theodore, thy widow'd spouse,
Listening the story of the cross, has more
Than angel importunity to urge
Submission. Who resist the blood-stain'd cross
Resist the uttermost that Heaven can do.
Faith must be free, not forced. Nor deem that she 690
Who bore thee, and who knows not yet thy doom,
If counted worthy of the gates of bliss,
Will need the ministry of angel hands
To stanch her wounds, or wipe her tears away:
Love, tenderer than the tenderest mother's, there
Comforts the weary heart and weeping eye.
Thy prayers to thy own bosom must return.
And yet, unhappy spirit, the Eye, which lights
Thy darkness with intolerable flame,
Doth not consume in thee the secret spring   700
Of pity whence those supplications flow'd.
For pity is of God, a fragment left
Even here of thy Divine original,
Not wholly crush'd. Nor can there be in God
Wrath against any Godlike lineament,
Wherever found, or howsoever dimm'd.
Not for thy pity art thou where thou art:
Not for thy pity rests the wrath to come
For ever on thy soul, but for thy sin
Indulged, embraced, enjoy'd, till sin and thou   710

No longer separable things became
Incorporate in one, one sinful life,
One ever-living sinner.   But the Day
Is coming, which will all to all declare.
And now, my mission done, my time elapsed,
I leave thee in thy Just Creator's hands.'

"So saying, through that lurid atmosphere
I rose, and through the flaming vault of hell,
And through the iron portals pass'd, which oped
And closed behind me of their own accord,   720
And through that dark ravine of midnight gloom,
And up that mighty highway of the heavens,
And by the passing stars and brightening sun;
Nor stay'd upon the battle-field of earth,
But upwards soaring with unwearied flight
Swift as the lightning toward the heaven of heavens
I bent my eager course, nor paused until
Kneeling before the everlasting throne,
And gazing on the emerald arch of love,
I soothed my bosom's agitated depths   730
In the calm presence of the light of God."

Then Oriel's voice was hush'd; and for a space
He seem'd as one communing with himself,
And nurturing his strength with memories
Of things that lived for ever in his soul,
The record of his ministry approved,
The beatific smile, the gracious words
Of benediction, and the choral songs

Of those who magnified his God in him:
But soon, mindful of my solicitude,   740
His awful story he resumed once more.

"Not then return'd I straight to earth; for then
Throughout the lower provinces of heaven
Was warfare. Michael and his angels fought,
Satan and his: no visionary strife;
But battle such as earth has never seen,
Seraph with seraph warring. And my lot
Was with Messiah's armies militant
To drive the rebel hosts from those fair realms
Their presence had too long defiled. Of this   750
I will relate hereafter. But, expell'd
From heaven, our foes and thine with doubled rage
Possess'd the lower firmament of earth.
And from that hour for fifteen centuries,
Not seldom with a band of spirits elect
Encamping, but more oft alone with God,
My charge was ministering to heirs of life.
Blest heirs, twice blessed minister! Nor came
My summons the third time to tread the shores
Of darkness, till the decade which forewent   760
My latest guardianship of saints — thyself.

"Already had the seven last angels, seen
By John in Patmos, from heaven's sanctuary
Come forth array'd in priestly robes of white,
Girdled with gold, and bearing in their hands
The mystic vials of the wrath of God.

Already had they pour'd those censers forth
Upon the earth, the sea, the river springs,
The sun's orb, and the great usurper's throne.
Two only' of seven remain'd. It was the year   770
When the last throes of laboring France were still'd,
And her proud despot, he for whom the world
Once seem'd too insignificant a throne,
Was banish'd to his narrow sea-girt isle
To chafe against the idle winds and waves ;
Then first I heard a chosen embassy
Of the angelic sanctities and powers
(Myself the twelfth) was order'd to descend
And traverse hell in all its length and breadth,
Announcing to the prisoners of wrath   780
The nearer advent of the day of doom.
Immediately, for angels never pause
To ask the wherefore of Divine behests,
Nor question their own aptitude whom God
Has summon'd as His aptest messengers,
We, on the wings of morning light. obey'd
And went. Swiftly, harmoniously we flew,
And each the other cheer'd with sweet converse
Of the Lamb's Bridal now at hand ; but soon,
At hell's inexorable gates arrived,   790
Our several and predestined pathways took
Through diverse fields of gloom and fiery woe,
Ordaining, when our dark sojourn was o'er,
To meet at last in that profoundest depth
Where rebel angels are immured in walls
Of darkness nearest to Gehenna's lake

" First to that mountain valley, where I left
Lost Theodore, I bent my course.   O God!
The solemn change which fifteen centuries
In hell had written on his fearful brow.   800
Unchanged in form, unchanged in hopelessness,
The same immortal heir of endless wrath,
But now the restlessness of agony,
The writhing of the miserable spirit
Under the first experience of despair,
Was scarcely visible.   Subdued he sate
Apart, crush'd, conscience-stricken, almost calm;
Oft gazing on that distant Paradise,
Which still appear'd within his vision's ken
And cast its reflex light upon his ruin,   810
But waken'd now no hope.   He mark'd my flight;
He heard my footstep in the vale ; he rose
In reverence : and, when he knew me, spake
In accents so chastised, they touch'd me more
Than loudest wailings or incessant tears

" ' O holy angel, is it thou ?   What brings
Thee to this dreadful prison-house again ?
I had not thought to see thee till I stood
Before the judgment-throne.   But I have learn'd
Much since I saw thee last.   My little span   820
Of mortal life, inured and stereotyped,
Is branded on the tablet of my soul
Each year, each month, each week, each day, each hour.
As drowning men have lived their bygone life
Again in one brief minute, so to me,

Each minute of these ages without end,
My past is always present. Now I see
Myself. 'Twas not apostasy alone
Damn'd me: this seal'd my ruin: but my life
Was one rebellion, one ingratitude.   830
God would, but could not save me 'gainst my will,
Moved, drawn, besought, persuaded, striven with,
But yet inviolate, or else no will,
And I no man — for man by birth is free.
Angel, He would, I would not. Further space
Would but have loaded me with deeper guilt.
Yea, now I fear that if the Eye of flame
Which rests upon me everlastingly
Soften'd its terrors, sin would yet revive
In me and bear again disastrous fruit,   840
And this entail more torturing remorse.
Better enforced subjection. I have ceased
Or almost ceased to struggle' against the Hand
That made me. For I madly chose to die:
I sold my immortality for death:
And death, eternal distance from His love,
Eternal nearness to His righteous wrath,
Death now is my immortal recompense.
I know it, I confess it, I submit.
But oh! the boding dread that I ere long   850
Must re-assume the flesh in which I sinn'd,
And naked stand before the judgment-throne.'

   " He ceased, and I replied: ' My mission is ·
To tell thee that the time is short

Before the dawning of that day of God,
Its Advent sunrise, its millennial sphere,
Its evening-tide of heaven and earth's assize.
I may not linger; for my journey tends
Throughout these desolate confines of woe
To hell's remotest verge ; but first to thee   860
(Thee only of the lost, my ward) I come
Permitted to advise thee this.   If here
The Uncreated Light, part seen, part veil'd,
Hath wrung this last confession from thy lips
That thy subordination, though compell'd,
Is better in its everlasting chains
Than dissolute freedom and unbridled guilt,
Will not its veilless and meridian blaze
(However terrible the fire that burns
The ineradicable germs of sin   870
For ever and for ever in thy soul,
Repressing their fertility with flame)
Be good, not evil? yea, the highest good
Thy guilt has render'd possible?   It will:
For God Himself has sworn that every knee,
Not only of the things in heaven and earth
But of the regions under earth in hell,
Shall bow beneath the sceptre of His Son,
And, willing or constrain'd, confess Him Lord.'

    " Nor paused I for an answer, but pursued   880
My way along that valley of the dead,
Only one valley of a myriad like,
But yet so vast, that, though its habitants

Were more than many a throng'd metropolis,
Scatter'd throughout its solitudes they seem'd,
Where'er I trod, but few and far betwixt
And seldom group'd in converse. Every one
Had his own chastisement to bear; on each
And every one the Eye of God was fix'd;
On every one the Hand of God was press'd.   890
And for the most part silence reign'd: few sighs
Were heard, or groans, or mutterings of remorse,
And chiefly these among the last arrived,
Who, when they knew themselves for ever lost,
Wept and bewail'd their ruin, till, their tears
And bitter outcries bringing no relief,
They, like their fellows, sank upon the ground,
Or wander'd to and fro in mute despair.
Most, peradventure, chose to be alone
From that sheer misery, which could not brook   900
Another convict's eye to read their woe.
But yet it was not always thus: at times
They met, and fearfully exchanged their pangs
And drear forebodings, which, from words I caugh
Centred on judgment and eternity.

" Lost souls of every type were there: and yet
The hell of one was not another's hell.
Nor needed separate prisons to adjust
The righteous meed of punishment to each.
As they had sinn'd, they suffer'd; for the flame   910
Of perfect righteousness abode on them,
God's righteousness on their unrighteousness.

Distinct, discriminate, distributive,
More tolerant of guilty ignorance
Than of intolerable guilty pride,
Restraining that which chafed against restraint.
Abhorring most the most abhorrent deeds,
Lighter on some, on others more intense;
Severest on the guiltiest, but to all
An earnest of the final lake of fire.   920

  " Some I beheld, who from the gayest haunts
Of fashion's revelries and pageantries
Were summon'd by the icy hand of death,
Blithe men, fair women, and, most piteous sight,
Children in years but not in wickedness:
And some, who fell asleep in sinks of vice,
Amid the orgies of their drunkenness
Breathing out curses in a harlot's ear,
And waken'd, unawares, amazed, to find
Damnation, oft invoked, at last their own.   930

  " I pass'd where two were standing side by side,
A princess, who had floated on through life
Wrapt in the perfumed incense-cloud of praise,
And a poor beggar's fallen child. They both
Had lived the living death of godless mirth;
Though variously in marble palaces
And wretched hovels matter'd little here:
One hour had made them comrades; one despair
Was written on their face; one sympathy
Drew them together; while in speechless woe   940
Each wrung convulsively her sister's hand.

" But heavier far their chastisement who drew
Their fellows to perdition from their greed
Of mammon, or from fleshly appetite.
In them the horrible antagonism
Betwixt the pure of God and their impure, —
His good, their ill, — His ruth, their cruelty, —
His heavenly love, and their most hellish lust, —
Bred an insufferable anguish words
May never picture, nor the heart of saint   950
Or any saintly' intelligence conceive.

" And there were hypocrites unmask'd and stripp'd ;
And haughty Pharisaic dignities
Low in the dust; and liars taught too late
To utter agonizing words of truth ;
And gamblers, who had staked their soul and lost ;
And perjurers compell'd at last to dread
God's oath ; manslayers, convict or escaped,
Confessing Hades had no shade secure
From blood's avenging cry ; and not a few   960
Diviners, necromancers, sorcerers,
Who once sought lawless commerce with the dead,
Now number'd with the damned dead themselves ;
And learned infidels, who proved a God
At least among improbabilities,
Aghast for ever underneath His frown.

" All these, and many more in that vast glen,
As I pursued my embassage, I saw,
And could narrate their names ; but better far

Buried in silence and oblivion's grave   970
Until the day of doom. They heard my voice;
And countless as they were, so manifold
The tokens of their anguish or dismay,
When I proclaimed the nearer dawn at hand:
Tears, tremblings, pallor which became more pale,
Moans, or more terrible than moans, the gaze
Of agony suppress'd, heart-rending sighs,
Or wailings of remorseless memory,
Or darker lourings of malign despite
Crush'd in a moment by the penal fire,   980
But each in his own way betokening
His terror of the unknown wrath to come.

"They miss the truth who meditate that death,
Or that which follows after death, can change
The native idealities of men.
These in the saved and lost alike remain
Immutable for ever. There is nought
In the unloosing of the mortal tent
To alter or transform immortal minds.
The gentle still are gentle, and the strong   990
Are ever strong. Innumerable traits
Each from the rest distinguish. It is true
There lies a gulf impassable betwixt
Salvation and perdition, heaven and hell;
But oh! the almost infinite degrees
Betwixt the lost and lost.

                    "All this I saw

In that one desolate valley of the dead,
And then to other hills and rocks and plains
Of that dark world I pass'd.   Nor boots it now
That I to thee, unwilling both, relate   1000
The progress of my terrible sojourn
In those drear regions.   God was with me there,
Or my celestial pinions would have droop'd
Unequal by my side.   But in His strength
I traversed all the provinces assign'd
To my celestial mission, nor surceased
My flight till every habitant therein
Heard from my lips (and none who heard gainsay'd)
Messiah's nearer Advent, and that soon
They might expect to see the Arch-fiend led   1010
In chains to his millennial prison-house,
A presage of his everlasting doom.

" Vast were the realms I trod, and to my eye
No bound apparent: but from clime to clime
Not many hours, as men count hours, elapsed
Without some ruin'd soul arriving thither
And swelling the dark aggregate of woe.
And then perchance there was a transient pause,
A momentary break: but soon the rest,
Their own cup full of misery, sank back   1020
In personal despair.   It was but once,
And then for a brief space, I saw the dead
Stirr'd with profounder feeling.   I was there,
What time a mighty conqueror came down
To limitless captivity.   He came,

Aforetime wont to lead his armies forth,
The god of pride, incarnate selfishness,
The nations trembling at his iron rod,
And tributary monarchs in his suite,
Now guided only by a stripling cherub,   1030
Yet in whose hand that vanquish'd victor's might
Were less than nothing.   For a little while
His fall was theme of converse with the dead,
But soon the voices sank; and hell resumed
Its dread monotony of crushing calm.

   " Terrestrial years pass'd by, as thus I trod
These regions, but my Captain's charge fulfill'd,
I came at last to that profound abyss
Wrapt in a tenfold gloom of darkening wrath,
Nearest Gehenna's lake, which first I saw   1040
When with a band of seraphim in arms,
I bore the captive angels, Samchasai
And Uziel, fallen potentates of heaven,
In chains, themselves and their rebellious hosts,
To their eternal banishment.   Since then
Four great millennial days had come and gone,
But there they lay immured in darkness, link'd
With adamantine manacles to rocks
Of adamant: and with them other spirits
Who, having fill'd their cup of wickedness   1050
Before the time, before the time were hurl'd
To this dark dungeon.   Such were those who sought
With suicidal prayer, Legion their name,
Driven from the human heart, their chosen seat,

To herd with swine ; and, their demand vouchsafed,
Rush'd headlong, they and all their bestial throng —
These into ocean depths and those to hell.
Nor were they solitary in their doom :
For think not He whose vengeance flashes forth
Upon the sons of men, and unawares   1060
Strikes down the sinner in his hour of pride, —
Think not He leaves the fallen hosts unwarn'd
By dread ensamples of His wrath, though such
No warning moves and no ensample' avails
To turn from final death. Yet once they stood
Pure spirits before the sapphire throne in heaven.
And many I knew in that their first estate,
And with them I had walk'd the golden streets,
And pluck'd the vintage of celestial grapes,
And tuned my harp in unison with theirs.   1070
But now, behold them — every lineament
Dimm'd with despair and utter agony.
For, as their guilt was deeper, fiercer wrath
Alone their unrepentant nature curb'd
From words and deeds of devilish violence.
That wrath was there. And of despite was heard
No whisper, nor a thought of open war
Express'd, nor breathed a breath of blasphemy.

"But them already advertised I found
By heaven's angelic principalities   1080
Of our great errand. So, our mission o'er,
Back from that bottomless abyss we turn'd,
And through hell's desolate champaigns arose,

8

Its iron portals, and its dark access;
And when, with footsteps nothing loath, we trod
The confines of most blessed light again,
Our Captain, as Melchisedec of old
Met Abraham with mystic bread and wine,
Himself came forth to meet us bearing fruit
Himself had pluck'd from heaven's ambrosial trees, 1090
And with His benediction wrote on all
The large experience of those years of gloom
The rainbow of His clear approving smile."

So Oriel spake, and ceased: and as he ceased
I felt his tears were falling on my hand.

END OF THE THIRD BOOK.

Book Fourth.

THE CREATION OF ANGELS AND OF MEN.

O TEARS, ye rivulets that flow profuse
Forth from the fountains of perennial love,
Love, sympathy, and sorrow, those pure springs
Welling in secret up from lower depths
Than couch beneath the everlasting hills:
Ye showers that from the cloud of mercy fall
In drops of tender grief, — you I invoke,
For in your gentleness there lies a spell
Mightier than arms or bolted chains of iron.
When floating by the reedy banks of Nile   10
A babe of more than human beauty wept,
Were not the innocent dews upon its cheeks
A link in God's great counsels? Who knows not
The loves of David and young Jonathan,
When in unwitting rivalry of hearts
The son of Jesse won a nobler wreath
Than garlands pluck'd in war and dipp'd in blood?

And haply she, who wash'd her Saviour's feet
With the soft silent rain of penitence,
And wiped them with her tangled tresses, gave   20
A costlier sacrifice than Solomon,
What time he slew myriads of sheep and kine,
And pour'd upon the brazen altar forth
Rivers of fragrant oil.   In Peter's woe,
Bitterly weeping in the darken'd street,
Love veils his fall.   The traitor shed no tear.
But Magdalene's gushing grief is fresh
In memory of us all, as when it drench'd
The cold stone of the sepulchre.   Paul wept,
And by the droppings of his heart subdued   30
Strong men by all his massive arguments
Unvanquish'd.   And the loved Evangelist
Wept, though in heaven, that none in heaven were found
Worthy to loose the Apocalyptic seals.
No holy tear is lost.   None idly sinks
As water in the barren sand: for God,
Let David witness, puts his children's tears
Into His cruse and writes them in His book; —
David, that sweetest lyrist, not the less
Sweet that his plaintive pleading tones ofttimes   40
Are tremulous with grief.   For he and all
God's nightingales have ever learn'd to sing,
Pressing their bosom on some secret thorn.
In the world's morning it was thus: and, since
The evening shadows fell athwart mankind,
Thus hath it always been.   Blind and bereft,
The minstrel of an Eden lost explored

Things all invisible to mortal eyes.
And he, who touch'd with a true poet's hand
The harp of prophecy, himself had learn'd　　50
Its music in the school of mourners.　But
Beyond all other sorrow stands enshrined
The imperishable record — JESUS WEPT.
He wept beside the grave of Lazarus ;
He wept lamenting lost Jerusalem ;
He wept with agonizing groans beneath
The olives of Gethsemane.　O tears,
For ever sacred, since in human grief
The Man of sorrows mingled healing drops
With the great ocean tides of human woe ;　　60
You I invoke to modulate my words
And chasten my ambition, while I search,
And by your aid with no unmoisten'd eye,
The early archives of the birth of time.

Yes, there are tears in heaven.　Love ever breathes
Compassion; and compassion without tears
Would lack its truest utterance : saints weep
And angels : only there no bitterness
Troubles the crystal spring.　And when I felt,
More solaced than surprised, my guardian's tears　　70
Falling upon my hand, my bosom yearn'd
Towards him with a nearer brotherhood ;
And, terrible as seem'd his beauty once,
His terrors were less mighty than his tears.
His heart was as my heart.　He was in grief,
No feigned sorrow.　And instinctively —

Love's instinct to console the one beloved —
I answer'd, " Oriel, let it grieve thee not
Thus to have told me of thy dark sojourn
In yonder world of death. I thought before   80
Of thee as dwelling ever in the light,
And knowing only joy ; but now I see
We both have suffer'd ; sinless thou, and I
Ransom'd from sin ; for others only thou,
I for myself and others ; — but yet links
Betwixt us of a tender sympathy
Eternity will rivet, not unloose.
And now, albeit, had I nursed a hope
For those unhappy prisoners of wrath,
Thy words had quench'd the latest spark, yet thou,   90
While quenching hope, hast hopelessness illumed.
Far visions throng my eye and fill my soul
Of evil overcome by final good,
And death itself absorb'd in victory.
But first I long to listen from thy lips
The story of creation's birth, whene'er
In the unclouded morning-tide of heaven
Thou and thy holy peers beheld the light."

And Oriel took my hand in his once more,
And from the summit of that cliff we turn'd,   100
And, with the ease of spirits, descending sought
A lower platform, whence the mighty gulf
Betwixt that shadowy land of death and ours
Was hidden, but afar pre-eminent
Over the realms of Paradise.   But soon

A train of silvern mists and airy clouds,
Only less limpid than the light itself,
Began to creep from every vale, where late
Invisible they couch'd by fount and rill,
Around us o'er the nearer hills, and hung   110
Their lucid veils across the crystal sky,
Not always, but by turns drawn and withdrawn
In grateful interchange, so that awhile
Rocks, mountains, valleys, woods, and glittering lakes,
And those uncounted distances of blue
Were mantled with their flowing draperies,
And then awhile in radiant outline lay ; —
Haply less lovely when unclothed than clothed
With those transparent half-transparent robes,
But loveliest in alternate sheen and shade.   120
I knew the token and was still : and there
Upon a ledge of rock recline, we gazed
Our fill of more than Eden's freshness, when
The mists of God water'd the virgin earth,
And gazing drank the music of its calm,
Silent ourselves for gladness.   But at last,
As if recalling his far-travell'd thoughts,
Not without deeper mellowness of tone,
Oriel resumed his narrative and spake :

" Yes, saidst thou truly, in the world of spirits,   130
As in the early Paradise of man,
Creation had its morning without clouds;
When first the bare illimitable void
Throughout its everlasting silences

Heard whispers of God's voice and trembled.   Then,
Passing from measureless eternity,
In which the Highest dwelt Triune Alone,
To measurable ages, Time began.
And then, emerging out of nothingness,
At God's behest commanding LET THEM BE,   140
The rude raw elements of nature WERE:
Viewless and without form at first.   But soon
God will'd, and breathed His will; and lo, a sea
Of subtle and elastic ether flow'd,
Immense, imponderable, luminous,
Which, while revealing other things, remains
Itself invisible, impalpable,
Pervading space.   Thus Uncreated Light
Created in the twinkling of an eye
A tabernacle worthy of Himself,   150
And saw that it was good, and dwelt therein.
Then, moulded by the Word's almighty hand,
And by the Spirit of life inform'd, the heaven
With all its orbits and the heaven of heavens
Rose like a vision.   There the throne supreme,
Refulgent as if built of solid light,
Where He, whom all the heavens cannot contain,
Reveals His glory' incomprehensible,
Was set upon the awful mount of God,
The Heavenly Zion: over it above   160
The empyrean of the universe;
And near it, or beneath it as it seem'd,
That mystic chariot, paved with love, instinct
Thereafter with the holy cherubim;

And round about it four and twenty thrones,
Vacant as yet — not long. God, who is Spirit,
Bade spirits exist, and they existed. Forms
Of light, in infinite varieties,
Though all partaking of that human type
Which afterward the Son of God assumed 170
(Angelical and human forms, thou seest,
Are not so far diverse as mortals think),
Awoke in legions arm'd, or one by one
Successively appear'd. Succession there,
In numbers passing thy arithmetic,
Might be more rapid than my words, and yet
Exhaust the flight of ages. There is space
For ages in the boundless past. But each
Came from the hand of God distinct, the fruit
Of His eternal counsels, the design 180
Of His omniscient love, His workmanship;
Each seraph, no angelic parentage
Betwixt him and the Great Artificer,
Born of the Spirit, and by the Word create.

" Of these were three the foremost, Lucifer,
Michael, and Gabriel: Lucifer, the first,
Conspicuous as the star of morning shone,
And held his lordly primacy supreme;
Though scarcely' inferior seem'd Michael the prince,
Or Gabriel, God's swift winged messenger. 190
And after these were holy Raphael;
Uriel, the son of light; Barakiel,
Impersonation of beatitude;

Great Ramiel, and Raamiel, mercy's child;
Dumah, and Lailah, and Yorekemo,
And Suriel, blessed Suriel, who abides
Mostly beside the footstool of God's throne,
(As Mary sate one time at Jesus' feet,)
His chosen inalienable heritage.
Nor these alone, but myriad sanctities,   200
Thrones, virtues, principalities, and powers,
Over whose names and high estates of bliss
I must not linger now, crown'd hierarchs;
And numbers without number under them
In order ranged, — some girt with flaming swords.
And others bearing golden harps, though all
Heaven's choristers are militant at will,
And all its martial ranks are priestly choirs.
And, even as in yonder Paradise
Thou sawest the multitudes of ransom'd babes   210
And children gather'd home of tenderest years,
So with the presbytery of angels, those
Who will appear to thee as infant spirits
Or stripling cherubs, cluster round our steps,
Each individual cherub born of God,
Clouds of innumerable drops composed,
Pure emanations of delight and love.

  "And yet, though only one of presbyters
There reckon'd by ten thousands, when I woke
To consciousness I found myself alone,   220
So vast are heaven's felicitous abodes,
As Adam found in Eden.   Not a sound

Greeted mine ear, except the tuneful flow
Of waters rippling past a tree of life,
Beneath whose shade on fragrant moss and flowers
Dreaming I lay. Realities and dreams
Were then confused as yonder clouds and rocks.
But soon my Maker, the Eternal Word,
Softening His glory, came to me, in form
Not wholly' unlike my own : for He, who walk'd   230
A man on earth among His fellow-men,
Is wont, self-humbled, to reveal Himself
An Angel among angels. And He said, —
His words are vivid in my heart this hour
As from His sacred lips at first they fell, —
' Child of the light, let Oriel be thy name;
Whom I have made an image of Myself,.
That in the age of ages I may shower
My love upon thee, and from thee receive
Responsive love. I, unto whom thou owest   240
Thy being, thy beauty, and immortal bliss,
I claim thy free spontaneous fealty.
Such it is thine to render or refuse.
It may be in the veil'd futurity,
Veil'd for thy good, another voice than Mine,
Though Mine resembling, will solicit thee,
When least suspicious of aught ill, to seek
Apart from Me thy bliss. Then let these words
Foreclose the path of danger. Then beware.
Obedience is thy very life, and death   250
Of disobedience the supreme award.
Forewarn'd, forearm'd resist. Obey and live.

But only in My love abide, and heaven
(So call the beautiful world around thee spread)
Shall be thy home for ever, and shall yield
Thee choicest fruits of immortality;
And thou shalt drink of every spring of joy,
And with the lapse of endless ages grow
In knowledge of My Father and Myself,
Ever more loving, ever more beloved.'　　　　260

" Speaking, He gazed on me, and gazing seal'd
Me with the impress of His countenance,
(Brother, I read the same upon thy brow,)
Until such close affinity of being
Enchain'd me, that the beauty' of holiness
Appear'd unutterably necessary,
And by its very nature part of me.
I loved Him for His love; and from that hour
My life began to circle round His life,
As planets round the sun, — His will my law,　　　270
His mysteries of counsel my research,
And His approving smile my rich reward.

"Then whispering, 'Follow Me,' He led me forth
By paths celestial through celestial scenes
(Of which the Paradise beneath our feet,
Though but the outer precincts of His courts,
Is pledge), each prospect lovelier than the last,
Until before my raptured eye there rose
The Heavenly Zion.

" Terribly sublime
It rose. The mountains at its base, albeit   280
Loftier than lonely Ararat, appear'd
But footsteps to a monarch's throne. The top
Was often lost in clouds — clouds all impregn'd
With light and girdled with a rainbow arch
Of opal and of emerald. For there,
Not as on Sinai with thick flashing flames,
But veiling His essential majesty
In robes of glory woven by Himself,
He dwells whose dwelling is the universe   ·
Of all things, and whose full-orb'd countenance   290
The Son alone sustains. But at His will
(So was it now) the clouds withdrawn disclosed
That portion of His glory, which might best
Fill all His saints with joy past utterance.
There were the cherubim instinct with eyes ;
And there the crowned elders on their thrones,
Encircling with a belt of starry light
The everlasting throne of God ; and round,
Wave after wave, myriads of flaming ones
From mightiest potentates and mid degrees   300
Unto the least of the angelic choirs.
Myself, nor of the first nor of the last
I saw ; but mingling with them was received
By some with tender condescending love,
By others with the grateful homage due
To their superior. Envy was unknown
In that society. But through their ranks
Delightful and delighting whispers ran,

Another brother is arrived to share
And multiply our gladness without end.'   310
Meanwhile, as I was answering love with love,
My Guide was not, and in that countless throng
I felt alone, till clustering round my steps,
With loud Hosannas and exuberant joy,
They led me to the footstool of the throne,
And there upon His Father's right He sate,
Without whom heaven had been no heaven to me,
Effulgent Image of the Invisible,
Co-equal co-eternal God of God.

" That day was one of thousands not unlike   320
Of holy convocation, when the saints
(This was our earliest name, God's holy ones)
From diverse fields of service far and near,
What time the archangel's trumpet rang through heaven,
Flock'd to the height of Zion — archetypes
Of Salem's festivals in after years.
And ever, as these high assemblies met,
New counsels were disclosed of love Divine,
New revelations of our Father's face,
New proofs of His creative handiwork,   330
Presentments at the throne of new-born spirits,
Wakening new raptures and new praise in us
The elder born.   No discord then in heaven.

" So pass'd continuous ages ; till at last,
The cycles of millennial days complete,
Mark'd by sidereal orbits, seven times seven,

By circuits inexpressible to man
Revolving, a Sabbatic jubilee
Dawn'd on creation. Usher'd in with songs
And blowing of melodious trumps, and voice   340
Of countless harpers harping on their harps,
That morning, long foretold in prophecy
(Heaven has, as earth, its scrolls prophetic, sketch'd
In word or symbol by the Prescient Spirit),
Broke in unclouded glory. Hitherto
No evil had appear'd to cast its shade
Over the splendors of perpetual light,
Nor then appear'd, though to the Omniscient Eye,
Which only reads the mysteries of thought
And can detect the blossom in the bulb,   350
All was not pure which pure and perfect seem'd.
But we presaged no tempest. We had lived,
Save for the warning each at birth received,
As children live in blissful ignorance
Of future griefs: nor even Michael guess'd,
So hath he often told me, what that day
Disclosed of war and final victory.

  "Such was the childhood of angelic life.
Such might not, could not always be. And when,
Ranged in innumerable phalanxes,   360
We stood or knelt around the sapphire throne,
The Word, the Angel of God's Presence, rose
From the right hand of glory, where He sate
Enshrined, imbosom'd in the light of light,
And gazing round with majesty Divine, —

Complacent rest in us His finish'd work,
His perfected creation, not unmix'd
With irrepressible concern of love, —
Thus spake in accents audible to all:

" ' Children of light, My children, whom My hand
Hath made, and into whom My quickening Spirit [370
Hath breathed an immortality of life,
My Father's pleasure is fulfill'd, nor now
Of His predestinated hosts remains
One seraph uncreated.   It is done.
Thrones, virtues, principalities, and powers,
Not equal, but dependent each on each,
O'er thousands and ten thousands president
No link is wanting in the golden chain.
None lacks his fellow, none his bosom friends,   380
No bosom friends their fit society,
And no society its sphere assign'd
In the great firmament of morning stars.
The brotherhood of angels is complete.
And now, My labor finish'd, I declare
Jehovah's irreversible decree,
With whom from Our eternal Yesterday,
Before creation's subtlest film appear'd,
I dwelt in light immutably the same,
Which saith to Me, " Thou art My Only Son,   390
From all eternity alone Beloved,
Alone begotten: Thee I now ordain
Lord of To-day, the great To-day of Time,
And Heir of all things in the world to come.

Who serve the Son, they too the Father serve;
And Thee, My Son, contemning, Me contemn.
My majesty is Thine: Thy word is Mine.
And now, in pledge of this My sovereign will,
Before heaven's peers on this high jubilee
I pour upon Thee without measure forth   400
The unction of My Everlasting Spirit,
And crown Thee with the crown of endless joy.'''

"So spake the Son; and, as He spake, a cloud
Of fragrance, such as heaven had never known,
Rested upon His Head, and soon distill'd
In odors inexpressibly sublimed
Dewdrops of golden balm, which flow'd adown
His garments to their lowest skirts, and fill'd
The vast of heaven with new ambrosial life.
And for a while, it seem'd a little while,   410
But joy soon fails in measurement of time,
We knelt before His footstool, none except,
And from the fountain-head of blessing drank
Beatitude past utterance.   But then,
Rising once more, the crown'd Messiah spake:

"'My children, ye have heard the high decree
Of Him, whose word is settled in the heavens,
Irrevocable; and your eyes have seen
The symbol of His pleasure, that I rule
Supreme for ever o'er His faithful hosts,   420
Or faithless enemies, if such arise:
And rise they will.   Already I behold

9

The giant toils of pride enveloping
The hearts of many: questionings of good,
Not evil in themselves, but which, sustained
And parley'd with apart from Me, will lead
To evil; thoughts of license not indulged,
Nor yet recoil'd from; and defect of power,
Inseparable from your finite being,
Soliciting so urgently your will　　　　　　　　430
(Free, therefore not infallible) to range
Through other possibilities of things
Than those large realms conceded to your ken,
That if ye yield, and ye cannot but yield
Without My mighty aid betimes implored.
From their disastrous wedlock will be born
That fertile monster, Sin.　Oh, yet be wise!
My children, ere it be too late, be warn'd!
The pathway of obedience and of life
Is one and narrow and of steep ascent,　　　　440
But leads to limitless felicity.
Not so the tracks of disobedience stretch
On all sides, open, downward, to the Deep
Which underlies the kingdom of My love.
Good, evil; life and death: here is your choice.
From this great trial of your fealty,
This shadow of all limited free will,
It is not Mine, albeit Omnipotent,
To save you.　Ye yourselves must choose to live.
But only supplicate My ready aid,　　　　　　450
And My Good Spirit within you will repel
Temptation from the threshold of your heart

Unscathed, or if conversed with heretofore
Will soon disperse the transitory film,
And fortify your soul with new resolve.'

"He spake, and from the ranks a seraph stepp'd,
One of heaven's brightest sanctities esteem'd,
Nought heeding underneath the eye of God
Ten thousand times ten thousand eyes of those
Who gazed in marvel, Penuel his name,   460
And knelt before Messiah's feet. What pass'd
We knew not: only this we knew; then first
Tears fell upon that floor of crystal gold —
Not long — a smile of reconcilement chased
Impending clouds, and that archangel's brow
Shone with the calm response of perfect love.

"Sole penitent he knelt, — if penitence
Be the due name for evil, not in deed,
But only in surmise. And for a space
Unwonted silence reign'd in heaven, until   470
The Son of God a third time rose and spake:

"'Angels, from conflict I have said no power
Avails to save you: here Omnipotence,
Which made and guards from force your freeborn will,
And never can deny itself, seems weak,
Seems only, — hidden in profounder depths.
But rather than temptation were diffused
Through boundless space and ages without end,
I have defined and circumscribed the strife

In narrowest limits both of place and time.   480
Ye know the planet, by yourselves call'd Earth,
Which in alternate tempest and repose
Has roll'd for ages round its central sun,
And often have ye wonder'd what might be
My secret counsel as regards that globe,
The scene of such perplex'd vicissitudes,
In turn the birthplace and the tomb of life,
Life slowly' unfolding from its lowest forms.
Now wrapt in swathing-bands of thickest clouds
Bred of volcanic fires, eruptions fierce   490
And seething oceans, on its path it rolls
In darkness, waiting for its lord and heir.
Hear, then, My word: this is the destined field,
Whereon both good and evil, self-impell'd,
Shall manifest the utmost each can do
To overwhelm its great antagonist.
There will I shower the riches of My grace
First to prevent, and, if prevention fail,
To conquer sin — eternal victory.
And there Mine enemies will wreak their worst: 500
Their worst will prove unequal in that war
To conquer My unconquerable love.
But why, ye thrones and potentates of heaven,
Say why should any amongst you, why should one
Attempt the suicidal strife? What more
Could have been done I have not done for you?
Have I not made you excellent in power,
Swift as the winds and subtle as the light,
Perfect and God-like in intelligence?

What more is possible? But one thing more,　　510
And I have kept back nothing I can do
If yet I may anticipate your fall.
Such glory have I pour'd upon your form
And made you thus in likeness of Myself,
That from your peerless excellence there springs
Temptation, lest the distance infinite
Betwixt the creature and the Increate
Be hidden from your eyes. For who of spirits,
First born or last, has seen his birth, or knows
The secrets of his own nativity?　　　　520
Nor were ye with Me, when My Father will'd,
And at My word the heavens obedient rose.
Come, then, with Me, your Maker, and behold
The making of a world. Nor this alone:
But I, working before your eyes, will take
Of earth's material dust, and mould its clay
Into My image, and imbreathe therein
The breath of life, and by My Spirit Divine
Implanting mind, choice, conscience, reason, love,
Will form a being, who in power and light,　　530
May seem a little lower than yourselves
(Yourselves whose very glory tempts to pride),
But capable of loftiest destinies.
This being shall be MAN. Made of the dust,
And thus allied to all material worlds,
Born of the Spirit, and thus allied to God,
He during his probation's term shall walk
His mother earth, unfledged to range the sky,
But, if found faithful, shall at length ascend

The highest heavens and share My home and yours. 540
Nor shall his race, like angels, be defined
In numbers, but expansive without end
Shall propagate itself by diverse sex,
And in its countless generations form
An image of Divine infinitude.
As younger, ye their elder brethren stand:
As feebler, ye their ministers. Nor deem
'That thus your glory shall be less, but more;
For glory' and love inseparably grow.
Only, ye firstborn sons of heaven, be true,   550
True to yourselves and true to Me, your Lord;
For as mankind must have a pledge proposed
(And without pledge the trial were the same)
Of their obedience, so mankind themselves
Are pledge and proof of yours. Only be true;
And the pure crystal river of My love
Widening shall flow with unimpeded course,
And water the whole universe with life.'

" So spake Messiah; and His words awoke
Deep searchings, *Is it I?* in countless hearts,   560
Hearts pure from sin and strong in self-distrust:
Nor holy fear alone, but strenuous prayer
For strength and wisdom and effectual aid
In the stern war foretold. And heaven that hour
New worship and unparallel'd beheld,
Self-humbled cherubim and seraphim,
And prostrate principalities and thrones.
And flaming legions, who on bended knees

Besought their fealty might never fail,
Never so great as when they lowliest seem'd.   570
Would all had pray'd!   But prayer to some appear'd
A sign of weakness unconceived : to some
Confession of an unsuspected pride :
And haply some rising ambition moved
To strive against the Spirit who strove with all
In mercy, forcing none, persuading most.
Yes, most yielded submiss.   And soon from prayer
To solemn adoration we uprose,
And all the firmament of Zion rang
With new Hosannas unto Him who saw   580
The gathering storm and warn'd us ere it broke.
New thoughts of high and generous courage stirr'd
In every loyal breast, and new resolves
To do and suffer all things for our Lord.
On which great themes conversing, friend with friend,
Or solitary with the King Himself,
That memorable Sabbath pass'd, a day,
Though one day there is as a thousand years,
Fraught with eternal destinies to all.

" Now dawn'd another morning-tide in heaven,   590
The morning of another age, and lo,
Forth from the height of Zion, where He sate
Throned in His glory inaccessible,
The Son of God, robed in a radiant cloud,
And circled by His angel hosts, came down,
Descending from that pure crystalline sphere
Into the starry firmament.   Not then

For the first time or second I beheld
Those marvels of His handiwork, those lamps
Suspended in His temple's azure dome,   600
And kindled by the Great High Priest Himself;
For through them I had often wing'd my flight.
But never saw I till that hour such blaze
Of glory: whether now the liquid sky
Did homage to its present Lord, or He
Our eyes anointed with peculiar power:
For to the farthest wall of heaven, where light
Trends on the outer gloom, with ease wᵃ scann'd
The maze of constellations : central suns
Attended by their planets ministrant,   610
These by their moons attended ; groups of worlds ;
Garlands of stars, like sapphires loosely strung ;
Festoons of golden orbs, nor golden all,
Some pearls, and rubies some, some emerald green,
And others shedding hyacinthine light
Far over the empurpled sky : but all
Moving with such smooth harmony, though mute,
Around some secret centre pendulous,
That in their very silence music breathed,
And in their motions none could choose but rest.   620

" Through these with gently undulating course
Messiah and His armies pass'd, until
They reach'd the confines of thy native orb,
The battle-field of Good and Evil, Earth.

" Wrapt in impervious mists, which ever steam'd

Up from its boiling oceans, without form
And void, it roll'd around the sun, which cast
Strange lurid lights on the revolving mass,
But pierced not to the solid globe beneath.
Such vast eruption of internal fires   630
Had mingled sea and land. This not the first
Convulsion which that fatal orb had known,
The while through immemorial ages God,
In patience of His own eternity,
Laid deep its firm foundations. When He spake
In the beginning, and His word stood fast,
An incandescent mass, molten and crude,
Arose from the primordial elements,
With gaseous vapors circumfused, and roll'd
Along its fiery orbit: till in lapse   640
Of time an ever thickening hardening crust
(So have I heard) upon its lava waves
Gather'd condense: a globe of granite rock,
Bleak, barren, utterly devoid of life,
Mantled on all sides with its swaddling-bands
Of seas and clouds : impenetrably dark,
Until the fiat of the Omnipotent
Went forth. And, slowly dawning from the East,
A cold gray twilight cast a pallid gleam
Over those vaporous floods, and days and nights,   650
All sunless days, all moonless starless nights,
For ages journey'd towards the western heavens : —
Unbroken circuits, till the central fires
Brake forth anew, emitting sulphurous heat.
And then at God's command a wide expanse

Sever'd the waters of those shoreless floods
From billowy clouds above; — an upper sea
Of waters o'er that limpid firmament
Rolling for cycles undefined, the while
God's leisure tarried.   Then again He will'd,   660
And lo, the bursting subterranean fires
Thrust from below vast continents of land
With deeper hollows yawning wide betwixt
Capacious, into which the troubled tides
Pour'd with impetuous rage, and fretting broke,
Returning with their ceaseless ebb and flow,
On many a sandy beach and shingly shore.
But soon, wherever the dank atmosphere
Kiss'd with its warm and sultry breath the soil,
Innumerable ferns and mosses clothed   670
The marshy plains, and endless forests waved,
Pine-trees and palms on every rising slope,
Gigantic reeds by every oozy stream,
Rank and luxuriant under cloudy skies,
Fed by the steaming vapors, race on race
Fattening, as generations throve and sank.
Their work was done ; and at the Almighty's word
Earth shudder'd with convulsive throes again,
And hid their gather'd riches in her folds
For after use.   But now a brighter light   680
Flushes the East: the winds are all abroad :
The cloud-drifts scud across the sky ; and lo,
Emerging like a bridegroom from his couch,
The lordly sun looks forth, and heaven and earth
Rejoice before him : till his bashful queen,

When the night shadows creep across the world,
Half peering through a veil of silver mists,
Discloses the pale beauty of her brow,
Attended by a glittering retinue .
Of stars. Again long ages glided by, 690
While Earth throughout her farthest climes imbibed
The influences of heaven.

               " Not yet the end.
For not for lifeless rocks, or pure expanse
Of the pellucid firmament, or growth
Of ferns or flowers or forests, or the smile
Of sun or moon far shining through the heavens
Was that fair globe created ; but for life,
A destined nursery of life, the home,
When death is vanquish'd, of immortal life.
But there is no precipitance with God, 700
Nor are His ways as ours. And living things,
When His next mandate from on high was given, .
Innumerous, but unintelligent,
Swarm'd from the seas and lakes and torrent floods,
Reptiles and lizards, and enormous birds
Which first with oaring wing assay'd the sky :
Vast tribes that for successive ages there
Appear'd and disappear'd. They had no king:
And mute creation mourn'd its want ; until
Destruction wrapt that world of vanity. 710
But from its wreck emerging, mammoth beasts
Peopled the plains, and fill'd the lonely woods.
But they too had no king, no lord, no head ;

And Earth was not for them. So when their term
In God's great counsels was fulfill'd, once more
Earth to its centre shook, and what were seas
Unsounded were of half their waters drain'd,
And what were wildernesses ocean beds;
And mountain ranges, from beneath upheaved,
Clave with their granite peaks primeval plains,   720
And rose sublime into the water-floods,
Floods overflow'd themselves with seas of mist,
Which swathed in darkness all terrestrial things,
Once more unfurnish'd, empty, void, and vast.

"Such and so formless was thy native earth,
Brother, what time our heavenly hosts arrived
Upon its outmost firmament; nor found
A spot whereon angelic foot might rest,
Though some with facile wing from pole to pole   730
Swift as the lightning flew, and others traced
From East to West the equidistant belt.
Such universal chaos reign'd without;
Within, the embryo of a world.

                      "For now
Messiah, riding on the heavens serene,
Sent forth His Omnipresent Spirit to brood
Over the troubled deep, and spake aloud,
'Let there be light;' and straightway at His Word,
The work of ages into hours compress'd,
Light pierced that canopy of surging clouds,   740
And shot its penetrative influence through

Their masses undispersed, until the waves
Couching beneath them felt its vital power.
And the Creator saw the light was good:
Thus evening now and morning were one day.

"The morrow came; and without interlude
Of labor, 'Let there be a firmament,'
God said, 'amid the waters to divide
The nether oceans from the upper seas
Of watery mists and clouds.' And so it was.   750
Immediate an elastic atmosphere
Circled the globe, source inexhaustible
Of vital breath for every thing that breathes:
And even and morning were a second day.

"But now again God spake, and said, 'Let all
The waters under heaven assembling flow
Together, and the solid land appear.'
And it was so. And thus were types prepared
For generations yet unborn of things
Invisible: that airy firmament,   760
Symbolic of the heaven and heaven of heavens;
The earth a theatre, where life with death
Should wage incessant warfare militant;
And those deep oceans, emblems of a depth
Profounder still, — the under-world of spirits.
But now before our eyes delighted broke
A sudden verdure over hill and dale,
Grasses and herbs and trees of every sort,
Each leaflet by an Architect Divine

Design'd and finish'd : proof, if proof be sought,   770
Of goodness in all climes present at once,
Untiring, unexhausted, infinite :
Thus evening was and morning a third day.

" And then again Messiah spoke, and lo,
The clouds empurpled, flush'd, incarnadined,
Melted in fairy wreaths before the sun,
Who climbing the meridian steep of heaven,
Shone with a monarch's glory, till he dipp'd
His footstep in the ruddy western waves,
And with the streaming of his golden hair   780
Startled the twilight.   But as evening drew
Her placid veil o'er all things, the pale moon
Right opposite ascending from the East,
By troops of virgin stars accompanied,
Arcturus and the sweet-voiced Pleiades,
Lordly Orion, and great Mazzaroth,
Footing with dainty step the milky way,
Assumed her ebon throne, empress of night.

"But now the fourth day closed. And at God's word
The waters teem'd with life, with life the air ;   790
Mostly new types of living things, though some
From past creations, buried deep beneath
Seas or the strata of incumbent soils,
Borrow'd their form.   Innumerable tribes
Of fishes, from the huge Leviathan
Roaming alone the solitary depths
To myriad minnows in their sunny creeks,

The ocean pathways swam. Nor less the birds,
Some of entrancing plumage, some of notes
More trancing still, awoke the sleeping woods   800
To gayety and music. Others perch'd
Upon the beetling cliffs, or walk'd the shore,
Or dived or floated on the waves at will,
Or skimm'd with light wing o'er their dashing foam,
Free of three elements, earth, water, air.
And, as the fifth day to the sixth gave place,
We gazed in eager expectation what
Might crown our Great Creator's work.

                                          " But first
All living creatures of the earth appear'd :
Insects that crept or flew as liked them best,   810
In hosts uncounted as the dews that hung
Upon the herbs their food ; and white flocks browsed,
Herds grazed, and generous horses paw'd the ground ;
And fawns and leopards and young antelopes
Gamboll'd together. Every moment seem'd
Fruitful of some new marvel, new delight,
Until at last the Great Artificer
Paused in His mighty labors. Noon had pass'd,
But many hours must yet elapse ere night :
And thus had God, rehearsing in brief space   820
His former acts of vast omnipotence,
In less than six days ere we stood aloof
From that tumultuous mass of moving gloom,
Out of the wrecks of past creations built
A world before our eyes. All was prepared :

This glorious mansion only craved its heir,
This shrine of God its worshipper and priest.

" Nor long His purpose in suspense. For soon
Descending from the firmamental heavens,
Where He had wrought and whence His mandates
 given,   830
Upon a mountain's summit which o'erlook'd
The fairest and most fruitful scene on earth,
Eden's delicious garden, in full view
Of us His ministering hosts, He took
Some handfuls of the dust and moulded it
Within His plastic hands, until it grew
Into an image like His own, like ours,
Of perfect symmetry, divinely fair,
But lifeless, till He stoop'd and breathed therein
The breath of life, and by His Spirit infused 840
A spirit endow'd with immortality.
And we, viewless ourselves in air, saw then
The first tryst of a creature with his God :
We read his features when surprise and awe
Pass'd into adoration, into trust;
And heard his first low whisperings of love, —
Heard, and remember'd how it was with us.

" But now, lowly in heart, Messiah took
Mankind's first father by the hand, and led
His footsteps from that solitary hill   850
Down to the Paradise below, well named
A paradise, for never earth has worn

Such close similitude to heaven as there.
The breezes laded with a thousand sweets,
Not luscious but invigorating, breathed
Ambrosial odors. Roses of all scents
Embower'd the walks; and flowers of every hue
Checker'd the green sward with mosaic. Trees
Hung with ripe clustering fruit, or blossoming
With promise, on all sides solicited   860
Refreshment and repose. Perpetual springs
Flow'd, feeding with their countless rivulets
Eden's majestic river. By its banks
The birds warbled in concert; and the beasts
Roam'd harmless and unharm'd from dell to dell,
Or leap'd for glee, or slept beneath the shade,
The kid and lion nestling side by side.

  " These, summon'd by their Maker, as they pass'd
Before his feet, the ancestor of men
Significantly named: such insight God   870
Had given him into nature: but for him
Of all these creatures was no helpmeet found.
And solitude had soon its shadow cast
Over his birthday's joy: which to prevent
God drench'd his eyes with sleep, and then and there,
Still in our aspect, from his very side
Took a warm rib and fashion'd it anew,
As lately' He fashion'd the obedient clay,
Till one like man, but softer gentler far
(The first of reasonable female sex,   880
For spirits, thou knowest, are not thus create)
                        10

He made, and brought her, blushing as the sky
Then blush'd with kisses of the evening sun,
Veil'd in her naked innocence alone,
To Adam. Naked too he stood, but joy
Not shame suffused his glowing cheek and hers,
The while their gracious Maker join'd their hands
In wedlock, and their hearts in nuptial love ;
Nor left them, till by many a flowery path
Through orange groves and cedarn alleys winding   890
At length He brought them to a fountain's brink,—
The fountain of that river which went forth
Through Eden, watering its countless flowers
With tributary rivulets, or mists
Exhaled at nightfall. There, on either side,
A fruit-tree grew, shading the limpid spring,
The tree of knowledge and the tree of life.

" Hither when they arrived, the Son of God,
With mingled majesty and tenderness
Their steps arresting, bade them look around   900
That garden of surpassing beauty, graced
With every fruit that earth could rear, and rich
With every gift that Heaven could give to man,
And told them all was theirs, all freely theirs,
For contemplation, for fruition theirs,—
Theirs and their seed's for ever. But one pledge
He claim'd of their allegiance and their love,
And, upon peril of His curse pronounced,
The awful curse of death, forbade them taste
The tree of knowledge. Then smiling He turn'd,   910

And told them of the other tree of life,
Of which divinest fruit, if faithful proved,
They by His pleasure should partake at length,
And without death translated, made like Him,
In heaven and earth, for earth should be as heaven,
Reap the full bliss of everlasting life.

" But now the evening sang her vesper song,
And lit her silver lamps; and vanishing
From view of thy first parents, not from ours,
Messiah rose into the heavens serene,   .   920
And, gazing on His fair and finish'd work
Outstretch'd before Him, saw that it was good,
And bless'd it, and in blessing sanctified;
Nor sooner ceased, than all the marshall'd host
Of angels pour'd their rapture forth in songs
Of Hallelujah and melodious praise.
No jar was heard. Then sang the morning stars
Together, and the first-born sons of God
Shouted for joy, a shout whose echoes yet
Ring in my ear for jubilant delight.   930
And He with gracious smile received our praise,
Lingering enamour'd o'er His new-made world,
The latest counsel of His love, the while
Your earth her earliest holiest Sabbath kept,
Gladden'd with new seraphic symphonies,
And the first echoes of the human voice.

" Too quickly' it pass'd. And then, ere we retraced
Our several paths of service and of rest,

Messiah call'd us round His feet once more,
And said to all, ' Angels, behold your charge,   940
Your pledge of fealty, your test of faith.
Thine, Lucifer, of heavenly princes first,
Earth is thy province, of all provinces
Henceforth the one that shares My first regards.
This is thy birthright, which, except thyself,
None can revoke: this firmamental heaven
Thy throne ordain'd; and yonder orb thy realm.
Thee, My vicegerent, thee I constitute
God of the world and guardian of mankind.
Only let this thy lofty service link   950
Thee closer to thy Lord; apart from Whom
This post will prove thy pinnacle of pride,
Whence falling thou wilt fall to the lowest hell;
But under Me thy seat of endless joy:
If faithless found, thy everlasting shame;
If faithful, this thy infinite renown.
For, lowly' as seems the earth compared with heaven,
We, the Triune, have sworn that through mankind
The angels and celestial potentates
Shall all receive their full beatitude;   960
Yea, that Myself, the Uncreated Word,
Join'd to mankind, shall of mankind elect
My Church, My chosen Bride, to share with Me
My glory and My throne and endless love.
I am the Bridegroom, and the Bride is Mine:
But yours, ye angel choirs, may be the joy
Pure and unselfish of the Bridegroom's friend.
Only be humble: ministry is might,

And loving servitude is sceptral rule.
Ye are My servants, and in serving men   970
Ye honor Me, and I will honor you.'

" So spake the Son, and forthwith rose sublime,
His pathway heralded with choral hymns,
Till on the heavenly Zion He regain'd
His Father's bosom and His Father's throne."

END OF THE FOURTH BOOK.

Book Fifth.

THE FALL OF ANGELS AND OF MEN.

"WHEN throned on that aerial firmament
Messiah singled out great Lucifer
As His vicegerent over all the earth,
Haply not one of the celestial hosts
But felt in that archangel's rule mankind
Had surest safeguard against harm. Such power,
Such glory, such supremacy of will
Was his. Even now his eclipsed majesty,
Though fall'n, o'ershadows potentates of heaven.
But I have seen him, when sublime he came   10
Forth from the presence of the Increate,
His eye glistening with joy for some design
Of lofty enterprise beyond our reach
Safely confided to his puissant arm;
Some new apocalypse of truth vouchsafed
To him, as prophet, to reveal to us.

Things which to other angels seem'd obscure,
Were crystal in his eyes: born to command;
In stature as in strength above his peers;
With whom and him comparison was not,   20
Except with Michael, next in princely rank,
And Gabriel the beloved; three hierarchs —
But Lucifer the chief. Nor odds appear'd
In outward state and circumstance of power
Betwixt him and Messiah, when the Word
Shrouding the awful blaze of Deity
Beneath angelic garb, as He was wont,
Mingled and communed with us face to face.
All gifts of form, all attributes of mind,
All high predominance of dignity   ·   30
Among his fellows, bound that lordly spirit
To Him who made him such. Oh wherefore not
The bond of everlasting gratitude?
Was it that knowledge with its dazzling light
Grew yet more rapidly with him than love?
God knows, God only, how and when his will,
Ranging through boundless latitudes of thought,
First tamper'd with tyrannic pride. Unfallen
He stood, though not unwavering, when the Son
Placed in his hand the sceptre of a world.   40
That crowning gift determined his resolve.
Then wherefore placed He' it? Brother, He foreknew
That arch-imperial will, crown'd or uncrown'd,
Would yield spontaneous and spontaneous fall
Untempted, unpersuaded, unseduced
Save by itself, chafing because controll'd,

And finite amid God's infinitudes:
Nor his alone, but myriad spirits of light,
Wavering like him, like him would fall. And, this
Foreknowing, nothing to Omnipotence   50
Remain'd but so to circumscribe the ruin,
That evil might succumb to good at last,
And darkness yield to everlasting light.
For this must Sin be known, her face unmask'd,
Her carcass stripp'd, her secret shame exposed,
And thus her loathsome harlotry abhorr'd:
Mask'd haply she had tainted all alike.
Hence to the prince of angels was mankind
Intrusted, and to man the fatal tree
Straitly forbidden, though accessible.   60

" Unfall'n had Lucifer received his charge ;
Unfall'n, not long. For, when Messiah rose,
His new creation perfected, to heaven,
He left as next associate in command
Gabriel my chieftain: and with him I sate
One eve conversing, on our watch intent
(Earth had not kept her circling birthday yet),
Upon that hill o'erlooking Paradise,
Where Adam was created, when we heard
Our leader's footstep, and together rose   70
To greet him. Salutation with salute
Freely he answer'd, but as one amused
With his own thoughts quickly address'd us saying,

" ' Brothers, I praise you and your faithfulness ·

No meagre proof of true humility
For thee, archangel Gabriel, thee of all
Heaven's principalities among the first,
Here set to guard this latest work of God,
This freak, this marvel of Omnipotence.
Yes, we are to believe this worm o' the earth,   80
A spark may be of immortality
Enshrined within a mortal coil of flesh,
Made of the clay we stamp beneath our feet,
Equal to us the first-born sons of light;
Nay more than equal, that through him at last
Beatitude shall flow to us, and man
Exalted to the everlasting throne,
The Bride, so spake Messiah, of Himself,
Shall see the peerless potentates of heaven
Standing far off in circles infinite,   90
Or prostrate at her Bridegroom's footstool. Sure,
If lowliness, as we have often heard,
Be measured by the depth that we descend,
This crowns that coy and virgin grace with praise.'

" And Gabriel in sarcastic war unversed
(The sword of sarcasm was not drawn till now)
Replied without suspicion ' Lucifer,
The smile upon thy mouth betrays thy mind.
Thou dost but try our fealty, and test
What answer we should make, if that unknown   100
Tempter predicted should assail our faith.
But wherefore should I weary thee, who knowest
The easy answer to such sophistries?

Our charge is not on man's behalf alone,
Or chiefly, though our power is likest God's
Whenever strength sustains infirmity;
But rather for His sake who made us both:
His work is wages, and His smile is heaven.
What then if we are call'd to stoop to man,
Our Maker, ours and his, stoop'd lower still   110
In making and preserving us when made;
Both in His glorious likeness wrought. Nor will
Our common Father raise these later born
To our disparagement, but higher bliss,
Through man more nearly' united with Himself.
And, when the fight foretold is fought and won,
We, mutable by birth, shall stand henceforth
For ever in our God immutable,
By His love and our own experience fenced.
Such arrows, Lucifer, thyself art judge,   120
Recoil soon blunted from the shield of faith.'

" To whom thus Lucifer, ' So let it be.
And, if my language seem too bold, reflect
It is the tempter, and not I, who speak.
But were I he, and wert thou, O my friend,
As thou art not, obnoxious to assault,
I would attempt thee thus. Two paths are ours :
That which for ages thou and I have trod,
The pathway of obedience. There remains
Untrodden that of disobedience. Why   130
Should one be always best ? God calls for praise :
Praising I please Him ; praising not, displease.

Why should I alway please Him? Say, I choose
To be my own eternal lord? What then?
Oh, by those burning thoughts, those hopes that rise
Within me subject to no will but mine,
I ask, why are we made thus circumscribed?
Are there not possibilities of being
Higher and nobler far than those we see?
Why are these myriads of the hosts of heaven　　140
So limited in power, that thou or I
Can scarcely find our mate? Why less than we?
Look at these vast innumerable worlds
Rolling around us; why not all the homes
Of sentient things? Man, male and female made,
Is in himself a fountain-spring of life;
And why not angels? Was the gift too great,
Too perilous for us? Remember, friends,
The things that might be always underlie
The things that are: things possible, things real.　　150
Say, thou art wise and happy, — it is well.
But why not wiser, happier? answer me.'

"'Let Oriel answer,' Gabriel interposed.

"'So hath it pleased Eternal Love,' I said,
'Perfect, Supreme, Unfathomable Love.
To ask why we have finite faculties
And diverse each from the' other, is to ask
Why all yon planets are not suns, and suns
All gorgeous as the heaven of heavens. Enough,
The universe is music as it is.　　160

Ye both are greater far than I; yet I
Would not be other than I am, whose cup
Already mantles to the brim with joy.
And why yon globes are yet untenanted,
Though not unuseful as the lamps of God,
I know no more than why my Maker fix'd,
As pleased Him, in the mighty Past my birth.
Nor care I further to inquire, but deem
His hour is not yet come of whose increase
Eternity itself shall see no end.   170
His time, His counsel must be best. Be this
Our wisdom with Omniscience to converse,
Our joy the beaming of Eternal Light,
Our strength to lean upon Almighty Power.'

" And Lucifer, as strangely moved, replied,
' I know He is Almighty: but I see
Another image of Omnipotence,
The awful Power of self-determined choice.
Suppose I choose to worship at that shrine,
What hinders? Will God drag me to His feet?   180
Forced adoration, what were this, and where
His own irrevocable gift, free-will?
Will He destroy me? Nay, Himself has said
We are endow'd with immortality.
That fatal dowry makes destruction null.
What then? He will beseech me to repent;
And, if obdurate, punish me? But how?
He spake of death: but what is death to us?
Beasts die and birds; man, made of flesh, may die;

But we are spirits, imperishable spirits.　　　　190
He spake of hell: but where or what is hell?
Gabriel, thy lightsome wing from star to star
Has spann'd creation's height, depth, length, and breadth;
Say, brother, hast thou ever seen this hell?
What is't? a place of chains? of punishment?
Can fetters bind ethereal essences?
Or would God make a creature who should live
For ever in perpetual torment? say,
Gabriel, is this like God, — God, who is love?
Nay, rather when mankind has broken loose　　　　200
From his poor pledge, as tempted he will break,
We shall be left sole arbiters of earth,
And all angelic natures, one by one,
Or flocking to our side in multitudes,
Will join us. If I fall, why should they stand?
They poorer, I have more to lose than they,
And yet risk all for freedom; so will they.
Ages may pass, but they will fall at last:
Finite their power, temptation infinite.
And God will exile me and them from heaven,　　　　210
And out of boundless space create new worlds,
New habitants, but henceforth will beware
How He endows with free-will like His own
Spirits mutable like ours. All such methinks
Sooner or later will forsake His throne.
Nor will our realms be limited, for wide
As stretches this star-spangled firmament,
The deep that lies beneath is wider still.
And there at least we shall be free, unwatch'd,

Lords of ourselves. His own essential form,   220
Though in the outer darkness, will make light
For each one to direct his steps at will.
Nor will my legions wholly be debarr'd
From fairer fields. This firmamental throne
Was given me as my proper seat, this earth
My destined empire, which I mean to hold
Against all foes secure. Nay, shudder not:
Not without God shall I with God contend.
Himself hath arm'd me for the awful strife.
He made me free, immortal, innocent: 230
He made abiding in His love the pledge
Of service; which whoever breaks becomes
His adversary. This mankind will do,
And straightway will be my allies, my bride,
Who, if prolific as foretold, shall fill
My kingdom with an offspring like their sire.
Say, Gabriel, wilt thou cast thy lot with me,
Equal associate? or return to joys,
Which only seem delightsome, till the higher
Delights of perfect liberty are known?   240
Wilt thou be chain'd or chainless? bond or free?'

    "Impetuous words hung on my lips: but me
Gabriel prevented: doubt obscured his look,
Never obscure till now, as thus he spake,
'Son of the morning, Lucifer, if thou,
Though for our safer guardianship, assumest
The tempter, let me answer thee as such.
False voice! that image of Omnipotence

That so allures thee, self-determined will,

Is but an image, at whose dreadful shrine   250

Whoever worships is the slave of self,

And must expect the portion of a slave,

Fetters and stripes. Thou say'st there is no hell:

Hast thou explored the secrets of that deep

Thou claimest as thy heritage and realm?

Or if no hell exists as yet, why not

Exist, as in a moment, if thou sin?

Thou canst not die, thou say'st: but what if death

Be immortality in mortal pain;

Not endless nothingness, but endless woe?   260

Thou pleadest God is love: but what if love,

Love to the universe, ay, love to thee,

Lest worse rebellion worse restraint demand,

Compel the flashing forth of those pure flames

Which — now there is no sin, no enemy —

Innocuous play around His awful throne?

All thou foreseest will yield like thee. False seer!

Hast thou forgotten that the hosts of God,

Premonish'd of the coming strife, besought

His prevalent aid? And what if some refused,   270

Weak in the fancied might of innocence,

The Same who warn'd us enemies should rise

Foretold their final overthrow. And thou,

Dost thou forecast the future, and in thought,

Piercing eternity, assay to clutch

Earth as thy empire and mankind thy bride?

False oracle! Shall His word be reversed

Who here ordain'd Messiah Heir of all?

Or wilt thou, wrestling with Omnipotence,
Wrest from His hands the sceptre, or usurp   280
The smallest foothold of His universe,
Who by Himself hath sworn that every knee
Of things in heaven and earth and under earth
Shall bow beneath His sceptre or His rod?
This, if thou wert the tempter, as my heart
Of thee abhors to think, were my response,
Now and for ever to reject thy thrall,
And in the liberty of truth abide.'

"The Arch-hypocrite replied, 'Gabriel, I said
Thy heart was proof against seductive wiles.   290
I did but try thee: untried faith is nought.
Pride has no charms for thee.   Impregnable
Thou standest.   Only thus maintain the strife,
And in the kingdom of eternal peace
No brighter coronal than thine shall blaze
Among the innumerable hosts of light.
Both have our task assign'd us.   Mine is now
To test the faith of others as thine own,
Detecting whose fidelity is stanch,
Or who are open to the coming foe.'   300

"So saying, he left us on that hill.   In muse
Sate Gabriel for long while contemplating
The moonlight sleeping on the woods and lakes
Of Eden: but his thoughts were otherwhere,
And at the last, heaving a heavy sigh,
He said, 'Oriel, the conflict thickens.   Days

Of peril are upon us.　Be it so.
Farewell, a long farewell, ye hours of peace!
Thou unsuspecting confidence, farewell!
And welcome, so the Master's will be done,　　　810
The strain of battle, and the patient watch
For hostile stratagem far worse than strength.
Now, brother, let us quit ourselves like those
Whom God has call'd to fight, and pledge our troth
As fellow-soldiers in the brooding war,
And fellow-heirs of everlasting peace.'

　" I gave him silently my hand, and there
Upon that mountain's brow we knelt and pray'd
For timely succor in our hour of need.
And, as we rose, the blessed Suriel came　　　320
Like lightning from the footstool of the throne,
And swift of wing spake to us winged words:

　" ' Gabriel, thy prayer is heard.　Messiah calls
Thee to a council of angelic thrones,
Held in His presence.　Oriel, it is thine
To watch mankind's first parents with a band
Of holy ones now camping round their bower,
And guard them from all ghostly violence:
Other temptations, warn'd, themselves must shun.
Brothers, my path is devious.　Fare ye well.'　　330

　" We parted, Gabriel to the heaven of heavens,
I to heaven's miniature, sweet Eden's vale.
There in a leafy arbor, side by side,

11

Half waking, half asleep, for early dews
Still drench'd the landscape, Eve on Adam's breast
Pillow'd her head.   Her loose dishevell'd hair
Part hid the scarlet of her cheek, and part
Curl'd like a wreathen chain about his neck;
While underneath her slender waist his arm
Embracing pass'd, until the listless hand   340
Rested upon her heaving bosom.   Round
A company of angels lean'd entranced.
Nor marvel: thou hast known in pilgrim days
Earth's princes, weary of their royal state,
Hang o'er the cradle of a sleeping babe,
Spell-bound.   And so in their most innocent loves
Was that which moved us more than all the blaze
Of seraphim, or song of heavenly choirs:
The very tenderness of flesh and blood;
The very weakness of humanity;   350
The unutterable sweetness of that bond
Which link'd them, bone of bone and flesh of flesh;
The promise of fertility to Eve;
The fresh bloom of that first and loveliest bride
Unfolding, like rose petals, to the joy
Of Adam, first and goodliest spouse; the rites,
Of their pure nuptial couch, a couch of flowers,
Known but unwitness'd (there are mysteries
Which holy angels guard, but gaze not on);
And the last awful issues, life or death,   360
With their fidelity or frailty link'd.

" But now the rosy-finger'd morn aside

The curtains of the sun's pavilion drew,
And he arose refresh'd.　So from their sleep
That innocent pair invigorated rose,
And from their arbor naked pass'd to pay,
As they were wont, their early orisons
Beside the fountain shaded by the trees
Of knowledge and of life.　Both loved the spot.
There oftenest God would walk at eventide,　　　370
Or dewy morn, or send some spirit elect
To gladden more their gladsome solitude :
A spot more sacred than the stony bed
Where Jacob slept, and visited more oft
With heavenly visitations.

　　　　　　　　" So that morn
Joyful they came.　But even as they knelt
And look'd adoring upward, Adam saw
Amid the foliage of that sapient tree
Two glowing eyes, and soon a serpent knew,
Amazed ; for heretofore nor beast would graze　　　380
Beneath it, nor bird light upon its boughs —
Such awe circled it round — but more amazed
To hear that sinuous snake utter a voice
Like God's voice, saying, ' Thou only follow me.'
And Adam, by preventing prayer unarm'd,
Obey'd and went, whispering to startled Eve,
' What this means it is mine alone to search :
Wait here my quick return.'　And through the walks,
Of Eden, gliding with contorted rings,
Now twisted in voluminous folds, and now　　　390

Shot forward like a bird upon the wing,
The serpent led the way, until his voice
Seductive, ever beckoning ' Follow me,'
Through many a labyrinth of fruits and flowers,
Roses with orange groves, myrtles with vines
Entwining, brought the ancestor of men
To the far distant gates of Paradise.
And then again the serpent spake and said,
' Here tarry, while I bring a mystic key,
Which shall unlock these envious gates, and yield   400
Thee access to the boundless world beyond
Of undefined delights.   Fear nothing.   God
Will guide thee forth, and angels guard thy way,
Eve thy companion.'

               " So the serpent leased,
And back with smooth and undulating course
Slid unimpeded by the tangled woods
To that salubrious fountain spring, where Eve
Waited impatiently.   Before her feet
He bow'd submiss, and to her gaze, which ask'd
Why Adam linger'd, with ambiguous words   410
Replied, ' He waits thy coming at the gates
Of Eden, whence ere long thy steps and his
Issuing shall tread the unexplored expanse
That lies beyond our narrow vale of bliss.
But this beware, those gates instinct with life
Will only on their golden hinges turn
To one who in his hand a cluster bears
Of this divinest fruit ; this fruit which first

Open'd my eyes to see, my tongue to speak.
Take, fairest Eve, and eat.'   420

                     " ' Enough,' she said,
' Our gracious Maker interdicts this tree.'

   " Whereat the serpent subtle' of heart replied,
' What, hath God placed you in this fruitful vale,
Fruitful but narrow, and not given you range
At least of every tree herein to eat?
It cannot be. Thou hast misdeem'd His voice.'

   " And Eve responded, ' Yea, of all the trees
Innumerable which here flower and bloom,
And with delicious fruitage tempt our taste,
We may eat freely. But this tree alone,   430
Planted as in a temple here by God,
He, knowing those who eat thereof will die,
In love denies us.'

                   " And the serpent said,
' Ye die? Die ye? Ye shall not surely die.
I ate and died not. I, a serpent, ate;
And lo, so far from dying, instantly
I lived a life to which my former state
Now bare existence seems. Then first I saw,
Then spake I, heretofore incapable
Of mental vision or articulate speech.   440
This was my only death. And what for thee
And Adam? Surely ye will be as gods,

Knowing all mysteries of good and ill,
Divine intelligences, and, no more
Within this garden's strait precincts confined,
Shall range at will your boundless heritage.
And this your Maker knows. Why otherwise
Placed He this tree within your easy reach?
Why, but to test if those sublimer thoughts
Within your bosom planted by Himself,   450
Thoughts ever stretching towards the Infinite,
By one bold venture daring death itself
(That is, a translation to a higher life —
There is no other death in yon fair fruit),
Were worthy of Himself? Take, Eve, and eat.
For what were all these trees, and what their fruits
Delightsome in one heap before thee piled,
Compared with this? They feed the body' alone:
This nurtures, elevates, expands the soul.
They with their ruddy bloom rejoice the eye,   460
And with their odorous scent the smell; but this,
At once in beauty and perfume supreme,
Clothes all terrestrial things with heavenly light,
And quickens by its spiritual essences
The heaven-implanted spirit. Of this, fair Eve,
This noblest boon of God to Paradise,
Freely and without fear partake with me.'

"Into her ear, into her heart the words
Of that first tempter stole. Now glow'd the fruit
Deliciously beneath the morning sun,   470
Sweet to the eye, and sweeter to the mouth,

Sweetest of all as promising unknown
Unending banquets to the craving spirit.
And so, with fatal and disastrous ease
Lifting her hand into the clustering boughs,
She touch'd, she took, she tasted.   One small taste
Sufficed.   Her eyes were open'd; and she seem'd,
The moorings cut which bound her to the shore,
Launch'd on an ocean of delights.   Alas,
Perfidious sea, on which the fairest bark   480
E'er floated suffer'd foulest wrong and wreck!

" Awhile as in a dream she stood, but soon
Her scatter'd thoughts recall'd, and from the boughs
Selecting one loaden with luscious fruit
She pluck'd it bower'd in leaves, and took her way
To seek her absent lord.   Him soon she met
Returning with no laggard steps; for when
The serpent slid with such strange haste away
The loitering minutes hours appear'd, and then
A strange solicitude unknown before   490
Began to creep around his boding heart,
And he retraced his path.   But when he saw
Eve with flush'd cheek and agitated mien
Advancing, in her hand that fatal branch,
His heart sank, and his lip quiver'd.   And when
She told her tale, the serpent's honey'd words,
Her brief refusal, his repeated suit,
Her answer, his reply, her touch, her taste,
Then first upon the virgin soil of earth
Fell human tears, presage of myriad showers.   500

But when again with pleading eye and hand,
Silent but most persuasive eloquence,
She pray'd him share with her the fruit she bore,
Then Adam wail'd aloud:

              " ' O Eve, my wife,
Heaven's last, Heaven's dearest gift, what hast thou
   done?
Me miserable!   Thou hast undone thyself,
Thyself and me ; for if thou diest I die,
Bone of my bone, flesh of my very flesh, —
Eve, in whose veins my heart's best juices flow.
What can I do, what suffer for thee?   Say   510
I rigorously refuse this fatal fruit,
What, shall I see thy warm and gentle limbs
Stiffen in death, and live myself?   How live?
Alone?   Or peradventure God will take
Another rib, and form another Eve?
Nay, we are one.   My heart, myself am thine.
Our Maker made us one.   Shall I unmake
His union? and transfer from heart to heart
My very life?   Far higher I deem of love,
No transferable perishable thing,   520
But flowing from its secret fountain, God,
Like God immortal and immutable.
But oh, what follows?   Adam, be thou sure
Of thy inflexible resolve — death, death :
Both cannot live, and therefore both must die.'

    " So saying, from her hand he took and ate,

Not circumvented by the serpent's fraud,
But blindly overcome by human love,
Love's semblance, which belied its name, denying
The Great Creator for the creature's sake.　　　530

"All this, and more than I can tell thee now,
Ourselves invisible we saw: and, when
Eve laid her hand on that forbidden fruit,
Not one but felt God's interdict alone
Restrain'd from dashing it aside.　This knew
The wily serpent lay not in our charge,
Enjoin'd to ward off violence, not fraud.
But little guess'd we what malignant foe
Lurk'd in that snake.　Nor marvel: who, though
　　　warn'd
Dark mysteries of evil were abroad,　　　540
Who ever surmised that God-like Lucifer,
The noblest of the first-born sons of light,
Would so debase his archangelic form
As into that sly reptile to descend,
And mingle his ethereal spirit one hour
With bestial instinct?　Little then we guess'd
To what abominations pride will stoop.
Nor only we, but heaven's sublimest thrones
Were here at fault.

　　　　　　"Three weary days and nights
We watch'd that miserable human pair,　　　550
Weeping their utter ruin.　Death had stolen
Into their bosom's sanctuary: and lo,

For love despite, for confidence mistrust,
And for the ringing merriment of joy
Mourning and heaviness; but not the death
For which in desperate expectancy
They waited. And when this came not, they strove
(And who that saw them could refrain his tears?)
To hide their shame with fig-leaves loosely strung,
Lamenting their rent robe of innocence,   560
Rent by themselves. But now the third day's sun
Was setting, and the wind of evening blew
Its cool refreshment over wood and wave,
When to our inexpressible delight,
But their quick fear, Messiah's voice was heard
Walking in Eden. In His eye was grief,
And on His holy brow displeasure, mix'd
With deep compassion, sate. With gentle voice
He summon'd those, who in their dread had sought
The shelter of a leafy labyrinth.   ·   570
Trembling and pale they came, expecting death
From Him their righteous Judge; but He, with all
A father's pity towards an erring child,
Father and Judge in one, inquired their shame.
Alas, their very words betray'd them, while
Adam on Eve, Eve on the serpent, threw
The load of guilt. But first upon the last
The crushing sentence fell, the curse of God.
No longer emulous of birds in speed,
Darting like light from tree to tree, henceforth   580
The serpent's belly to the dust should cleave,
Dust be its nauseous meat, until at length

The woman's Seed beneath His bruised heel
Should bruise its head for ever.   Mystic words,
Which, even as utter'd, fill'd our hearts with awe!
Then, turning to the serpent's victims, God
Assign'd to each their lot retributive:
To Eve were sorrows of the womb and breasts
Foretold, and multiplied from age to age,
With strict subjection to her husband's law —   590
A lot unsoften'd till the Son of man
Was of a woman born: to Adam, toil
And bread wrung hardly from his native earth,
Fruitful of thorns and water'd with his sweat,
Till dust should to its kindred dust return.

  " And then mankind's first Priest and Minister
Before them slew some firstlings of the flock,
And pour'd their blood upon the thirsty soil,
And having flay'd the carcasses consumed
The flesh upon a sudden hearth of coals: 600
First altar, and first holocausts, which taught
The sinner that through sacrifice alone,
The guiltless for the guilty slain, was now
For man access to God.   This having done,
He took those skins and fleeces, nor disdain'd
To fashion garments for their trembling limbs.
Type of His spotless robe of righteousness,
And clothed them.   Nor till then the Son of God,
Before He re-assumed His Father's throne,
In pity lest in some rash hour they dare,   610
Fall'n as they were, to touch the tree of life,

And thus (disastrous victory) achieve
An immortality in mortal sin,
Drave them before Him, weeping as they went,
Forth from that happy garden, through its walks
Of fruit-trees, by its crystal rivulets,
And past its countless bowers of blossoming shade.
To Eden's distant gates.   These opening wide
Disclosed what seem'd a tangled wold beyond, —
Dark forests with their sparse and scanty plots   620
Of pasture.   But no choice remain'd them now.
Loath went they forth.   And at the portal blazed
The flaming circling sword which warn'd their steps
From nearer access to the tree of life,
And cherubim of glory shadowing
The mercy-seat, the footstool of God's throne.

"The sun was set.   The mists hung heavily
Around the mountain-tops : Adam and Eve,
Without the gates but near them as they might,
Were sleeping for sheer sorrow ; when my prince,   630
Gabriel, who with Messiah came from heaven,
Call'd me.   Together silently we roam'd
The lonely walks of Paradise, through trees
Which to our pensive musing seem'd to droop
Their foliage as we pass'd ; until we came
To Eve's now solitary nuptial bower.
No happy hearts beat there ; no angel guards
Kept vigil : not a sound ruffled the air —
Till Gabriel pointing to the desolate couch
Said, ' See what Sin hath wrought.   The die is cast, 640

The vast conspiracy is now abroad,
The conflict is begun. Of all the thrones
Summon'd to meet in council before God,
Not one was there but Lucifer had tried
Their faith as ours — whether in truth or not,
None knew — such subtle ambiguity
Had clothed his words. Nor only potentates,
But all the legionary hosts of light,
Since his vicegerency began, have known
Struggle with doubts of outer darkness born.   650
Myriads have fall'n : myriads twice told are firm.
Thus far the Word reveal'd. But when we ask'd
Who was the tempter? Who had fall'n? Who stood?
How first the war arose, and how would end?
He answer'd that the strife would shortly prove
His friends and foes, assaying every spirit ;
And warn'd us that rebellion, now awork
Among the hosts of heaven, would forthwith cast
Its shadow upon earth : that man would fall :
That days of foul ingratitude would seem   860
To blot His love : that angels would be devils,
Traducing God and all that breathed of God :
That devils would become from age to age
More devilish ; and mankind likewise : that Sin,
Deadlier eruption than when hidden fires
Bursting from earth's entrails have wrapt in night
Former creations, over all would cast
The mantling pall of death, dreadful eclipse :
That He, foreseeing all this ruin, had form'd,
Deep in the unfathomable depth that lies   670

Beneath the ocean veiling things unseen,
Two vast receptacles sunder'd though near;
One luminous, one dark: the first He named
After this lovely Eden, Paradise,
Henceforth the outer court of heaven itself;
The other, precinct to the fiery lake
Of dread Gehenna, Hell: and, ever as death
Touch'd with his icy spear the sons of men,
Thither their spirits dismantled should descend,
And there await His judgment-bar, when they   680
And rebel angels should receive their doom.

" ' Thus while Messiah spake, who should approach
His throne, as wearied with unwonted speed,
But Lucifer? his brow contract, his eye
Flashing with indignation, which at once
Burst from his lips — " Mankind, Thy chosen race,
Ingrate, and only by a reptile urged,
Have eaten of the fruit proscribed.   Wilt Thou
I smite them, so that in the threaten'd day
Of their transgression they may perish, Lord?"   690
" Myself will judge them," in calm majesty
The Son replied — " Myself will judge them soon.
Meanwhile their sin will be its chastisement.
Sheathe thou thy sword, and to thy charge return."

" ' And forthwith Lucifer obey'd; and then
The everlasting Son, as if, methought,
Reposing on our loyalty and love,
Turn'd to us saying, " My children, be not ye

Stagger'd or troubled overmuch.   Or ever
The cloud arose, I warn'd you of the storm.   700
And fiercely will the tempest rage ere long,
And the proud billows toss themselves on high,
And seem to mingle heaven's serene expanse
With nether darkness.   Fear not ye.   For I
Am throned above the angry waterfloods,
Compassionate because Omnipotent,
Patient because Eternal.   Sons of God,
Be ye, too, patient.   Not by power alone
Must this great fight be foughten, or My foes
Beneath the glory of My countenance   710
Would melt like yonder incense clouds away.
Howbeit not by power, but love with hate
Conflicting, and humility with pride,
Matchless humility with matchless pride,
My Spirit shall wrestle with the spirit of evil
In what may seem long while an equal war,
But shall not prove so in the event.   Hereby
Shall the allegiance of My saints be known.
There will be adverse powers, yet high in rank,
The thrones and principalities of hell,   720
Who shall bear rule through their appointed times,
And challenge, as My representatives,
Observance.   Evil shall have scope enough,
And range through heavenly places unconfined,
The sons of darkness robed as sons of light,
Until their hideous nature be declared
And branded with the brand of wickedness,
(Nor sooner their commission I revoke,)

Gods of an evil eminence. Till then
Their eminence observe, their evil abhor.   730
Avenge not ye My cause. Vengeance is Mine.
And when My time is come I will arise
And with the blasting of My breath of wrath
Scatter My foes, and all My Father's smile
Reflecting on My saints, angels and men,
Fill heaven and earth with everlasting joy."

    "' So spake Messiah. And such pure delight
In blessing and responsive blessedness,
Such calm assurance, such triumphant love
Breathed in His aspect, none who saw but clave   740
To Him with new intensity of zeal;
And, arduous as the strife foretold might prove,
All felt beneath the banner of His love
Labor was bliss, and battle victory.
And soon the council was dissolved. The rest
Thou know'st : man's summons to his Maker's feet;
His and Eve's sentence, and expulsion hence :
But tell me how the guileful serpent led
Those guiltless to transgress , for much I deem
Angels from men as men from angels learn.'   750

    " Then I to Gabriel told what now to thee
Of Eden's wreck. Nor then alone, but oft
That great archangel summon'd me to rove
With him among those solitary walks,
And talk of happier days. But time would fail
Here to retrace the ages, age by age

Darker and more defiled, until the earth
Was fill'd with lust and rapine. Not at once,
In men or angels, the abhorrent plague
Appear'd in all its loathsomeness. But as   760
In some fair virgin's bosom a small spot,
As if a thorn had prick'd the delicate skin,
Rises and spreads an ever-fretting sore,
Creeping from limb to limb, corrosive, foul,
Until the miserable leper lives
A dying life, and dies a living death:
So there. What though the cherubim diffused
Their glory at the gates of Paradise,
Earth's altar-hearth of worship: what though men
Peer'd through those golden bars on heavenly fields: 770
What though they knew the tree of life within
Shed month by month its beatific fruit,
Unpluck'd but unremoved, a silent pledge
Of immortality not wholly lost:
What though thy eldest ancestors, themselves
The firstfruits of redeeming pity' and love,
Their children and their children's children told
(A few millennial lives link'd all to each)
Of man's primeval state: all was in vain.
The babe whom Eve, drying her woful tears,   780
Clasp'd as the promised Seed, while angels stood
Around unwitness'd sponsors to his name,
Arrived at years, too soon betray'd himself
Begotten of the Serpent's venomous brood,
His brother's murderer: I was one who bore
That protomartyr to his saintly rest:

12

Dark omen of dark days to come. Arts grew
Apace, but chiefly minister'd to arms;
Till Earth grew sick with deeds of violence,
Sick at the heart. And when a holy seer,   790
Who walk'd with God amid a godless world,
Stood forth, and by the Prescient Spirit foretold
Jehovah's Advent with His myriad saints
To judgment, soon the madden'd multitude
Had torn that prophet limb from limb, except
The Master whom he served had stoop'd, and borne
His servant in His whirlwind chariot home.

"And then the darkness deepen'd. Men with men
Wrought wickedness. Nor less the spirits malign,
The which when first they fell, as I have known,   800
Compassionated even the wreck they made,
Grew in malignity, till crime and craft
Became to them what virtue once had been,
Their joy, their nature, their essential life:
Lovers of darkness, foul, obscene, impure;
Some darker, fouler than the rest. Of whom
Were Uziel and Samchasai his mate,
By birthright sons of God, now sons of wrath,
Who, prompted by the boast of Lucifer,
Mankind should be his bride, and stung with lust,   810
Mix'd with the daughters of unhappy Eve,
Heirs of her beauty, not her penitence,
In wedlock. Fatal league! whence soon arose
The monstrous brood of giants, ruthless race,
Offspring of human and angelic kind,

Who now confusion more confused, and stain'd
The fairest homes with violence and blood.
Rapine ran riot on the earth. Alas,
Was this the earth, whose birth we blithely sang ℓ
Hell gloated o'er the ruin : till the Arch-spirit,   820
Who ever at heaven's circling festivals,
Cloaking his malice under show of zeal,
His bitter accusations plied, at last
Affirm'd all godliness extinct, and pray'd
For vengeance on the wretched sons of men
To vindicate the majesty of heaven.
False spirit, in after ages *Devil* call'd,
The lying father of all lies ! But then
He seem'd to triumph when the Word replied,
One saintly patriarch alone was left ;   830
And, if mankind refused his warning voice,
Then after respite due the wrath should fall.

" Fresh respite only fresh rebellion bred.
Earth fainted at her children's deeds. And **God**,
With whose unalterable attributes
Grief jars not, grieved within His heart, that man
Was made for disobedience to unmake.
Judgment awoke, and watch'd with tearful eye
The cup of crime fast rising to the brim,
And trembling on the very edge. Meanwhile   840
At His command the ponderous ark was built,
That jest of scoffers, on the wooded plains
Of Asshur. Little reck'd the sons of men ;
The shipwrights lightly jested as they wrought,

And ask'd if that huge vessel were to mount
The hills or navigate the sandy wastes?
They ate, they drank, they wooed them wives and won,
They builded palaces, they planted trees,
Rich with far distant promise.   Drop by drop
The measure of ungodliness was fill'd.   850
It overflow'd.   And forthwith Lucifer,
Whether his eye, burning like coals of fire,
With indignation gleam'd, or proud despite,
Some doubted, claim'd the overhanging wrath
Should fall as threaten'd on his guilty realm.

 " His triumphing was short.   For now the Son
Came by a legion of His armed saints
Attended (I was there), and sent us forth
To seize amid their foul indulgences
(So Phinehas the lustful Zimri smote)   860
First victims, Uziel and his cursed crew
Surprised, and bring them fetter'd hand and foot
Before Him.   As He spake, so was it done.
And these Messiah, in the sight of all
Fall'n and unfall'n alike, adjudged to lie
In chains of darkness in the lowest hell,
Reserved unto the dreadful day of doom.
Immediately we led them forth.   No hand
Was raised for rescue, and no pleading voice
For mercy.   Terror shook the adverse ranks   870
To see some of their mightiest thus arraign'd,
And cast to punishment condign : nor less
Forebodings of like vengeance on themselves
Disturb'd their guilty thoughts.

"While startled heaven
Thus first beheld empyreal thrones dethroned,
Earth trembled underneath her Maker's frown.
The ark received her freightage, Noah last:
Then God shut to the door: and massive clouds
From treasure-houses inexhaustible
Mantled the firmament in black, and burst   880
In torrent floods on the soon sated plains.
The rivers spurn'd their custom'd banks. The sea
Roar'd, and enormous waves, crested with foam,
Broke with incessant flow o'er sands and cliffs, —
Vain barriers! Whether now the ocean beds,
By subterranean fires upheaved and raised,
Disgorged the secrets of their pathless depths ;
Or whether, as the moon's calm influence draws
The refluent tides in daily ebb and flow,
So now she or some planetary orb   890
Displaced, or in malign conjunction set,
Drew more than half their waters from those seas
Which more than half submerge thy native globe,
Charging the heaven with clouds, and wrapping earth
From pole to pole in one unbroken flood,
A dreary waste of ocean without shore,
And only by the solitary ark
Relieved, the second cradle of mankind.

"So saw I it, returning with my peers
From our sad quest to Hades. Not that those   900
Alone within the patriarch's vessel hid
Found mercy. They alone were saved from death.

But others, when the flood of waters rose
From shores to plains, from plains to upland slopes,
From slopes to craggy rocks, from rocks to hills
Still fugitive, at last betook themselves
To agonizing prayer, their sin and guilt
With bitter anguish not unmix'd with faith
Bewailing, ere the lamp of life was quench'd;
Too late for rescue from the whelming waves,   910
But not for that Almighty love they sought
To snatch them from a lower depth beneath.
And these, a remnant of that ruin'd world,
Surnamed the disembodied spirits in ward,
Were convoy'd to a lonely vale distinct
With its own walks and gates in Paradise:
Nor mingled with the other Blessed Dead,
Till He, who grasp'd the keys of death and hell,
Himself unbarr'd those portals, and proclaim'd
The everlasting triumph of the cross.   920

" Justice had had its way; and Mercy's voice
Was now heard pleading in the ear of God
Well pleased. Heaven closed its windows, and the deep
Restrain'd its fountains, while the arid winds
Swept o'er the floods, until the floating ark
Grounded on Ararat, whose haughty peaks
Soon from the tide emerged, islands of rock
'Mid those subsiding waters. Day by day
The thirsty sun drank seas. And when the dove,
A second time returning to her roost,   930
Brought in her mouth a tender olive-leaf,

Emblem of peace, then Noah and his sons,
With living tribes innumerous, beasts and birds,
Forth from the ark came flocking. And ere long
The smoke of sacrifice arose, and God
Smell'd a sweet savor of obedient faith,
And set His opal rainbow in the clouds,
A token when His judgments are abroad
Of His perpetual covenant of peace.

"Thus have I at thy suit in brief retraced   940
The early annals of Creation's birth,
Its cloudless sunrise, cloudless soon no more,
Obscured and dark, but in its darkness spann'd
By the pure arch of promise. Time remains
(Thine eye forbids me think I weary thee)
To tell thee of another better ark,
Like Noah's, cast upon the stormy floods,
But sheltering One who gave His life for man,
A nobler Victim on a holier mount,
The fragrance of which perfect Sacrifice   950
Breathes infinite beatitude, and spans
The clouds of judgment with eternal light."

Thus Oriel spake, and after grateful pause,
Sweet silence, and yet sweeter interlude
Of music on melodious strings, resumed
The story of the great To-day of Time.

END OF THE FIFTH BOOK.

Book Sixth.

THE EMPIRE OF DARKNESS.

"THE rainbow, that o'er Noah's sacrifice
Stamp'd on the morning clouds the smile of God,
Had scarcely hidden in the amber light
Its unremaining hues, when Lucifer
Summon'd his scatter'd armies to attend
His presence on his great viceregal throne,
Set in the airy firmament. Far off
The signal of the archangelic trump
Rang through the void of heaven, and all his hosts
Flocking in numbers without number stood,   10
Cohorts and fiery legions arm'd for war,
At awful distance from the standard waving
Hard by his seat. Around it thrones were set
In imitation of the mount of God,
And soon a clarion blast resounding call'd
The rebel chieftains from their serried ranks

To close about their Prince. Congress malign
Of powers in common covenant with death,
Gloomy conspirators, despair of good
Graved on their brow, and in their baleful eyes   20
Hunger for mischief! But their robes of light
And coronets of glory flashing fire
Dazzled the empyrean, nor bespoke
Less than a synod of apostate gods;
Whom Satan, over all predominant
In cruelty and craft and fiendish pride
As in infernal splendor, thus address'd:

  "'Virtues of heaven, my comrades, who with me
Have rather chosen liberty and war
Than vassalage and ease, noble have been   30
And vast beyond my highest hopes achieved
Our triumphs. Where is now that innocent world
Which God created for His pastime? Where?
Destroy'd, except a miserable few
Hardly escaping with their skins, and they
Sure victims in their turn to our intrigues.
Messiah said that life should fight with death,
And good with evil. They have fought. But whose,
Proudly I ask, the victory? ours or God's?
Not God's, but ours. One solitary seer,   40
One only has been snatch'd from death and us.
Is this the uttermost the Prince of Life,
Aided by Michael and his peers, can do
For His poor servants? Nay, I wrong His rule :
Some obscure suppliants age by age have foil'd

Our efforts immature as yet. The rest
Have rather seem'd to court our tutelage
Than we to proffer it; and greedily
Have revell'd in what we misdeem, no doubt,
Hard servitude with scanty wages paid.   50
So fertile in that cursed soil have proved
The germs of sin. Darkness, tremendous Power,
I see it written on the scrolls of fate,
Must reign for ever there. But not from this
My only confidence of empire. God,
As I forewarn'd you, wars with God: and hence
Interminable strife, or endless truce.
What are they but His attributes in us
That baffle Him? Had He not fashion'd us
Free and immortal, He had forced our love,   60
Or in a moment quench'd our feeble hate.
But now Omnipotence hath bound itself,
Nor can Omniscience pierce the shrine of thought
Itself has made inviolate. Think you
Messiah knew me, when of all His hosts,
Of all His flaming myriads, me He made
God of the world and guardian of mankind,
And for His viceroy chose His bitterest foe?
Ah, friends, He was too prodigal of gifts,
And now repents too late. Wisdom and might   70
Have here outwitted and outdone themselves.
But now, ye gods, advise how best to wage
Protracted warfare: for it seems mankind,
As from a second centre, shall proceed
To propagate their race — matter to us

Of future triumph.   Let them multiply:
They only multiply our wealth in slaves.
Were they upright as Adam, ere he fell,
And pure as was their unstain'd mother, Eve,
Did innocence secure those guileless hearts   80
From guile?   And these, impair'd by sin, will prove
An easier booty.   That pellucid belt,
Slung on the clouds, forbids us hope or fear
Another flood of waters.   And henceforth,
Safe from such vast catastrophe of ruin,
Though sweeping millions into hell at once,
We weave our snares, and ply our arts to draw
From their allegiance all the sons of men,
Not one like that grave patriarch unseduced
(For see how God's love lingers over one):   90
Then shall we reign without a rival here,
This firmament our throne for ever.   Say,
What counsel or what might were best employ'd
For this great enterprise, in which we stand
Equal antagonists to heaven in arms?'

" He ask'd, and Baalim arose, who next
Shone in that fallen hierarchy sublime:
Himself the prince of three, who with him wrought
In all things, Belus and Beelzebub,
A triad of angelic thrones.   For God,   10C
Who, when He lit the firmamental dome,
Hung in the heavens a thousand double stars,
Triple, quadruple, multiple, around
Each other or a common centre poised,

With colors complementary to each,
Associate suns of glory, — God who group'd
The Pleiads in their glittering sisterhood,
Thus in the birthtime of creation wove
Innumerable bonds 'twixt spirits and spirits,
Source of untold delights in holy hearts,   110
Sweet concords, charities, and tender loves,
As with the fourfold cherubim, instinct
With One presiding Spirit: but in the rest,
Apostate, breeding worse conspiracies;
Which now appear'd, when Baalim, his brow
Clouded with counsel, pride impersonate,
A trinity of wills in one express'd,
Thus open'd to his peers in crime his mind:

" ' Well hast thou summon'd us, O Lucifer,
To consultation.   Hitherto the war,   120
Though crown'd with victory beyond our hopes,
Has lack'd deliberate plan.   And now mankind,
Afflicted by the recent flood, will prove
Less facile to our desultory' assaults.
My counsel is, mindful how we ourselves,
Combining and conspiring, spirit with spirit,
Under thy subtle leadership, O Prince,
Escaped the yoke, whenever flesh and blood
Have swarm'd into a multitude again,
To bind their scatter'd tribes and families   130
In one confederate nation.   Let one name
Unite them.   Let one vast metropolis
Foster one common pride.   Or, if ye will,

Incite them to erect some mountain pile
Whose top shall reach to heaven in their surmise,
And let this be their citadel of strength
For after ages.   So shall deeds of wrong,
Which timid hearts had shrunk from if alone,
Be wrought together in defiant league.'

" So counsell'd Baalim ; and after him   140
Rose on his right Apollyon, truculent
His eye, and on his flaming sword half drawn
Rested his restless hand. ' Comrades,' he said,
' If Baalim's design prevail, and one
Colossal empire stride athwart the world,
What room were left for war?   What space for fields,
Where I have reap'd the richest sheaves of death,
And mingling with the hostile ranks infused
Infernal hatred into human hearts?
Nay, be it ours to nurture rival realms,   150
Ourselves o'er them presiding (we shall love,
As loves the prowling wolf its chosen flock,
Each one his kingdom), and then sow betwixt
Suspicions, hatreds, lusts, whence wars are spawn'd,
Until we lead their armies fired with rage
To mutual slaughter, foiling Him who made
All of one common blood.   Ye have my mind.'

" Apollyon sate, gloomy as death.   But now
Near him arose, the loveliest in form
Of all the lost archangels, Ashtaroth, —   160
The corypheus of a band of spirits,

Six spirits, himself the seventh, and the rest
Only less lovely than their chosen chief, —
Of winning voice and sweet attractive grace ;
So gentle, that his worshippers on earth
Deem'd him a goddess, though none such exist
Among the fallen or unfallen hosts ;
In diverse countries known by diverse names
Hereafter: by the virgin troops of Tyre
Surnamed Astarte, but in Nineveh   170
Mylitta call'd ; along the isles of Greece
Invoked as Aphrodite ocean-born,
As Venus by the stately dames of Rome ;
But in all lands adored with moonlight rites
And softest hymns melodious. Ah, false fiend,
In whose perfidious eye damnation lurks,
A chalice in his hand of sparkling wine
Whereof who drinks must die, and on his lip
Kisses and smiles and everlasting woe !

  "'Thine, lordly Baalim, the task severe   180
Of building vast confederacies of pride :
And thine, Apollyon, jarring wars to breed
Among the nations. But to me belongs,
To me and to my legionary band,
The smoother but the not less onerous work
Of garlanding with buds and flowers and fruits
The paths of pleasurable youth. I hang
Around the traveller's footsteps day and night
Singing my dulcet songs, and few are they
Who close their ears against the charmer's voice.   190

Each victim draws his mate : the throngs increase :
They cluster round my cloud-like draperies :
They press around my glancing feet: as moths
That scorch their wings against the ardent flame,
But stay not till with many an airy flight
They plunge at last into their fiery tomb.
Men call me Love, the deity of love.
And thus it happen'd ; when I saw that lust
Conceiving brought forth sin, and sin alone
Could wrest from God the empire God had made,   200
I thought the best perverted would be worst,
And chose the holiest of connubial rites,
The mutual laying open each to each
Of life's profoundest purest sanctities,
And deem'd infusing poison there to mar
The river at its fountain. The event
Hath not belied my hopes. Friends, I have breathed
Upon the lamp of hymeneal joy,
And it hath sicken'd, sicken'd and expired,
Almost as soon as lighted. Oftener yet   210
Have I beguiled unstable hearts to seek
In license pleasures God has link'd to love,
And blown upon their innocence, and bent
In triumph not unmix'd with pity' and scorn
O'er the unhallow'd couch. Men arm'd in proof
Against all other wiles have yielded here,
And, conquer'd by a glance, a blush, a sigh,
For one brief hour upon a stranger's bosom
Have barter'd immortality of bliss.
And haply in my woven chains of flowers,   220

Chains light as gossamer, I, Baalim,
Have bound more captives to our prince's car
Than thou hast held in fortresses of power,
Or thou, Apollyon, slain on fields of blood.'

" And, as the fallen seraph sate, he threw
A glance of such bewitching tenderness
Around the assembly, none who caught his eye
But felt, and with involuntary assent
Did homage to the spell: his radiant form
Recline or standing seem'd embodied grace,   230
And the melodious treble of his voice,
Like the far echo of seraphic harps,
Rang in their ears : when on a sudden one,   ·
In stature low for gods, of downcast look,
Rose from the furthest of those golden thrones,
Mammon his name.   His slow and painful words
At first seem'd clinging to his lips, but soon ·
Fell on that council with momentous weight,
Nor least upon its haughty president :

" ' I too have poised the heart of man, and watch'd
With sleepless eye what avenue may best   [240
Yield us access.   And here I answer, Gold.
Smile not that yellow dust should have such power ;
For what is man but dust ?   What marvel then
Dust over dust holds sway ?   The blighted earth
No longer yields him her spontaneous fruit.
Poor wretch, his sweat moistens his daily bread.
Labor is bread, and bread is life : and thus

He lives a pensioner for every breath
Upon Another's bounty — yoke to us   250
Insufferable, not the less to man.
But gold appears a tower other than God,
With honors, pomp, and endless pleasures stored,
Impregnable while life shall last. Poor fool,
He knows not in the lowest keep a fire
Smoulders in its own ashes self-conceal'd:
It glows; it flames; it never says, Enough —
More is more fuel — till the shrivell'd soul,
Alive but wrapt in cerements of death,
Breathes out itself upon that funeral pyre.   260
Whatever counsels may obtain this day,
Let mortals worship at this golden shrine,
They will not fail of hell. What would ye more?'

    "So Mammon sate; and opposite arose
Moloch, tremendous deity, who thus
Louring address'd his peers:

                        "'There is a power
Mightier than pride, or war, or pleasure's thrall,
Or greed of gold, — the intolerable pangs
Of conscience seeking rest and finding none,
The terror which hath torment. Slighting this,   270
We do ourselves, we do our cause much wrong.
Friends, I have seen the wretched outcast rove,
Driven by the anguish of tyrannic guilt,
From land to land self-exiled. I have seen
Parents imbrue their clench'd hands in the blood

                        13

Of their own children. Nor do I despair
Of more. So dreadful are the shadows cast
From the dark outlines of that prison of death
Whence never yet a prisoner return'd,
That unknown all-embracing dungeon house,   280
What likelier in process of time than they
Of men most miserable, finding God
Deaf to their rebel importunities,
Should call upon the dead? a bootless cry,
Which nathless we will condescend to hear,
And by permission answer those who sell
Their souls for hidden lore, ordaining them
Not without dismal rites of sorcery
Our priests and priestesses. So shall we wield
An enginery of next to' Almighty power.   290
For conscience hath in it the strength of God,
Which can creation uncreate, and make
A hell of heaven. It is God's oracle:
And if our voice be but mista'en for God's,
The terror-stricken worshipper is ours,
Body and soul, for ever and for ever.'

"As Moloch spake, his gloomy words though brief
Such echo found in lamentable hearts
Once calm as yonder firmament, but now
Vex'd and disquieted and ill at ease,   300
(For what was man's unrest to theirs, though like?)
That misery held them mute. Which soon their chief
Perceiving, fearful lest remorse might lead
Any to mourn their choice (example dire),

Majestically rising from his throne
Around the council threw his scornful eye
Burning with pride, and thus resumed debate ,

"'Thrones, virtues, principalities, and powers,
Titles vouchsafed us not in vain by One
Who never of His words or gifts repents,   310
Ours therefore by inalienable right,
Ye hear your brethren. Well have they advised.
Let Baalim his empire raise supreme,
Or empires out of ruin'd empires build,
Each greater than the last (for who can doubt
That God will cross our counsels? vain attempt),
Each worse, — a worse must still be possible, —
Our scale of greatness. Let Apollyon whet
The keen edge of intestine feuds and wars.
Let Ashtaroth in chains of love or lust   320
Lead forth his groups of willing prisoners,
Gay captives, garlanded with fading flowers,
Behind our chariot wheels. Let Mammon heap
Fuel for fire on stubborn hearts, and there
Foster the secret flame unquenchable.
And last, though loftiest enterprise, be thou,
O Moloch, as a god to men, and grasp
Their conscience with the iron gripe of fate.
We need your banded strength. Nothing, O peers,
Nothing is done while aught remains to do.   330
We have not trodden yet the unseen shades,
Divided, if report speaks true, betwixt
A paradise of bliss and prison of woe;

To us alike impenetrable. At least
I own my uttermost of effort foil'd,
By some obscure necessity debarr'd,
Some limit against which I dash'd my wings
As against viewless crystal. Be it so.
We have not yet achieved the battle-field,
Nor can expect the provinces beyond.   340
Earth once our trophy, we shall conquer peace,
And soon behold the regions under earth
Abandon'd by their Maker, nothing loath,
Being we leave the walls of heaven unscaled.
Earth, earth must first be ours. But, friends, for this
We must defile mankind ere we destroy :
Evil must go before us, death behind.
God has not yet forsaken man, nor yet
Suffers that we assail the fleshly tent
Of his short pilgrimage. Herein beware.   350
Here Samchasai and Uziel with their hosts
Erring have fall'n; a fall to be avenged,
Not follow'd. What, shall we, celestial powers,
For the brief lust of carnal pleasure mar
Our mighty future? Tush, leave this to man,
Your dupes and drudges. Or if thoughts of joys,
Forbidden to angelic natures, stir
Within your bosom, only' abide your time,
And when the realms of darkness are defined,
And God has yielded this fair earth to us,   360
As He must yield when utterly corrupt,
Then shall ye and your legions, as ye list,
Act by mankind, your conquer'd heritage.

I will not question how ye treat your slaves.
Meanwhile be this our sleepless care to' estrange
Them and their God, rousing His wrath, their hate.
How think ye? Had He not at Eden's gate
His mercy-seat and altar blazing nigh,
Whereat who knelt with sacrifice and prayer
Alone repulsed our arms? Henceforth, O peers, 370
If men will worship, let them worship us,
Despite the everlasting interdict
Which severs things unseen and seen. Why not?
Let them make images of wood and stone,
Brass, iron, silver, gold, and call them gods,
Adoring us in them by countless names.
My counsel moves your laughter. But if once
The Almighty, jealous of His name blasphemed,
Swear in His wrath that He disowns mankind,
Our work is done, the empire is our own. 380
Be it thy charge, O subtle Sammael,
Thou master of the spells of ignorance,
To blind their eyes and indurate their hearts.
For now our watchword must be fraud, not force ;
Darkness our panoply: and of success
The past affords us no uncertain pledge.'

" He spake, and murmurs of assent not loud
But deep, — as is the ocean's sudden roar,
When a careering blast with tempest charged
Down rushing through the mountain gorges strikes
The waters of a rocky bay, whose cliffs [390
And caves re-echo when the storm is past. —

Spread in interminable waves of sound
Along those countless ranks. Gladly they crouch'd,
As weaker spirits will crouch, beneath the shade
Of wickedness more wicked than their own,
And call'd upon their prince as God: when, lo,
A cloud impenetrable to all light,
At first not larger than the mystic hand
The prophet's servant saw from Carmel's rocks,   400
Hung poised above the throne of Lucifer,
And, spreading with the speed of thought, o'erhung
The apostate armies, shroud of dreadful gloom,
Darkness that might be felt.   Nor dark alone,
But soon sharp lightnings flash'd abruptly; bright
Startling the black a moment, and then quench'd;
While volleys of tremendous thunder shook
The furthest empyrean, and the hearts
Of that rebellious host.   Speechless they stood
And stricken, as if every peal announced   410
The crash of worlds.   In horror Lucifer
Gazed upward, sinking on one knee appall'd.
For still the darkness deepen'd, and the wrath
Apparent stamp'd on every guilty brow
Its scathing impress ineffaceable,
The death-brand on the children of despair.
And for one dreadful hour, one of heaven's hours,
None from his seat arose, or station stirr'd,
Or moved his lip, or trembled.   Terror froze
Their hearts insensible, until a sound,   420
More terrible than thunder, vibrated
Through every spirit, Jehovah's awful laugh,

Mocking their fears and scorning their designs,
The laughter of Eternal Love incensed.
It pass'd ; and then as suddenly the sky
Was clear, and save the graven brand on each
No vestige of that cloud of wrath remain'd.

" Nor was it long before the rebel host
Resumed their courage, and in marvel gazed
Each on the other that the vengeful flame   430
Had smitten none amongst them, and ere long
Jested at their own fears, but vainly' assay'd
To rase the ineradicable sign
Too deeply on their cursed brow inured ;
But, finding all their efforts useless, laugh'd
At this dark badge, which Satan told his mates
(Satan henceforth his name, and demons theirs)
Was the predestined bruise on him and his,
The serpent and its seed : — cheap penalty,
He vaunted, for a world, and gladly paid,   440
A warrior's honorable scar, the pledge
Of daring and of desperate revenge.

" So in their fiendish pride they schemed.   But this
Shadow of things to come was but the first
Faint pressure of God's hand, a transient breath
Blown from that wrath which to the lowest hell
Burns and shall burn for ever, — though by them
Discredited, when forth in swarms they went
From that infernal senate, as they thought
To wrest the sceptre from Almighty power,   450

And baffle the All-wise in counsel.   Fools,
And blind !   Vainly, when plann'd by Baalim
The city of confusion rear'd its brow
Towards heaven, a whisper of God's voice perplex'd
The builders' language and their works at once.
When Ashtaroth, standing himself aloof,
Through some of his perfidious crew defiled
With lust and blood the cities of the plain,
Vainly the fiery wrath too long provoked
Fell undistinguishing on men and fiends,   460
And made of earth's most fragrant flowery vale
A picture of Gehenna's burning lake.
And when at last the prince of darkness, couch'd
In symbol of the great leviathan,
The dragon of the river floods of Nile,
Harden'd the heart of Pharaoh, scourged by all
Heaven's plagues, until it grew like adamant,
And led him to assay the ocean depths
And satisfy his lust on Israel there,
Vainly God moving in the pillar cloud   470
Smote with His glittering sword that monster's head,
And with the wreck of chariots and of arms
And horsemen overta'en in baleful rout
Cumber'd the waters and confused the shores.
All was in vain.   Each desperate repulse
But seem'd to kindle fiercer subtler hate
In those infatuate spirits, till I have seen
The cheek of Michael alter with distress,
And all the hosts of heaven astonied stand,
As couriers in successive hours announced   480
Hell's endless crafts, each deadlier than the last.

" The clouds yet brooded upon Sinai's peaks,
And twice ten thousand chariots flashing fire
Attended Him, who plants His steps serene
Upon the whirlwind and the storm, and there
Was communing, as communes friend with friend,
With Amram's princely son, when Sammael,
(In Egypt as the great Osiris known,)
By all the judgments on his countless fanes
And Satan's ghastly wound unterrified,   490
Moved Israel and their timid priest to cast
Their idol god, and interweave with songs
Their naked dances round the golden calf; —
Vision to us of horror and of grief,
Presaging woes. Ah, faithless children ! Still
The manna fell around their pilgrim tents ;
The living water from the smitten rock
Still track'd their devious steps ; the fiery cloud,
Shadowing the tabernacle, still bespoke
Jehovah's awful Presence ; — when they turn'd   500
(Hard to believe, though seen) and chose for gods
Grim Moloch's shrine and Remphan's lurid star.
But Mercy strove with Judgment, and prevail'd,
And led them to the promised land, a land
With milk and honey flowing, redolent
With Eden's fragrance in a fallen world,
The glory of all other lands. But there
Abandoning ere long the holy tent,
In Shiloh first, after on Zion pitch'd,
Throngs of insensate worshippers besiege   510
Lewd Baal's gates in Bethel and in Dan.

But little boots it to recall those scenes
Of foul apostasy, though here and there
Illumined with celestial lights of faith
And virtue militant. Once only' it seem'd,
When saintly David fell on sleep, and left
To Solomon his sceptre, prince of peace,
Angels might yet behold upon the earth
A nation witness for the truth. Ah, brief
And fleeting vision! Soon on Salem's height   520
Gaunt altars rose to every hideous god.
And thenceforth, on through weary centuries
Of vigil, oft the blessed stars appear'd
As blotted from the very firmament
Appall'd. What time of Israel's chosen tribes
Ten, like a loosen'd cliff, crumbled and sank
Into the surging tide of heathen lands,
Who shall relate the scoffs of fiendish mirth,
That taunted our persistent ministries
Camping around God's hidden ones? And when, — 530
Albeit awhile the sudden blast of death,
As Michael waved his keen far-reaching sword
Over the armies of Sennacherib,
Shielded the royal city, — when at last
The cup of Israel's wickedness was full,
And Asshur, trampling on Jerusalem,
Led forth her trembling prisoners to hang
Their harps beside the proud Euphrates' banks,
Then shouts of nearer victory fill'd the air,
And Satan's firmamental kingdom rang   540
With praises of their leader's matchless craft,

And loudly-mutter'd blasphemies of Him
Whose patience they misreckon'd impotence.

"So dream'd they dreams, which nothing but the
    strains,
Breathed from the solemn harp of prophecy,
Disturb'd; — mysterious harpings on the wind,
Not now first mingling with the jarring sounds
Of earth and time, for they had ever rung,
Since Enoch laid his hand upon the chords,
Echoes of heavenly voices in faith's ear,   550
Still clearest in the hour of sorest need,
But never more distinct than now.

                                        "The sun
Still couch'd unrisen beneath the dawning hills,
But far and wide the heavens were all aglow
With saffron lights and hues of roseate pearl,
Shedding upon the towers of Babylon,
Its massive walls, and gates of burnish'd brass,
And gardens in the golden morn suspense,
Nor least upon the river's amber waves,
A thousand changeful splendors. On a roof   560
Beneath the open sky a young man lay
And slept; serene his brow; and on his face
Even in his sleep a smile of holy joy
Play'd inexpressible, which, when he rose
With morning from his calm unruffled couch,
Flow'd from his lips in praise. Gabriel and I
Had watch'd his slumbers, and, so order'd, hung

On his unfaltering steps, as through the ranks
Of courtiers, follow'd by a trembling group
Of magi, sorcerers, astrologers,   570
Who gazed on him incredulous, he pass'd,
And calmly faced his monarch's baffled pride.
And as, instructed by the Spirit of God,
He in their audience (nor in theirs alone)
Renew'd the faded image, excellent
In brightness and in stature terrible ;
And then, as God's ambassador, reveal'd
The import of the head of gold, the breast
Of silver, and the loins of brass, and legs
Of iron and of miry clay compact,   580
Portending ruin, till a mystic stone,
Quarried and fashion'd by no human hand,
Smote that colossal idol, which straightway
Crumbled to dust and vanish'd as the chaff
Driven idly from the summer threshing-floor,
The while that rock grew vaster and more vast,
A mountain whose circumference was earth.
And whose eternal canopy the heaven ;
As thus that youthful seer, dauntless in heart
And mien, cast his prophetic eye of fire   590
Athwart the changes of tumultuous time,
And in the illimitable distance saw
Eternal love triumphant, Gabriel look'd
On me and smiled, and we refresh'd our faith
With strength in mortal weakness perfected.
Hard by us Baal stood, and Ashtaroth,
And Moloch, kept in terror by the sword

That waved in Gabriel's hand; but oh, the scowl
Of cruel disappointment on their lip
And baffled vengeance, till obscure they shrank   600
To nurture worse designs; while songs of praise,
Flowing spontaneously from angel harps,
Were wafted to the ear of God in heaven.

" Nor learn'd we less of faith's omnipotence,
When Shadrach, Meshach, and Abednego
Chose for their dying couch the fiery kiln,
Rather than vile prostration to the god
Chaldea's monarch, brooding o'er his dream,
Not uninspired by Belus, rear'd aloof
On Dura's sultry plain, finding amid   610
Those thousand forked tongues of hungry flame
An unsuspected Paradise more sweet,
Than sinless Adam when he walk'd with God
In Eden.   But enough, brother, thou knowest
All that befell that haughty monarch driven
From palace halls with flocks and herds to graze,
A bitter school.   Thou knowest the weary lapse
Of those predestined threescore years and ten
Of Israel's woe and Babylonia's pride,
Even to their latest bourn, that impious feast   620
By those brief characters of doom perplex'd,
When Persia grasp'd the sceptre Asshur dropp'd.
Thy heart has been with Daniel in the den
Of lions.   I was by his side that night.
And when he wrote upon his mystic scroll
The visions of his lonely bed, wherein

Earth's proudest realms as ravenous beasts appear'd,
Assyria, Persia, Macedon, and last
One diverse from all others, iron-tooth'd,
Ten-horn'd, dreadful and strong exceedingly,   630
Far ranging o'er the desolated world,
Till earthly thrones all sank in ruinous heaps
Before the Ancient of eternal days,
I saw the joyous eloquence, that flash'd
From that lone prophet's eye undimm'd by age,
And lighted up his wrinkled countenance
With glories from the everlasting hills.
Nor was I absent, when his prevalent prayer
Clomb to the highest heavens, and Gabriel came,
Descending with the speed of seraphim,   640
The herald of evangel grace, though link'd
With mystic times and numbers, seventy sevens;
Nor wholly clear nor dark, faith's chosen light.
And I was there what time a mightier One
Than Gabriel, having striven, self-limited,
With Persia's guardian fiend three weeks of days,
Till Michael sped, permitted, to his aid,
Beside the crystal waves of Hiddekel
Reveal'd His glory and the scroll of time
Till time should be no more.   650

                "The light of heaven
Soon faded, and the transitory rent
Through which it stream'd was block'd with denser
    cloud :
But it had lit imperishable hopes

In human hearts and ours.   How could we faint,
Or how despond, when men of flesh and blood,
Weaker than we in power but strong in prayer,
Wrestled and wrought and vanquish'd?   Oft herein
They minister'd to us as we to them.

" Without us haply human faith had fail'd,
Without them ours.   For still the gloom increased. 660
What though a band of stricken fugitives
Return'd to lorn Jerusalem and built
Their wall and temple gates in troublous times;
What though in faded splendor Judah held
His trembling sceptre; darkness wrapt the earth.
Apollyon, Baalim, Beelzebub,
Bel, Dagon, Chemosh, Nisroch, Arioch,
Merodach, Moloch, these and countless more,
With hosts of spirits subordinate to each,
They to their princedoms, these to Satan bound,   670
Ranged in imperious tyranny abroad,
And chose their various realms as liked them best,
And parcell'd out the kingdoms of the world
Amongst them as their rightful heritage.
Each region had its dynasty of gods:
Primeval Asshur hers, whose altars blazed
Upon the plains of Shinar: Persia hers,
Beside her founts of liquid fire : and where
The mighty Indus rolls its tide of wealth,
Innumerable shrines, sparkling with gems,   680
Studded the odorous banks.   But none like Greece
Could boast its names of graceful deities

For every fountain, and for every breeze,
For every stream, and wood, and ocean shore,
For night and day, for sunshine, and for storm,
For every changeful phase of Nature's moods,
For every passion of the human heart,
For wine, for war, for laughter, and for tears,
For nuptial dances, and for funeral dirge,
For all things from the cradle to the grave   690
And past the grave in Hades, — over all
Were gods, or goddesses, or demigods,
Sylphs, nymphs, fawns, muses, graces president;
For here the sevenfold power of Ashtaroth,
Encamping with his limitary hosts,
First fix'd his seat, in after years removed
Where Tiber rolls beneath the walls of Rome.

" Amongst them Satan ranged pre-eminent,
Incessant; and, denied ubiquity,
Yet seem'd the more to multiply himself,   700
And almost with the speed of thought to be
(For narrow is the breadth of earth to spirits
Accustom'd to celestial latitudes)
Where most the struggle lack'd his puissant arm,
Or archangelic counsel.   Nor the less,
When to the heaven of heavens the sons of God
Were summon'd, sate he on his ducal throne.
Arch-adversary was his name, well earn'd;
And well by all his ministers of state
And legions seconded.   710

"Yet deem not we
On God's behalf were idle.   O'er the world
Death reign'd, but underneath its sable shroud
Life wrought in secret, as serenest gems
In darkest caverns oft are found anneal'd,
Crystalline amethysts, or roseate quartz,
The pure quintessence of incumbent rocks
Distill'd by extinct fires.   And it was ours
To watch these priceless jewels carved and set,
As finish'd, in that diadem of glory,
Wherewith in fulness of predestined time   720
Messiah shall appear for ever crown'd."

END OF THE SIXTH BOOK.

14

Book Seventh.

REDEMPTION.

As one, who having climb'd the livelong day,
Not unaccompanied by friendly steps,
From the rock-girdled marge of gay Lucerne
By Altorf's memorable walls, and glens
Through which the headlong Reuss rushes amain,
Scarce under skyey Hospenthal one hour
Sojourning, stands at last with weary feet
Upon the summit of Saint Gotthard's wilds,
And sees the intricate ravines, that slope
Down to the sunny vales of Italy,   10
And smiles to see them, yet before he wends
Along the young Ticino's purling brook,
Pauses, and with inquisitive retrospect
Speaks with the toilworn comrade by his side
Of defiles they have pass'd to right and left,
And chasms, and rainbow-haunted cataracts,

And vistas through the dawning hills, the which
Their onward track forbade their steps explore; —
So paused Oriel, my guardian, here.   And long
We spake of sacred stories, such as oft   20
In pilgrim days I loved to meditate,
Now by his transitory words illumed
With unsuspected glory : of Jacob's dream
Scaling the heavens, and built of things that are,
Of those funereal rites on Pisgah's brow,
When Michael in Jehovah's name rebuked
The daring prince of hell; of that Arch-fiend
Repairing with the other sons of God
To heaven's high festivals, ere leave obtain'd
To breathe disaster and eclipse of joy   30
Upon the patriarch in the land of Uz;
Of David moved by him in evil hour
To count the tribes of Israel; of the strife
On Carmel's rocky sides, when Baalim,
By bloody supplications importuned,
Raved all in vain to answer; of the car,
That fiery car by fiery chargers drawn,
Which stooping o'er the Jordan's wilderness
Wafted Elijah to the rest of God;
Of that false emissary, who assumed   40
To lure forth Ahab to the field of doom;
Of Joshua, son of Josedech, withstood
By Satan, but upheld by Satan's Lord; —
Of these and other marvels, when the veil
Was rent betwixt the things unseen and seen,
Shedding bright beams of glory on the earth

What time the clouds were darkest, for a while
We communed, till my heart afire with hope
Besought him to resume where last he left,
Upon the extreme verge of better days,   50
Time's awful drama, which he thus vouchsafed:

" One night, when night was listening for the dawn,
Aloof upon the brow of Olivet
I gazed on sleeping Salem.   In the East
Flush'd a faint streak of pearl: the distant hills
Slumber'd in shadow, and the vales in mist:
When haply prompted by the hour, or thoughts
Of loftier vigilance, for many signs
In heaven and earth as in the middle air
Of late had quicken'd us to keener guard,   60
Musing I utter'd half unconsciously
The prophet's words, ' Watchman, what of the night?'

" Sudden I heard the rush of angel wings,
And Gabriel stood beside me, saying, ' Brother,
The morning cometh, and the night: beyond
All is unclouded everlasting day.
This very hour the Sun of Righteousness
Peers o'er the horizon.   Virgin-born to-night
Within the crowded gates of Bethlehem
A Babe, who owns no human sire, is lying   70
Upon His mother's bosom.   It was mine,
Some space agone, to tell that lowly maid
Of David sprung, in David's house betrothed,
The awful secret of Messiah's birth,

The advent of the Holy Quickening Spirit,
The overshadowing Power of the Most High,
Herself the chosen vessel; and to watch
The deepening blush of childlike innocence,
As slowly to herself she realized
'The bliss immense vouchsafed her, not unmix'd   80
With bitter anguish from a faithless world.
It has been mine to guard her low estate,
As month by month within her virgin womb
She bore the promise of her Lord.   Nor now,
Albeit the mystery of mysteries,
For which eternity has waited, dawns,
Is the veil rent in twain.   The tree of life
Must strike its roots in secret in the earth:
The well-spring gush from hidden depths.   Not all
Heaven's radiant ministries, but spirits elect   90
As yet are advertised, the Son of God
Incarnate tabernacles among men:
Far less the powers of darkness, now elate,
Finding the rigid interdict relax'd,
Or rather with less pains transgress'd, that fenced
The bodies of their slaves from violence.
Demons possess demoniacs: thou hast seen
Their victims toss'd and driven by fiends malign
To worse than frenzy: and on this intent
For the most part the myriads of the damn'd   100
Heed not this fateful hour.   Far otherwise
Their leader and his fallen thrones are fill'd
With torment and remorseless fear, and scheme
Their uttermost to thwart Eternal Love:

Which work to counterwork is ours. But now
Come, brother, let us hasten where the tryst
Of friends awaits us on the grassy slopes
Of Bethlehem, and, as is meet, announce
Messiah's humble birth to humble men,
The shepherds, who there hold nocturnal watch.'   110

" So swifter than the eagle's flight we flew
Over the shadowy landscape, and there found,
As he had said, a heavenly cohort arm'd,
And keeping by command that region free
From footstep or from wing unblest. Forthwith
Gabriel diffused unwonted lustre round,
And in the glory of that light appear'd,
Though softening all the terrors of his brow,
Not less than heaven's elect ambassador,
Heralding tidings of eternal joy ; —   120
Which, even as he utter'd, all the band
Of angels, suddenly apparent, caught
And set to music of seraphic harps,
Pure crystal symphonies of joy and love,
Until the waves of Hallelujah moved
The orient clouds, and gathering strength rang out
Among the golden stars, and travelling on
Held for a space the tongues of cherubim
Mute for delight before the throne of God.

" Soon from that throne, through clouds of glory
     stealing,   130
The whispers of the Spirit of God were heard ;

And Suriel moving at that still small voice
Took of the lamps, that ever blaze beside
The altar of celestial frankincense,
Symbols of love enkindling endless praise,
And from that lucid sphere descending sloped
His course to earth, where on the nightly plain
Chaldea's watchers read the starry heavens ;
And holding in his hand that torch, which seem'd
As if a planet brighter than its peers   140
Had wander'd from its path, viewless himself,
Allured their steps, whose minds were taught of God,
Until their weary pilgrimage at last
Was ended with unutterable joy
Before the Royal Babe of Bethlehem.

" Why should I tell thee what thou know'st? His
     flight
To Egypt's house of bondage ; and return
'Neath angel wings to lowly Nazareth ?
No palace home was His. No menials nursed
His childhood. Mary kept her secret close,   150
Or only breathed thereof in prayer to God,
Yet watch'd her gentle meditative Child,
Unlike yet like His brethren (for they err
Who deem her firstborn Son her only one),
With love beyond a mother's. Holiness
Breathed in His meek aspect. No passion wrought
To fret His bosom. Never a word of guile
Sullied His lips. Pure, harmless, undefiled,
He loved of all things best to be alone.

And oft would hie Him to the fields, and there   160
Ponder and pray.   And, when the Sabbath came,
Such gleams of glory in the synagogue
Play'd on His blessed countenance, as if
Conversing with the Invisible, mouth to mouth,
That I have seen His virgin mother's eyes
Fix'd on Him, till they flow'd with tears of joy.
But chiefly, when the yearly festivals
Drew them to Zion, a mysterious awe,
A child's most tender awe, the awe of love,
Seem'd to dilate His swelling breast, the while   170
He trod, as One at home, His Father's courts.

"Years pass'd; and still He grew in grace: yet still
His brethren knew Him not.   His perfect love
Disturb'd them; and they oftener chose consort
With those, whose goodness was not all unstain'd.
They quail'd before His gentleness.   But when
Their father sank beneath the weight of years,
As sinks the sun behind the autumn hills,
Then in that darken'd home the Light of Light
Diffused its softest radiance.   He it was,   180
Who bound up with the tenderest balms of love
His mother's bleeding heart; who mix'd His tears
With those that chased adown His sisters' cheeks,
Till sorrow's self grew calm; and He, who first
Summon'd His brethren to the needful toil,
Toil shared by Him, their common heritage.
And when He spake with such unfaltering faith
Of that celestial Paradise, wherein

Their father now was walking, even as One
Familiar with its living founts and fruits,   190
The bitterness of grief was gone, and death's
Dark portal was the golden gate of life.

" But if they saw and marvell'd, how with us
Who knew Him what He was, the Son of God?
Brother, our hearts were bow'd within us.   Pride,
That deadliest upas, that sought cast its shade
Over angelic natures though elect,
Wither'd before that wondrous spectacle.
It was not only grace we saw, but grace
That fail'd not in a world of selfishness ;   200
Nor only light, but light in poisonous air
Miraculously burning, self-sustain'd ;
Nor faith alone, but faith, emptying itself,
Itself to strengthen in Another's might ;
Self-limited Omnipotence, that deign'd,
Weak even as man is weak, to lean on God.
Messiah praying : — brother, I have watch'd
His lips moving, until my very soul
Clave to Him with intensity of love ;
And heard Him plead for those He came to save,   210
Until of all hard tasks the hardest seem'd
Not to go trumpet-tongued, and summon all
To fall and worship at His sacred feet.

" But now His time was come : His herald, John,
Who, like Elias, in the wilderness
Had nursed his kingly soul to kingly deeds

Heroic, came, the voice before the Word,
Crying, ' Repent, the kingdom is at hand.'
God's Spirit echoed the warning, and the cry
Struck sharp on human hearts, like steel on flint :   220
And crowds, their sins bewailing, throng'd the man
Whose hand explored the secret womb of thought.
And in whose dreadless eye eternity
Glared upon time.   Men ask'd men, ' Is there space
To flee the wrath to come?'   Jerusalem
Hurried to Jordan.   Ah, what deeds of wrong
Lips, counted by their fellows pure as babes,
Flung there upon the startled winds!   What filth
Was wash'd away from penitential hearts
In that baptismal stream!   But now, behold,   230
To our amaze among the crowds we saw
The spotless Son of Mary.   John, abash'd,
Shrank from the suit He urged.   But He refused
Refusal.   And, as from the shallow ford
Returning on the bank He knelt in prayer,
Lo, on a sudden the blue heavens were rent,
Unfolding to the very throne of God,
And (time and space subjected now to love)
The Spirit descending in corporeal shape,
Dove-like alighted on His sacred head,   .   240
A Dove of plumage whiter than the light:
And from the depths of glory came the Voice
Of the Eternal Father, ' This is He,
My well-beloved, My Son, My soul's delight.'
This voice celestial, this celestial form,
Alone of all those thronging multitudes

John heard and saw ; while Gabriel with his hosts
Shielded the spot from hell's malignant thrones,
Who pined in vain, confounded auditors
Of words which knell'd their doom.　But straight their
　　prince,　　　　　　　　　　　　　　　　　250
Like some great warlike chief repulsed, who makes
His failure instant cause for fresh assaults
Or deadlier stratagems, recall'd his peers .
To their dark council chamber wrapt in clouds,
Whence issuing after long consult, a smile
Of baleful hope upon his faded brow,
He sought the designated Son of God.

" Meanwhile from Jordan's farther banks the Christ,
With His own thoughts communing, thoughts im-
　　pregn'd
And glorified by the incumbent Spirit,　　　　260
Which in His sevenfold plenitude of grace,
Life, light, power, wisdom, counsel, fear, and love,
Immeasurable on Him abode, was led
Eastward towards the wilds of Araby.
Hour after hour He walk'd lonely, nor felt
Or weariness or want : such bursting hopes
Of His unparallel'd emprise surcharged
His bosom.　And, when nightfall unawares
Came down upon the rocky wilderness,
He, like the solitary Jacob, laid　　　　　　270
His head upon a stone and slept : but dreams
Diviner than the pilgrim patriarch saw
Visited His bleak couch, we camping near.

And, when the morning broke, He rose refresh'd,
His first thoughts like the fragrant incense borne
Up to His Father's presence. Onward still,
As One guided invisibly, He press'd,
Nor ate nor hunger'd. Thus a second day
Pass'd, and a third; till Nebo's barren cliffs
And rugged precipices barr'd in front   280
His prospect. But, as night again descended.
And on a stony pillow as before
Messiah sought repose, we were aware
Of change and peril imminent. Thick clouds,
Dragging their vaporous skirts along the hills,
Blotted the stars; and distant thunders roused
The beasts of rapine from their lairs, whose roar
Seem'd ever nearer on the moaning blast.
The darkness was not all of earth : wing'd forms
Unhallow'd pass'd us in the thickening gloom.   290
We watch'd in doubt, unweeting what designs
The foe was hatching. But, when morn approach'd,
And Jesus through the twilight walk'd abroad,
Far other visions than the last appear'd
To' have haunted His night hours. His calm aspect
Was troubled; and in place of joy His eye
Flash'd with the wrath of tempted innocence
Indignant. Not the brooding wintry storm,
That beat in gusts upon His sacred head,
Vex'd Him whose spirit was swept with fiercer winds,
Nor yet the lion's baffled growl, that slunk   301
From Gabriel's sword into the tangled brake;
Nor pangs of hunger, for in that stern strife

He felt them not. But now the Arch-fiend wove
His subtlest machinations, flinging shafts
Incessant of all racking doubts and fears,
The tempter wielding archangelic powers,
The Tempted in weak human flesh enshrined.
Night came, but night was terrible as day ;
And sleep, but sleep was worse than waking thoughts :
Nor one day only, nor yet seven, nor seven   311
Twice told or thrice ; but forty days and nights
That conflict inexpressible was waged,
No avenue of reason unassail'd,
No bolt from that wide quiver's mouth unshot :
All, all in vain. Then inly to himself
The devil mutter'd, as I caught the words,
' My ghostly weapons fail, let sight and sense
Avail me, as in Eden,'—and relax'd
His onset.   320

               " Then it was, the urgent stress
Of battle interrupted, hunger seized
The fainting Saviour. And His foe and ours,
No longer unapparent, what remain'd
Of his original lustre re-assumed,
And in his proper shape approach'd, his aim
Dissembling. ' If Thou art the Son of God, —
Nor other can I deem Thee, who hast foil'd
My uttermost attempt, — our duel now
Is ended. I confess discomfiture.
One only proof I ask, not for myself   330
Who know Thee, but for those who know Thee not,

One act as innocent in Thee to grant
As it is reasonable in me to crave;
Nay further, necessary for Thy wants,
Who here wilt perish in the wilderness.
Change by Thy word this rocky stone to bread.
Vouchsafe me this; and henceforth I and mine
Will leave Thee undisturb'd, the Christ of God.'

" So glozed the tempter. But the Son of Man,
As man clad in the panoply of faith,   340
Drew from its sheath the sharp sword of the Spirit,
And answer'd, ' It is written, Man shall live
Not by bread only, but by every word
Spoken by God.' And Satan shrank abash'd:
For on these very rocks, when bread was not,
The food of angels, at His voice who spake,
Had fallen round the tents of Israel.

" But from the deserts now the spirit of evil,
God's Spirit permitting, led the Saviour forth
Invisible, and with speed miraculous   350
Brought Him to Salem's sanctuary sublime,
Where over Kedron's vale the dizzy porch
O'erhung the valley. It was then the feast
Of tabernacles, and the crowds were spread
Like aloes by the rivers far beneath,
While others from Siloah's fountain fetch'd
The mystic water in a golden ewer,
And pour'd it in the temple forth with songs
Of Hallelujah and exuberant joy.

There, as they stood upon the utmost ridge,　　　360
Thus spake the tempter — ' Be it as Thou sayest:
Thy faith forbids Thee work a work to still
The cravings of Thy mortal need.　For Thee,
Whether by famine or by violence,
Death has no terrors.　Be it so.　But now,
Not for Thyself, but for Thy chosen race
I ask Thee, show Thyself the Son of God.
Cast Thyself down from hence.　Angels of light,
Thou knowest, are about Thee: they will bear,
As promised in the oracles of truth,　　　370
Thee in their hands.　I meanwhile will direct
All eyes upon this lofty battlement;
And joyful Israel shall behold her Prince
Descending with His radiant ministries
About Him, and shall crown Thee, as foretold,
The Son of David upon David's throne.'

" Messiah answer'd, — ' It is written again,
Thou shalt not dare to tempt the Lord thy God.'
Brief words but keen : beneath whose subtle edge
The devil writhed in anguish.　But yet one,　　　380
One last and damnable assault remain'd ;
And from the holy city quickly' he bore
The Saviour to that mountain peak, which look'd
Far over His late solitary watch,
Whence Moses, ere he fell on sleep, beheld
The hills and valleys of the land, with milk
And honey flowing, to the western sea
And goodly Lebanon.　But now (such skill

That mighty regent of the air had learn'd)
Whether by optical illusion wrought,   390
Like some mirage of cataracts and lakes
And gardens in Arabia's barren sands,
Or suns in mockery flushing Zembla's snows,
Refraction on refraction multiplied, —
Or haply' air pictures cunningly disposed
Within the eye's transparent microcosm, —
The mode I know not — but the dædal earth
With all its mighty realms from pole to pole,
Illumed with sudden supernatural light,
Seem'd lying, kindreds, peoples, nations, tongues,   400
A gorgeous panorama, scene on scene
Reflecting splendor, at Messiah's feet,
And in the twinkling of an eye condensed
The glories and the miseries of man,
As in a focus, on His startled soul,
Moving compassion and amaze at once.

"Then spake again the tempter, 'Not for Thee,
Whose meat it is to do Thy Father's will,
Nor yet for Israel, far too scant a field
For Thy illimitable sovereign schemes   410
Of goodness, do I now prefer request;
But for the world, the universal world,
To me committed, as Thou know'st, by One
Who never of His words or deeds repents : —
Let these four thousand years of wreck and ruin
Bear witness. I had fondly thought to hold
This sceptre as mine own. But let it pass.

Rather than wage interminable war,
I yield Thee my dominion.　I shall find
Some other orb untenanted as yet,　　　　　　420
Whereon to fix my throne.　And for the gift,
Vouchsafed me first, mine therefore to restore,
This coveted inheritance, I ask
But one brief passing act of homage done,
One transient recognition whence Thou owest
Thy kingdom.　At my feet receive the boon.
Thou shrinkest?　Why not?　I have seen Thee bow
To earthly rulers, — by Thy mother's side
Have seen Thee kneeling.　Having stoop'd so low,
Stoop once again to less indignity　　　　　　430
By far than prophecy assigns Thee.　Thou
Already' hast suffer'd much ; Thy gentle spirit
Amongst ungentle children ; Thy pure youth
Alien amongst impure ; Thy ripening faith
Exotic in a faithless world ; but all
Is nothing, less than nothing, to the doom
Before Thee chronicled in scrolls of fate,
If Thou refuse my offer.　Thou wilt stretch
Thy weary hands, loaden with gifts of life,
To disobedient and gainsaying men :　　　　　　440
Thine own will not receive Thee: cruel craft
Will dog Thy footsteps: till Thou sink'st at last
Under distress, dismay, derision, death.
What, death for Thee, the peerless Prince of life?
Truly, though I have done fell deeds, — in war
All things are lawful, — I, though damn'd should grieve
To see death's ghastly weapon pierce Thy heart.

15

My Liege, to Thee I owe my being: what
Of great I am is Thine: why then abhor
In me to honor Thy own workmanship?   450
Fear not, though I have woven countless snares,
And tangled countless hearts, angels and men,
With Thee all snares were useless; and I swear,
In this my offer lurks nor lure nor guile:
One insignificant act of homage paid,
And I retire, and with me all my hosts,
From earth and earth's precincts. Sole sovereign here
May'st Thou achieve Thy God-like enterprise,
Thy Good Spirit recreate this shatter'd world,
And earth re-echo Thy Great Father's name.   460
Nor ever again will I disturb Thy realm:
I have my gloomy bodings, even as Thou,
What may ensue, thus struggling without end:
Weary of horrid war, I long for peace.
One little act, and I resign Thee all.'

" Messiah's words anticipate our thoughts,
His hand still cleaving to the two-edged sword,
' Hence, Satan: it is written, Thou shalt serve
The Lord thy God, and worship only Him.'
And by the lightning of the Saviour's eye,   .   470
Bent full upon the Adversary, we saw
His desperate repulse. The naked truth
Had rived his bosom. Gnashing with remorse,
Slowly, reluctantly, he sank, as sinks
The angry tide from off a lighthouse rock,
Which it has drench'd in blinding spray and foam.

Leaving the light unscathed.   And it was ours
To cluster round that humble Victor's feet,
And offer fruitage from the vines of heaven,
And water from the rivulets of life,   480
And blossoms gather'd on their marge ; from me
He took with smiles a flower of amaranth —
(As Oriel spake, a blush of deeper rose
Crimson'd his cheek at the remember'd joy) —
Yea, and to tender sympathies more sweet
Than flowers, or fruit, or fountains gushing life,
Wherewith refresh'd ere long Messiah bent
His footsteps to the plains of Galilee.

" Full of the Spirit He came : His sinless powers
All quicken'd to the uttermost of man :   490
His faith transparent without clouds : His love,
Clear radiance on the altar of His heart,
Fire without smoke of darkness : prophecies
Of everlasting joy kindling His soul :
Pure perfect Manhood.   We had often wept
Tears of delight to see celestial grace
Struggling and triumphing in weakness ; but
Some stains had ever with the saintliest saints
Blotted the story of their life.   What need
To speak of Noah, and of Abraham,   500
Of Moses, David, Hezekiah, Job,
Who sometime trail'd their garments on the earth,
Though whiter now than snow ?   But here was One
Faultless though compass'd with infirmity,
In human weakness sinless, who had stoop'd

Lower than angelhood in might, but dwarf'd
In uncreated goodness infinite
The loftiest seraphim : no stern recluse,
As His forerunner ; but the Guest and Friend
Of all who sought Him, mingling with all life   510
To breathe His holiness on all.   No film
Obscured His spotless lustre.   From His lips
Truth limpid without error flow'd.   Disease
Fled from His touch.   Pain heard Him, and was not.
Despair smiled in His presence.   Devils knew,
And trembled.   In the omnipotence of faith
Unintermittent, indefectible,
Leaning upon His Father's might, He bent
All nature to His will.   The tempest sank,
He whispering, into waveless calm.   The bread,   520
Given from His hands, fed thousands and to spare.
The stormy waters, as the solid rock,
Were pavement for His footstep.   Death itself
With vain reluctancies yielded its prey
To the stern mandate of the Prince of life.

" Not that these things are hid from thee : but, brother,
None but an angel can methinks conceive
What angels felt, as over Him they stoop'd
Lost in adoring contemplation.   Oft
Has Gabriel call'd me to his side in awe   530
At His Divine humility ; which once,
Once only in His earthly pilgrimage,
Suffer'd the shrouded glory to escape
Its fleshly veil.

"Once only, on the crest
Of snowy Hermon as He knelt in prayer,
His chosen witnesses beheld His form
Apparell'd in its own celestial light,
More dazzling than the snows on which it shone,
When Michael, who on Satan's fall assumed
At God's command the hierarchal primacy,   540
The same who guarded Moses' funeral rites
And bore Elijah in God's chariot home,
Brought them, one bodiless, embodied one,
From Paradise before the other dead,
To commune with their Lord on His decease
Now nigh at hand.   Then the Shekinah cloud
Descending, wrapt them in its radiant folds,
And from its excellent glory came a Voice
'This is My Son Beloved, hear ye Him.'

"This Voice we heard, nor we alone who knelt   550
Near as permitted: fiendish auditors
Beyond us, in the dusky air suspense,
Heard it, and quaked in silence: Satan heard
Confounded, and now, desperate of fraud,
Seem'd only' intent to deal the cruellest bruise
Immedicable on his Victim's heel,
His Victor soon.   Ranging abroad he stirr'd
The hosts of darkness to maligner hate,
Saying, Now was the hinge of battle, now
The fated hour of doom: one effort more,   560
And earth, their destined heritage, was theirs.
Then round him cluster'd, gloomy body-guard,

His peers, into whose venomous breasts he fused
Fresh venom, urging some to wreak worse ill
On their demoniac slaves, others to wind
Their coils of envy around priestly hearts,
And others in the path of ruthless men
To dig quick pitfalls of insensate pride :
Himself, with Mammon for his minister,
Tracking the Saviour's steps, and beckoning on,   570
With lures of miserable gold, a wretch
Who sprang well pleased into his cursed embrace,
Judas, the heir of everlasting shame.

"Once he was cow'd; when seated with his mates
In council (such were daily now convened)
Quick tidings reach'd him, that his fiercest spirits
Quail'd at the name of Jesus breathed in faith
By humblest lips.   Instantly, whether rage
O'ermaster'd him, or shadowing fear surprised,
Down like a meteor or a lightning flash   580
From that aerial height he sank, he fell, —
Not unobserved by Him whose piercing Eye,
Scanning the ages, in that lapse beheld
A presage of his endless fall from heaven
To the abysmal pit.   But Satan soon,
Collecting his dejected legions, cried,
The while he spat defiance on his Lord,
' Do Thou Thy worst: Thou hast not tasted ours ' —
And without further cause of hate pursued
His drear deliberations, boding death.   590

" The hour was almost come. Six days had pass'd,
Since from the lonely Ephraim the Lord
Had sought the house He loved at Bethany,
Where Martha and her sister dwelt, and he,
Whose disembodied spirit we some time kept
Lull'd by the wafting of angelic wings,
As in a dream of undefined delight,
Until the Word recall'd him: six brief days,
But every moment big with destiny:
The Sabbath of unbroken peace and prayer: 600
That evening,— was it much for her, whose heart
Was crush'd, to crush the alabaster vase?—
Mary, with love's foreboding instinct, pour'd
The precious myrrh upon His head and feet,
And wiped them with her rich dishevell'd hair.
The midnight watches spent with God: the ride
Of lowly triumph dash'd with tears, and songs
Woven with sighs, into Jerusalem ;
The weary Wayfarer's return afoot
Over the ridge of wooded Olivet   610
At nightfall ; the surprise of early dawn
Startling His orisons ; the lonely curse,
Pregnant with gracious warning, which His lips
Pronounced ; the sanctuary cleansed anew ;
The nightly calm ; the morrow's stern contest
With stubborn hearts, sheathed in dark unbelief
Or darker superstition, - - crystal truth
Confuting guile, pure love predicting woes
Upon impure malignity ; the cry
' We would see Jesus,' breathed by Gentile lips,   620

While on His prescient troubled soul there fell
The first dark shadows of the vale of death,
Rugged with tempest; the suspended prayer,
Whose dread alternative was death or life,
Which rested ' Father, glorify Thy name ; '
The Voice responsive from the Throne, which fill'd ·
The hearts of prostrate seraphim with awe,
But fell unheeded upon mortal ears ;
Until the Lord o' the temple, not before
He made the widow's heart to sing for joy,   630
Forsook His house.   As once Ezekiel saw
The symbol of His awful Presence pause
Reluctant o'er the threshold, cherub-borne,
And o'er the city brood like guardian fire,
And move, and rest upon the hill that lies
Fronting the dawn, — so then on Olivet
The weary Saviour rested and forecast
The anguish coming on Jerusalem,
The birth-pangs of evangel life, nor left
That mountain's brow, nor limited the range   640
Of His prophetic vision, till He spake
Of His great Advent in the clouds of Heaven.
One day of calm seclusion ; and a night
And morning all unvex'd, albeit the powers
Of evil throng'd the air ; but, as the sun
Swerved westward, Jesus, with the Twelve, set forth
Towards the city which He loved, the while
We hung around their footsteps, till they sate
In silent thought around the Paschal board.

"Thou knowest all.   But when the Son of God, 650
Equal Assessor of the Father's throne,
Author and Heir of all things, girt Himself,
Stoop'd, and the Servant of His servants, wash'd
Their feet, we gazed upon the awful scene
In terrible amazement, till His words
Recall'd us to the Infinite of love
Which dwelt within Him and in which He dwelt,
Making, it seem'd, all other humbleness
Appear too high, all other love too low.
But now the Paschal lamb was eaten, now   660
The wine-cups fill'd and drunk; when He, who knew
What was in man, and from that hour look'd forth
Upon the ages of all time, ordain'd
Those holy mysteries of bread and wine,
The banquet of His body and His blood,
The ever fresh memorials of His death
To faith instinct with life, and quick with love,
Symbols of eucharistic sacrifice,
The sacramental oath of fealty,
The bond of brotherhood, the pledge of heaven.   670

"Alas, far different fruit those emblems now
Wrought in the traitor!   Satan, who ere this
Had visited his heart nor met repulse,
Now readily assumed the ready throne,
And sway'd him willing to his will.   The light
Was torment: and alone he stagger'd forth
Into the darkness on his dark intent.

"And now from lips, which spake as never man,
Flow'd words of inexpressible tenderness
Mingled with power, while more than human love, 680
Clothing itself in human language, pour'd
Immortal comforts into mortal hearts,
Until they overflow'd in tears.   And then
The Great High Priest, with eyes uplift to heaven,
Standing as if the mystic veil were rent
Before the seat of mercy, in full view
Of those He loved, pleaded their cause with One
Who loved them even as Himself; nor stay'd
Before He breathed that wonderful ' I will '
Which draws His children hither as their work   690
Is finish'd, spring of countless tears on earth,
And harvests sown in weeping reap'd in joy.

"Meanwhile the moon had risen full-orb'd: and they,
Passing through lights and shadows, bent their steps
Along the city's now deserted streets
To Kedron's vale ; over the brook ; where wound
The mountain path to Olivet: and there
Upon the right a garden, into which
They enter'd, olive-set Gethsemane.

"But wherefore now with trembling lips recall   700
That scene of unimaginable woe ?
The summons of the chosen three ; the moan
Of mortal anguish from the Lord of life ;
The vigil, tenderly enjoin'd in vain ;

The agony of prayer; the bloody sweat,
Wrung from His sacred brow and trembling limbs
By griefs, which no created mind can sound;
The cry, when that exceeding bitter cup
Sear'd as hot iron His lip; the human soul
Quivering, until from the unfolding heavens   710
A seraph (which of the empyreal thrones
We knew not, for upon that awful quest
His mantling wings had too securely veil'd
His presence and his face perplex'd with tears,
And his dear Master's look sufficed for praise)
Descending knelt beside that kneeling Form
And strengthen'd Him: and through the moonlight
          stole
The slow, the tremulously balanced words,
' Not My will, O My Father, Thine be done,'
Once and again.

          " The first sharp paroxysm,   720
As Death infix'd his keen envenom'd sting
Full in the bosom of Eternal Life,
Was over.   Follow'd now the traitor's kiss;
The binding of Omnipotence; the stroke
Of Peter, kept from rash repeat by words
That thrill'd our hearts, and sheathed more swords
          than his
Each in its scabbard; the apostles' flight;
The hurried Sanhedrim; the viewless fiends,
Thronging that hall and plying all their arts
On men abandon'd to their cursed will;   730

The strength of one, who lean'd upon himself,
Found wanting; meantime falsehood bearding Truth;
The Lamb of God silent; the faith which look'd
From that tribunal to the final bar:
And, as the cold gray morning struggled through,
The guiltless Sufferer bound, and rudely dragg'd
From court to court, abhorr'd, accused, reviled,
Until that proud contemptuous Roman heart
Yielded to those infuriate cries, and gave
The Man of sorrows up to bitter death.   740

"Woe, brother, woe for those, who against hope
Ere this in hope persisted! One of us
Was summon'd to the wretched traitor's end,
And by command led forth his damned spirit
To its own place of doom. But we, the rest,
Forbidden longer to oppose the worst,
Could only follow with those weeping few
Who hung around the footsteps of their Lord,
Amazed, appall'd. We saw the weary cross
Laid on His fainting strength, His sacred limbs   750
Ruthlessly stripp'd, His quivering hands and feet
Pierced with the cruel nails, while words of love,
Father, forgive who know not what they do,
Fell from His agonized lips. And now
The cross was raised. And there betwixt two thieves
The Increate Creator of all worlds,
The Son of the Eternal Father, hung
Betray'd, bereft, beleaguer'd, crucified.

"Thou weepest, brother: well thou may'st. My
　　tears
With thine are flowing.　But in that first hour　　760
No angel wept.　Sorrow itself was numb'd
Within us : while the bitter jests and taunts
Of soldiers, priests, and reckless passers by,
And curses mutter'd from between clench'd teeth
Fell ever on the meek Redeemer's ears,
A pitiless storm.　But, when upon His right,
Gazing upon His superhuman love
Till the hard stone was crush'd and contrite, one
Of those who hung beside His cross rebuked
His fellow, and cried, 'Lord, remember me,'　　770
And, firstfruits of His dying anguish, drew
Life from that bleeding sacrifice ; and when
The Saviour, looking on the faithful group
That cluster'd at His feet, tenderly gave
His mother to His friend, — the sight unseal'd
The frozen springs of sorrow, and we wept.

"Was love stronger than death ?　Upon that cross
They grappled as in final strife.　For now
Hell put forth all its malice, and let loose
Its gather'd vengeance.　All the air was dense　　780
With fiends ; and blackness, blacker than the night
Which Moses' rod on smitten Egypt drew,
Dismay'd the heavens : such delegated power
Had Satan, regent of the air, and all
The gloomy hosts of darkness at his beck
Hemming the Saviour round.　And, as the load

Immense, intolerable, of the world's sin,
Casting its dreadful shadow high as heaven,
Deep as Gehenna, nearer and more near
Grounded at last upon that Sinless Soul   790
With all its crushing weight and killing curse,
Then first, from all eternity then first,
From His beloved Son the Father's face
Was slowly' averted, and its light eclipsed;
And through the midnight broke the Sufferer's groan,
Eli, Eli, lama sabachthani?
The echo was the mockeries of hell,
Reverberate in human lips. We heard,
And shudder'd. Gabriel lean'd on me a space,
And hid his face within my vesture's folds,   800
As if the sight were all too terrible
Even for archangelic faith. But now
Once more the agonizing Victim moan'd,
Uttering His anguish in one dreadful plaint,
I thirst; His last: for, when the cooling sponge
Had touch'd His lips, a loud and different cry,
As if of triumph, *It is finish'd,* rang
Upon our startled ears; and with a child's
Confiding tender trustfulness, that breathed
Father, tc Thy hands I commend My spirit,   810
He bow'd His head, and yielded up the ghost.

  " Earth quaked. The rocks were rent. The graves
        of saints
Were open'd. And the temple's mystic veil
Was riven in view of worshippers and priests,

Disclosing things unseen. Ere long the spear
Open'd the fountain in the Saviour's side,
And soon that holy tabernacle lay,
Like a deserted temple, cold and still,
In Joseph's rock-hewn tomb. But, brother, who
Of angels can describe what next ensued,   820
When Jesus breathed His last upon the cross,
In the throng'd firmament of spirits? Straightway
Around His disembodied soul the powers
Of darkness swarm'd, and Satan face to face
With burning falchion barr'd His path. One look,
Mere virtue bent on mere maliciousness,
Pierced him like lightning, and shot withering fire
Among his blasted hosts. Distraught they stood,
Insensible, one moment ; and then fell
From round Him, as the billow's cloven pride   830
Falls in thick spray from off the vessel's prow
By northern blasts, as by the arm of fate,
Driven towards the port of refuge. Fain had we
Accompanied His steps. His warning hand
Restrain'd us. Lonely He had fought the fight ;
And lonely He must stoop to strip the slain,
And lonely gather up the spoils of death.

  " Immediate, quicken'd in His human spirit,
More swiftly than the swiftest seraph's wing,
With speed akin to thought journeying He pass'd   840
Adown the firmamental heavens, and through
The maze of constellations, and, or ever
His stiffening corse was from the tree unloosed,

Had traversed the dark avenue that leads
Straight to the adamantine doors of hell.
These open'd to His advent, and beneath
Their awful archway He descended; and,
As downward through the lurid air He oped
His discontinuous path, beneath Him lay
The ruins and the wrecks of sin.　And then　　850
Full on His naked soul His Father's Eye
Rested with uneclipsed unclouded blaze,
Rested and found no flaw, no film of dark,
No jar, no discord, no antagonism,
But light to light responsive, beam to beam,
And love in faultless unison with love,
Perfection imaging Perfection: whence,
Not agony as with the damn'd perforce,
But trust, and peace, and joy too deep for words.

"Around Him devils and lost souls stood thronging.
Under God's custody compell'd that hour　　[860
To gather from the farthest vaults of hell,
And witness His descent, whose calm aspect
Might crush all hope, not wholly dead before,
That Satan in the conflict waged on earth
Should win some transient triumph, and unbar
Their prison.　But when now they saw their Lord
Strengthless, for so He seem'd, as they themselves,
Dark thoughts possess'd them to seize fast their prey.
And hold Him hostage for their own escape —　　870
Proof that no hell can change the lost.　But lo,
The Son of God upon that cursed soil,

In human weakness though Almighty, knelt,
And gazing up into His Father's face
Pleaded for rescue from that dark sojourn
Among the dead.   And instantly His prayer,
As Jonah's issuing from the ocean depths,
Rose like a cloud of incense high within
Heaven's temple.   Then the empyrean shook ;
The everlasting hills trembled ; the heavens   880
Were bow'd beneath His glory, who came down
Upon the wings of Cherubim, in wrath,
Darkness beneath His feet, lightnings before,
And round about Him clouds, which from their skirts
Shot hailstones and thick burning coals of fire
Among His enemies : while at their feet
The solid yawn'd with fissures, and disclosed
A lower depth of fire unquenchable,
Gehenna's lake, soon hidden ; but the sight,
Once seen, was shadow of the second death.   890
And now the right hand of Omnipotence
Was laid in love upon His Only Son,
And drew Him from among His stricken foes,
And from that vast profound, and o'er that gulf
Untravell'd by created wing, that lies
Betwixt that land of utter death and ours,
Athwart that billowy chasm, over these hills
And triple battlements of Paradise :
And, ere on earth the Sabbath eve began,
The Saviour met the sinner He had saved,   900
And welcomed him beneath the trees of life.
16

" Now was there joy and jubilant delight
In that fair Eden. Now was come the hour,
For which four thousand years had look'd and long'd,
Since first the solitary Abel trod
These hills and plains. Placid had been that rest,
And calm that haven after life's rough sea,
Each one at will in holy solitude
Reposing, or with the other saintly spirits
Walking in blissful converse. Age by age   910
Earth yielded hither her choicest and her best,
And here the angels on their ministries
Pass'd ever to and fro. But till the Word
Had conquer'd death, He came not to the dead
In excellence of glory manifest,
Though there, as every where, in power and spirit:—
Haply such advent had not all beseem'd
The Lord of life:—howbeit they saw not God,
As saints thereafter saw His face and lived,
But rather walk'd by faith like those on earth;   920
And oftentimes the craving cry ' How long? '
Of souls beneath the altar rose to heaven.
Judge then their ecstasy of joy, when now,
Apparent in a human form like theirs,
The Saviour stood amongst them, and proclaim'd,
The fight was foughten, and the victory won.

" From realm to realm of that great under-world
That day He journey'd. No one but received
Some token of His love. And, as He pass'd

That lonely vale with its own gates recluse, 930
Wherein the disembodied spirits in ward,
Who once were disobedient ere the flood,
Waited His advent with intenser hope,
He enter'd and reveal'd Himself, their Lord,
Besought, too late, for rescue in the ark,
But not for mercy ere they died, which same
Now bade them join the other Blessed Dead.

"This was His latest work. For now the hour
Predestined summon'd Him again to earth:
And, follow'd with innumerable songs 940
Of blessing, through the gates of Paradise,
And all along its glorious avenue,
Lonely He pass'd, and through the subject heavens
(His foes still cowering from their sore defeat)
To the lone chamber of the tomb.

                              "The sun
Had not yet risen; but in the golden East
The morning star was tricking his soft lamp,
Like some fair pearl with amber overlaid,
When through the twilight slid the hurrying steps
Of women bearing to the sepulchre 950
Unguents, and spice, and balm. Suddenly the' earth
Trembled and shook: and Gabriel, such his charge,
Descending from our airy watch roll'd back
The sealed stone, and, with his glory, cast
In a dead swoon the guards. Abash'd, confused,
The women, seeing, saw not; hearing, they

Heard not: save only she of Magdala
Hasted, and ran, a breathless messenger,
To those who mourn'd Him sorest. Quickly these
Ran, love outstripping ardor, to the spot,   960
And found the empty sepulchre. Love mused;
Faith marvell'd; but persistent Grief remain'd,
Weeping beside that desolated tomb.
Her heart lay buried there. He was her all,
Who in her helpless hopeless misery
Had sometime pass'd her by, and spake the word,
And set the hell-bound captive free. Henceforth
She loved Him with a holy clinging love,
Stronger than death. With broken heart she stood
Brokenly moaning at His cross: she heard   970
His dying cry. Alas, the weary night!
The long interminable day of rest!
The mournful task of mingling that rich myrrh!
The stifled doubt, could a dead Saviour save?
She crush'd the maddening thought, and only clung
The closer to the sepulchre: and now
Weeping she lean'd upon the cold gray stone,
And, stooping, look'd within.

                         " There two of us,
Where the dear body of our Lord had lain,
Sate robed in radiant white. Little she reck'd   980
Of angel ministries who sought her Lord:
And when we ask'd, ' Woman, why weepest thou?'
She utter'd her one plaint, ' He is not here.'
But turning mournfully away beheld

One whom she knew not, for the sluice of tears
Had drench'd her eyelids : and He likewise ask'd,
' Woman, why weepest thou ? whom seekest thou ? '
She answer'd ; when the Stranger turn'd and said,
' Mary.' She started, and, in one deep cry,
Breathing her incommunicable bliss,   990
' Rabboni,' fell before His feet, and fain
Had clasp'd them.

         " But not now as heretofore,
The human intercourse vouchsafed on earth ;
Nor was He to His Father's throne in heaven
That hour ascending. Yet a little space
Emmanuel tabernacled among men
To solace and sustain His orphan Church,
To heal the bleeding heart of penitence,
To cheer the downcast wayfarers, to stand
Suddenly as a spirit, but very Man   1000
Among His brethren, and imbreathe on them
The benediction of His peace and power,
To transform human fear to heavenly faith,
To conquer doubt by love, a second time
To teach His chosen fishermen to cast
The drag-net of the kingdom, to reveal
Himself unto His own in Galilee,
Where He had lived and labor'd longest ; thence
Returning to Jerusalem, once more
To lead His loved apostles o'er the slope   1010
Of Olivet to sacred Bethany ;
And, ere He left them in that world of sin

Irradiate with the bow of heavenly hope
Their watchings, and their warfare, and their woes.

"It was a golden eventide. The sun
Was sinking through the roseate clouds to rest
Beneath the Western waves. But purer light
And vestments woven of more glorious hues,
Albeit invisible to mortal eyes, [1020
Gladden'd the heavens. For there the hosts of God,
Ten thousand times ten thousand, tier on tier,
Marshall'd by Gabriel, fill'd the firmament;
The lowest ranks, horses and cars of fire,
Circling Mount Olivet; and next to these
A body-guard of flaming seraphim,
And hierarchal thrones; and after them
Celestial armies without number stretch'd
In infinite ascent aloft, their swords
Sheathed by their side (for, like an eagle scared,
No foe on that great triumph moved the wing, 1030
Open'd his mouth, or peep'd), and in their hand
The palm of victory and the harp of praise:
While through their thronging multitudes there oped
A path of crystal glory, all perfumed
With love and breezy raptures, such as heaven
Had never known. But every eye was bent
Upon the Saviour, as He stood amongst
The apostolic group, and lifted up
His hands and bless'd them, and in blessing rose,
No wind, no car, no cherubim of fire 1040
Ministrant, in His Father's might self-moved,

Into the glowing sky ; until a cloud
Far floating in the zenith, which had drunk
Of the last sunbeams, wrapt His radiant form,
And instantly became like light itself,
Then melted into viewless air.   But we,
Closing around His path, with shouts of joy
Rose with Him through the subjugated heavens,
The desolate domains of Lucifer,
And through the starry firmament, whose orbs,   1050
Vibrating with the impulse of our march,
Resounded Hallelujahs and flash'd fires
Of welcome — a procession such as earth
Saw never, nor had heaven beheld till now —
Observing each his place, yet each one near
The Prince of glory, who was near to each,
His Omnipresent Eye on every face
Shedding His rapture ; ever soaring higher,
And singing as we soar'd, until we reach'd
The confines of the third celestial sphere,   1060
Shut in by gates of pearl, transcending these
Of Paradise, as these surpass the porch
Of the first Eden.   There aloof, around,
Thronging the arch on this side and on that,
Was Michael with a host equal to ours,
Sent from the heavenly Zion.   Onward still
We swept like clouds over an azure sky,
And to the sound of martial trumpets sang
Exultingly, ' Lift up your heads, ye gates !
Be ye lift up, ye everlasting doors !   1070
Up, and the King of glory shall come in.'

Immediate, like an echo from those ranks
Guarding the heavenly citadel, the voice
Of myriads perfectly attuned as one,
Came back the peal of joyful challenge, 'Who,
Who is the King of glory?'—and from ours
The jubilant response, 'The Lord of hosts,
Mighty in battle' against the powers of hell,
Jehovah, King of glory! Lift your heads!
Be ye lift up, ye everlasting doors!   1030
Up, and the King of glory shall come in.'
'Who is the King of glory?' yet again
Peal'd from those opening gates. 'The Lord of hosts ·
He is the King of glory,' broke once more
In waves of thunder on those jasper walls,
Which never shook till now. And, host with host
Commingling, through the portals on we swept,
And through the city of the King of kings,
The streets of golden crystal tremulous
Beneath the nimble tread of seraphim,   1090
And eager principalities and powers,
And cohorts without number, till we came
Into the heavenly temple (space enough
Beneath its comprehensive dome for all
God's ministries and more than all twice told
In order ranged): and then the Great High Priest
Alone advancing with His precious blood
Touch'd, as it seem'd, the spotless mercy-seat;
And lo, the Everlasting Father rose,
Diffusing beams of joy ineffable,   1100
Which centred on His Son, His only Son,

And rising to His bosom folded Him
(If acts of Him the Increate can thus
Be duly in our language shadow'd forth)
And set Him at His own right hand: while clouds,
Breathing Divine ambrosial fragrance, fill'd
The temple, and awoke in every heart
Bliss inconceivable of silent praise.

" Much, brother, could I tell what then and there
Befell in heaven: and chiefly how the Son　　　1110
Cleansed with the virtue of His blood those courts
Which had defilement from the access thither
Of spirits accurst, and having cleansed them bless'd
With unction of the Holy One, and then
Utter'd His irreversible decree,
Which henceforth from those holiest precincts barr'd
Entrance of ill.　But yet remains untold
The warfare which ensued in earth and heaven:
And in the age of ages yet to come
Often shall we resume the wondrous tale,　　　1120
Which now I touch so briefly, of the past."

END OF THE SEVENTH BOOK.

Book Eighth.

THE CHURCH MILITANT.

AVAUNT thee, horrid War: whose miasms, bred
Of nether darkness and Tartarean swamps,
Float o'er this fallen world and blight the flowers.
Sole relics of a ruin'd Eden! Hence
With all thy cruel ravages! fair homes
Rifled for thee of husband, brother, son;
Wild passions slipp'd like hell-hounds in the heart,
And baying in full cry for blood; the shock
Of battle: the quick throes of dying men;
The ghastly stillness of the mangled dead;   10
The crumbling ramparts breach'd, the city storm'd,
The massacre of unresisting age,
The shrieks of violated innocence,
And bloom, almost too delicate for the print
Of bridal kisses and the touch of love,
Ruthlessly trampled underneath the heel

Of armed lust; and, pitiful to see,
The mother's womb ripp'd by the pitiless sword,
And life — her unborn offspring's and her own —
Shed in short mortal travail; lurid flames,　　　　20
Wrapping the toils of arduous centuries
And hopes of ages in one funeral pyre ;
Gaunt famine after, and remorseless plague,
Reaping their myriads where the warrior's scythe
Had been content with thousands ; leaving scars
Upon a nation's heart, which never time
Wholly can heal: hence horrid, horrid War !
But, as I mused, there crowded on my spirit
The lofty virtues nursed in strife ; the will
That breaks but bends not; goodness even in death　30
Abhorring evil; right defying wrong;
The stern self-sacrifice of souls afire
For perill'd altars and for hearths profaned ;
The generous chivalry, which shields the weak,
And dares the oppressor's worst; love guarding love
From rapine, or, as God's executor,
Dealing forth vengeance on the stubborn foe,
And mercy to the vanquish'd; all along
The ages, names the noblest and the best
From Israel's chiefs to those brave men whose swords　40
Have been the bulwark of my native isle ;
Till musing I excláim'd, O righteous War,
Thou immemorial school of deathless deeds,
Not thee I censure, nor thy sons, but those
Dark powers of evil, who awoke thee first
From thy eternal slumbers undisturb'd,

Leaning remiss upon thy stainless spear
Hard by God's seat : not thee or thine I blame,
Not thee, — Jehovah is a man of war,
Nor thine, — Jehovah is the Lord of hosts.   50

Howbeit not of war in earth or heaven,
After a grateful interlude, where thought
Flow'd onward to its own sweet rhythm, at first
Oriel discoursed ; but of the Sevenfold Spirit
Who, in similitude of burning lamps,
Burning before the sapphire Throne, appear'd
At signal of His voice who sate thereon
To move, His glory's effluence part veil'd
And part translucent in a radiant cloud,
While through the ranks of prostrate hierarchs   60
Descending from the heaven of heavens He came.
And with a sound of mighty rushing wind,
And likeness as of fiery tongues, diffused
In His Divine munificence of gifts
The brightness of His Presence, and enwreath'd
Each suppliant's head with flame.   By the same
      Spirit
Impregn'd, as if his lips were touch'd with fire,
My guardian spake with an enthusiast joy
Of those first Pentecostal days, that morn
After such long millennial watches hail'd,   70
That burst of dewy spring unchill'd by frost,
That garden water'd by the early rain,
And tended by the risen ascended Lord,
The rosy childhood of His bride, the gush

Of pure first love untinctured by the world,
When silvery Hope whisper'd in angel hearts,
The time was short, the kingdom was at hand.

" Where, brother, thou wilt ask," Oriel pursued,
" Where, meanwhile, lurk'd the powers of darkness ?
  Crush'd
They lay, and scatter'd for a week of years,   80
And of their buoyant life utterly drain'd
By that intolerable mortal stroke
The Saviour's spirit, enfranchised on the cross
From the rent tabernacle of His flesh,
Dealt in one gaze around. Six years and more,
Smit by that scathing agony, they cower'd,
Irresolute, disheartened, disarray'd,
The spoilers spoil'd, the thrones of hell dethroned,
And all their routed hosts wandering astray,
In earth or air, a spectacle of shame.   90
But then (so Wisdom Infinite ordain'd),
Time soothing their disastrous wound, of all
Satan the first recall'd his drooping pride,
And, gazing on earth's battle-field, renew'd
His desperate counsels. All appear'd not lost,
While ruin out of ruin yet might rise,
As thus, conferring with his own dark thoughts
And gathering courage from his daring words,
Upon the height of Lebanon he mused :

" ' Satan, bethink thee who thou art. To faint   100
Were weaker than thy vassal's weakness. Man

For a few years' abandonment to lust,—
Prodigious venture,—risks eternal flames.
And shalt thou yield, thus alway respited
From age to age? Who knows not, but for ever?
Omniscience, as it seems, can only read
Futurity but dimly. Hath the Cross
Drawn, as foreshadow'd by the Crucified,
All to His footstool? I trow not. To thwart
Love's best, to baffle Mercy's uttermost,   110
This were revenge indeed, worthy the name,
For the corroding fire His Dreadful Eye
Has kindled in my secret bosom. Thou,
Arch-adversary, be thyself once more.
The crisis challenges despatch: for lo,
Heaven's sapling strikes its roots deeper each day;
The fount of life unseal'd on Zion's hill
Is ever sending forth fresh rivulets
Of blessing,—blessing which to me is curse:
Be mine to blight that tree: be mine to shed   120
A secret poison in that crystal spring.
Despair, as hope, breeds counsels. I have found
Anguish no sluggish spur to thought. Despatch—
Yet for despatch delay. My faithful hosts
Are scatter'd, and my princes, Baalim,
Apollyon, Ashtaroth, and all their peers,
Cower till the storm be overblown: with them
Let me advise how easiest to retard
The Gospel chariot wheels. Tides flow and ebb:
This now hath reach'd its flood. The Son hath gone 130
With His bright ministries to heaven. and there

By sore experience taught, I dread Him less
Than walking on this earth in mortal flesh.
Nor fear I greatly His vicegerent Spirit,
Whose tongues of harmless lightning seem to' announce
A different war. Here I put off the last
Soft remnants of compunction. I have been
Too generous, too gentle heretofore;
But henceforth, rather than the sinuous snake,
Assume the fiery dragon. If this fail,   140
As likely' it may, my quiver is not void.'

" So saying, his dusky pinions he outspread,
And rose sublime into his ancient throne
Set in the starry firmament, and thence
Call'd his afflicted mates, who soon, though shorn
Of their late glory, with unbated rage,
And eyes that flash'd implacable revenge,
Came at their leader's summons, and ere long
In dire deliberations sate absorb'd.

" The shadow of that council fell on earth   150
When Stephen, on whose lips the Spirit had breathed
More of the fire of love than on the rest,
Was dragg'd before his nation's Sanhedrim,
And with seraphic radiance on his face,
Pleaded his Master's cause, heaven's advocate
Confronting hell's inexorable bar
In vain: but, from that presbytery malign
And ruthless judge averting his rapt gaze,
Behold the heavens were open'd to his view.

And with the eagle eye of faith he saw   160
Within the veil the holy cherubim
Shadowing the glory of the mercy-seat,
And on the right the Great High Priest of God,
Messiah, ministering (vision of bliss
Ineffable), and, calmly kneeling down,
Amid those cruel taunts and crushing stones,
The dying martyr breathed his spirit forth,
And fell in his Redeemer's arms asleep.

" This was the signal of that bitter war,
Which Satan and his re-assembled hosts,   170
Now urging, now relaxing, the contest,
Waged to the death for nine long months of years,
War which upon its scroll of heroes 'nscrihed
Apostles, prophets, seers, evangelists,
Princes, and peasants of a princely heart,
Matrons, and maids, and children, till the cross
Was planted on the battlements of Rome.
Sore was the tempest; but the rooted oak,
Though loaden with the stormy winds and bruised,
Only more widely cast its acorns round,   180
The seed of after forests.   On our part,
Like lightnings on our ministries of love,
Moved by the Omnipresent Spirit we flew.
Heaven put forth all its ghostly strength as hell,
Counsel with counsel militant: what time
The snow-white horse and its imperial lord,
Apollyon's symbol (worshipp'd there as Mars)
Chosen in defiance of the King of kings,

With eagles crown'd by Capitolian Jove,
Went conquering and to conquer forth.   Ere long   190
That hue triumphal changed to fiery red,
The rider and his horse incarnadined
By fratricidal slaughter.   And again,
Lean hunger prowling o'er the Roman world,
That mystic horseman and his crimson'd steed
Grew black as night : all faces gather'd gloom ;
The new wine languish'd, and the mirth of harps
Was quench'd, and all the merry-hearted sigh'd :
Presage of worse.   For that black phantasm soon
Assumed a livid pale, most ghastly steed,   200
Bestridden by the king of terrors, Death,
And follow'd by the shades of hell.   Through all
We pitch'd our tents around the saints of God,
Alike in prisons and in palaces,
In cities, and in lonesome dens and caves ;
And, when the fadeless crown of martyrdom
Was wreathen for the martyr's holy brow,
The Captain of our armies oft ordain'd
No slender band of spirits, but legions arm'd,
And turms of the celestial chivalry,   210
Such as in Dothan camp'd about the seer,
To' attend His dying servants ; or Himself
Descended in His chariot paved with love
To bear them straightway home.

                        " But time would fail
To speak of all who trod in Stephen's steps,
Who for their Master's sake endured the worst

17

Of vengeance men could wreak on fellow-men,
Shame, taunts, revilings, hunger, nakedness,
Bonds, dungeons, scourges, tortures, till at last
They yielded up their bodies to be burn'd,   220
Or bow'd their neck to the devouring sword.
By many, with my bright compeers, I stood
In their last agony. Some I had watch'd
Like thee, from earliest infancy of faith,
My chosen wards : of whom thou know'st by name,
Perpetua, beautiful Perpetua, pride
Of Carthage. I was by her side that hour
When she a wife, a mother, stood unblench'd,
So young and fair, so tender and so true,
Before the proud Hilarian. In mine ears   230
Vainly her father urged his passionate suit,
And pleaded his thin silvery locks in vain.
And when the shouting theatre received
Her and her sister saint, Felicitas,
A princess and a slave (rank weigh'd not then),
And with them other three — when ruthless hands
Stripp'd from her gentle limbs her robes, and gave
To the rude gaze of thousands charms which love
Had scarcely seen, — I heard her low-breathed cry
For patience, by her Lord vouchsafed, though now 240
The scourge made furrows on her quivering flesh,
And soon the madden'd and infuriate bull,
Wild with affright, forth rushing from its den
Gored all her tender side ; until herself,
Triumphant in the hour of mortal pain,
Guided the gladiator's trembling blade

Straight to her bursting throat : then it was mine,
Attended by a glorious retinue
Of angels, to await her parting spirit,
And lead her, heralded with songs of praise,　　250
Through heaven's glad portals to her Lord's embrace
In yonder bowers of beatific joy.

"Martyr'd Perpetua was but only one
Of thousands not unlike : until the cry,
Swelling from year to year, from age to age,
Rose ever louder and more loud from souls
Beneath the altar crying, 'How long, O Lord,
Most Holy, dost Thou not avenge our blood?
How long, O Lord, how long?' A little space
God's patience suffer'd. Then the Pagan earth　　260
Trembled as smitten with His hand : the sun
Became as sackcloth, and the moon as blood :
The stars fell ruinous from heaven, as when
A fig-tree, shaken of a mighty wind,
Casts its untimely figs : the firmament
Was shrivell'd as a scroll : the island rocks
Fled, and the everlasting mountains sank
Appall'd. Jehovah had arisen, and man
Was prostrate at His feet.

　　　　　　　　　"The earthquake ceased ;
And all things had ere long resumed their calm,　　270
When lo, the mystic Bride appear'd in heaven
Clothed with the sun, the moon beneath her feet,
And on her head a coronal of stars,

Exceeding fair. But, even as we gazed,
Her hour was come, and travailing in birth
She cried aloud, with bitter pangs and throes
Tormented. And, or ever we were 'ware,
Right opposite a fiery dragon roll'd
His baleful eyes, all ravenous to devour
Her helpless babe when born : portentous sign   280
Of woe and warfare imminent, which soon
Darken'd the fields of heaven. Her new-born babe
In sooth was caught up to the throne of power;
And upon eagle wings the woman fled
Into the lonely wilderness, and there
Abode for six times seven months of years,
Until the time appointed her of God.
But now the dragon and his hosts must drink
More deeply of the bitter cup of shame,
And taste from our avenging swords that wrath   290
Which they had braved too fiercely and too long.

" It was the year that Constantine avow'd
Allegiance to the conquering Cross, when I,
Returning from my solitary charge
With the lost Theodore to Hades, found
War, open war, already pre-announced
In heaven. For though Messiah, when He rose
Triumphant from Mount Olivet, had cleansed
The Heavenly Zion and its vast precincts,
Nor suffer'd from that hour unholy feet   300
To tread those temple courts, there lay betwixt
Wide champaigns, lower than the heaven of heavens,

But loftier than the earth; and these the foe,
Recovering from their fatal bruise, possess'd,
Wide regions of the starry firmament,
Not without orbs and embryo worlds, the which
They fortified with munimental walls
Of fire and darkness, fastnesses and forts
Innumerable, but chiefly' around that pole
Far stretching toward the regions of the North,   310
Where Satan fix'd his capital supreme,
By mortals Pandemonium call'd, for there
He and his rebel potentates were wont,
A gloomy consistory, to sit immured,
And thence descending in quick raids to ply
Their devilish arts upon mankind: as when,
To liken things in heaven to things on earth,
A pirate chieftain in the Egean lurks
By Lesbos or its tributary isles,
And sweeps the ocean from his secret lair.   320
Moreover from those dark palatial halls,
Where fallen gods in synod sate enthroned,
Invective blasphemies against the saints,
Exaggerating or inventing ill,
Cruel, obscure, vindictive, false, malign,
Rose day and night to God: never more loud,
Never more loathsome than when Cæsar's crown
Wreath'd Christian brows, and Satan knew his seat
Was crumbling underneath its idol weight.

"But now the inevitable hour had struck   330
Of conflict., Hell's iniquity once more

Had risen and trembled on the utmost brim.
Nor was it longer possible for ours,
Who for four thousand years and more had fought,
Opposing stratagem to stratagem,
Manœuvre to manœuvre, toil to toil,
But from the forceful violence of war
By God's command refraining, not to feel
A stern and holy joy, when now the word
Came from the height of Zion, by the mouth   840
Of Suriel, to equip themselves for fight,
And where the standard of great Michael waved,
A sheet of flame athwart the northern heavens.
To muster their innumerable ranks
For battle, following where he led the way.

" But ere that burning messenger resumed
His station at the footstool of God's throne,
Unarm'd, and unaccompanied, he pass'd
(Such is the fearless confidence of love,
And such amazement fearless love compels —   350
So Moses stood unmoved in Pharaoh's court)
Within the triple walls of darkness piled
By Satan round his vast metropolis,
And through the throng of ruin'd seraphim,
And lurid cohorts round about them ranged,
And, suddenly amid that council hall
Apparent, for His Lord spake winged words :

" ' Ye fallen principalities of heaven,
Wrath is impendent. Michael and his hosts

Already by command are on their way   360
To cleanse these heavenly regions. Ere the sword
Drive you and yours to ignominious flight
Or worse —'

         " But Satan, rising from his throne,
Scarce in his fury finding words, brake short
The warning voice of heaven's ambassador,
' Whence art thou, cherub? Are not heaven's domains
Sufficient for thy nimble wing, that thou
Must violate my realms? Michael, thou sayest, —
He first, or I, of the archangelic three ?
His armies — are they more or less than mine ?   370
But let him come, with all the hosts of God
Number'd tenfold, — I fear, I fly him not.
Whatever it avail in idle peace,
Love is no equal match for hate in war,
Nor truth for guile, nor courage for despair.
Meanwhile for thy insultant ambassage,
Until the cohorts of thy friends are driven
From our imperial battlements confused,
Within the darkest dungeon they conceal,
Cherub, abide in chains, a spy's desert.'   380

  " So saying, the Arch-fiend stretch'd his puissant arm,
To grasp that fearless spirit, but grasp'd him not,
For God around him cast His shield of power
Invisible; and through them forth he pass'd
(As once Messiah through the furious crowd
Of Nazareth pass'd scathless) through the guards

Who vainly throng'd his path, and through the maze
Of bastions — none could stop his way — nor paused
Until he came within angelic ken
Of the bright legions now from far and near   390
Assembling round the hierarchal tent
Of Michael. Goodly was the sight and brave.
Far as the eye could reach, beneath him lay,
In turms and squadrons and battalions rank'd,
The armies of the living God. Like light
Their helmets shone ; like lightnings flash'd their
    swords ;
While over them their ensigns waved like fire :
Warriors innumerable, of whom the least
Thus militant appearing among men
Would loose the loins of thousands. On the right 400
Was Gabriel marshalling his endless hosts ;
Nor less upon the left was Raphael's charge ;
Michael the centre held : while far in front
Ten thousand times ten thousand chariots blazed,
And horsemen clad in armor white as snow,
Who oft to right and left disparting show'd
The forest of impenetrable spears behind.

" Straight to those guards of flaming seraphim,
Where Michael stood alone pre-eminent,
Directing with his eye, and hand, and spear,   410
The glorious tryst, sped Suriel and announced
The scornful answer of the foe : whereat,
From chief to chief, from armed rank to rank,
And from brigade to battailous brigade

Rolling, arose a shout of martial wrath
Indignant. Thrice it rose, and thrice it fell.
A mighty wave of multitudinous sound,
And broke far off amid the troubled stars :
And, as the latest echoes sank, I came
From Zion's height, and took, at Gabriel's beck,   420
My post upon his distant right reserved.

  " But now, at secret signal from the Throne,
Sounded the archangelic trump.   Forthwith
That hosts of hosts, as by one breath inspired,
In silence voiceless as the hush of night,
Moved on with unimaginable speed,
Smooth and unbroken (as the peopled earth
Unjarring and unjarr'd moves evermore
Along her heavenly orbit), through the realms
Of light, until frowning before them lay   430
Outstretch'd in almost limitless extent
The empyreal kingdom of the prince of hell,
Immured in gloom, meet ramparts for meet foes,
Walls of what seem'd impenetrable dark,
Blind fissures yawning here and there betwixt,
Inviolate, embrasures none above,
Foundations none below, to mine or scale :
Nothing to mark where lurk'd the unseen foe ;
No whisper heard within.

                        " Thither arrived
Michael his legions wide aloof disposed   440
To search if guarded portal, or ravine,

Or secret avenue, might tempt approach.
But none appear'd ; though twice ten thousand leagues
Each touching each his millions stretch'd, such clouds
And exhalations had the Apostate Fiend
(In likeness of the judgment clouds that roll
Veiling the Light of Light from creature gaze,
Though those be pure and these impure and foul)
Around his throne of evil circumfused.
But as we stood at gaze, a furnace blast   450
Rush'd from those bastions forth, and storms of hail,
As sharp rocks hurl'd from countless catapults,
With whirlwind fury on our armies smote ;
Nor intermitted, while above our heads
Hot clouds of fiery ashes, black as night,
Discharged their ominous burden : such as once
Vesuvius travailing in earthquake pour'd
On Herculaneum's idle battlements,
And doom'd Pompeii's last festivities.
Horrible tempest: but for us that hour   460
Innocuous, who with instinct's quick surmise
(So flashes before thought the closing lid
That guards the apple of the human eye)
All cover'd by our golden shields received
Those levell'd thunderbolts ; and on our helms,
And mail of proof those burning ashes fell
Harmless as rain, which we beneath us shook —
Not without scorn.   Haply to one who watch'd
From Pharos or from Egypt's plain it seem'd
Far in the Northern heavens a nebulous mist   470
Streak'd with strange fires, which vanish'd as he gazed.

But, when that terrible Simoom had pass'd,
No sun of light had moved, none crouch'd with fear,
None counsell'd base retreat. Such lofty strength
God in the hearts of all infused. And lo,
Michael stretch'd forth his spear; and instantly,
Quick as the lightning's flash, from east to west
The watchword ran; and even as we were
We plunged into those beetling clouds — no thought
Of dastard terror, though it seem'd as well   480
Plunge into Etna's crater. For each one
His armor, forged of diamond and light,
Made luminous a foothold; and for each
The breath of his own lips before him clave
A dubious path, dubious and throng'd with foes,
Who now half hidden, half apparent now,
With arms of darkness in the darkness aim'd
Their deadly thrusts. Wounds were received and
    given
By weapons upon diverse anvils wrought,
Keen, ghastly, fiery wounds. Nor deem it strange 490
That sinless angels bear some marks of war,
A transient anguish for eternal gain.
Has not the King of glory in His hands,
And feet, and side, prints which eternity
Will not efface? Why not His angels? Is
The servant greater than his Lord? Were we
By hearing and by sight alone to know
His sympathy with pain?"

As Oriel spake,

He laid his hand upon a scar that seam'd
His forehead, which not unobserved before   500
Only appear'd a line of deeper thought,
No foul disfigurement, but added power
And more majestic royalty of mien

" This from the furious Moloch's blade, who deem'd
With shout of victory and redoubled stroke
To end our duel; but Gabriel succor'd me,
And bore the fiend on his avenging spear
Back to his cloudy ambush. Few of ours
In that dread battle but received some sign
Of like endurance, honorable scars,   510
More precious to the warrior's glistening eye
Than spoil or jewell'd diadem: and few
But in extremity of peril owed
Their safety to a comrade's generous arm.
Deeds of high courage and renown were wrought,
And links enwove by stern self-sacrifice
Brother to brother binding, binding all
The closer to the Prince of all, whose eye
Nothing escaped, and whose recording hand
Wrote every act of loyalty and love   520
In heaven's unfading ageless chronicles.
The war was hand to hand: albeit at times
The storm-clouds scatter'd by God's breath reveal'd
A cubic phalanx of the foe, more densely'
Embattled than the guards of Macedon,
Who for great Philip's greater son subdued
Wan Persia 'neath the leopard's feet. And then

Oft have I seen some mighty seraph, arm'd
In adamantine armor, throw himself
Into those serried hostile ranks alone,   530
While, following in the path that fiery sword
Made for itself, others to right and left
Have dealt their indiscriminate vengeance.   Thus
Or singly, or in groups, or marshall'd charge,
As time and place befell, that conflict raged:
Millions of flaming spirits on either side,
And heaven, with planetary orbs for towers,
The ample battle-field.   But from the first
Darkness succumb'd to light: though not one day,
As mortals reckon days, nor one brief year   540
Look'd forth the sun on the revolving earth,
But seven times seven her annual circuit mark'd,
The while from battlement to battlement,
From cloudy lair to lair, from orb to orb,
From plain to plain of dismal overthrow,
The foe borne slowly backward fell.   In chains
My chieftain led Apollyon breathing fire,
And with him his quaternion body-guard,
Four angels fiercest of hell's brood, and bound
After the battle, for worse fate reserved,   550
These last in fetters by Euphrates' banks;
But hurl'd their leader to the abysmal pit,
To moan his fall with Uziel and his hosts.
Nor less Michael encounter'd Baalim
With Belus and Beelzebub, who drave
Consentient in tempestuous hurricane
Their fiery cars against his single might.

But found the race not always to the swift,
When, cleaving through their shields and useless helms
Those twain, our archangelic hierarch   560
Smote Baalim as with a stroke of fate
Inevitable, and dragg'd him from his throne
Above that flaming chariot, and consign'd
Him, maugre his relentless blasphemies,
To durance by Gehenna's brazen doors.
These our sole captives: for the rest our charge
Was not to capture but to drive them forth
From that supernal firmament. So God
Commanded, so His ministers obeyed.
For, as the trumpet of the jubilee   570
Blown on the height of Zion rang through heaven,
Their latest stronghold storm'd, their proud array
Pierced and transpierced on all sides, and their chiefs
Staggering with ghastly wounds, and pale with rage,
While now the breath of the Eternal Spirit
Cleansed all that sulphurous atmosphere, the crowds,
Of those rebellious, gnashing with remorse,
And inextinguishable pride, were seen
Driven to the uttermost precincts, that lie
Betwixt celestial and terrestrial things ;   580
While Michael and his peers advancing bore
Their mangled cohorts down, a hideous rout,
Falling, like meteors quench'd, from heaven.   Nor
    was
One province, lost in that disastrous fight,
Ever by the infernal powers regain'd :
For, while his armies march'd triumphant on

To songs of undeclining victory,
Messiah seal'd the glorious realms they trod
Against the foes' return.   And, in the year
The apostate Julian breathed his last on earth,   590
The rearmost of those ruin'd ones, despite
The cloudy covert of the Arch-fiend's shield,
Was driven from the empyreal regions down
To lower worlds.   And heaven had rest from war.

" Scarce in the limitless demesnes of space
Echoing had our triumphal pæans sunk
To whispers, ere a strange refrain of woe,
Foreboding ill to dwellers on the earth,
Rose from the Prescient Spirit: and, without pause
Of service, we on God's behalf resumed   600
Our stations militant about the saints :
Nor needless, nor too soon.   For Satan now,
Dislodged from heaven with all his powers accurst,
Driven headlong, and tormented with quick wounds
(For not to them were healing leaves of life
Brought in that battle from the trees that bloom
Around the heavenly Zion), urged their flight
Through the terrestrial firmament, nor stay'd
Till shrouded by the vaporous skirts of clouds,
That for seven moons had hung like ominous death   610
Over the frozen regions of the North,
They cluster'd shivering with despair and shame,
A ghastly rabblement of angels — small
And great were there — the mightiest as the least
Confounded.   But as when a stranded bark

Is beating on the surge-swept rocks, the crew
Pale with near death around their captain throng,
The while he schemes some miserable raft
Only less hopeless than the ravenous waves,
So they around the lost Archangel flock'd,   620
Who, with intensity of stifled rage,
Not fear, pallid and trembling, for his time
He knew was short, lest premature despair
Should, ere the fated hour had struck, consign
Him and his armies to the bottomless pit,
Opening designs, which on himself and them
With tenfold vengeance should recoil, thus spake:

" ' Comrades in arms, and in this sore defeat
Equal companions, sinister this day
Hath been to us the sword's arbitrament.   '   630
Such is the lot of war.   But not the less
Stands adverse our unconquerable will,
Against which iron obstinate resolve
Omnipotence is shatter'd.   Friends, herein
Let us make virtue of necessity.
The door of mercy hath long since been shut;
And soon, after a respite pre-ordain'd,
If rightly' I read the oracles of fate,
The portals of the vast abysmal deep
Will open, and the victor hosts of heaven,   640
Or heaven's High King Himself descending, drive
Us from our native light to the dark realms
Of chaos, there to' abide disconsolate,
Disown'd of God. disherited of heaven,

Unless in sooth we make a hell of earth,
And thus anticipate a lower fall,
Embracing (our primeval hope) this orb
Within the empire of eternal night.
Nor call I now a secret consistory
Of potentates, and seraphim, and thrones: 650
My comrades, be ye all my counsellors —
Thus much your zeal, your faith, your sufferings claim.
Not wisely has One deem'd Allwise, methinks,
Suffer'd our weary multitudes to rest
Midway on this vex'd globe, whose former wrecks
Shall be forgotten, overlaid with more;
Nor will the hostile legions find their charge
So light as their untimely shouts misdeem.
Much may in brief be done. First let us loose
The barriers of those Northern floods that chafe   660
Around the confines of the Roman world,
An angry fretting sea, which loosed may sweep
That Woman (ye that hear me, understand),
Her with the starry crown and new-born child,
To utter death. But failing this, — and this
Is but the prelude of my last revenge, —
Our triumphs in the past, and they have been
Such as have shaken the Eternal Throne,
Have sprung from fighting God with God-like arms:
Now let us counterfeit Himself, Triune.   670
Comrades, for this I willingly forego
My solitary regal state supreme,
And for the common sake of all resign
My archangelic primacy, and give

18

My sceptre to another. Which, ye gods,
Which of ye will ascend my throne, and share
With me its everlasting royalty?'

"He ask'd, but for a space no whisper broke
The gloomy silence, — such far-shadowing fears
Fulfill'd all hearts, — till Ashtaroth, still sore   680
With wounds unclosed and torments unassuaged,
Groan'd forth, 'If only Baalim were here!'

"And Satan, as a prescient god, return'd —
'Thy prayers shall be accomplish'd. Baalim
In the ripe fulness of predestined years
Shall rise — so fatal oracles ordain —
Rise from the dark abyss : and him I set
Vicegerent on my throne, by virtue earn'd,
Messiah's not unmeet antagonist,
Subdued and risen against subdued and risen,   690
And with him thee, my faithful Ashtaroth,
Indomitable in thy sevenfold might.
Henceforth my glory is to glorify
You twain, you only. Let us, three in one,
If not in essence yet in will triune,
Triunity of darkness, counterwork
The Trinity of light. My soul forecasts
The shadows of the future. Is the cup
Of vengeance sweet? Comrades, it shall be fill'd
Full and for ever to the cruel brim.   700
Messiah hath espoused a Bride on earth:
We will defile that Bride. His Church of old

Fell easily in our lascivious arms ;
But this chaste matron, nurtured at the Cross,
And overshadow'd by the Dove, and school'd
In suffering, will be far more rigid found :
Yet not impregnable, we copying Him.
Doth He work slowly ? slowly we must work :
And secretly ? we must in secret work :
And patiently ? we patiently must work.   710
And if at last within His temple courts
His well-beloved, by us betray'd, debauch'd,
Decking herself with scarlet, gems, and gold,
And all the blandishments of harlotry,
Have dalliance with the nations and their kings,
And offer them her honey'd cup of loves,
Drunken herself with sweeter nectarine,
The life-blood of the martyr'd saints of God,
Were not this vengeance which might soothe our pangs
Here, or in dread Gehenna, to recall ?   720
Let Him chastise as likes Him. Let Him crush
Our hatred underneath His burning feet.
We shall have marr'd His bridal. What amends
Were to the injured spouse the worst of ills
Heap'd on the loathed adulterer ? Likelier far,
Weary and sick at heart of those ingrate,
Messiah will forsake that ruin'd race,
Them and their tainted home, and leave us here,
Apostate gods of an apostate world.'

   " So spake the lost Archangel ; and his hosts   730
Infatuate on their bucklers clash'd applause.

" Ah subtlest, snared in thine own subtleties!
False spirit, by thine own falsehoods circumvent!
Folly impersonate! And deemedst thou
In thy blind madness to defile the Bride,
Whom from eternity the Father gave
Affianced consort to His only Son?
Defile her? or, if not defile, destroy?
Go, ply thy devilish arts, thou shalt but grasp
An unsubstantial phantom, or at most,   740
Polluting more thy loathsome seed, advance
A harlot to the world's hierarchal throne:
The Bride is hidden in the wilderness.
Go, heat thine idol furnace sevenfold,
And, baffled of the Bride, her children cast
Into the burning kiln, it shall not singe
The tender blossom on their cheek; for lo,
Walking at large as sons of God with God
Through fire and fume, their white asbestos robes
Grow only purer with intenser flame.   750

" Dead calm before the tempest: a strange hush
Upon the expectant deep: the winds enchain'd,
Till from the mystic Israel's tribes the saints
Were seal'd in secret with the seal of God;
And visions of the upper Paradise, —
Palm-bearing, white-robed multitudes who sing
Salvation, pastures of unwithering bloom,
And fountains of perennial living joy, —
Drew homeward pilgrim hearts. 'Twas done: and
    heaven

In solemn awe kept silence for a space :   760
While now seven angels stood with trumps in hand ;
And habited in light, as man's High Priest
Standing before the golden mercy-seat,
The Christ, the Angel of the Covenant,
Offer'd in sacrifice rich fragrant clouds
Of incense with the struggling prayers of saints, —
Propitious eucharist.   But, this rite done,
The Angel in His golden censer took
Fire blazing from that altar hearth, and cast
Earthward the flaming coals, which as they fell   770
Kindled the tempest-charged electric air.
And the first angel blew his trump ; and lo,
Forth rushing from the North a hailstorm burst
Upon the Roman earth, and fire and ice
(More terrible than that which smote the pride
Of Egypt at the beck of Amram's son)
Fell mix'd with blood.   Nor long delay : for now
The second angel sounded, and forthwith
A mountain, belching lava streams and smoke,
Torn from its dark foundations, slowly sank   780
Into the angry seas, and dyed their waves
With ruddy fires.   And lo, an ominous star,
As the third trumpeter his clarion blew,
Sloped through the startled firmament and fell,
Bitter as wormwood, in the crystal springs :
Whence after flow'd not life, but death.   But, ere
This plague was past, the fourth celestial watch
Sounded his boding cornet, and behold
The sun and moon endured dismal eclipse,

And through the heavens a third part of the stars   790
Grew pale: while flying with disastrous wing
An eagle cleft the troubled sky and scream'd
Its triple dirge prophetic, Woe, Woe, Woe !

" Like buried Nineveh, or Carthage, Rome
Had sunk for ever underneath these plagues,
But on the verge of ruin, as forecast
By Satan, Baalim, heal'd of his wound,
In likeness of a ravenous beast of prey,
Rising from the abysmal waters, ranged
The desolated shores, ten-horn'd, ten-crown'd,   800
And on his heads the names of blasphemy:
To him the dragon tender'd all his power.
While sevenfold Ashtaroth, with beauty smirch'd
In battle, but with undecaying wiles,
Couching his fell designs in lamb-like guise,
Sent through all lands his legionary spirits,
And led the shepherds of the silly sheep
Blindfold, and blinding others, to adore
The beast whose deadly wound was heal'd, and make,
By his perfidious miracles beguiled,   810
A bestial vocal image, who as God
Upon the altar seated in God's house,
Holding the keys of Peter, should receive
The homage of the world.   Thus Phœnix-like
On the rent walls and smoking towers of Rome,
In hideous mimicry of Him who built
His church on Salem's crumbling battlements,
The Arch-adversary for his harlot bride

Builded a mystical metropolis,
The haunt of devils, Babylon the great,　　820
Whence in her pride and pomp she might allure
The nations, as the peerless queen of heaven,
Mother and mistress of all lands.　Alas
For miserable Christendom!　The East
Gloom'd underneath the shadow of new gods,
Sculptured, or cast, or pictured: and the West
Drave out Olympian deities to' instate
Angels and saints within their vacant shrines,
Blaspheming God and them at once.　Meanwhile
Apollyon, otherwise Abaddon call'd,　　830
Who sank with Baalim, equal in crime,
Nor had in the abyss unlearn'd revenge,
Oped, when his chains were loosed, the infernal pit,
From whence, as from a furnace, fiery smoke
Rose, darkening the terrestrial firmament;
And locust legions issuing, mail'd for war,
None such before or after them, swarm'd forth
Embattled from the wilds of Araby,
And with their lion teeth and scorpion stings
Tormented them that dwelt upon the earth　　840
For twice five months of years.　Nor had this scourge
Pass'd ere the sixth prophetic trumpet clang'd,
And the four spirits, Apollyon's fourfold guard,
Bound in Euphrates, by command were loosed,
And straightway from the famed Bagdad led forth
Myriads of myriads, turms of horse, twice told,
In sulphur clad and hyacinth and fire,
Over the devastated earth which shook

Beneath their trampling : but the rest, whose names
Were not engraven in the book of life,   850
In foul idolatries and endless lusts
And devilish incantations lived and died.

" The roots of fairest bloom lie sometime hidden
The deepest underneath the soil : the stones
Of purest crystal are from gloomiest mines :
The tenderest pearls are won from roughest seas :
And stars of colors dipp'd in Iris' vats
Beam from unfathomable distances,
Ere they disclose their radiance.   And when night
Hung darkest o'er the struggling Church, — when faith
Was weary wrestling, not with heathen foes,   [860
But, mystery of mysteries, with her
Who claim'd allegiance as the Bride of Christ, —
When Satan and his fellow-fiends devised
Daily new tortures, and relentless scythes
Mow'd swaths of martyrs in the Alpine glens, —
When fronting all the powers of Antichrist .
Christ's feeblest braved their fiercest, — then and there
Were vessels fashion'd for the Master's use
Of unexampled beauty and of price   870
Beyond all price.   The Comforter was there,
And in His tender ministries we learn'd
Patience and grace not dream'd of hitherto.
Angels hung clustering round an infant's sleep ;
And seraphs waited for a child's response ;
And legions watch'd who deem'd themselves alone.
Love baffled hate ; and never a trembling lamb

Was from the Heavenly Shepherd's bosom torn.
Eternity irradiated time :
A Father's smile outweigh'd earth's myriad powers ;
A Saviour's love was country, kith, and home ;   [880
The weakest, in the Spirit's might, were strong.
Ah! brother, there are tales of secret grace,
Written in heaven, which shall suffuse thine eyes
With tears of joy hereafter.

                " But those days
Were number'd of rebuke and blasphemy.
And even as Rome in her infatuate pride
Vaunted the last faint witnesses were crush'd,
Lo, from the heavens descended One whose face
Shone as the sun, cloud-mantled, rainbow-crown'd,   890
And set His fiery right foot on the sea,
His left on earth, and with His lion voice
Waking far thunders in the clouds that hung
Around the throne of judgment, sware by Him
Who lives for ever and for ever, time,
As meted on His chart, should be no more,
Save only till the great archangel blew
The latest trumpet of the seven, and then
The mystery of God should be complete.

    " Askest thou, who it was, thus robed in light ?   900
None other than Messiah. For they err
Who deem, because the Word as man's High Priest
Within the Holiest Sanctuary abides,
That never, as before His days of flesh,

He, Omnipresent, as in heaven, on earth
Reveals His glory to the sons of men
Or angels.   Show'd He not Himself to Saul
Of Tarsus, as he near'd Damascus' gates?
And fell not John in Patmos at His feet?
And when unhappy Salem sank, as sinks   916
The blood-red sun in clouds of fiery storm,
Came He not in His royalty descending,
Smiting His foes, and rescuing His own
According to His word?   Nor otherwise
When dragon ensigns fled before the Cross,
The Incarnate Lamb, beaming His beams of wrath,
Was present in the awful strife.   And now
What time this last confederacy of hell
Was stricken to the heart, He stood and cried,
By man, but not by us unseen, unheard.   920

" That Morning Star, herald of dawn, diffused
Its radiance on all lands and distant isles,
Nor, brother, least on thine.   Never again
Such midnight darkness whelm'd the earth.   Far
    streaks
Of glory flush'd the heavens.   Yet not the less
The powers of hell conspired to dim or quench
The God-enkindled flame.   But stifled here,
The bright fire burst forth there in tenfold strength.
And when with better augury they breathed
Over the toilworn Church a sultry heat,   930
Mephitic, somnolent, the winds of God
Rushing tempestuous, and with lightnings wing'd,

Scatter'd the deadly sloth. For now appear'd,
Emerging from the heavenly sanctuary,
Seven angels, clad in priestly robes of white,
Each holding in his hand a golden vase,
Full of the wrath of God. These as they pour'd
Forth from their fiery censers one by one,
The earth was smitten by a noisome plague,
The sea became a pool of stagnant gore,   940
The rivers and the fountains flow'd with blood,
The old Euphrates dwindled in its bed
And ran a puny stream a child might wade,
While spirits malignant, by hell's triad urged,
Sped forth, gathering the nations and their kings
To Armageddon's battle-field. The while
Another angel, flying in mid-heaven,
Preach'd as he flew to every tribe and tongue
Evangel tidings of eternal love.
And on from watch to watch adown the streets   950
Of Zion pass'd the cry, ' Arise, behold
The Bridegroom cometh,' and the virgins rose
Who for long hours had slept, and trimm'd their
     lamps
And ready stood, waiting their Lord's return.

" Thus, brother, have I at thy suit retraced,
Though but in briefest retrospect, the fight
The militant Church hath foughten. Nor remains
Save that the latest censer of God's wrath
Be pour'd into the aërial firmament
Ere the shout echoes round the startled world,   960

'Great Babylon is fallen!' and the Prince
Leads forth His armies with triumphal palms
And hymning Hallelujahs, while His foes
Are crush'd before Him, and Himself assumes
The sceptre of His rightful universe."

    So Oriel spake; and while he spake mine eye
Moved not from reading his; such glorious thoughts,
Passing his own angelic tongue to' express,
Were written on his countenance. The more
He spake to me, the more I long'd to know,   970
And fain methought had listen'd on and on
In raptured audience evermore. But now
After sweet interval in which he touch'd
The light chords of what seem'd a golden lute,
And to spontaneous gushing melodies
Sang from heaven's psalter one of those refrains
Whose faint far echo ravish'd David's soul; —
. This ended, he turn'd to me and besought,
As he had open'd things unknown by me,
I would vouchsafe his earnest suit, and tell   980
What he had watch'd and guarded from without
But knew not from within, — my spirit's life
From its first dawn to noon: this he besought
With such unfeign'd humility, such grace,
Making it easy to refuse or grant,
That all my bosom open'd to his love,
So far as one may know another. Depths
There are in all no creature eye can read,
Sacred to God. But, as I told him all

That love may ask of perfect confidence,   990
Our hearts were knit for ever. I henceforth
Had claims on him who thus drank in my words,
A mute rapt listener. As the astronomer,
Who on the starry heavens the livelong night
Has gazed unwearied, in the dewy dawn
Returning homeward, plucks a simple flower,
Primrose, or cowslip, or anemone,
And in its tender beauties peering finds
More calm delight than in those mighty orbs
With all their pendent satellites: so then   1000
My guardian with an elder brother's joy
Rested upon me in his love, the while
I told the humble story of my heart.

How long might there elapse of earthly time,
As thus upon that mountain range we sate
Communing, I knew not. But suddenly
A clear deep musical sound about us breathed,
Like to a silver trumpet blown far off,
From rocks to distant rocks reverberate,
As though the hills, instinct with harmony,   1010
Themselves were live and vocal. And my guide
Sprang to his feet, and gazed intently' and long
Upon the blissful Paradise that smiled
Beneath us, while a flush of eager joy
Crimson'd his cheek, and quick words from his lips
Dropp'd hurriedly, — " Brother, this is the first
Of the three trumpet signals fore-announced,
That usher in the long-expected close.

The first portends our tryst on yonder plains;
The second our ascent beneath the sword   1020
Of Gabriel to the confines of the earth;
The third, the Bridal of the Lamb.   But now
They need our presence yonder.   Let us go."

So saying, again he took my hand in his;
And swifter than the light of morn we pass'd
Down from those airy battlements, and soon,
Albeit the intervening space was far
As Atlas from the snowy Himalays,
Rejoin'd the multitudes of the redeem'd
With angels intermingled, rapidly   1030
From every distant realm of Paradise
Within what seem'd one endless vale of flowers
Assembling, joy in every bounding step
And love past utterance stamp'd on every brow.

END OF THE EIGHTH BOOK.

𝔅𝔬𝔬𝔨 𝔑𝔦𝔫𝔱𝔥.

THE BRIDAL OF THE LAMB.

O MYSTERY of love, whose simplest signs
Are hieroglyphics of another tongue
Love only can interpret, from a babe's
First smile of joyance at its mother's voice,
To the warm ruddy glow of frostless age;
A web of heavenly warp and earthly woof;
Affections twined, and intertwined; gold threads
Woven, unwoven, and again rewove;
Links riveted, and loosen'd, and relink'd,
Imperishable all, — what shall I say?   10
How speak of thee in language worthy thee?
My spirit is willing, but my flesh is weak.
I see thee through a glass but darkly, — beams
From the great Fontal Orb of love, which shone,
Ere the foundations of the heavens were laid,
Self-luminous, self-centred, self-contain'd,

In its own increate immensity,
Perfect, incomprehensible, Triune;
But which in fulness of the age of ages
Brake effluent forth, the exuberance of life   20
Creative, till the universe of things
Rose underneath the hand of God, instinct
With His own nature, sinless, undefiled;
And, when foreseen but not the less abhorr'd
Evil arose from good, and cast its pall,
The pall of death, over the birth of life,
Which, not one ray of glory quench'd or dimm'd,
Ceased not to shine, immutably the same,
Through clouds of judgment and quick flames of wrath
On worlds perplex'd with tempest.   Holy love,   30
Which out of that corrupt creation deignedst
To build a new creation incorrupt,
And link thyself thereto by sinless bands
Incarnate, that Godhead to manhood join'd,
And through mankind to all material worlds
(Wondrous espousals), might at last present
His chosen Bride in virgin white array'd
Before the Eternal Throne : — how shall I speak
Thy fulness, who can scarce conceive thy least?
How gaze upon the sun, when one bright beam   40
Dazzles my feeble sight?   Spirit of love,
Hear me, who humbly supplicate thine aid;
That which is gross in me, etherealize;
That which in me is carnal, spiritualize;
That which is earthly, elevate to heaven;
The weak enable, and the dark illume,

Till love, which is of God, abides in me,
And I abide in God, for God is love.

Oh, precious foretaste of the feast at hand!
Oh, blessed prelibation of the draughts   50
Of everlasting joy!   When I return'd
With Oriel from our lonely mountain watch
To that fast-filling vale of Paradise,
Who first of all those white-robed multitudes
Should greet me, but my own, my sainted wife, —
Her spirit like mine dismantled of the flesh,
But radiant with the likeness of her Lord;
Our infant cherubs clinging to her skirts,
The mother with the children (how not so?);
And by her one whom I had seen, but scarce   60
Remember'd, till his grateful smile revived
The memory of his watch the night I died?
My wife — yet deem not by that name, her soul
Had not put off its earthly, and put on
Its heavenly.   In a moment I was 'ware
She was for ever altogether mine ;
Not spouse, but what is symbolized by spouse;
Not consort, but what consort typifies ;
The meaning now made fact ; the ideal here
Transparent in our real unity ;   70
A reflex glory' and image of myself;
An help meet for me in the house of God.
Oh, never in her loveliest on earth
Of bud or bloom appear'd she lovely' as now :
Nor ever had I loved her as this hour,

When hanging on my neck, as she was wont,
She look'd up with her tender pleading face,
And sobb'd for very ecstasy, not grief,
"My husband!" This was all, but this was heaven.

Nor was there longer interval for muse,   80
Ere Gabriel with a royal retinue,
Passing, as so it chanced, adown those ranks,
Amid those princely hierarchs a prince,
Advanced to meet us: — majesty of rule
Engraven on his awful brow and mien,
Temper'd with grace; and military power,
Mix'd with such gentleness as might beseem
The Bridegroom's friend. With open hand and heart
He hail'd us, and to Oriel spake, and said,
"Yonder midway, where trends towards the right   90
This happy vale, brother, assign thy group,
Till the next trumpet sound. The time is short."

So saying he pass'd, he and his gorgeous suite.
And as he said, we did. Whither arrived
I stood a brief space gazing right and left,
Fulfill'd with joy. Far as the eye could reach,
Stretch'd that illimitable valley, named
In flowery Paradise the Vale of Flowers:
For here whatever Eden's walks could boast
Of fair or fragrant, asphodel or rose,   100
Lily or orange bloom, or citron fruit,
Myrrh, spikenard, cinnamon, or frankincense,
Grew in tenfold luxuriance unsurpass'd,

Fearlessly opening to that crystal light
Its perfume and its purity. But now
Nor flower nor fruit could fix the lingering eye :
For here in numbers without number flock'd
The saints of every age ; the Bride was here,
Clothing herself with light; no bower of bliss
But hither sent its blessed habitants :   110
So shrill the archangel's clarion rang through heaven.

    They came in multitudinous throngs ; but soon
Celestial order reign'd, nor one appear'd
But necessary where he stood, albeit
Wide gaps were here and there discernible,
Room, as I deem'd for struggling saints on earth,
We without them not perfect. But behold,
More frequent every moment were the shouts
Along the victor armies, welcoming
Saints newly' arrived from earth. For now their foes, 120
Knowing they stood upon the brink of fate,
Redoubled their blind rage. Disguise was not :
The dust instead of water drank in blood ;
And fiery persecution in all lands
Lit up the lurid flames of hell. The whole
Creation in birth-pangs travail'd and groan'd ;
While Satan inly tortured, with a fiend's
Dark jealousy contemplating the power
Of Baalim and envious Ashtaroth,
Though by himself advanced, as yet subserved   130
Their banded domination. Antichrist,
All hollow subterfuges cast aside,

Usurp'd the throne of Christ. And there was woe
Intense, insufferable, such as earth
Saw never, such as heaven shudder'd to see.
For as these tidings came, and every hour
Disclosed some new atrocity of crime,
The language of all hearts, angels and saints,
Thrilling with cries of martyr'd innocents,
Swell'd in one tide of prayer adown that vale,   140
And clomb the highest heavens — " Arise, O Lord !
Arise, O God of vengeance, show Thyself !
Make bare Thine arm, and lift Thy glittering spear !
Awake, awake, Almighty One !   How long
Shall the ungodly triumph, and Thy foes
Trample Thy heritage beneath their feet ?
How long, Eternal, tarriest Thou ?   Arise !
Jehovah, God of vengeance, show Thyself ! "

    And He, whose ear is never heavy, heard ;
And He, who never slumbers, woke.   But yet   150
A transitory pause, a breathing space,
A silence terrible as sound before,
Until a cry of anguish and alarm
Rose from the lowest vaults of Tartarus,
" Alas ! the dreadful day of wrath has come."

    It pass'd, and silence reign'd.   And far and near
Messiah's Presence, though unseen, was felt
Amongst us, shedding secret power on all.
Angels on saints, and saints on angels look'd
Expectant ; when lo, Gabriel by command   160

Put to his lips the trump of God, and blew
A blast so long and clear and musical,
That none drew breath until its echoes ceased.
And straightway, even as we were, we rose
(So rises from an Alpine vale the mist
At daybreak by the golden sun allured)
Self-poised, or rather by the Spirit upborne
Into that ambient atmosphere of light,
Angels and principalities and thrones
Mingling and ministrant. Slowly we rose   170
Towards the upper gates of Paradise,
Gates of pellucid pearl, which as we near'd
Seem'd to dilate themselves, the while our hosts,
Myriads abreast, pass'd through them singing songs
Of irrepressible joy, or friend with friend
Sweetly communing. Eagerly I ask'd
Of her, who like a sunbeam moved beside me,
What had befallen our sweet lambs, since I
Their shepherd left them in the wilderness
These many years; for years I found had flown,   180
While I, unconscious of their flight, had hung
On Oriel's lips, or follow'd where he led.
Let it suffice that all had faithful stood,
Much tried, much toiling, but all leal and true,
And children's children walking as they walk'd.

Thus all along that bright ravine we moved,
Expanded to what seem'd an hundredfold
Its former breadth upon our easy march
Ascending, nor too swiftly for the flight

Of the innumerable babes, that swell'd 190
That vast procession of the sons of God,
And with their innocent rapture woke new joy
In all. But now, this zone of mist travèrsed,
Forth issuing from its roseate avenue
Into the open firmament we pass'd,
And unimpeded held our way, — as though
That nebulous belt of stars, that girdles heaven,
Were seen moving among the other orbs,
And with a closer cincture binding earth.
How diverse from my last descent, alone 200
With Oriel and his courier seraphim,
Down this celestial roadway, to a world
I knew not, lit with passing splendors ! Now
It seem'd as heaven itself were scaling heaven
For love, not war.

     But half remains untold.
While thus along the star-paved firmament
The Bride, awaken'd from the holy rest
Of ages, hasten'd to her mother earth,
There to assume her hymeneal robes,
And, with the residue of God's elect 210
Made perfect, wait the advent of her Lord,
Himself the Bridegroom on the right of power,
Where in the heaven of heavens He sate embosom'd
Rose in His awful Majesty, and deign'd
Ascend the chariot of Omnipotence,
Borne onward by cherubic shapes.

As when
To the lone seer, by Chebar's waves exiled,
There came dense cloud and whirlwind from the North,
And fiery wreaths of flame, fold within fold,
And brightness as of glowing amber round   220
Those living creatures inexpressible,
Of human form apparent, clad with wings
Of Seraphim, like burning coals of fire
Or lamps or lightnings flashing to and fro,
Straight moving where the Spirit will'd : beneath
Wheels rush'd, set with innumerable eyes,
Wheel within wheel of beryl, and instinct
With One pervading Spirit; and overhead
The firmament of crystal, terrible
In its transparent brightness stretch'd : they rose   230
And lo, the rushing of their wings appear'd
The roll of mighty waters, or the shout
Of countless multitudes : but, when the voice
Of God above them sounded eminent,
Straightway they stood and droop'd their awful wings;
And far above the firmament, behold
The likeness of a sapphire throne ; and there,
Mysterious presage of the Incarnate, shone
The likeness of a Man.   Human He was
In every lineament, yet likest God,   240
Flame-girdled, like a sardine stone afire,
Pure bright amid impenetrable dark,
Insufferably radiant, till it wrote
Mercy's great symbol on the clouds of wrath,

And with its arch of soften'd rainbow hues,
Gold, emerald, and vermilion spann'd the throne.

    Thus came He to that solitary seer.
But who of men or angels can relate
His coming with the sanctities of heaven,
This day of His espousals?   Such estate   250
And pomp and presence, as might best comport
With Filial Majesty, Supreme, Divine,
Were round about Him pour'd.   Eternal love,
Rejoicing in its well Beloved, breathed
New raptures o'er His blessed countenance ;
While in His Father's glory and His own,
By thousand times ten thousand ministries
Attended, through the holiest heaven of heavens
He came, and through the multitudinous maze
Of jubilant constellations.   But, or ever   260
His armies, following underneath the sign
Of Michael's archangelic standard, touch'd
The confines of the sun's crystalline sphere
Earthward descending, on the other side
The hosts of the redeem'd, by Gabriel led,
Advancing from the opposite aspect,
Not without songs of triumph heard far off,
Stood on what seem'd the nether edge of space
Bordering earth's airy firmament.   So stood
Israel aforetime, from the ocean depths   270
Emerging, by the clouds of spray baptized,
Beside the marge of Idumea's sea,

And sang the song of Moses to the sound
Of Miriam's timbrel, or disposed themselves
In loose array along those hoary rocks
Fretted by waves, which here and there cast up
The bodies of their late blaspheming foes.
Not otherwise that hour nor with less joy
We, all invisible to mortal sight,
Enwrapp'd the circling earth from pole to pole,   280
A thin pure veil of disembodied spirits
(Scarcely less subtle than the luminous hair,
Dishevell'd, streaming from a comet's brow,
Through which the faintest star shines on undimm'd,)
And nearing now our birth-land, at a word
That with electric speed circled the globe,
Bore downward through the realms of air (as once
The lambent fiery tongues of Pentecost
Fell straight from heaven) where waited each the germ,
Once sown in weakness, to be raised in power.   290
The motion was as thought.   Howbeit nor I,
Nor any, lost one moment's consciousness.
It was a village churchyard where I lighted,
My wife, my babes, beside me, on the left
My parents, and my chasten'd sister's spirit,
Our angel guardians hanging on our steps.
But, even as we touch'd the solid earth,
The Lord Himself descended with a shout,
Loud as of torrent floods, into mid-heaven,
His bright cherubic chariot veil'd in clouds   300
Of dazzling glory.   And at His command
The voice of Michael, like the knell of doom,

Broke on the slumbers of a guilty world,
And on the last conspiracies of hell ;
And flashes of incessant lightnings wrapp'd
The incandescent sky from East to West,
Where night was, making night itself as noon,
And where was day, blinding the sun with light :
A thunder sound, but no articulate words ;
A lightning glory, but no lineaments   310
Apparent to the habitants of earth,
Save on the hills of Zion, where the tribes
Of Israel, gather'd from all lands and seas,
Heard what the nations heard not, and beheld,
Astonied, Him whom they had pierced ; — as once
To Saul, alone of all that stricken band,
His persecuted Lord appear'd and spake.
But now Gabriel a third time blew his trump,
Given him from the celestial sanctuary
Against this Bridal hour.   And in a glimpse,   320
In the individual twinkling of an eye,
The ground, on which we stood, trembled and clave ;
And I, a sense of rapture like new life
Through every limb discoursing, found myself
Apparell'd in celestial robes, what once
Was mortal clothed in immortality,
What was corrupt in incorruption lost.
So were all clad.   But angel whispers now
Spake welcomes scarcely audible ; for still
The echoes of the Bridal trump rang out,   330
And still the Bridegroom's voice resounded and
Straightway, as if the altar of the earth

Exhaled one cloud of incense, we rose up
Towards the sapphire throne ; but scarce had risen,
Ere thousand times ten thousand living saints,
Changed and transfigured, from all lands and seas,
Like Enoch and Elias, without death
Achieving deathless life, translated rose
And swell'd our soaring multitudes, and fill'd
Whate'er was wanting to the Bride.　Behold　340
The Church of the Firstborn at last complete !
The while, with Hallelujahs on our lips,
Still on and on towards the throne we swept
Through the aërial regions, every eye
Bent on the King, and every instant rich
With new delights ; until His hosts and ours
Seem'd two fraternal armies edge to edge
Approaching, nothing save His car of fire
Flashing prismatic flames betwixt.　As when
(If such celestial mysteries may bear　350
Earthly comparison, nor suffer loss),
Emergent from his eastern couch, the sun
Pours forth at last his horizontal beams
Between two banks of clouds, above, below,
Rubied with light, a flood of golden day,
Till closing round his chariot they imbibe
The full effulgence of his ardent wheels,
Leaving the hills in gloom : so clustering round
Messiah, who descended from His throne
To greet us, as the bridegroom greets the bride, — 360
Love omnipresent, inexpressible,
Welcoming all as each, and each as all, —

We from His smile drank in beatitudes
Beyond all words to picture. But what more
Befell us in those high aërial realms
Was closely mantled from unholy gaze.

Earth trembled at the sudden night. The Bride
Was not. They sought her, but she was not found;
And for a space in mute amaze men ask'd
Each of his fellow, where were those they loathed,   370
Yet loathing fear'd? But soon far other scenes
Engross'd all hearts: for lo, great Babylon
Trembled, as smitten with the curse of God,
And fell in ruinous heaps, and sank, as sinks
A millstone in the mighty waters, down
Into a dreadful chasm of fire, which oped
Beneath her battlements, while overhead
The sky rain'd burning sulphur, till the smoke
Of her great torment clomb into the heavens;
And all her merchants standing far aloof,   380
Bewail'd her, casting dust upon their heads.
But not on Satan and his peers that hour
The wrath-beam fell: whereat greatly rejoiced
The rebel triad, and, embolden'd more
By what had cow'd less than infernal pride,
From every shore their thronging armies drew,
Weening to' erect, where Zion's temple stood,
The throne of wickedness, and set thereon
The proud son of perdition, in whose breast
They three might tabernacle, as the Arch-fiend,   390
Sole monarch, once in wretched Judas dwelt.

There was a sound of weeping on the slopes
Of Zion, not the children's hungry cry,
Or wail of women over slaughter'd babes,
Or the loud groans of linked prisoners,
Albeit the eagles of destruction swoop'd
Wheeling in ever nearer circles o'er
Emmanuel's land.   Their hour was not yet come.
But all the air breathed sadness.   Sobs and sighs,
Vainly suppress'd, were heard in every home.   400
A nation was in tears.   For they had seen
Their Prince the Lord of glory, and had heard
Him saying, " I am Jesus, whom ye pierced,"
And, pierced themselves, in bitterness of soul
Mourn'd for Him, as men mourn an only son,
Mourning in solitude ; or, if they met,
None to his fellow spake except in sighs,
And smiting on his breast would go his way.
But one among them moved, of nobler mien,
Veiling in mortal guise immortal power,   410
And like another Baptist bow'd all hearts,
Priests, people, parents, children, as one man,
Till, gazing on the cross their fathers rear'd,
Israel beheld the Crucified and lived.

Such things were wrought on earth.   But who of
        saints
Or seraphs may with chasten'd reverence
Disclose what holy mysteries ensued
Within the veil, when now the rest withdrawn
Past earshot, not beyond angelic view.

Retiring till their robes and wings and crowns   420
Appear'd as hangings wov'n of richest dyes
Star-spangled, like the temple curtains twined
With purple, crimson, blue, and gleaming forms
Cherubic curiously traced in gold,
The Bridegroom met the Bride alone?   Himself
In glorified humanity supreme,
Incarnate Light: and she like Him in glory,
No spot or wrinkle on her holy brow,
No film upon her robes of dazzling white,
Most beautiful, most glorious: every saint   430
Perfect in individual perfectness ;
And each to each so fitly interlink'd,
Join'd and compact, their countless millions seem'd
One body by One Spirit inspired and moved,
The various members knit in faultless grace,
The feeblest as the strongest necessary,
Nor schism, nor discord, nor excess, nor lack ;
The Ideal of all beauty realized,
The Impersonation of delight and love.

And the Lord look'd on her ; and in His Eye   440
Beam'd admiration infinite, Divine.
She was His chosen, His elect.   When cast
Abroad a foundling infant in her blood,
Hers was the time of love: no eye but His
Had pity : but He took her to His heart,
And nurtured all her helpless infancy,
And taught her gentle childhood, and at last
Betroth'd her virgin beauty to Himself,

And, being that another claim'd her life,
Had with His heart's blood ransom'd her from death,
For her descending from His throne to die,   [45r
And re-ascending to prepare her home,
Had won her tender maidenhood to long
For this chaste Bridal.   Now His time was come;
And all her coy and childish bashfulness
Had ripen'd into womanly reserve.
Pure and intense affection o'er her threw
A veil of soften'd light.   To share His throne
Was little in her eyes, whose glory' it was
To hear Him whisper, " My beloved is Mine,"   460
To lean upon His bosom, and reflect
The sunshine of His everlasting joy.

And still He look'd on her; and silently
Drank in her beauty, as once Adam look'd
On Eve, till underneath His searching Eye,
Conscious of loving, confident of love,
Quick flushes of delight suffused her heart
And shed new charms about her, when it seem'd
(I speak of heavenly things in earthly words)
As if He drew her nearer to Himself,   470
And folded her to His Eternal breast,
And spake to her, and said, " My love, My dove,
My beauty be upon thee.   Thou art Mine.
Thou art all fair.   There is no spot in thee."

When in the nether Paradise He stamp'd
Me with the impress of His gaze of love,

My cup, methought, ran over, nor could hold
Another crystal joy.   But now His Spirit
Empower'd my spirit to receive new streams
Of gladness, which from all sides flow'd on me.   480
The throbbing pulses of the Bride's great heart
Seem'd from the joy, that coursed through every vein,
To gather new intensity of life,
While glowing, like the morning sky, she blush'd
Beneath the sun-smile of His holiness,
Who look'd on her, revealing evermore
New wonders of unfathomable grace,
Grace blent with glory, tenderness with truth,
Light without shade of dark, love without end.

Wife of the Lamb, known only by His name   490
Oh finite image of the Infinite :
Oh holy creaturehood, perfect at last :
Oh true Self raised to true unselfishness,
Living for Him alone, who is thy life,
All and in all for Him as He for God.

But now, at secret signal from Himself,
The saints dispersing, like a golden cloud
Of incense blown among the orange groves,
In twos or threes, or groups, as liked them best,
He walking in the midst, to each and all   500
Most affable and most accessible,
Held converse : and the angels gather'd round,
Rejoicing greatly for the Bridegroom's joy,
And soon at His permissive voice disposed

And piled the banquet of His love with fruits
And nectar from ambrosial vines distill'd.

   Then first, for interval ere this was none,
Turning I look'd upon my wife to read
My immortality of bliss in hers
Reflected.   O my God, the glad surprise   510
Thou hadst prepared for us!   Never in thought
Or dream or waking vision had such bloom,
As I in her, and she in me beheld,
Floated across our meditative eye.
Our spiritual body was the same in type,
In face and form and fashion, as on earth,
Yet not the same, — transfigured: suited this
For the quick motions of the new-born spirit,
As that for all the functions of the flesh ;
Obedient to our faintest wish, as was   520
Sometime the disembodied soul ; yea, more,
So willingly responsive, that it woke
Wish to exert, where exercise itself
Was pleasure.   Would I speak, my tongue was fain;
And language copious, yet precise and clear,
Embracing all the loftiest thoughts enshrined
In all earth's dialects, flow'd from my lips
Spontaneously, catching the finer tints
Of mingled light and shade, like photographs
Of contemplation.   Would I touch my harp,   530
The very touch was music, and enticed
Melodious words.   The opening eye drank in
Such scenes of beauty, and the listening ear

Such trancing harmonies, audience and sight
Seem'd sweet necessity.   Or would I move,
Volition, without wings, or nimble tread
Of footsteps, wafted my aërial form,
Swifter than sunbeams glance from East to West,
Whithersoe'er I would, as mortals move
Their hand or foot by motion of swift thought.   540
A body meet for heaven, as that for earth;
One from the other nascent: that the root,
This the fair flower: even as the hyacinth,
With its pavilion of green leaves, and wealth
Of blossom and rose-tinted petals, springs
From a dull dismal bulb, which none who saw,
And knew not of its latent power, could dream
The cradle of such loveliness, yet each
Meet for its home, for the rain-nurtured soil,
And the soft kisses of the playful air;   550
And each to each indissolubly join'd.

And when instinctively we raised our eyes
From contemplation of the heavenly forms,
Now ours for ever, to the Prince we loved,
To thank Him who had made us thus, behold
These bodies of our glory could sustain
More of His glory than the naked spirit;
Our pure affections His affections clasp'd :
And every power within us had some hold
On His omnipotence.   Like imaged like.   560
And, as with us, so was it with the rest:
To all a vast promotion of their bliss,

To each the increase, as each sow'd on earth.
Love only can know love.   And as they loved,
They knew Him.   As they knew Him, they return'd
His lineaments of beatific light:
So glory is proportionate to grace.

But, hearken, now a concert of sweet sounds
On all sides imperceptibly arose,
From twice ten thousand flutes the ravish'd air   570
Soliciting, and whispering in all hearts,
The marriage supper of the Lamb was come.
And, even as we were, we saw what seem'd
A banquet of all heavenly fruits and food,
And chalices of crystal wreath'd with flowers,
Before us.   And what seem'd, was there.   And lo,
The Prince, at once our Minister and Host,
Assign'd to each his festal couch, whereon
No sooner were the happy guests recline
Than He Himself crown'd every cup with joy,   580
And charged attendant seraphim to keep
The tables loaded with the choicest bloom
Celestial walks could yield.   They, nothing loath,
Bore from the Paradise of God such rich
Exuberance of vernal promise, mix'd
With the ripe fruits of summer (for in heaven
Summer and spring dance ever hand in hand),
As heaven itself had never seen till now
Pluck'd in one hour and on one board profuse,
Yet presently repair'd its gift, nor seem'd   590
The poorer.   These the blessed angels piled,

In large unsparing hospitality,
Before the presence of their guests. Nor lack'd
Greetings, nor glad surprises, nor fond eyes
Flashing their welcome to beloved ones round:
Whether the bliss of guardian spirits or saints
Was greater, whether children most rejoiced
In parents, or their parents most in them,
I know not: this I know, all hearts were full.
Angels and principalities and thrones   600
Confess'd, they never tasted joy like this ;
While youthful cherubs without number flew,
Shaking a dewy fragrance from their wings,
And in their rosy fingers bore to each
Some token of the Royal grace. And soon
The genial flow of converse, like the sound
Of many waters heard far off, appear'd
A multitudinous tide of mirth and love.

The crystal river of eternal life·
Flows ever deeper on ; and since that hour,   610
It may be, I have witness'd other scenes
Of majesty and grandeur more august ;
But purer rapture could not be. The first
Unfolding of the blossom to the sun ;
The leaping of the spring, when first unseal'd ;
The young bride's incommunicable joy,
When first the words, My husband, cross her lips ;
The first babe folded to the mother's heart ;
These have a rapture all their own. And we,
Methinks, of that delicious feast of love   620

Had never wearied (half a week of years
As meted by the sun, so I have heard,
Pass'd by the while: they only seem'd like days),
But now Messiah rising from His throne,
In the calm awe of His Omnipotence,
Address'd us, saying,

        "My Father's will be done.
His will is Mine.   The fated hour has struck
Of battle.   On mine ears but now there fell
The short sharp cry of Israel's travail-pangs.
Come with Me, saints and angels, and behold   630
My foes and yours prostrate beneath our feet.
Now is the day of vengeance in My heart,
And now the year of My redeem'd is come."

    He spake; and lo, that festive scene of love
Quickly appear'd a camp of mustering war,
From whose cerulean gates, wide open thrown,
Messiah seated on a snow-white horse
Of fiery brightness, as the Lord of hosts,
Apparell'd in a vesture dipp'd in blood,
And many crowns upon His sacred head,   640
Rode conquering and to conquer forth.   And those,
Who lately at His marriage feast reclined,
Appear'd an army, clothed in robes of white,
And mounted like their Lord on steeds of fire,
A glorious retinue.   On either side,
Like wings of light-arm'd troops, innumerable,
The hosts of angels, ranged in order, march'd,

And, as they march'd, to sound of martial trumps,
Pour'd forth prophetic strains of Jubilee :

" Hail, Prince of life ! Hail, virgin Princess, hail ! 650
Thou fairer than the sons of men, Thy lips
Drop with the fragrant honey-dews of grace,
For God, Thy God, hath blessed Thee for ever.
Almighty, gird Thy sword upon Thy thigh.
Ride, in Thy Majesty, Thy glory, forth :
In truth, in meekness, and in righteousness
Ride on and prosper ! Thy right hand alone
Shall teach Thee deeds of vengeance, and Thy shafts
Shall drink the life-blood of Thy vaunting foes.
Thy throne, O God, from everlasting years   660
Hath been, and is, and shall for ever be.
Thy sceptre is a rod of righteousness.
Right loves Thee, and wrong dreads Thee : wherefore
        God,
Thy God, anoints Thee with the oil of joy
Immeasurable. From Thy Bridal feast
Thou ridest forth to conquer ; whiles Thy robes
Of myrrh and cassia smell and mingled spice,
And love and gladness glisten in Thine eye.
O Blessed Bridegroom ! O thrice-blessed Bride !
Happy art thou, O fairest among women.   670
Follow where triumph waits thee. All thy tears
Shall be forgotten in thy Husband's smile,
Resting upon thy perfect loveliness :
Thy Husband is the Lord, the Lord of hosts.
And be it ours in countless multitudes

To throng around thy steps, and lavish love
On the Beloved of the Lord we love:
Until the palaces of glory, fill'd
With ever-during infinite delights,
Receive thee in their golden gates, and there,   680
Peerless Queen-consort of the King of kings,
Thy virgin ministries about thee drawn,
Thou dwellest in His mansions evermore,
Sharing His throne, and from the well of life
Diffusest living streams through earth and heaven."

END OF THE NINTH BOOK.

Book Tenth.

THE MILLENNIAL SABBATH.

A SABBATH morn — softly the village bells
Ring out their welcome to the sacred day.
The weary swain has drunk of longer sleep,
And now, his children clustering round him, leads
The happy group from under his low porch
And through their little garden, where each plucks
A rose or pansy, to the school they love:
The busy hum delights his ear; and soon
The morning hymn floats heavenward; but himself,
Holding the youngest prattler in his arms,   10
Waits in the churchyard, where about him lie
His father and his father's fathers, till,
The children following in their pastor's steps
Whose gray locks flutter in the summer breeze,
All pass beneath the hallow'd roof, and all
Kneeling, where generations past have knelt,

Pour forth their common wants in common prayer.
A rural Sabbath — nearest type of heaven :
Yet scarcely less beloved in toilworn courts
And alleys of the city.   What true heart   20
Loves not the Sabbath ? that dear pledge of home ;
That trysting-place of God and man : that link
Betwixt a near eternity and time ;
That almost lonely rivulet, which flows
From Eden through the world's wide wastes of sand
Uncheck'd, and though not unalloy'd with earth
Its healing waters all impregn'd with life,
The life of their first blessing, to pure lips
The memory of a bygone Paradise,
The earnest of a Paradise to come.   30
Who know thee best, love best, thou pearl of days,
And guard thee with most jealous care from morn
Till dewy evening, when the ceaseless play
Hour after hour of thy sweet influences
Has tuned the heart of pilgrims to the songs
And music of their heavenly fatherland.
But mortal ears are heavy', and mortal eyes
Catch only glimpses dim and indistinct
Of things unseen, beauteous but far away ;
Enough to quicken, but not satiate love :   40
And the soon weary spirit exhausted sighs
For wings to flee away and be at rest,
Or solaces its musings, there remains
A Sabbath for the toiling Church of God.

It dawn'd at last.   But not, as many thought
And fabling sang, the amber twilight glowing

More and more radiant in the Eastern heavens,
Till almost imperceptibly the sun
Should glide above the golden hyaline,
And straightway what remain'd of dark be light.   50
But rather now the angry thunder-clouds,
Which for six thousand years in broken drifts
Had roll'd athwart earth's troubled firmament,
Portended unexampled storms; so dark
The masses of disastrous gloom, that hung
Over all lands.   Was it heaven's blessed light,
That shone behind and through their sulphurous folds?
And could this bloody fiery haze be day?

Ah, woe for Zion! for the hills that rise
Like ramparts round about Jerusalem;   60
Where, as a flock of timid goats or sheep
Driven by fierce wolves together to one fold
Ill-fenced for such an onset, Israel cower'd,
Contrite and crush'd in bitterness of soul!
Jerusalem, thy hour is come.   Lo, Gog,
The prince of Rosh, Meshech and Tubal's prince,
In panoply of impious pride leads forth
His hungry myriads to Emmanuel's land,
Gomer and all its swarming multitudes,   ·
Togarmah and its rugged uncouth hordes,   0
Elam, and Phut, and Lud, and Javan's isles,
Asshur, and Shinar, and the tents of Cush,
Myriads of myriads, numbers numberless,
From North and South and East, three dreadful hosts,
The least of which earth never saw the like,
Muster'd by hell to quench on Zion's heights,

Despite that lonely prophet's words, the last
Faint glimmering brands of truth.   So Satan ween'd,
And in their aid had gather'd from all lands
And airy realms, where they in secret wrought,   80
The spirits of ill.   Not one was wanting there:
Foul and obscured by centuries of crime,
But with unmitigated rage they came,
Unweeting for their common doom compell'd.
Scent they afar the field of blood? for now
Those chafing hosts, by wrath and lust inspired,
Like beasts of ravin, burst on Israel's camp,
And gorge themselves with slaughter.   Woe for thee,
O Zion! woe for thee, Jerusalem!
Thy birth-pangs are upon thee; and thy cries   90
Reach to the heavens.   Jerusalem is fallen.
The iron rives her heart.   Her little ones
Are dash'd in fury on the cruel rocks.
Her virgins, and her mothers great with child,
Speak not of them.   Her priests and elders lie,
Their silvery reverend hair defiled with blood,
Even where they fell, upon the ghastly hills.
Fire wraps her ramparts round: the clouds are live
With vengeance; and the stars shoot withering flame;
And her slain armies block the narrow gates   100
And causeways of the city: for the cup
Of her last agony is in her hand,
And now she drinks it to the bitter dregs.

A shout of fiendish triumph!   They have storm'd
With ruinous battering-rams the temple doors,

And now upon the holiest mercy-seat,
Betwixt the golden cherubim, install
The proud usurper of Jehovah's name :
And out of human lips there came a voice,
Like man's voice, from the trinity of hell   110 ·
Within that breast, three voices heard as one,
Most terrible: " This is the hour of fate.
God has abandon'd earth; and I assume
The vacant throne of vanquish'd Deity.
Worship me, all ye gods." Straightway arose
The swell of adoration ; and the hosts
Of darkness, mingling with the sons of men,
Sang triumph to the three in equal strains,
" Hail, Satan, Ashtaroth, and Baalim !
Triunity of darkness, hail, all hail !"   120
But, even as the echoes sank, behold,
Tyrannic jealousy, too long suppress'd,
Burst forth, as nitrous powder touch'd by flame,
In Satan's heart; — torment intolerable ! —
Ah, fool ! to think that concord, born of heaven,
Could bind in lasting league infernal hate ! —
Thus pondering, — " Was it then for this I left
My archangelic primacy of light?
In realms of darkness to be one of three ?
One of three only ? I, who know myself   130
Worthy of monarchy? Monarch I am,
And will be: none shall share my gloomy throne,
Dark, solitary, unapproachable."

Nor Baalim, meanwhile, that lordly fiend,

Conceived less envy of great Ashtaroth,
Nor Ashtaroth of him: which Satan saw
Well pleased, and now dilated rose sublime,
Hovering on what appear'd cherubic wings,
Above the clouds, and fostering, as he rose,
The horrid feud in his associate gods,   140
Till envy grew to wrath, and wrath to rage,
And rage to deadly warfare. They, for oft
Passions with spirits are instantaneous acts,
And thoughts are deeds, in no unequal strife
Guile match'd with guile, might militant with might,
Wrestled within that narrow battle-field,
The impious breast of Antichrist, until
Their miserable victim foaming writhed
Convulsed, and strengthless lay as dead; and then,
Each on his fellow scowling dire revenge,   150
Forth from that fleshly tenement they came,
And parted right and left.   Flock'd around each
An army of the rebel spirits.   Swords flash'd
Infernal fires; and in the sulphurous air
The embattled clouds were squadrons lock'd in fight,
By Satan both infuriate, who thus
Madly against himself divided fought
A duel ghastlier far than that which drench'd
The ramparts of Jerusalem with blood,
And from the trembling fugitives, who cower'd   160
Behind Elijah's mantle, wrung the cry,
"How long, O Lord, how long? Why tarriest Thou?"

That hour, what time the hideous din of war,

Fiends in their fury' o'ershadowing furious men,
Was at its worst, a blast more terrible
Than all the dread artillery of earth,
Vomiting iron hail in one discharge,
Appall'd the firmament. A silence fell
Sudden, as if all hearts had ceased to beat,
Upon the madding combatants : and lo,   170
The sound of distant chariot-wheels was heard
Rolling in heaven.   Nearer and nearer still
The rush of flaming millions, and the tramp
Like as of fiery chivalry.   But, hark !
A voice : it is the shout of God.   Behold !
A light : it is the glory of the Lord.
And thither, where the marshall'd hosts of hell
Opposed the densest gloom, onward He rode
Almighty, — a devouring fire, — no room
For flight, no space for idle penitence,   180
No thought of prayer, no lurking-place to shun
The lightnings of His omnipresent Eye.
First as it seem'd (though sequence in the acts
Of the Eternal needs not lapse of time)
Upon the rebel spirits He rain'd His wrath,
Till from the mightiest to the least they lay
Under His fiery horse-hoofs crush'd.   Of all
From hell's dark triad singling Baalim
And Ashtaroth in everlasting chains,
Chains such as spiritual essences may hold,   190
These twain He bound, and, stamping with His foot,
Asunder by the act appear'd to cleave
Whate'er subtle or solid lay betwixt

His presence and Gehenna's burning floor:
And in the right hand of Omnipotence
Grasping huge Baalim, and in the left
The lustful Ashtaroth, He hurled them down
Like meteors through the lurid vault, and fix'd
Their adamantine fetters to a rock
Of adamant, submerged but unconsumed   200
Beneath the lake of fire.   Nor paused He then,
But pointing where the vanquish'd Arch-fiend lay
Crouching in agony, bade Michael seize
The spiritless spirit of evil, and convoy
Him and the countless myriads of the lost
In chains to their Tartarean prison.   Straightway
The God-like chief descending with the key
Of Hades and a ponderous chain, to which
Earth's mightiest cable were a strand of tow,
Grasp'd his dread captive, once his peerless peer   210
In glory, now his miserable prey,
And bore him manacled and fetter'd forth,
And with him his dejected hosts, beneath
An equal escort of angelic guards,
To their own place of doom.   Oh dreadful march!
O yet more dreadful issue!   Hell had seen
Terrific sights ere now, within her depths
Receiving hecatombs of dead at once,
But never ruin like this.   For lo, meanwhile
The King of glory, on the chariot clouds   220
Riding serene, shot blasts of flaming fire,
As from a furnace, from His opening lips
On Israel's conquerors.   The murderer's arm

Was stricken in the very act to strike :
The ravisher was rapt by death, and lay
Blasted before his shrieking captive's feet:
And to the wild and dissonant cries of men,
Calling upon their gods, the sole response
Which heaven, too long insulted, now vouchsafed
Was storm, and tempest, and hot burning coals —   230
Horrible hail.   Nor only on the hills
Of Judah fell the whirlwind of God's wrath,
But through all lands and seas (for the whole earth
From pole to pole was wrapt in clouds and flame)
Whoever bore the mark of Baalim,
Or bow'd the knee to Ashtaroth, on him
The wrath-beam fell, distinguishing the rest
Who, though they knew not fellowship with God,
Knew not communion with the spirits of hell.
Wherefore not ruin'd fiends alone that day   240
Were captive led captivity, and throng'd
The roadway to the abysmal pit with groans,
But with them crowds of disembodied souls,
Such as till now the portals of the grave
Had never received, a hideous spectacle,
Each heart a fathomless profound of woe,
Each spirit the wreck of everlasting life.

How art thou fallen, Lucifer, from heaven,
Son of the Morning!   Hell beneath is moved
To meet thee at thy coming ; and the dead,   250
The chiefs and potentates of elder time,
Stirr'd from the silent calm of their despair,

Flock round thee.   Narrowly they scan thy face,
And ask, astonied, " Art thou one of us ?
All heartless, nerveless, passionless as we ?
Thou that would'st wrestle with Omnipotence,
And plant thy seat above the stars of God,
And soar beyond the azure clouds that veil
The throne of the Eternal ? "

                             Through their ranks
By Michael led, with downcast louring looks,   260
Answering them never a word, he slowly pass'd
To his own place of woe.   Over against
The fissure, where the brazen floor of hell
Yawn'd to receive his ruin'd mates in guilt,
And yawning closed again, there was he bound
In adamantine fetters, and beneath
The unclouded terrors of the Eye of God.
And next to him was Moloch, his swarth brow
Darken'd with tenfold gloom : and next to him
Mammon, whose boundless wealth of artifice   270
Purchased no solace in this house of chains :
And next, ruthless Apollyon, — he who show'd
No mercy found none here.   Nor far away
Was Sammael, blind leader of the blind ;
Nor Lailah, prince of night.   But why prolong
Memorials of the damn'd, or fiends, or men ?
Or measure their immeasurable loss,
Immeasurable, hopeless, limitless,
Who lay in torments, prisoners of wrath,
Waiting the judgment of the last assize ?   280
                    21

Meanwhile Messiah, from the tempest clouds
Descending, calm'd the terrors of His brow,
And drew His garment of celestial light
About Him, rainbow-fringed, until His feet
Rested on Olivet.   Beneath Him lay
Jerusalem in flames, and all the air
Glow'd with intensity of heat.   But lo,
His people underneath his shadowing wings,
And hidden in the hollow of His hand,
The remnant which the sword of war had left,   290
Felt not the breath of those devouring flames,
Heard not the roar of those wild cataracts
Of fire, nor knew what time the solid earth
Was moved as ocean by the wintry wind.
They only saw Messiah's glorious form;
They only heard His voice; they only knew,
As the three children in the burning kiln,
That they were with their Lord, their Lord with them.
Other spectators than the Bride were none,
When now, as once in Egypt's royal courts   300
Young Joseph drew his brethren to his heart
And kiss'd and wept upon them tears of joy,
The Prince of glory veil'd His glory' anew
In tenderness of most forgiving love.
But when the dreadful cloud of fire and smoke,
Which brooded on those hills, was clear'd, behold
The mountain of the Lord had risen sublime
Above the mountains: Olivet was cleft
Asunder to the North and to the South;
And a vast vale, with sudden verdure clad,   310

Stretch'd toward the former and the hinder sea,
A paradise of fruits.   And far aloof
Mount Zion, marvellous to see, was crown'd
With a resplendent city (whether this
Were the immediate handiwork of God,
Or of angelic ministries) where shone
Like gold a temple supereminent
In dazzling sheen, and thence on either side
A river of perennial waters flow'd
In ever-deepening waves of crystal life.   320

   The voice o' the Lord is on the waters !   Hark,
Not now in thunder with red lightnings wing'd,
Making the everlasting mountains bow
And the scathed forests shiver: but hark, a Voice
Is heard above the troubled elements,
A low clear Voice, which whispers, " Peace, be still."
And all the winds have sunk to gentle breaths,
And, as on vex'd Gennesaret of old
When He rebuked the raging winds and waves,
There is a mighty calm.   The broken clouds   330
Melt into colors, like a dream.   The Sun
Of righteousness with healing in His wings
Has risen upon a world weary of night,
Most glorious, where emergent from the flood,
That from far Lebanon to Kadesh roll'd
Its waves of fire baptismal, Zion rose
In perfect beauty.   There the Light of Light
Entering His temple courts assumed His throne,
And from the unveil'd golden mercy-seat,

His Bride beside Him, and His angel guards   340
About Him in their radiant phalanxes,
A pattern on the earth of things in heaven,
Sent forth His embassies of grace.   No shade
Obscured His beatific countenance ;
For in that holy temple all was love,
And in that holy city all was light,
Which lighten'd, far as human eye could reach,
The outmost confines of Emmanuel's land.

Yet deem not of His Presence as restrict   ·
There only, where those pure Shekinah beams   350
Gladden'd Jerusalem, nor limited
By measurable accidents of time,
Who fills all space Incomprehensible,
And dwells the Highest in the highest heavens,
And spans the breadth, and circumscribes the depth,
Inhabiting eternity.   For now,   ·
While quickening the Millennial earth with life,
And sending forth ambassadors of peace
From Zion to all lands and seas, the Prince
With us, His Bride, was custom'd to withdraw,   360
Where far above the clouds His throne was set
Within the purple curtains of the sky,
But lower than the starry heavens, and there
Commune with us of all the solemn past
And all the dawning future.   One by one
We stood before Him.   One by one He spake
With us, conversing of our mortal life
And heavenly home ; and words of grateful praise,

As the fidelity of each appear'd,
Fell from His lips.   Nor were His servants' falls   370
Wrong done and good undone, conceal'd that day:
But being all was now forgiven and cleansed,
And being it was the Bridegroom's Eye that judged,
And being we were members of one Bride,
Brothers and sisters in one home of love,
The retrospect but bound us, each and all,
Closer to Him who wash'd us in His blood,
And closer to each other, when we saw
Our debt of service by another paid.
For envy had no foothold there.   Pure love,   380
Beaming upon regenerate spirits, had left
No film of that pollution.   What was most
For His eternal glory whom we loved,
And for our brethren's purest happiness,
Fulfill'd all hearts with rapture to the brim,
And more than fill'd: they overflow'd with love,
And drank in light till they could hold no more,
All full, though fulness not the same to all,
As dewdrops, fountains, streams, and argent lakes,
Albeit with diverse breadth and brilliancy,   390
Reflect one rising sun.   If grief were there,
In memory of so little done for Him
Who had done all for us, it was that grief
Which, while it chastens, only deepens joy,
Seeing the mantle of His love was thrown
Over the past, and henceforth it was ours
To see, adore, and serve Him without end.

And there and then, as when a monarch's son,
The heir apparent of a mighty realm,
Well pleased in that his father's will is his,   400
Fixes his love upon some lowly maid
Of noble ancestry though faded wealth,
But, ere he brings her to her palace home,
Instructs her in all gentle courtesies,
And in such queenly graces, as beseem
The bride of one whom nations own their prince,
But chiefly tells her of his father's love,
His glory, and his goodness, and his grace,
Until her heart travels before her steps
To see the sire beloved of her beloved;—   410
So, hour by hour, through that millennial day,
In the pavilion of the heavens recluse,
As in the active royalties of earth,
Messiah taught His virgin Bride to long
For full fruition of the light of God,
A rapture inconceivable before,
And only from His own lips to be learn'd.

Meanwhile on earth the Sabbath morn, that rose
In its first freshness on Emmanuel's land,
Scatter'd its glory o'er the nations. Realms,   420
For ages mantled with the pall of death,
Woke and arose to life. The ocean waves
Caught the far splendor, and the winds of heaven
Wafted the tidings on. Evangelists,
Of whom the least was mightier in God's might
Than that prophetic voice by Jordan's banks,

Went forth from Salem. All the powers of hell
Were bound, and not a rebel spirit abroad:
But angels plied their ministry uncheck'd,
Untired. And human hearts, weary of sin,   430
Weary of warfare, weary of themselves,
Welcomed with shouts the messengers of peace
Upon the morning mountains. Beautiful
Their steps, and beauty follow'd where they trod;
For ever, like a crown of holy flame
Wreathing their brows, the Pentecostal Spirit
Moved in the wastes of darkness; and again
God said, Let there be light: and there was light.

Creation, which had groan'd in travail-pangs
Together with her children until now,   440
Ceased from her groaning. Long-forgotten smiles,
The smiles of her sweet childhood's innocence,
Stole o'er her happy face. The wilderness
Rejoiced, and blossom'd as the rose. The curse,
Which for six thousand years had sear'd the heart
Of nature, was repeal'd. And where the thorn
Perplex'd the glens, and prickly briars the hills,
Now, for the Word so spake and it was done,
The fir-tree rear'd its stately obelisk,
The cedar waved its arms of peaceful shade,   450
The vine embraced the elm, and myrtles flower'd
Among the fragrant orange-groves. No storms
Vex'd the serene of heaven: but genial mists,
Such as in Eden drench'd the willing soil,
Nurtured all lands with richer dews than balm.

Earth breathed her thanks.   Rivers of living waters
Broke from a thousand unsuspected springs ;
And gushing cataracts, like that call'd forth
On Horeb by the rod of Amram's son,
Gladden'd the mountain slopes, and coursed adown   460
The startled defiles, till the crystal wealth,
Gather'd in what was once an arid vale,
A lake of azure and of silver shone,
A mirror for the sun and moon and stars.

  Peace reign'd.   Antipathies of kind were now
Things of the past.   The wolf and yearling lamb
Were playmates ; and the leopard and the kid
Gamboll'd together on one knoll ; the steer
And lion grazed one herbage, and the ox
Couch'd with the bear on one luxurious sward.   470
Nor of the advent of the Prince of peace
Lack'd the calm sea its symbols, nor the sky.
Dolphins and sharks in many a sunny creek
Together bask'd at noon ; and glittering shoals
Made mirth around the huge leviathan.
Nor less, as I have seen, the king of birds,
Would bear the cushat dove upon its wings
Into the morning sunlight ; while beneath
The swallow and the vulture only vied
In speed, disporting o'er the woods and waves.   480
And now in air and ocean, as on earth,
A holy fear of man, Nature's true priest,
Subdued all creatures to his will.   His word
Was law.   Even the infant stretch'd its hand,

Its tiny hand, towards the cockatrice,
Now seen, now hidden in its den; and babes
Play'd with the innocent asp, wreathing a coil
Of burnish'd gold and opal round the neck,
Or as a bracelet round the dimpled arm.
Freed from the curse, the grateful garden gave   490
Its fruits in goodly revenue.   Nor frost
Nor blight nor mildew fell; nor canker-worm
Nor caterpillar marr'd one ripening hope.
The clouds dropp'd fatness.   The very elements
Were subject to the prayerful will of those,
Whose pleasure was in unison with God's.
There winter was as summer: summer there,
Attemper'd with soft dews and cooling winds,
Appear'd in sevenfold glory; for the moon
Was as the sun in that pellucid air,   500
The sun as seven day's light in one condensed.
And when the sun had set nor moon had risen,
The lesser glories of the stars shone forth,
As flames fair Venus in the Eastern heavens,
Or lordly Jupiter.

                    War was unknown;
The brotherhood of nations unrelax'd:
Swords now were ploughshares, spears were pruning-
          hooks,
And all the enginery of battle shown
As trophies of the victory of love.
Babel's confusion was unlearn'd.   And one   510
Melodious language, wherein every thought

Found utterance, overspread the circling globe,
A language worthy of the sons of God.
No labor now was lost. Commerce diffused
From pole to pole the gifts of every clime,
And spread her sails to every wind that blew,
Though love, not greed of lucre, held the helm.
But chiefly to Jerusalem and fro
The drift of ceaseless traffic set; for there
David, vicegerent, sate on David's throne;   520
And on their thrones of judgment round about,
Judging the tribes of Israel, the twelve,
Who sometime suffered with a suffering Lord,
Reign'd in His glorious reign. Mercy and truth
Met in His presence: righteousness and peace
Kiss'd each the other underneath His eye.
His people were a royalty of priests,
And offer'd in His temple ceaseless prayer
And incense of uninterrupted praise.
Thither the nations flock'd. There every doubt   530
Was solved: there perfect equity held sway.
No wrong, but there was instantly redress'd;
No right, but there was gloriously confirm'd:
For Zion was the mercy-seat of earth,
The footstool of the throne of God; where faith
Had clearest evidence of things unseen,
And hope climb'd easiest up the golden stairs
Scaling the heavens, and love, pure passionate love,
Saw the Beloved One and was at rest.

Yet deem not this millennial Sabbath knew   540

The perfectness of that which was to come,
Save in Emmanuel's land. There all was light :
And all the holy race of Abraham
Were clothed in priestly robes, spotless as snow.
But elsewhere good was prevalent, not perfect,
Not universal. Evil lurk'd unseen
In hearts that strove against the striving Spirit,
And at rare intervals appear'd; though wrath
Then quickly flashing from Messiah's throne
Branded the sinner with a curse like Cain's ;   550
And vice crouch'd before virtue. Nor was death
Wholly unknown; though now, as ere the flood,
Decades were centuries of life. Enough
Remain'd to witness of the awful past,
And warn the nations of the dread To be.

Nor prophecy was mute. But, fill'd with joy,
Little thought men of twilight shadows ever
Falling upon their day of rest : so bright
The morn; so cloudless the meridian sun ;
So calm the after ages as they roll'd.   560
Earth teem'd with life. Connubial love recall'd
The freshness of the bowers of Paradise ;
And rosy infancy and childhood smiled
In every homestead; and the heart of youth
Open'd its buds and blossoms to the light,
Unchill'd by devilish lust. Disease had fled.
Nor wounds, though rare, lack'd healing from the leaves,
That grew beside the crystal stream of life
Forth issuing from Emmanuel's throne. But who

May tell the stillness, who the melodies   570
Of that great Sabbath's sabbaths, when the voices
Of the whole world were hush'd in silent prayer,
Or in successive Hallelujahs roll'd
From shore to shore along the circling hours?
But chiefly' in thee, O Zion, where the Prince
Held court, and His seraphic minstrelsies
In mortal hearing touch'd immortal harps,
And fill'd earth's temple with the sounds of heaven.
There on their thrones the crowned hierarchs
Sate in due course: and oftentimes it seem'd   580
As if the deep-blue sky was rent asunder,
Till they who worshipp'd, through cherubic wings
Unfolding like a woven veil of light,
Beheld Messiah and His Bride in glory,
And angels up and down those radiant stairs
Ascending and descending, on their quests
Of mercy and high embassies of power.

Thus visions seen far off, and sung of old
By holy seers and prophets, grasp'd by faith
And long'd for, though the half could ne'er be told   590
In language, nor by hope itself conceived,
Had now accomplishment — a waking bliss,
The rest foreshadow'd for the Church of God,
The golden eve of everlasting day.

END OF THE TENTH BOOK.

Book Eleventh.

THE LAST JUDGMENT.

WHEN first the armies of the blest, recall'd
By Michael's trumpet, left the gloomy depths
Of Hades, where the damned, fiends and men,
Lay in the gulf of Tartarus o'erthrown,
There was an outcry as of those who wept,
And gnashing as of teeth, and passionate groans
Of spirits in pain, and clanking as of fetters,
That fill'd those dolorous abodes, though used
To every sight and every sound of woe,
With unimaginable dread, the first   16
Loud wail of endless bottomless despair.
But when, as those Sabbatic ages roll'd,
The Omnipresent Eye of Righteousness
Rested on each, nor moved, nor swerved, nor changed,
Nor of its terrors mitigated aught, —
Eternal Equity enveloping
The passions of iniquity with flame, —

The cries grew fainter and more faint, until
Oppressive silence like a leaden weight
Brooded upon the Deep unbroken, save   20
When some dark memory of forgotten guilt
Flash'd on a tortured conscience, and a low
Moan of remorse bewail'd in that red stain
An added anguish for eternity.

   Yes, there was silence, silence but no sleep:
Sleep on the weary eyelids of the lost
Hath never rested, nor can rest: and thought
Was terribly awake in every heart,
Traversing and retraversing the past,
And auguring at times with frightful truth   30
The interminable future. But in none
Tyrannic conscience stirr'd such inward storm
As in the Arch-apostate. For long while
Nor moan, nor motion in his fetter'd limbs,
Nor sign upon his faded brow betray'd
The suppress'd agony: but at the last,
Like Pharaoh scourged by those resistless plagues
Which crush'd, but could not kill his obstinate pride,
In a low whisper that yet thrill'd through hell,
As one communing with himself he said,   40
"The Lord is righteous; I and mine have sinn'd."

   And now that he had spoken, others spake ·
And each, beneath his individual load
Of guilt and punishment and fear, confess'd
The madness and the bitterness of crime.

Their words were few: but in that heavy air
They sounded like the muffled bell, that tolls
Above a murderer ere he dies.   Sometimes
A fiend in torments thought of early days
And raptures now for ever lost, and moan'd,   50
" Fool, fool, to barter heaven for endless hell ! "
And sometimes one with fearful balancing
Would weigh the pleasures 'gainst the pains of sin,
And with a sigh of desperate remorse
Inly would murmur, " Tekel."   But with most
The judgment and the wrath to come fulfill'd
Their dark imaginings with darker dread, —
" The worst not come; yet what of terrible
Can ever be more terrible than this ? "

Thus centuries roll'd slowly by: and now   60
Earth's holy Sabbath of Millennial rest
Was drawing to its outmost verge, when lo,
Once more through those vast depths reverberate
The voice of the Arch-adversary pierced,
Though weak and painful, fearfully distinct;
As not in guile, for guile was useless now
When God's Eye through and through search'd out
    the folds
Of next to infinite duplicity:
Submiss, but not in penitence or grief,
He thus gave broken utterance to thoughts,   70
Fruit of a thousand years of agony :

" Yes, we have sinn'd, I most, I chiefly ; and ye,

My comrades in apostasy and pain,
Have sinn'd in following me.　Madness to deem
We could do battle with Almighty Power,
Or with a measurable guile elude
The counsels of immeasurable Light!
Enough : I see it now.　Yet what remains?
The past is even to Omnipotence
Irrevocable.　Shall we humbly sue　　　　　　　80
For mercy, and fall low before the throne,
And all on bended knees send up one cry,
' Spare us, O Lord! who bitterly repent
Of our stupendous folly and misdeed,'—
And urge the prayer, if it must needs be so,
For ten times ten Millennial days like this,
Or that re-multiplied a thousand times
Ten thousand (an eternity beyond
Would swallow this as ocean sucks a shower),
Until our tide of importunity,　　　　　　　90
Swelling above the songs of Cherubim,
Obtain at last from wearied Justice that
Which Justice might unblamed deny to less
Unconquerable resolve?　But is it true
We bitterly repent us of our deeds?
Ah! comrades, search your hearts as I search mine.
The issue we repent, but not the act.
Of all our multitudes, rack'd as we are,
Is there one grieved for having grieved his God?
Is there one bosom that could ever glow　　　100
With love towards Him who cast us hither down?
One right hand that could ever touch again

The string of Hallelujah?   I trow not.
Others may do' it — think of them if ye will,
Haply with envy — but not we.   Our spirits
Are wrench'd for ever and averse from God.
Thus much at least this torturing flame reveals.
And knowing no repentance, in God's ear
What would avail us words of penitence?
Tush, would Eternal Justice be cajoled,   110
Or wearied with our importunities?
It cannot be: there is no streak of light.
For man, tempted by us, by us seduced,
The Son of the Eternal must needs die,
Die in his stead, ere Mercy could prevail,
And God's Great Spirit descending recreate
His marr'd and shatter'd image.   But for us
No Christ has shed His blood; no Spirit of love
In my obdurate conscience or in yours
Awakens one response.   It cannot be.   120
Our lot is irredeemable : our fall
Is final: we are damn'd for evermore."

    Again was silence for a space in hell,
So terrible, that only the quick breath
Of spirits in pain was heard like tongues of flame
Sibilant in the sultry atmosphere :
But shortly, Satan sighing thus resumed:

  "That which is done can never be undone.
Believe me, I who led you on to ruin,
And as is righteous suffer most, have tried   130
                        22

All pathways of return, and thought, and thought,
Till thought itself was vacancy and reel'd
Upon the giddy pinnacle it clomb, —
There is no hope. How is that possible,
Which we can never ask, nor God vouchsafe?
Friends, reconciliation cannot be,
Nor war, nor peace: one thing alone remains, —
Submission. Underneath His scorching Eye
Who knows what anguish this averment costs,
Who knows herein I utter all my heart,   140
I say submission to His iron rod
Whose golden sceptre we have spurn'd for ever;
Here lies the only unction for our woes:
Submission, which persisted in, despite
All cravings from without and from within,
May bring at least escape from this abyss,
And from the fiercer lake which burns below.
Hearken, ye know upon the scrolls of truth
It stands recorded when the Sabbath rest
Is o'er, we shall be loosen'd from our chains   150
A little season. Wherefore? for man's sake?
Not wholly: God deals equally with all.
One trial more is there accorded us.
'Tis true, the Oracle proceeds, that we
Shall quickly with mankind conspire again
To mar His reign, and lead the apostate earth
Against the embattled army of His saints:
But this is ours to do, or not to do.
There is no Fate, as once I madly thought,
Which writes decrees immutably ordain'd   160

Other than creature will, and increate
Foreknowledge of the workings of that will
In Him who governs all. And for myself,
This by my right hand have I straitly sworn, —
Never, if instant monarchy were mine,
Never to gratify revenge or pride
Never, ye all soliciting the deed,
Insensate, never will I raise an arm
Against Omniscient and Eternal Power."

He paused, and hollow murmurs of assent,   170
Such murmurs at midnight the desert wind
Wakes in Gomorrah's dead mephitic sea,
Crept over the abyss: so pleasing seem'd
The least abatement of their vivid pangs.
And readily they pledged their dismal oath,
If only' escape from this Tartarean pit
Were granted, never more to violate
With deeds of rapine or designs of wrong
The kingdom of the Prince of Peace. Ah, fools,
Tempters too long, who now misdeem'd themselves 180
In their own might against temptation proof!

But barely had the echo of their words
Died in the gloomy distances of night,
When lo, the thing they long'd for, was: their chains
Were loosen'd: the terrific flame of fire
Assuaged its lightnings: the infernal gates
Recoiling by some viewless hand were thrown
Wide open; and a Dreadful Voice proclaim'd,

"The roadway of return to earth is free :
But touch not mankind lest far worse ensue."   190

Straightway, like that Apocalyptic smoke
By John seen rising from the bottomless pit,
Whence issued swarms of locusts on the earth
All arm'd for battle, — through the open gates
Of terror-stricken Hades they ascended,
And through that lustreless defile of clouds
Which led to the expanse, and through the fields
Of ether, and the blasted stars which paled
Sensibly as their ruinous train swept by,
Startling the sons of men. But 'mongst them soon 200
Arriving, to their old familiar haunts
Of earth, or air, or ocean, they repair'd —
Unheralded, except Creation sigh'd
Through all her lengths and breadths and depths and
          heights
A sigh prophetic of her latest pangs.

Three days the prince of darkness, day and night,
Though night was now what day had once appear'd,
Flew with disastrous pinion to and fro
Over the renovated earth. No shore
Escaped his gloomy visitation. Straight   210
From Arctic to Antarctic climes he pass'd,
And in the dubious light from East to West.
Only so steering his pernicious course
As to avoid Emmanuel's saintly land,
Outstripp'd the rising sun. The glorious sight

Fill'd him with envy and amaze: so soon
His footprints, as it seem'd, had been effaced:
So transient evil's film; so naturally
Goodness and mercy had reclaim'd their own.
Not that the sparse and rare remains of ill   220
Escaped his sympathetic eye, or fail'd
To' awaken pleasure in the Evil One:
But these were few and far.   The earth was full
Of gladness; and her hymns of ceaseless praise,
Rich with the music of his Rival's name,
Grated worse discord in his ear than all
Hell's wailings.   But for full three days and nights
The memory of his dark Millennial prison
And his late dominant resolve suppress'd,
Albeit with inward agony untold,   230
Utterance of hatred or by deed or word
Or louring frown.

                    But then, as morning broke,
It chanced he lighted there where Penuel, —
The seraph who first dropp'd on heaven's bright floor
Such contrite tears as the unfall'n may weep, —
Shed fragrance on the bridal couch of two
Only last eve united in the links
Of marriage.   Through her half-closed lids the bride
Glanced bashfully upon her sleeping spouse
As glad to find him not awaked, that she   240
Might gaze embolden'd with less burning cheek
Upon his lofty brow.   Sweetly she quaff'd
The odors, and imbibed the quicken'd air,

Nor knew the perfume was from heavenly bowers,
Nor human love was fann'd by angel wings.
It was a scene of which the happy earth
Had myriads not unlike. But Penuel's watch,
So like his own in Eden o'er the sleep
Of our first parents, stirr'd such fell despite,
Such envy' and enmity and withering pride   250
In Satan's breast, that, when the seraph flew,
His errand done, swift as a beam of light,
To Zion's golden gates and thence to heaven,
The fiend no more refrain'd himself, but scowl'd
Defiance on the sky, and spake aloud:

" God, this is worse than hell. Here rent in twain
Myself against myself wage deadly strife.
What see I here but love? innocent love?
Love, which I share not, nor can ever share,
But crave with inextinguishable desire   260
To shrivel all its beauty like a scroll
Now and for ever. Rest, proud heart, be still.
How rest amid this restless rising tide?
Anguish intolerable : not these twain,
Nor millions like upon this peopled world.
One world might be endured. But, maddening
          thought,
These are but firstfruits of the things to be.
Love must needs multiply. Nothing but sin
Can kill its growth. Prolific tree of life,
Whose seed is in itself upon the earth !   270
And Earth, her granaries overstock'd ere long,

Doubtless will sow the starry heavens with love,
New worlds on worlds impregning (who shall fix
A term to that increase?) while I and mine, —
They multiplying more and more, we not, —
Become through endless ages less and less,
Less great, less formidable, less observed,
Nothing or worse than nothing; — gazing-stocks,
At which the elect will point and cry, Behold
The fruit of disobedience, and fear;   280
Poor motes, floating amid a flood of light;
And every new apocalypse of grace,
To Michael and his peers new bliss, new heaven,
To us and ours new shame, new loss, new hell;
Our torment more, our power to injure less.
Better strike now.   Better to be abhorr'd
Than pitied.   Mar this second paradise,
And perish rather.   What forefends?   Not God,
Or He had never brought me hither again.
Nor His bright winged ministries: mine arm   290
Hath not yet lost its native puissance:
Nor men, too easy victims, flesh and blood,
Unfenced in spotless purity like those
Who fell in Eden, and through long disuse
Untaught to cope with cruelty and craft.
What hinders?   Nothing but my mighty oath,
Sworn only to myself and mine, from which
I therefore can absolve myself and them;
And they, so willing, loose themselves and me.
Ha! my strong lust wrestles with my resolve,   300
Which waxes weak and weaker every pulse.

The inevitable end approaches.   Death,
Whatever death may be to spirits like us,
Were easement to this riven and ruptured life.
But haply, ere we perish, we shall drink,
Sweeter than nectar to our lips, the cup
Of desolating desperate revenge."

And like a cloud with tempest charged, which rolls
Suddenly o'er the azure firmament
Its darkness in the teeth of wind, he swept   310
Over a sleeping world.   Little reck'd men
Of danger.   But his gloomy hosts he found
Beyond his utmost expectation ripe
For new revolt.   Their will, less strong than his,
Had struggled less against temptation's tide:
Their foresight less was sooner at a fault:
Brief respite banish'd centuries of pain.
Had they not fasted a Millennial fast
From deeds of violence and wrong?   And now,
As prowls a pack of lean and hungry wolves   320
Driven by fierce winter from Siberian steppes
Around a camp's fast waning fires, they fix'd
Their ravenous glances on a world which lay
Basking in unsuspicious Sabbath rest, —
Near and delicious booty.   Every hour
Inflamed them; and their fretting cowardice
Only awaited one to lead them forth,
Fit captain for fit crew.

                              The time was short;

But fiendish malice made short work. The earth
Was of one speech and language. Myriads teem'd 330
In former wilds: and all the sons of men
Were link'd in countless bonds of intercourse.
No wasting war check'd the full tide of life.
Oceans were walls no more, but voyaged now,
No storms occurrent, with electric speed
Were highways of the nations. Science ask'd
Of Nature's limitless munificence
Vast largesses, nor met refusal: love
Won easily what she had grudged to lust;
Millennial life ripening her fruits. All lands 340
Were wont to gather now in holy tryst
At Zion's glad memorial festivals
With greater ease than Israel of old
Flock'd to the temple gates of Solomon.
Thought circulated like the light. Mankind
Was one great family, and earth one home:
Source of innumerable joys, when all
Was purity and evil was unknown,
Or known was instantly repress'd with good;
But of infectious pestilence, if once 350
The foe infuse his venom unobserved
Into the human heart, — which now befell.

Watchman, what of the night? Night is far spent:
Morn is at hand, the morn of endless day.
Broods yet a tempest? Yet the last, hell's last
Expiring struggle, heaven's last victory:
Beyond is cloudless light and perfect peace.

Yet seem'd it passing miracle, that they,
Who lived beneath the shadow of the throne,
And saw the glory of the Prince, and knew   360
That Canaan, of earth's provinces elect,
Was as His temple, Israel His priests,
The Church His Bride, and holy seraphim
The servants of His pleasure, they should heed
Infatuate the Arch-tempter's glozing speech
And yield — how easily deceived, how soon
Deceivers! It was passing miracle.
God only knows the fathomless profound
Of man. Yet peradventure otherwise,
Maugre the lessons of six thousand years,   370
Earth, mother of the human race, and nurse
Of countless generations yet unborn,
Had rested in her native strength, nor learn'd
The creature by itself can never stand,
Mutable, fallible, and on its God
For righteousness dependent as for life.
Pride falls for ever now: and lowliness
Meekly receives her amaranthine crown.

But the last strife was terrible. Each fiend
Was now as Satan, train'd in guilt and guile,   380
Student and scholar of the human heart,
And skilful when and where to show himself
Clad in angelic light. Quickly they saw
The perilous exaltation free from fear
Of those who revell'd in Millennial peace.
They mark'd the easy avenue, they gauged

The powers of man, the limits of his power,
And what beyond was feasible to hope:
Long life was his, not immortality;
Swift motion, but not flight; far-reaching fields   390
Of knowledge, but yet wider lay beyond;
Earth was earth; men were men, not angels; saints,
Not seraphs; though celestial intercourse
Was oft within terrestrial homes vouchsafed.
Hence first the spirits of evil in men's hearts,
Echoing the serpent's lie a million times,
Clandestinely infused mistrust, and plied
The vacillating will with hateful doubt:
Could that be love which circumscribed their power?
Why were they fetter'd to this narrow orb?   400
Why not, as angels, free to range the heavens?
Why this delay of glory?   Could it be
That He, who gave so much, begrudged them more?
Nor marvel, if such thoughts, which once avail'd
To drag archangels from their.thrones, had power
To baffle unsuspecting human hearts,
To try their faith who lean'd upon their God,
And taint the rest.   No longer instant wrath
Visibly on transgression fell.   For now,
As once on Sinai in awed Israel's sight,   410
God had retired into His secret place
Of thunder, and had wrapt His glory round
In swaddling bands of darkness.   Hell meanwhile
Embolden'd show'd its lying signs of power
And fiery portents in the sky : till earth,
Heaven's mirror late, became again the haunt

Of fear, suspicion, hatred, violence, —
All save Emmanuel's land.   Yet think not all
Fell from their loyalty.   Myriads were found
Faithful in every region under heaven.   420
And speedily, for half a week of years
Saw this rebellion schemed and swoll'n and crush'd,
War reassumed her bloody car, her sons
Wielding infernal powers unguess'd of yore,
And drave the saints before her: not a few,
Like Enoch, rapt from the tumultuous strife
To the calm presence of the Prince of Peace,
Companions of the Virgin Bride: the rest
Flocking by day and night, by land and sea,
Under the shadow of that holy cloud   430
Which o'er the height of Zion hung sublime.

But now the foe infuriated draws
All nations from the fourfold winds, himself
Incarnate, and in blasphemous despair
Or bitter mockery of his last defeat,
As Gog and Magog, leads his armies forth
To compass the beloved city.   Earth
Groan'd underneath the tread of armed men :
The winds and oceans chafed to bear their fleets .
The very sky was frighted by the rush   440
Of fiendish wings.   Baleful conspiracy !
Devils and men at last in open league
Assuming empire with a front, to less
Than strength Almighty, irresistible.
Darkening all lands they come, but densest where

Euphrates roll'd her ancient tide of wealth
Through Shinar's plains: for in their pride they ween'd
To storm the citadel of heaven and climb
The ladder of crystalline gold there set,
And leading higher than the stars of God.   450

Ah! blind rebellion, madness to the last,
Infatuate, suicidal, desperate!

The latest band of unpolluted saints
Was gather'd now beneath the shadowing wings
Of that Shekinah cloud which stretch'd its shade
From Lebanon to Nile; and now the hosts
Of Satan flock'd around the holy realm
By foot unblest as yet inviolate;
When from the frowning heavens again that sound,
Which shook the first fell council of the damn'd,   460
More terrible than thunder vibrated
Through every heart, Jehovah's awful laugh,
Mocking their fears and scorning their designs,
The laughter of Eternal love incensed.
From pole to pole it peal'd.   And lo, the cloud,
Whence it appear'd to issue, spread abroad
Over the rebel hosts its pregnant gloom,
And, louring, in the twinkling of an eye
Flash'd into flame.   The dreadful storm of fire
Bore ever down, precipitately down,   470
Scathing the spirits of evil first (of power
These everlasting burnings to destroy
Spiritual and carnal essences alike),

Still down, — though not before a whisper ran
Through those pale ranks like that which blanch'd the
    lips
Of Pharaoh's bravest in the yawning deep, —
"God fights for Zion; let us flee His face."
It was too late: for down, still ever down,
The arrows of destruction fell, the flames
Baffling escape or flight. And now the Lord   480
Himself on the Arch-adversary laid
The right hand of Omnipotence. The touch
Alone was foretaste of the second death,
Such death as damned spirits for ever die.
He shudder'd and was still. Nor less his hosts,
Whelm'd by the glory' of God, and manacled
Beneath angelic wardenship, were ranged
Far to the left of the consuming fire
Burning around the central throne, and there
In speechless horror waited, till the Judge   490
Should summon each to His eternal bar.

But first Messiah spake again, His voice
Resounding from the jasper walls of heaven
To hell's profoundest caves. And lo, the Deep
Grew darker at the summons. Hades shook
Through all her strong foundations, as of old
Sinai beneath the feet of God. Nor now
Was key or loosen'd bar or facile bolt
Needed to ope her adamantine doors;
For, as it seem'd, the firmament, which arch'd   500
That prison of the damn'd with lurid gloom,

To right and left was rent: and Death and Hell
With dreadful throes and agonizing groans
Disgorged their dead, the lost of every age,
In myriads, small and great confusedly. These,
As shivering on the bare expanse they stood,
Ejected prisoners but not escaped,
The angels in dead ominous silence led
Back to their mother earth, where waited each
His ruin'd spirit's tenement, made fit   510
To' endure the terrors of the wrath to come,
The body of his sin, and from this hour
The body of his everlasting woe.
Thus clothed with shame not glory, came they forth
From graves innumerable by land and sea,
And took their station, so the Judge ordain'd,
Behind the accursed angels, who first sinn'd
And, as was meet, must first receive their doom.

    Hades was empty. Not a sound or sigh
Or whisper of a living thing was heard   520
In the sepulchral air. That gloomy prison
Had done its work. And suddenly, behold,
What seem'd its floor of solid adamant
Heaved, — as in Zembla's seas at summer prime
A mighty floe of ice disruptured heaves
Beneath the chafing tide, and in an hour
Its glens and bergs and frozen fastnesses
Break in a thousand fragments, the vex'd waves
Betwixt them washing to and fro. So now,
As it appear'd, the keystone of that crypt,   530

Which overarch'd the fiery gulf below,
Was crush'd: and. like a sinking dome, the vault
With rout insufferable and hideous noise
Fell sheer into the bottomless pit.   But huge
As was that ruin, loom'd more huge, more vast
That shoreless fathomless abyss of fire,
Which swallow'd up in its remorseless waves
Whatever lay beyond the mighty gulf
Coasting the triple wall of Paradise.

Meanwhile on earth the quick tempestuous flames,
That overthrew the rebel armies, spread   [540
From fell to forest, and from clime to clime,
From shore to shore, from island on to isle,
And burning continent to continent;
While from beneath the ocean lava floods
Surged up until the very waters roll'd
Aflame; and clouds of smoke and seething steam
Darken'd the sky — a space: then I beheld,
And lo, the firmamental heavens themselves
Were kindled, and the primal elements   550
Melted with heat, and one vast sea of fire,
Its waves darting their hungry tongues aloof,
Baptized the unregenerate earth in flame.
One land alone, — like Goshen, when the shroud
Of palpable darkness wrapt the Memphian plains,
Sunning its pastures in the smile of God, —
One land remain'd unscathed, and over that
Nor firebrand shot, nor smell of burning pass'd.

And there in heaven, immediately above
The holy hills of Zion as it seem'd,   560
Though peradventure airy semblance veil'd
A distance greater than the solar orb,
When now the blasts of lightning wrath were spent,
From out the dazzling glory' at last emerged
The likeness of a great white throne, more bright
(If time may render such similitude
To mysteries not born of time) than when
A vaporous sea of mist, shrouding the Alps
From Viso to the far Tyrol, an hour
Ere sunset, lifts its giant gloom, and melts   570
In showers, save where the victor king of day
Rides on the uppermost ravine of cloud
And brightens it to brightness till it glows
Whiter than light itself. And on the throne,
When strengthen'd by the Spirit I look'd, behold
One seated, from whose unveil'd face the earth
As mantled with its former robes, and heaven,
Its azure curtains shrivelling like a leaf,
Melted as melts a dream o' the night. But lo,
Before the throne in countless millions stood   580
New risen the dead, all of them, small and great,
Speechless with terror, by the angels soon
Far to the left reduced: while on the right
Advanced the saints in blissful multitudes;
And round about the throne were seraphim
And cherubim of glory, and the chiefs
Of the celestial host; meanwhile the rest
Stretch'd like a fringe of light beyond the saints,
28

Beyond the ruin'd dead, beyond the spirits
Accursed in concentric walls of flame.   590
And then and there the likeness as of books
Before the awful Presence of the Judge
Was seen, the massive chronicles of time,
The law, the Gospel, and the book of life.

This the last open'd was first read. And as
The names engraven on its crystal leaves
Fell singly from Messiah's lips, the saints
From martyr'd Abel to the youngest babe
Caught heavenward for the joy of His espousals
Stood forth apparent in that holy light,   600
Their blood-wash'd robes purer than driven snow,
Palms in their hands, and woven in their hair
Garlands of amaranth. And one by one
The beams o' the Divine glory seem'd to rest
On each: and in the twinkling of an eye,
In sight and audience of the universe,
That one became the object, whereon all,
Forgetful of themselves and all besides,
Gazed. Not the faintest film of guilt remain'd
Beneath the scrutiny of Perfect Love,   610
Such was the virtue of His blood, and such
The lustre of His seamless robe of light.
But every thought, and word, and act of grace,
Writ in the book of His remembrance,.shed
A halo of such radiant holiness
O'er every member of the mystic Bride,
That all, not saints alone but seraphim,

With shouts of lofty joy congratulant,
Nor seraphs only, but the lost perforce,
Both men and devils, as the Son of God　　　620
Proclaim'd the righteousness of saints, and placed
A crown of glory on the brow of each,
Echoed the verdict of the Throne, Amen.

Those numbers had no number: but ask not
How long their judgment lasted; for methinks
Time and its ages then were felt to be
Creatures of the Eternal, in whose Eye
And Presence moments are as years, and years
As moments.　But to me at least it seem'd
Only the fragment of a day, before　　　630
The latest saint received his blest award;
And the King stooping from the snow-white throne
Held forth the sceptre of His grace, dove-tipp'd
(As once of yore Ahasuerus calm'd
Young Esther's beating heart), and bade us touch
The symbol, and draw nearer while He spake:

"Come, all ye blessed of My Father, come
Inherit ye the royalties and realms,
Ere the foundations of the world were laid
For you prepared and destined.　Heirs of God,　　　640
Joint heirs with Me, receive your heritage;
Come ye, who bore My cross, and wear My crown;
Come share My glories ye who shared My griefs;
But first assessors to My throne abide,
The while I judge Mine enemies and yours."

So saying, He drew us nearer to His side,
And placed us on His glorious right. O scene
Of solemn unimaginable awe!
Ere this, though nurtured in Millennial wonders,
The saints were with themselves absorb'd, nor dared 650
Look otherwhere than on their peers and Judge.
But now it seem'd we were again the Bride,
And seated by the Bridegroom's side; for lo,
The likeness as of countless thrones appear'd
On that unutterably radiant cloud
Which was Messiah's judgment-throne — nor think
Room wanting in that vast sidereal dome —
Each in its order'd place, tier above tier,
Rank above rank, so marvellously set,
Or such the virtue here of sight and sound,   660
We saw the shades that pass'd on every brow,
We heard the whisper of the faintest sigh.
Before us first the hosts of rebel spirits
Under angelic wardens: next to these
Their miserable victims, of mankind:
And still beyond them angels numberless:
Beside us, to the right hand and the left,
The diverse glories of the stars : and far
Below our feet our mother planet, earth,
Glow'd in the embers of her final fire,   670
Except the solitary land conceal'd
Beneath the shadow of the hand of God.

And now the Anointed Judge, fronting the left,
Summon'd the apostate spirits one by one

Before Him.   Face to face with us they stood,
Whom they had wrestled with in dubious fight
And plied with hellish crafts in pilgrim days.
Dreadful it was to see them now unmask'd,
And, as the story of each appear'd, to learn
What poisonous arrows they had shot, what snares   680
Had strew'd, what pitfalls of iniquity
Had digg'd for us, albeit Heavenly Love
Led our unwary footsteps safely home.
Now we beheld the secret springs of ill
Which moved the mighty drama of the world,
And saw how often proud infatuate men,
Like Ahab by the lying fiend beguiled,
Were dupes of hell.   On each the judgment fell :
As he had sinn'd, so was to each the weight
And measure of eternal punishment,   690
Weigh'd in the scales of Perfect Equity,
Poised to the small dust of the balances,
And meted to a gossamer's viewless breadth ;
And with such clear necessity adjudged
By One, whose long forbearance had been drain'd
To the last drop, by Love, Almighty Love,
Uttering its slow irrevocable words
In tones of wrath so strangely blent with grief,
So calm, so true, so just, that even the damn'd
Could only answer, "Thou art righteous, Lord : "   700
And, as the awful sentence fell on each
Of chains and everlasting banishment
To his own portion in the lake of fire,

As by the Spirit of holiness compell'd
We and the blessed angels said, Amen.

The Arch-tempter was reserved for judgment last.
Silent he stood. Upon his haggard brow
Nor hope nor fear was visible, nor guile,
Nor lust, nor hate: an utter blank it seem'd,
A passionless vacuity of thought: 710
But when the concentrated light of God,
As sunbeams in a burning-glass condensed,
Fell on his naked spirit, it touch'd, it woke
The dormant sense within him ; and a moan
Stifled was heard; and mighty shudderings
Shook his colossal frame : for in that light
His pride was despicable littleness,
His wisdom idiot folly, and his lies
Rent cobwebs in the torturing glare of truth.
And now the strong was weak, the haughty' abased,
The rebel crouching at his Conqueror's feet,   [720
The shameless clothed with everlasting shame.
Prostrate he fell before the throne ; and there,
In sight of all, Messiah on his neck
Planted His burning heel, and in the act
For ever crush'd the accursed Serpent's head .
Life not extinct, but crush'd; and sin not slain,
But bruised and ready for the second death :
I look'd again ; and lo, among his own,
Convict and chain'd, the strengthless Arch-fiend lay.
And for a space no sound was heard. But then   [730

It seem'd the crystal empyrean clave
Beneath them, and the horrid vacuum suck'd
The devil and his armies down (as once
Korah and all his crew, quick as they were,
Sank from amid the camp of Israel)
To bottomless perdition.　None escaped.
And, as their cry of piercing misery
From out that yawning gulf went up to heaven,
Standing upon its rugged edge we gazed　　　　740
Intently' and long down after them; and there
They sank and sank, the forms more indistinct,
The cries more faint, the echoes feebler, till
The firmamental pavement closed again :
And silence was in heaven.

　　　　　　　　　　Nor longer pause,
For now the everlasting Son of God
Summon'd the millions of the dead, the lost,
Each to appear before the great white throne.
And lo, the angels round about them urged,
Urged and compell'd obedience, or they　　　　750
Had gladlier sunk that hour to utter night.
And all the other angels, from their charge
Of the rebellious spirits for aye released,
Disposed themselves around the judgment-seat
In fashion of an emerald rainbow, built
Of loftiest arch what time the sun is low ;
Or intermingling with the saints communed
In whispers to the rest inaudible
Of the dread issues of this last Assize.

Of these was Oriel.　To my side he flew　　　760
And press'd my hand for gladness at my crown,
And, like an elder brother, by my side
Half leaning, ever and anon he spake
With tears of that which pass'd beneath our feet.

　　Yes, there was Cain the fratricide, the brand
Of murder still upon his brow; and they
Who mock'd the saintly Enoch; and the brood
Begotten of the fallen sons of light,
Giants in sin as size; and they who sank
Blaspheming heaven around the ark they built;　　770
And they who in another deluge found
Untimely burial, Pharaoh and his chiefs;
The rebel sons of Reuben; and the seer
Who loved the wages of unrighteousness,
The son of Bosor; multitudes of slain
From the polluted homes of Canaan;
And he who fell upon the bloody heights
Of Mount Gilboa, Saul the son of Kish;
And crowds of miserable idolaters,
Of whom I mark'd lascivious Jezebel:　　780
Sinners of every age and every type;
The proud, despiteful, fierce, implacable,
Unthankful, and unholy, and unclean;
And they who lived in pleasure, dead the while;
Haters of God; and whosoever loved,
And whosoever wrought the devil's lie.

　　Time's river in that awful retrospect

Was flowing swiftly by; when lo, I heard
The traitor's name, and from among the dead
He stagger'd shuddering to the judgment bar,   790
And eye to eye met Him whose sacred life
He sold for lucre: infinite contempt
Was branded on his brow, who knew at last
Good were it for him had he ne'er been born.
Nero was there; and none appear'd to shrink
More terror-stricken from the face of God;
In vain: and many, who with lighter guilt
Had yet imbued their hands in holy blood,
Nor wash'd them in the only fount: and when
The persecuting priests of Carthage came   800
For judgment forth, my guardian touch'd my hand
And pointed to a rank of glorious saints,
Far, far aloof, and nearer to the throne,
Where sate the beautiful Perpetua clothed
In amaranthine bloom, though pity fill'd
Her heart with tenderness, her eyes with tears.

Thus pass'd the centuries with ruin vex'd
And visited with wrath: when lo, a name
Startled me, so familiar was the sound;
And Oriel faintly whisper'd, " It is he,"   810
As Theodore approach'd the throne, and stood
Trembling at that tribunal.   Not a trace
Of pride or blasphemous despite survived
Upon his hopeless brow, only despair,
Who now beneath the terrors of God's Eye
For two Millennial days and half a third

Had lain submiss.   One hurried glance he stole
Upon a form below us, — could it be
His mother? — but no breath of useless prayer
Escaped his lips, compress'd in agony ;   820
Until the irrevocable sentence fell
Upon him, and methought I caught the words,
" O God, I bow beneath Thy rod for ever."
And Oriel whisper'd in my ears, " Amen.
Omniscient Love ordains it.   All is well."

But who of saints or angels could revive
All the dread scenes of that tribunal?   Time
In that judicial retrospect appear'd
To bare itself before eternity ;
Though as the ages onward roll'd, they each   830
Yielded an ever larger harvest-field
To the keen scythe of death.   But when at last
The period of my mortal pilgrimage
Arrived for judgment, I beheld the forms
Of many I had known from youth to prime,
Sheep, wayward sheep whom I had vainly sought,
Now fronting the Chief Shepherd face to face.
And now the fold was closed : and it was mine
To witness I had call'd in vain.   O God,
Thou know'st, Thou only, what sustain'd me then.   84ʊ
Still the dark plots grew darker, as the end
Drew near, and tangled labyrinths of crime
More intricate : all were unravell'd now ;
And deeds, scarce trusted to the subtle winds
And whisper'd in the ear with bated breath,

Were now in presence of the universe
Proclaim'd.   Rebel ingratitude had kept
Its worst, its blackest for the close of all:
But when the last impenitent, who died
With devils leagued and devilish arms in hand   350
Fighting against apparent Deity,
Had all received the terrible award
Of Justice, and among their comrades slunk,
Once more was silence for a space in heaven ;
Until the Judge arising from His throne
Bent on the countless multitudes convict
His visage of eternal wrath, and spake
In tones which more than thousand thunders shook
The crumbling citadel of every heart, —
" Depart from Me, ye cursed, into fire,   360
Fire for the devil and his hosts prepared,
Fire everlasting, fire unquenchable;
Myself have said it : let it be : Amen."
And from the upper firmament there came
A Voice Almighty, " Let it be: Amen."
And all the trembling angels said, " Amen."
And the pale Bride repeated, " Yea, Amen."

God spake, and it was done.   Again the floor
Of solid crystal where the damned stood
Open'd its mouth, immeasurable leagues ;   370
And with a cry whose piercing echoes yet
Beat through the void of shoreless space, the lost
Helplessly, hopelessly, resistlessly,
Adown the inevitable fissure sank,

As sank before the ruin'd hosts of hell,
Still down, still ever down, from deep to deep,
Into the outer darkness, till at last
The fiery gulf received them, and they plunged
Beneath Gehenna's burning sulphurous waves
In the abyss of ever-during woe.   880

All shook except the Throne of Judgment.   That.
Built on the righteousness of God, nor shook
Nor faintest tremor of vibration felt:
The Hand that held the scales of destiny
Swerved not an hair's breadth: and the Voice which
      spake
Those utterances quail'd not, falter'd not.
But when the fiery gulf was shut, and all
Look'd with one instinct on the judgment-seat
To read His countenance who sate thereon,
He was in tears — the Judge was weeping — tears 890
Of grief and pity inexpressible.
And straightway we remember'd who had wept
Over Jerusalem, and is the same
For ever as to-day and yesterday ;
And in full sympathy of grief the springs
Gush'd forth within us ; and the angels wept :
Till stooping from the throne with His own hand
He wiped the tears from every eye, and said,
" My Father's will be done ; His will is Mine ;
And Mine is yours : but mercy' is His delight,   900
And judgment is His strange and dreadful work.
Now it is done for ever.   Come with Me

Ye blessed children of my Father, come;
And in the many mansions of His love
Enjoy the beams of His unclouded smile."

So saying, as once from Olivet, He rose
Majestically toward the heaven of heavens
In the serenity of perfect peace:
And we arose with Him.

                    But what of those
Who, from the place of final judgment hurl'd,   910
Had each his portion in the lake of fire?
No Lethe roll'd its dark oblivious waves,
As some have feign'd, betwixt that world of woe
And ours of bliss. But rather, as of old
Foreshadow'd in the prescient oracles,
The smoke of their great torment rose to heaven
In presence of the holy seraphim,
And in the presence of the Lamb of God,
For ever and for ever. At the first
Nothing was heard ascending from the deep   920
Save wailings and unutterable groans,
Wrung from them by o'ermastering agony;
But as His Eye, who is consuming fire,
Unintermittently abode on them, —
Truth, cleanness, justice fastening like flame
On all that was untrue, unclean, unjust,
And thus to each awarding his due meed, —
The outbreaks of the rebel will were quell'd,
The quick activities of sin were crush'd,

No word of wrathful blasphemy was heard,   930
No violence was wrought; but order rose
From that profound confusion unconfused,
Order and forced submission; and ere long
Swaying her sceptre through the lurid gloom,
And curbing every utterance but truth,
Silence assumed her adamantine throne.

Now were the works of Satan brought to nought;
His vast conspiracy dissolved for ever;
Pride, the first fatal lure, abased for ever;
Hell's transient eminence destroy'd for ever;   940
The haughtiness of man bow'd down for ever;
The lips of idle falsehood seal'd for ever;
Tyrant oppression now oppress'd for ever;
Hatred was still; and murder was no more;
And lust had wrought its latest shame.   The germs
Of evil, ineradicable germs
(Grace only in the day of grace has power
To purge the ill, and recreate the good),
Could never strike one poisonous root again
Beneath the curse of God, nor germinate   950
In that devouring atmosphere of fire:
And, being that repressive fire was there
For ever, Sin the vanquish'd monster lay
For ever powerless in the jaws of Death;
And to our eyes, who saw the light of life
And stood upon the shore of glory, Death
Itself was swallow'd up in victory.

Well I remember, — ages then had roll'd
Out of a measureless eternity, —
Standing with Oriel on that outmost verge   960
Of Paradise, the lowest court of heaven,
Where once to me a bodiless spirit he spake
Of yesterday: the morrow now long since
Had dawn'd: there standing, suddenly we heard
A voice from an unfathomable depth
(And Oriel touch'd me saying, " It is the voice
Of hell's dethroned monarch ") as it seem'd,
In shame and humiliation infinite,
Making confession to himself and God:

" For ever lost: this is the second death: 970
Meet end for me who whisper'd in the ear
Of fragile man, Ye shall not surely die.
So flattering falsehood spake to me.   Man fell;
And falling, as I knew too well, he died.
The Lord is righteous; I have sinn'd and die.
Lost, lost: nor could I crave it otherwise.
What would I otherwise? escape from chains?
Were not we loosed from prison, I and mine,
And only madly heap'd upon ourselves
Fresh torment by fresh crime?   Nay, in our death   980
Eternal Justice hath alone fulfill'd
The equal sentence of Eternal Love.
Me miserable! freedom were worse than bonds;
And life to me more terrible than death.
Myself alone am cause of all my woe.
Mercy constrain'd the stroke.   Left to itself,

My maniac suicidal wickedness
Had still inflicted worse upon itself,
And upon all beneath its cruel rule.
Goodness has hung these chains around my limbs.   990
O God, I bow for ever at Thy feet,
The only Potentate, the only Lord.
I see far off the glory of Thy kingdom
Basking in peace, uninterrupted peace :
But were I free, and were my comrades free,
Sin mightier than myself and them would drag
Our armies to perplex those fields with war.
Only thus fetter'd can we safely gaze
On this the final victory of love,
Virtue and goodness triumphing, and grace   1000
Evolving out of darkness light in heaven.
Thus only to the prisoners of despair
Can Mercy, which is infinite, vouchsafe
Far glimpses of the beauty' of holiness,
Albeit a beauty which can never clothe
Ourselves, the heirs of everlasting wrath.
Woe, woe, immedicable woe for those
Whose hopeless ruin is their only hope,
And hell their solitary resting-place.
Lost, lost : our doom is irreversible :   1010
Power, justice, mercy, love have seal'd us here.
Glory to God who sitteth on the throne,
And to the Lamb for ever and for ever."

The voice was hush'd a moment; then a deep
Low murmur, like a hoarse resounding surge,

Rose from the universal lake of fire :
No tongue was mute, no damned spirit but swell'd
That multitudinous tide of awful praise,
" Glory to God who sitteth on the throne,
And to the Lamb for ever and for ever."   1020

END OF THE ELEVENTH BOOK.

24

Book Twelfth.

THE MANY MANSIONS.

Yet once more, Harp of prophecy, once more
Fondly I come soliciting thine aid ;
By whose celestial minstrelsy inspired
The saintly Enoch walk'd with God and sang
At cloudy morning-tide of evening light.
Thine were the strains that floated o'er tne waves
From Miriam's timbrel and from Moses' tongue;
And thine the suasive melodies, that made
The royal shepherd on his lute forecast
The golden morrow from the vex'd to-day.　　10
Nor was he in thy tuneful lore unlearn'd,
Who interwove the lyrics of the Bride
And idyls of the Bridegroom.　Taught by thee,
Isaiah gazed with eagle eye athwart
The conflicts of a thousand years thrice told ;
And Jeremy, and rapt Ezekiel,
And all the prophets prophesied ; and chief

The seer who, moated by the fretting waves
In Patmos, open'd his responsive breast
To the pure impulses, which only thou   20
Canst echo from eternity to time.
But not, as these great masters of the lyre,
Invoke I thee: for they at God's own voice
Came near and laid their fingers on thy chords,
And by the Spirit empower'd drew forth the tones
Immediate from the sacred fount of song.
And I would only sit beneath their feet,
And earnest catch the echo of their strain,
And with faint imitative notes attempt
To win the pilgrim's ear, who listening me   30
Haply may ask whence I such music drew,
And so become a votary of thine,
As I am. From a boy I loved to sit
The while thy numbers thrill'd my soul, and since
Life with its ruder noises and rough cares
Has somewhat dull'd mine ear, thine, prescient harp,
Thine oftentimes has been the only spell
Of virtue to arouse my laggard spirit.
And now once more in this my last assay,
Only this once, I ask thy heavenly aid   40
(My task is almost done, a task, and yet,
When thou hast breathed, a sweet necessity),
That I may catch, if few and far away,
Some glimpses of the infinite To be.

The judgment had an end. The great white throne
Was hidden in excess of light. And lo,

The earth, emerging from her flood of fire
Baptismal, by a new and heavenly birth
Arose regenerate. The dews of God,
As once in Eden, cool'd the ardent soil ;   50
And rivers from innumerable springs
Flow'd intersecting every gorgeous clime
With living waters. Like a smile of light
The Sun of Righteousness in rising shed
Healing from His benignant wings ; and earth,
Who came forth naked from her bath of flame,
Felt His rich blessing at her heart, and smiled
Responsive, and in blushing haste put on
Her beautiful robes of immortality.
Her late apparel was not found. But now   60
The azure hyaline, in which she moved,
Was not more pure than was her virgin dress.
No trace of her great sufferings remain'd;
No wrecks of time were strewn upon her shores ;
No monuments of ruin ; — saving one : —
Where Satan with his rebel peers had erst
Built on the mystic Babylon his throne,
There rose a solitary mountain peak,
The one volcano of that new-born world,
Thrust from beneath by struggling fires, and thence 70
Ever by day and night, world without end,
A thin white wreath of smoke went up to heaven,
And quickly melted in the golden beams
Which ever from the height of Zion flow'd :
Symbol of deeper things. The sea was not:
Its salt and barren waters were consumed

In that last fire; and all its fruitless wastes,
Once fruitless, now with profuse verdure clad,
In undulating hills and valleys, bared
Untrodden landscapes to the light. Nor deem   80
Because the ocean was no more, earth lack'd
Her noblest type of the profound and free,
Nor heaven its mirror. For the streams of life,
Flowing incessant, stored their crystal wealth
In countless pools and lakes and inland seas,
Wherewith the sportive breezes wantoning
Drave billows crested with their diamond foam
On emerald shores, or in whose lucid calm
The stars slept imaged. Earth from pole to pole
Was one illimitable Paradise;   90
Albeit Emmanuel's land was as that spot
In Eden, where the blossoming tree of life
Grew with the tree of knowledge intertwined,
The presence-chamber of the King of kings,
The temple of the world. And thence the saints
(As sometime from Armenian Ararat,
The sons of Noah) spread o'er every clime,
Good without fear of evil beckoning them,
Life without fear of death embracing them,
All pleasure without pain refreshing them,   100
All sunshine without sorrow in their hearts,
All music without discord in their homes.

So they on earth: but where were we the while?
When from the judgment-throne Messiah rose
To glory, we arose with Him; the heavens

Pealing their jubilant welcomes as we pass'd ;
And all the armies of the sons of God
Clapping their wings of fire before the Bride,
And shouting for the Bridegroom's voice, with sound
Of trumpets and melodious harps; until   110
The everlasting arches rang again,
And that Light-sea which floods the universe
Trembled with its impulsive waves for joy,
And Heaven in ecstasy of rapture ask'd,
What were those echoes of triumphant mirth
That thrill'd creation from the central throne
To its remotest bound. So pass'd we on,
Until the ramparts of the heaven of heavens
Stretch'd like a wall of fire along the expanse,
And those great portals carved of solid pearl   120
(Through which had flown no wing unhallowed, since
The Son of God ascending cleansed with blood
And seal'd the Holiest) now wide open thrown,
Nor henceforth closed, for foes were now no more,
With songs received our singing multitudes;
And through the provinces of bliss we swept
On towards the city of the living God.

Before us now it rose, builded aloft
Upon the heavenly Zion. Never eye
Of mortal man had seen, nor ear had heard,   130
Though ravish'd with the distant fame thereof,
Glory like this; the handiwork of God,
And fashion'd of heaven's choice material, light,
Through which the Light of Light translucent shone ;

The mansion of Creation's Architect;
The palace of the Everlasting King:
Its gates of pearl, its edifice of gold;
Its very streets of pure crystalline gold;
Its walls on twelve foundations superposed
(Of which divine realities the earth   140
Can only lend its feeble semblances),
The jasper streak'd with many a tender dye,
The sapphire of celestial blue serene,
The agate once Chalcedon's peerless boast,
The fathomless repose of emerald,
The ruby, and blood-tinctured sardonyx,
The chrysolite like amber sheathing fire,
The beryl emulous of ocean's sheen,
The opal-tinted topaz clear as glass,
The soft pale purple of the chrysoprase,   150
The Melibœan hyacinth, and last
The lucid violet of amethyst.
But not of pearly gates, or golden streets,
Or bulwarks, or foundations built of jewels
Thought we that day, or linger'd to admire;
For we were on our way to meet our God.

The city had no temple; for itself
From wall to wall, from base to pinnacle,
Was one harmonious veilless sanctuary,
One Holiest of all: of which the shrine   160
Reveal'd amid the clouds of Sinai
Yielded the earliest pattern. This the house
Which Israel's royal seer in symbol saw,

And by the Spirit's hand on his described.
This the beloved apostle, rapt in spirit
To some high watch among the lasting hills,
Beheld. Most blessed, beatific sight!
Here veil'd in radiant clouds, clouds only call'd
From the supreme of brightness they enfolded,
Was set the throne of Majesty in heaven.   170
In front seven ever-burning lamps of fire,
Which are the Spirits of God: and round about
Mysterious cherubim, instinct with eyes,
Fourfold in glory, symbolized in forms
Of lion-like imperial royalty,
Of patient sacrificial ministry,
Of human, more than human sympathy,
Of soaring eagle-plumed intelligence,
Most highest of all creatures, whereof each
Caught and reflected some peculiar rays,   180
Some distinct aspect of his Lord; but all
Uniting in one everlasting song,
Cried, " Holy, Holy, Holy, Lord of hosts."
And here around were four-and-twenty thrones
In wider circuit, like a starry belt,
And on them four-and-twenty hierarchs
In priestly' apparel, but with kingly crowns,
Sitting sublime. And in mid view, behold,
What seem'd the likeness of a sea of glass.
But not on glassy sea, or royal priests,   190
Or cherubim of glory gazed we then;
For we were on our way to meet our God,
Children about to see their Father's face.

Parent and child, O purest fount that flows!
Earth, fallen earth, had known thy heavenly spell:
In whose deep waters selfishness dissolved
And was not, like the sicknesses that fled
At touch of angel-moved Bethesda's pool,
Though tinctured then by many a noxious plant
That grew upon its trampled marge, of power   200
To dim but not destroy its healing life.
A babe upon its mother's breast, a child
Lock'd in a father's arms — oh, things that are!
Love coming forth of love and meeting love;
Love resting in its love and satisfied.
And knew the earth such mysteries? what now
When through the temple courts fragrant with praise
The Bridegroom led His own, His only Bride,
Into His Father's presence, His and ours?
Were they the parted wings of cherubim,   210
Or opening clouds of glory which disclosed
Such lineaments of love unutterable,
Attemper'd as the spirit of each could bear?
No pain, no shrinking from excessive bright,
No sense of discord, no tormenting fear
(For filial love had cast out servile fear),
The Spirit's grace within us meeting grace
Unfathomable, and we His holy ones
Drinking our fill of perfect holiness.
Yet seem'd it every thought in one was lost, —   220
Whether the words were audible to those
Who stood around in endless ranks of light
I know not, but they echoed in my heart, —

It was my Father's voice saying, "My child:"
And every power within me vibrated
To those divinest words, — whether I spoke,
Or whether others spoke, I never knew, —
"My Father, O my Father!"   Beams of love,
The repercussion of His beams of love,
Fill'd every chamber of my soul with light,   230
As in pure waves face answers back to face;
Nor though eternity unfold the powers
Of knowledge, — and to know Him is to love, —
Can beatific blessedness transcend
The rapture of that welcome, that response,
"My child . . . . My Father."   Heaven has nothing
          higher.

The angels gazed in silent ecstasy:
For now it seem'd as if Jehovah turn'd
The glory of His countenance full-orb'd
Upon the Son ; that glory, which on us   240
Shone only as each child could bear its light,
Resting upon the Everlasting Son
In all unveil'd effulgence : not one beam
Of its unmitigated splendor lost,
But from His face reflected, beam for beam,
In the One Spirit's communion infinite,
Uninterrupted fellowship.   And then
(Alas ! the feebleness of words to tell
Those wonders passing wonder) but it seem'd
The Eternal Father slowly rising placed   250
A crown, which in itself was many crowns,

Upon the head of the Eternal Son :
And from amidst the throne a Voice was heard
Commanding Hallelujah. And forthwith
From cherubim and burning seraphim,
And from the hierarchal presbytery,
And from the Bride low at her Bridegroom's feet,
And from the principalities and powers,
And hosts of angels rank'd in endless files,
As sounds the roar of mighty multitudes,   26C
Or rush of many waters in still night,
Or thunders echoing from hill to cloud,
Arose that pealing coronation hymn —
" Crown Him for ever, crown Him King of kings ;
Crown Him for ever, crown Him Lord of lords ;
Crown Him the glorious Conqueror of hell ;
Crown Him the Everlasting Prince of Peace ;
Crown Him Jehovah, Jesu, Lamb of God,
Hallelujah ! Hallelujah !   Amen."
But, ere the sound of their great anthem sank,   270
In waves of rapture on the walls of heaven,
The Son Himself appear'd on bended knee
Stooping before His Father's throne to kneel,
And place that diadem of many crowns
Upon that radiant footstool, then and there
Presenting us and all the ransom'd Church,
Yea and Himself as Man, to God submiss,
Filial obedience as conspicuous now
As had been filial power, His Father's gift.
This adoration paid as man, as God   280
He at His Father's bidding re-assumed

His session on the throne of Majesty,
Radiance with radiance interfused, great depths
Of light, known only to the Spirit of light.
And as in silent awe we knelt and gazed,
And gazing worshipp'd, we beheld no more
The glory of the Father, Son, and Spirit,
Each by itself distinct, but all Triune,
The Trinity in Unity express'd,
One Uncreated, One Almighty, One   290
Eternal, One Incomprehensible,
One Lord, One God.   And God was all in all.

Time measured not such raptures.   But at last
It seem'd as rising from the sapphire throne
Messiah led us forth at large to view
The city' Himself had builded and prepared
After His Father's counsel for His Bride, ·
A city, or a temple, or a home,
Or rather all in one.   Enrich'd it was
With every exquisite design of love,   300
And every form of beauty.   Not a film
Stain'd its bright pavement of transparent gold ;
Not a harsh murmur vex'd its silences,
Or with the melodies of angels jarr'd.
No cloud darken'd its empyrean.   Joy
Held court here in its own metropolis.
And through the midst the crystal river flow'd
Exhaustless from the everlasting throne,
Shaded on either side by trees of life
Which yielded in unwearying interchange   810

Their ripe vicissitude of monthly fruits
Amid their clustering leaves medicinal;
Of fruits twelve manner; for eternity,
Measured by ages limitless to man,
Has intervals and periods of bliss
And high recurring festivals that stand
On the sidereal calends mark'd in light.
Through these celestial groves the Lamb of God
Led us delighted.　Every sight and sound
Ravish'd the sense: and every loving heart　　　320
Reflected joy to joy and light to light,
Like crystals in a cave flashing with fire,
And multiplied our bliss a million-fold.
O blessed royal priesthood! priests and kings
Under the Great High Priest and Prince of Peace,
Who now in tender grace assign'd to each
His priestly' abode within the House of God
(So Solomon around his temple built
The chambers for its stated ministries)
Where each might be alone with God, or mix　　　330
In converse with his fellow-saints at will,
Adorn'd with those peculiar gifts He knew,
Who knows us better than we know ourselves,
Would gratify those tastes and feelings most
Himself had planted: delicate delights;
If little, loving from their littleness,
Which nought but Love could ever have devised;
If rich and large, more precious from the love
That gave them than from excellence or cost;
The bounties of a Father's thoughtfulness,　　　340

The tokens of the Bridegroom's tenderness,
Gifts of the Spirit and with His love instinct.

Oft in my mansion would some elder saint
(For dignity was there humility)
Linger and tell his story, or ask mine:
Or I would listen from an infant's lip
A tale of such delightsomeness as pour'd
New meaning into words henceforth. And oft
A group of the beatified, enlink'd
In all the bonds of holy lineage,   350
Would cluster underneath the trees of life,
One eye kindling another, one deep thought
Waking another thought, and this another,
Until all bosoms overflow'd with love,
And all perforce would hasten to the throne,
And at their Father's footstool pour their hearts
In one full tide of common rapture forth.

Sweet was the intercourse of saint with saint;
Nor less of saints with angels. Now appear'd
The lustrous promise which ordain'd at first   360
That in Messiah's Bridal angelhood
Should find its perfected felicity:
Whether rejoicing in the Bridegroom's joy;
Or drinking in the beauty of the Bride;
Or with some ward, as Oriel oft with me,
Retracing in astonish'd retrospect,
How good from evil, light from darkness sprang
By counsel of All-wise Almighty love.

Nor wanted heaven its hours of such repose
As added zest to ministry, or walks   370
Of patient meditative solitude,
Thought following thought through links of argument,
The heart retiring in itself to muse
On God, His works and ways.   Much as we knew,
Infinite marvels were unknown.   As one
Who climbing some far height at break of day
Among the Alps or lonely Apennines
Sees ever at his feet new landscapes spread,
New vales, new glittering lakes, new summits piercing
The roseate sky with pinnacles of snow,   380
The air still purer crystal, and the arc
Of fresh horizons widening every step,
Yet at the highest touches not the fringe
Of heaven's blue curtains, and when seeing most
Sees but a narrow fragment of God's world:
So ever learning more we never stood
Nearer the limits of His love, whose name
Is always through all ages Wonderful,
And, as it has been, shall be: things reveal'd
Only discovering more beyond our ken: 390
There, as on earth, experience working hope,
Celestial hope who knows no blush of shame,
The child of patience.   Hence they err'd, who taught
That in His presence faith and hope are lost
Who is the God of patience and of hope.
Things once invisible were visible;
Things hoped for present: but beyond them all
Illimitable fields untravell'd lay;

And over these faith saw God's rainbow cast,
And young-eyed hope wing'd many an airy flight. 400
With these dwelt love, by men call'd charity,
And of the peerless sisterhood herself
Was chief; her sweet pre-eminence then seen,
When unawares, as oft, the Prince Himself
Gladdening our lonely meditation came,
And from things past would teach us things to be,
Till in the sunshine of His smile we saw
Darkly no more, no longer in a glass,
But gazing face to face, and eye to eye,
Knew the Beloved as ourselves were known. 410

By such delicious solitude refresh'd,
Not loath we sought society again;
For here we never from His Presence went
Who is the glory of heaven's light: but chief
What time the trump of God, by Michael blown,
Summon'd our glad rejoicing multitudes
To holy convocation. And had hearts
Of weary pilgrims in the wilderness
Oft fainted for His courts of prayer, and found
His earthly tabernacles amiable, 420
Uttering their wants in broken sobs and sighs,
And listening the story of His love
From tremulous lips? Had many a spot appear'd,
Where two or three thus gather'd in His Name,
The house of God and very gate of heaven?
O far exceeding weight of glory, when
Angels and saints, commingling hosts of light,

No laggard heart, no voice unmatch'd or mute,
We knelt before our Father's visible throne,
And saw the Sevenfold Spirit as lamps of fire,   430
And read our names upon Messiah's breast,
And heard the music of His robe (the while
He pass'd the crystal sea bearing aloft
The incense of His meritorious love),
And saw Him touch the golden mercy-seat,
And worshipp'd, as the Oracle of God
Came, from amid Cherubic wings, proclaiming,
" This is My Son Beloved ; hear ye Him."
And when the Prince, the Prophet of His Church,
Spake of His Father in our ears, and show'd   440
The unfathomable glories of His Name,
Until the love which dwelt in the Triune
Dwelt in our hearts, — Emmanuel, God with us ; —
And oftentimes, Chief Minstrel as Chief Priest,
While every heart was vibrating with love,
Himself sang Hallelujah, to the sound
Of thousand times ten thousand angel harps
Which instantly in perfect unison
Roll'd from the golden floor their waves of joy
Against the empyrean's crystal roof ;   450
Then who could choose but swell the mighty tide
Of music with concerting harp and voice,
Until the courts of Zion were fulfill'd
With fragrance of delight and songs of praise ?

From such a Sabbath festival it was
(After what blissful ages know I not),

25

Messiah from the Bridal city led
Down through the starry firmament His Bride,
Not unaccompanied with angel choirs
And gorgeous trains of seraphim and thrones,   460
Towards her native earth.   Flushes of joy
Suffused her cheek with gladness.   To compare
Celestial and terrestrial things, as when
The consort of some mighty Emperor,
Raised by his sovereign will to share his throne,
After long years revisits with her lord
The sweet home of her childhood, and with all
A child's first ecstasy and bloom of joy
Wanders from room to room, and walk to walk,
And each dear spot indelibly engraved   470
On memory's tablet, saying, " Here it was
My father taught me first to lisp his name :
Here first my mother clasp'd my hands in prayer :
This was my favorite knoll; and in this glen,
Well I remember, thou didst speak to me
That summer evening what was in thy mind,
And win this timid heart, — O foolish heart !
Fearing to trust its happiness with thee,
My lord, and better than my lord, my love."
Not otherwise, nor less delightful seem'd   480
To us returning from the heaven of heavens
Our birthplace earth.   And easily we found
Each haunt to memory dear of pilgrim days,
Each hill and valley; for the flood of fire
Which wrapt the earth in its baptismal robe,
Had purged, not changed its lineaments : as once

The deluge of great waters overwhelm'd
All life, except the cradled Church, but left
Creation's landmarks and the river beds
Coasting the land of Shinar undisturb'd.   490
The wastes of ocean only were no more,
Nor wastes of sand, nor aught of barrenness;
And yet the earth through all her vast expanse
Of golden plains and rich umbrageous hills
Already seem'd too narrow for the growth
Of her great human family; so quick
The virtue of her Maker's law, when once
Sin's crushing interdict was disannull'd,
That primal law, " Be fruitful; multiply
Your joys; replenish and subdue the earth."   500
Blest mandate! blest obedience! Earth was full
Of goodness, full of glory, full of grace:
A perfect image of high heaven: the globe
One temple, all mankind for worshippers,
Israel for priests: and now the prayer we used
To pray, "Our Father, Hallow'd be Thy Name;
Thy kingdom come; Thy will be done in earth,
As by Thy angel ministries in heaven,"
Was turn'd into a thousand forms of praise,
And sung from hill to hill, from clime to clime,   510
Innumerable infant choristers
Swelling the deeper tones of youth and age,
In holy matins and in vesper hymns.

Great thoughts were stirring in the hearts of men,
And hopes too big for utterance: yet were none

Who deem'd their present rapture capable
Of such enlargement as was theirs, when now
Messiah, who had heretofore reveal'd
His Presence in Jerusalem alone,
Came with His Virgin Bride and angel choirs,　　520
And tabernacled upon earth again,
And visited not only His own land,
But every country, every home, and left
Some token of His love in every heart,
The Son of Man among the sons of men.
Not least their rapture when as He was wont
He touch'd their eyes with heavenly balm ; and lo
They saw in heaven the city of His Bride,
Its gates of pearl, its streets of limpid gold,
Its walls on bright foundations built, and walks　　530
By crystal streams shaded by trees of life.
Nor, if the rebel Regent of the air
Once had such power to represent the world
Comprised as in a moment to His eye,
Marvel that He the rightful Prince had power
To show His children that Jerusalem
Of glory, which is mother of us all,
Descending out of heaven from God it seem'd,
Though distant far.　And, while He show'd it them,
He told them of its undeclining light,　　540
And blessed vision of His Father's face,
And royalty of service, promising,
Their earthly ministry approved, to' enroll
Their names among the citizens of heaven
And freemen of His sinless universe.

Haply such perfectness of earthly bliss
And such far vistas of celestial light
Had overcharged their hearts.　But not in vain
The awful chronicles of time.　And oft,
When dazzled with the glory and the glow　　　550
That stream'd from Zion's everlasting hills,
Messiah or His ministers would tell
Rapt auditors how Satan fell from bliss,
The story of a ruin'd Paradise,
The foughten fight, the victory achieved,
But only with the endless banishment
Of damned spirits innumerable and men
From heaven and heavenly favor which is life.
Nor seldom He, who strengthen'd human sight,
As with angelic telescope, to read　　　　560
The wonders of the highest firmament,
Would bid them gaze into the awful Deep
Couching beneath; and there they saw the lost
For ever bound under His dreadful Eye
Who is eternal and consuming fire,
There in the outer darkness.　And the view
So wrought in them, that perfect self-distrust,
With pity not unmix'd and tender tears,
Lean'd ever on their God for perfect strength.

That which men witness'd of the damn'd in hell,　570
By unction of the Spirit at God's command,
Was in our gaze at will, whene'er the smoke
In mighty volumes rising from the Deep,
Blown devious by God's breath athwart the void,

Dispersed.   Nor turn'd we always from the sight,
Although it touch'd the inmost springs of grief,
And stirr'd our bosoms from their depths.   Hell was:
The fact, and not our vision of the fact,
Was their unending anguish and our grief,
A grief which chasten'd but not jarr'd our bliss.   580
Should not the children share their Father's thoughts?
Should not the Wife her Husband's counsels learn?
Learn ever more and more?   Let it suffice
That in the depth, as in the height above,
God was Supreme; His righteousness confess'd
In dread Gehenna as His love in heaven;
Absolute order reigning; of the lost
Some scourged with many stripes, with fewer some,
All underneath the footstool of His throne
Subdued, submiss.   This we beheld and knew.   590
And in the cloudless joys of heaven and earth
Haply this sight and knowledge were to us
The needful undertones of sympathy
With Him, who was in days of mortal flesh
A man of sorrows conversant with griefs,
The necessary fountain-spring of tears,
The sign and sacrament of pride abased
And creature humiliation without end.

      Cloudless indeed our joys in earth and heaven,
Ceaseless our ministry, and limitless   600
The increase of that government and peace,
Messiah's heritage and ours.   For as
Our native orb ere long too strait became

For its blest habitants, not only some
Translated without death, for death was not,
As Enoch, join'd the glorified in light;
But at the voice of God the stars, which roll'd
Innumerous in the azure firmament
By thousands and ten thousands, as He spake
Six words of power, the seventh, it was done,   610
Were mantled and prepared as seats of life:
And it was ours to bear from earth and plant,
Like Adam, in some paradise of fruits
The ancestors of many a new-born world;
Like Adam, but far different issue now,
Sin and the curse and death for ever crush'd.
And thus from planet on to planet spread
The living light.   As when a white-robed priest
Himself, surrounded by his acolytes,
In some vast minster, from the altar fire   620
Lighting his torch, walks through the slumb'rous
      aisles,
And kindles one by one the brazen lamps
That on the fluted columns cast their shade
Or from the frescoed ceiling hang suspense,
Until the startled sanctuary is bathed
In glory, and the evening chant of praise
Floats in the radiance: so it was in heaven:
God's temple, the expectant firmament,
Hung with its lamps, innumerable stars;
The Priest, Messiah; earth, the altar flame;   63C
Angels and saints, the winged messengers;

And that great choral eucharist the hymn
Of all creation's everlasting praise.

Such are the many kingdoms of God's realm;
And in these boundless provinces of light
We who once suffer'd with a suffering Lord
Reign with Him in His glory, unto each
According to his power and proven love
His rule assign'd.   But Zion is our home;
Jerusalem, the city of our God.   640
O happy home!   O happy children here!
O blissful mansions of our Father's house!
O walks surpassing Eden for delight!
Here are the harvests reap'd once sown in tears:
Here is the rest by ministry enhanced:
Here is the banquet of the wine of heaven,
Riches of glory incorruptible,
Crowns, amaranthine crowns of victory,
The voice of harpers harping on their harps,
The anthems of the holy cherubim,   650
The crystal river of the Spirit's joy,
The Bridal palace of the Prince of Peace,
The Holiest of Holies — God is here.

THE END.

NOTES.

NOTES.

BOOK I.

THE SEER'S DEATH.

St. Paul's adoption of the word *prophet* to describe the Cretan bard Epimenides (Titus i. 12) appears to justify the use of *seer* in an equivalent sense. Compare 1 Sam. ix. 9.

Line 1. *The last day of my earthly pilgrimage.*
From Homer downward, it has been usual for those who would picture the unseen world to imagine the descent of a living man to Hades. This, so far as we know, has never happened, and cannot happen. And it seemed to me more natural to make the attempt at least of conceiving that which is taking place almost every breath we draw, I mean the passage of a disembodied spirit to the world of spirits.

Line 25. *I was scarcely more, &c.*
See Dante, Inferno, Canto 1, line 1.

Line 78. *Its true gauge.*
" In His unerring sight who measures life by love." Keble.

Line 321. *Of him who call'd his son " a stranger here."*
Compare Exod. ii. 22 with Ps. xc. 1.

Lines 327—334.
See John xiv.—xvii.

Lines 335—346.
See 1 Cor. xv. 20—57.

Line 850. *The vision,* &c.
Rev. xxi. 2.—xxii 5.

Line 892. *A Presence.*
See Isa. xliii. 2.

Line 406. *They err who tell us, that the spirit unclothed,* &c.
The historic narratives of Samuel's disembodied spirit appearing
and speaking to Saul (1 Sam. xxviii. 14), and of Moses, whose body
was buried by God (Deut. xxxiv. 6), being seen by the three Apostles, and discoursing with our Lord on the Mount of Transfiguration
(Luke ix. 81), may confirm the statements here made.

Line 438. *Saintly apparel.*
See 1 Sam. xxviii. 14. Rev. vi. 11.

Line 446. *All ear, all eye, all feeling, and all heart.*
See Paradise Lost, Book vi., line 850.

Line 499. *The angelical convoy.*
Luke xvi. 22.

Line 505. *Ere we set forth, rise brother, and look round,* &c.
The numerous and well authenticated appearances of the human
spirit, within a few hours of death, seem to indicate that God does
sometimes permit such a lingering on earth as is here described, ere
the soul enters the unseen world.

Line 518. *There were more spirits than men,* &c.
Compare the following Scriptures: " The angel of the Lord encamp-
eth round about them that fear Him " (Ps. xxxiv. 7). " The mountain was full of horses and chariots of fire round about Elisha" (2
Kings vi. 17). "Are they not all ministering spirits, sent forth to
minister to them that shall be heirs of salvation?" (Heb. i. 14.)
" We wrestle against principalities, against powers, against the rulers
(τοὺς κοσμοκράτορας) of the darkness of this world, agai ıst spiritual
wickedness in high places (τὰ πνευματικὰ τῆς πονηρίας ἐν τοῖς ἐπου-
ρανίοις, ' the spiritual hosts of wickedness in the heavenly regions.'
Ellicott) " (Eph. vi. 12). Also 1 Cor. iv. 9. 2 Cor. ii. 11. 1 Thess.
ii. 18.

Line 583. *The fallen wore,* &c.
" Satan himself also is transformed into an angel of light." 2 Cor
xii. 14.

Lines 559—567.
Compare 2 Tim. ii. 26.

Line 571. *An angel stooped,* &c.

See Ps. xci. 11.

Line 625. *Distemper'd phantasies, or spirits unblest.*

One or other of these disastrous alternatives must, I fear, explain the reputed wonders of spiritualism, wherever they are not wilful impostures.

Line 671. *The road to Paradise a long descent.*

The almost uniform testimony of Scripture points to Hades as a region below. The dying are spoken of as " going down to the pit," or "going down into silence." Samuel's spirit said to Saul, " Why hast thou disquieted me to bring me up?" (1 Sam. xxviii. 15.) So we read " David is not yet ascended into the heavens " (Acts ii. 84). Our Lord says of Himself, " The Son of Man shall be three days and three nights in the heart of the earth " (Matt. xii. 40). And St. Paul writes of Him, " He descended first into the lower parts of the earth " (Eph. iv. 9).

From these and similar Scriptures, some have thought that the Paradise of the Blessed Dead, as well as the prison of the Lost, was actually situate within the crust of our terrestrial globe. But this Divine language may only be an accommodation to our earthly thoughts of height and depth. And there is one deeply interesting passage of Holy Writ, which appears to indicate that the Hades to which our Lord's disembodied human spirit went betwixt His death and resurrection is as much to be regarded *below* our earth, as the heavens of glory to which He ascended from Olivet are to be regarded *above* it. I refer to 1 Pet. iii. 18—22. As the local structure of my poem in some measure depends upon it, I may be permitted to make an extract from my Commentary on the New Testament—
" *Because even Christ suffered once on account of sins* (περὶ ἁμαρτιῶν — i.e. an atoning sacrifice for sins, the usual name for the sin-offerings in the LXX version being τὰ περὶ ἁμαρτιῶν), *the just on behalf of the unjust* — a Sinless Victim in the stead of sinful mankind — *having been put to death in* (His human) *flesh, but quickened in spirit* (πνεύματι, omit τῷ with best MSS.) — i.e. His disembodied human spirit — *in which* (human spirit) *also He went a journey* (πορευθείς, compare πορευθεὶς εἰς οὐρανόν ver. 22) *and preached* (ἐκήρυξεν, as a herald proclaiming tidings) *to the spirits in prison* (φυλακῇ, compare Job xiv. 18; ἐν ᾅδῃ με ἐφύλαξας, LXX), *which* (spirits) *were sometime disobedient* — refusing to repent before the door of the ark was shut — *when the long-suffering of God was waiting* (ἀπεξεδέχετο, so the best MSS.) *in the days of Noah, while the ark was a preparing where*

into (εἰς ἦν) entering — *few persons, that is eight souls, were saved*
(διεσώθησαν, 'thoroughly saved,' perhaps implying both in body and
soul) *by means of water* — for the water which buried the rest of the
world upbore the ark of their salvation.

"That the time here spoken of is the interval betwixt the death
and resurrection of our Lord, during which His human spirit was
separated from His human flesh, appears from the emphatic contrast
of His death with respect to one, and his life in the other (θανατωθεὶς
μὲν σαρκί, ζωοποιηθεὶς δὲ πνεύματι). Compare Rom. i. 3, 4, and 1
Tim. iii. 16. That an actual journey from place to place is described
(ver. 19) is evident from the use of the same word (πορευθείς, 'having
travelled') there, and in ver. 22, where it must signify a local transi-
tion from earth to heaven. The comparison of one verse with another
precludes any metaphorical adaptation of the term 'journeyed.'
That this mission of Christ to the souls in Hades is nowhere else
recorded by the Holy Spirit will never stagger those who believe
that every word of God is true. That by the phrase 'He preached'
(ἐκήρυξεν) is intimated the announcement of the work of redemption
is almost certain from other passages where it thus stands by itself,
and from a comparison of the answering term (εὐηγγελίσθη, ch. iv. 6).
That the day of grace, the time of salvation, is every where in Holy
Scripture limited to the brief space of life is true; but this hinders
not such a proclamation of mercy to those who, after the door of
temporal safety was shut, may have truly repented of their guilt, and
found forgiveness with God before they were overwhelmed with the
rising waters. That the destruction of the body is not inconsistent
with the salvation of the soul, in the case of repenting sinners, we
know from other instances of Divine compassion. And, finally, that
the descent of Christ to Hades, a fact which, like His death, stands
alone and admits not of repetition, should be illustrated with signal
acts of royal clemency is only in accordance with those miracles of
mercy which ever attended His steps.

"For further notes upon this difficult, but most interesting, portion
of Holy Writ I must refer the reader to Wordsworth's cautious and
reverent exposition — an exposition entirely in harmony with the
third article of the Church of England as first published, viz., 'That
the body of Christ lay in the grave till His resurrection, but His
spirit which He gave up was with the spirits which are detained in
prison, or in hell, and preached to them, as the place in St. Peter
testifieth.' These words were afterwards omitted, but our Church
sufficiently indicates her interpretation of this Scripture by appoint-
ing it to be read as the epistle on Easter even."

From this it appears that the Divine Spirit describes our Lord's descent to Hades by the same word (πορευθείς) which relates His ascent to heaven. In both cases He went a journey, first descending, afterwards ascending. And as in the latter case our thoughts travel upwards with Him who passed through the heavens (διεληλυθότα τοὺς οὐρανούς, Heb. iv. 14) to the throne of glory, so in the former they travel downwards with Him to the Deep into which He descended for our sakes.

Line 676. *Oriel*, i.e. "Light or flame of God."

The Hebrew word might be indifferently rendered *Uriel* or *Ooriel*: but I have selected this modification, the name "Uriel" having been traditionally appropriated to one of the seven chief angels; which tradition I observe, Book iv., line 192.

Line 787. *One world, but widely sunder'd by a gulf.*

Compare Luke xvi. 22, 23.

BOOK II.

Line 23. *Back with melodious sound they softly flew.*

See Paradise Lost, Book vii., line 207.

Line 149. *Without Him heaven were but a desert rude.*

See Keble's Christian Year, Fourth Sun. after Easter, line 9.

Line 166. *His brightness shone, &c.*

Dan. viii. 15—18; and x. 5—17.

Line 169. *The Apocalyptic seer.*

Rev. i. 17.

Lines 181—188.

"We shall be like Him; FOR (ὅτι) we shall see Him as He is." 1 John iii. 2.

Line 854. *A babe in glory is a babe for ever.*

This seems a necessary inference from such Scriptures as declare that the harvest hereafter is according to the seed sown here; Gal. vi. 7. 2 Cor. ix. 6, &c.

Line 372. *A link betwixt mankind and angelhood.*

This thought, and the one below of infants in glory resembling the lilywork in Solomon's temple, were suggested by a friend.

Line 462. *The strange salute of father.*

See 1 Cor. iv. 15. 1 Thess. ii. 19, 20. The joy of this spiritual relationship has its earnests on earth, which we may well believe will be deepened in Paradise, though awaiting the resurrection for its full glory.

Line 554. *While words, &c.*
Rev. i. 5, 6.

Line 587. *The Increate alone is self-sustain'd.*

See Paradise Lost, Book v., lines 404—433, and especially the words,

" For know whatever was created needs
To be sustain'd and fed."

The passage had escaped my memory while writing my lines, which were probably an unconscious echo of Milton's.

Line 600. *They who weep on earth shall laugh, &c.*
Luke vi. 21.

Line 623. *A cloud of witnesses.*
Heb. xii. 1.

Line 642. *He knew who spake of trees.*
1 Kings iv. 33.

Line 667. *Saints wait their bright apparelling.*
2 Cor. v. 4.

Line 786. *All are not equal there.*
" For orders and degrees
Jar not with liberty, but well consist."
Paradise Lost, Book v., line 792.

Line 801. *Many first were last, &c.*
Matt. xix. 30.

Line 828. *Of such babes as these, &c.*

Matt. xix. 14. When we remember what multitudes of little children, not only from Christian but also from heathen lands, are gathered home before they have committed actual sin, and are thus saved in Christ for ever, may we not believe that there is a direct historic fulfilment of these words of our Lord, as well as a spiritual meaning underlying them?

Line 889. *A mystic time and times and half a time.*
Compare Dan. vii. 25 with Rev. xi. 8.

Line 852. *Antipas.*
Rev. ii. 18.

Lines 875, 876.
See Eph. iii. 18, 19.

Line 884. *The voice.*
Matt. iii. 8.

Lines 890—892.

" No wonder that even the holy mother when she gazed on that august assemblage, when she saw, as perchance she might have seen, the now aged Hillel the looser, and Shammai the binder, and the wise sons of Betirah, and Rabban Simeon, Hillel's son, and. Jonathan the paraphrast, the greatest of his pupils, when she saw these and such as these, all hanging on the lips of the Divine Child, no wonder she forgot all." Ellicott's Historical Lectures, p. 92.

Line 934. *The matins of the Church.*
Gen. iv. 26.

Line 980. *They are not perfect here.*

For the testimony of Scripture to the state of the disembodied saints before the resurrection, the writer would venture to refer his readers to a little work of his called " The Blessed Dead."

Line 1002. *Two diverse from the rest.*

It appears from the words of our Lord to Nicodemus (John iii. 18), that, when they were uttered, no man had ever ascended to the heavens of glory; and, if Enoch and Elijah had not then ascended, we may well believe they still await this lofty privilege with all the other saints of God. See note on Book vii. 595.

———

BOOK III.

Line 21. *Tartarean night.*

I have throughout this poem attempted rigidly to abstain from interweaving classical mythology with Scriptural realities. It has not been always easy to observe this restriction with phrases and stories familiar from childhood. But the above expression is no exception

to the rule I imposed upon myself, of only introducing those terms
for the usage of which I could appeal to Holy Writ; for St. Peter,
speaking of angels who sinned, says, that "God having cast them
down to Tartarus (ταρταρώσας), delivered them into chains of darkness." (2 Pet. ii. 4.)

Line 25. *Yet deignest in the contrite heart to' abide,* &c.
See Paradise Lost, Book i., lines 17—23.

Line 77. *A horrid chasm.*
See Luke xvi. 26.

Line 93. *Darkness alone,* &c.
"A land of darkness, as darkness itself; and of the shadow of
death, without any order, and where the light is as darkness."
(Job x. 22.)   ·

Line 131. *Needs not the shining of created light.*
In this, as in some other points, I have ventured to believe that
Paradise will anticipate the glory that is to be revealed, for in Para-
dise we shall be with Him who is the true, the archetypal Light.

Line 142. *A shield,* &c.
See Exod. xiv. 20.

Line 144. *Who fain would pass,* &c.
See Luke xvi. 26.

Line 149. *Listening we might catch,* &c.
So Abraham is represented by our Lord as hearing the words of
the rich man in Hades.

Line 191. *Those angels who forsook their high estate.*
See note on Book v., lines 807—817.

Line 225. *God's gift.*
See Gen. xxv. 21. Esau and Jacob were both of them given by
God to Isaac in answer to prayer.

Line 230. *The moated fortress of a faithful house.*
See Ps. xci. 9—11. Prov. iii. 33.

Line 253. *Maxentius hurried, vowing to his gods,* &c.
"When Maxentius went forth to battle, he went fortified by
heathen oracles, the champion of heathenism against the champion
of the cross." Elliott's *Horæ,* Vol. i., p. 243.   .

Line 286. *Not circumvented,* &c.
See 1 Tim. ii. 14.

Line 310. *The labarum emblazoned with the cross.*

"From as early a date as that of the great battle with Maxentius, according to the testimony both of Lactantius and Eusebius, Constantine adopted the cross as his distinctive military ensign. That object of abomination to the heathen Romans was seen glittering on the helmets, engraved on the shields, and interwoven with the banners of his soldiers. The Emperor's own person was adorned by it wrought of richest material and of finest workmanship. Above all, in his principal banner, the *labarum*, he displayed the same once accursed emblem, with a crown of gold and gems above it, and the monogram of the name of Him who after bearing the one now wore the other." Elliott's *Horæ*, Vol. i., p. 239.

Line 514. *With ponderous noise,* &c.

See Paradise Lost, Book ii., line 880.

Line 536. *And then and there upon that guilty man,* &c.

This thought was first suggested by Southey's Kehama, xxiv. 18.

Line 579. *Know that Omnipotence can but perform,* &c.

From the words, "He cannot deny Himself" (2 Tim. ii. 13), we learn there is that the Almighty cannot do. He cannot deny Himself, either falsifying His word, or acting contrary to the counsels of His own infinite wisdom and righteousness. Omnipotence, therefore, is not the power of doing whatever blind man may conceive possible, but of accomplishing all that Omniscient Goodness sees to be right. I would refer the reader to some noble thoughts on this in Birks' Difficulties of Belief.

Line 596. *And not in utter solitariness.*

Compare Job iii. 18. Ps. xlix. 14. Isa. xiv. 16.

Line 624. *He caught a glimpse,* &c.

Luke xvi. 28.

Line 700 *Doth not consume in thee the secret spring.*

On the request of the rich man to Abraham that Lazarus might be sent to his brethren lest they also should come to that place of torment (Luke xvi. 27—31), Matthew Henry writes, "He desired the preventing of their ruin, partly in tenderness to them for whom he could not but retain a natural affection; he knew their temper, their temptations, their ignorance, their infidelity, their inconsideration, and wished to prevent the destruction they were running into; partly in tenderness to himself, &c." Holy Scripture does not oblige us to believe, with some theologians, the utter extinction of all natural feelings in the lost, but rather leads us to infer that, in proportion as they have depraved and vitiated those feelings on earth, do they suffer everlastingly. So Milton says —

> " For neither do the spirits damned
> Lose all their virtue."

Paradise Lost, Book ii., line 482. And doubtless that Perfect Equity which distinguishes on earth the right acts of evil men (see for example, Jehu, 2 Kings x. 80, 81), must ever distinguish degrees of guilt.

Line 750. *Of this I will relate hereafter.*
Book viii. 291—594.

Line 762. *The seven last angels, &c.*
Rev. xv. and xvi.

Line 780. *Announcing to the prisoners of wrath, &c.*

I have ventured to believe that the Advent cry, " Behold He cometh with clouds," which has been so often raised in Christendom during the last half-century, has not been without its echo in the underworld of spirits. Such reverberations seem to be according to the analogy of Providence.

Line 831. *God would, but could not save me 'gainst my will.*

Compare " The Pharisees rejected (ἠθέτησαν, in margin ' frustrated') the counsel of God" (Luke vii. 30); and also the pathetic words, " How often would I (ἠθέλησα) . . . and ye would not (οὐκ ἠθελήσατε)," Matt. xxiii. 37.

Lines 862 to 874 beginning *If here, &c.*
See Book xi., where this thought is further unfolded.

Line 875. *For God Himself has sworn, &c.*

See Phil. ii. 9—11, where we read, " That in (ἐν) the name of Jesus every knee should bow, of things in heaven and things in earth, and THINGS UNDER THE EARTH (καταχθονίων), and every tongue confess that Jesus Christ is Lord." The expression " the things under the earth " Wordsworth, in his Notes on the Greek Testament, interprets " especially of Death and the Grave . . . and Satan himself and all the powers of darkness; " and says, " The sense is best explained by Rev. v. 13, where the creatures beneath the earth join in ascribing honor to the Lamb." The momentous addition here of the things under the earth, compared with their equally notable absence in the parallel passages, Eph. i. 10. Col. i. 20, seems to import that, while lost angels and men are never reconciled to God or gathered together in Christ, but are consigned at the judgment to everlasting punishment, they will be for ever reduced to compulsory submission, and in this state of absolute order will ascribe glory to God. There will be no anarchy even in that world of outer gloom. The days of regnant rebellion are numbered. Christ must reign, till He hath put all enemies under His feet. See further notes on Book xi.

Line 891. *Silence reigned.*

Compare " The wicked shall be silent in darkness," 1 Sam. ii. 9

Line 910. *As they had sinn'd, they suffer'd.*
Luke xii. 47, 48.

Line 1024. *What time a mighty conqueror, &c.*
Compare Isa. xiv. 4—20.

Line 1042. *The captive angels, &c.*
See note, Book v. 807—817.

Line 1052. *Such were those who sought, &c.*
See Luke viii. 31, " They besought Him that He would not command them to go out into the deep (εἰς τὴν ἄβυσσον, rendered " bottomless pit," Rev. xx. 3). The entreaty betokens, as expressed by another Evangelist, their fear of " torment before the time " (Matt viii. 29.)

BOOK IV.

Line 11. *A babe of more than human beauty wept.*

Exod. ii. 6. In Acts vii. 20, we read the infant Moses was " exceeding fair " (ἀστεῖος τῷ Θεῷ, "fair to God," or fair in God' sight ").

Line 15. *Rivalry of hearts.*
1 Sam. xx. 41.

Line 18. *Who wash'd her Saviour's feet.*
Luke vii. 37, 38.

Line 37. *Let David witness.*
Ps. lvi. 8.

Line 46. *Blind and bereft.*

Paradise Lost, Book iii., lines 51—55.

Line 49. *And he, who touch'd,* &c.

" The Winter Walk at Noon." Cowper.

Line 56. *He wept with agonizing groans.*
Heb. v. 7.

Line 93. *Of evil overcome,* &c.

1 Cor. xv. 25, 26. 54. Rev. xx. 14.

Lines 136—138.

Compare Heb. i. 2 and xi. 8, " He made the worlds " (τοὺς αἰῶνας)
or " the ages."

Lines 171, 172.

See Gen. xviii. 1, 2; xix. 1; and Acts i. 10, &c.

Line 182. *No angelic parentage.*

Hence angels are called the sons of God (Job xxxviii. 7), as is
Adam (Luke iii. 38).

Line 186. *Lucifer, the first.*
Isa. xiv. 12.

Line 189. *Michael the prince.*
Dan. x. 13; xii. 1.

Line 190. *Gabriel, God's swift winged messenger.*
Dan. ix. 21.

Lines 191, 192. *Raphael* and *Uriel.*

These, with the two last named, were according to the rabbins the
four angels who surround the throne of God. R. Bechai: the book
Zohar.

Lines 192—194. *Barakiel, Ramiel,* and *Raamiel.*

Among the angels whose names have come down to us by Jewish
tradition. Layard's " Ruins of Nineveh and Babylon," pp. 509—
523.

Lines 195, 196.

Dumah or *Duma* (silence) the angel who presides over the dead:
Lailah (night) the angel who presides over conception: *Yorekemo,*
the angel who is lord over the hail: and *Suriel* (access to God), an
angel called " prince of the face," because he is continually in the
presence of God. I am indebted for these Talmudic names to my
learned friend, the Rev. John Ayre, whose kind interest in this poem,

before its publication, I must take this opportunity of gratefully acknowledging.

Line 201. *Thrones, virtues, principalities, and powers.*
" Whether they be thrones (θρόνοι), or dominions (κυριότητες), or principalities (ἀρχαί), or powers (ἐξουσίαι)," Col. i. 16.

Line 220. *I found myself alone.*
See Milton's exquisite description of Adam awaking to life Paradise Lost, Book viii., lines 250—337.

Line 233. *An Angel among angels.*
" The Angel of His Presence saved them." Isa. lxiii. 9.

Lines 295—301.
On the interpretation of the living creatures and crowned elders, as being angelic, not human, I must venture to refer to the notes in my Commentary on Rev. iv. 4—6 and v. 9, 10, the reading now generally approved of the last passage running thus, " Thou redeemedst *them,* i.e. the saints, to God by Thy blood, and hast made them (αὐτούς) unto our God kings and priests, and they reign (βασιλεύουσιν) on the earth." If this reading be adopted, the testimony of Scripture elsewhere is uniform in favor of their angelic nature.

Line 306. *Envy was unknown.*
So Plato, " Envy stands aloof from the celestial choir " (φθόνος γαρ ἔξω θείου χοροῦ ἵσταται. Phædrus, iii. 247).

Line 322. *Our earliest name.*
Deut. xxxiii. 2. Jude 14.

Line 336. *Mark'd by sidereal orbits.*
" The same principles of the intersections of the solar and lunar periods, by which the units of the ordinary calendar are determined, when carried further up the ascending periods of time, produce even from the abstract relations of the celestial periods, the larger but corresponding units of 30 and 360 years, or the prophetic month and time. . . . A Divine ladder of time is set before us, and, as we rise successively from step to step, days are replaced by years, and years by millennia; and these perhaps, hereafter, in their turn by some higher unit from which the soul of man may measure out cycles still more vast, and obtain a wider view of the immeasurable grandeur of eternity." Birks' Elements of Prophecy, pp. 371, 372.

Line 383. *Firmament of morning stars.*
Job xxxviii. 7.

Line 390. *Which saith to Me, Thou art My only Son.*

See Ps. ii. 6, 7. " Yet have I set ('anointed' *Hebrew*) My King upon My holy hill of Zion. I will declare the decree: the Lord hath said unto Me, Thou art My Son; this day have I begotten Thee." Here the words " Thou art My Son " appear to proclaim the Eternal Godhead of the Word as being from everlasting to everlasting the coequal Son of the Father; and the words " This day have I begotten Thee " to declare His manifestation as the Christ IN TIME, a manifestation crowned and consummated by His resurrection (Acts xiii· 83). Thus in Hebrews xiii. 8, where we read "Jesus Christ *is* the same yesterday, to-day, and for ever," *yesterday* seems to respect the infinite past, *to-day* the course of time, and *for ever* the ages of an eternity to come.

Lines 403—409.

" God, even Thy God, hath anointed Thee with the oil of gladness above Thy fellows " (Ps. xlv. 7). And the Second Psalm quoted in the last note appears to point to some declaration of the Eternal Father's sovereign pleasure respecting the Eternal Son, the Heir of all things, as the occasion, or at least one occasion, of such anointing.

Lines 422—449.

See Birks' Difficulties of Belief, " On temptation in free agents," and " On the creation and fall of angels."

Lines 534—545. *Made of the dust, &c.*

" Man in virtue of his original creation occupies a central place among all the works of God. His immortal spirit links him with the hosts of angels, and he is only a little lower than they. Yet his animal life links him equally with the whole circle of animated and organized being, while his body formed of the dust, is linked with all the planetary spheres by the laws of material gravitation. . . . The nature thus assumed [by the Son of God] in its original constitution admits of a perpetual increase, by which it may reflect, in the largest measure any created being is capable of doing, the absolute infinitude of the Uncreated Being." Birks' Ways of God, " On the Incarnation," pp. 108—111. And with respect to man's central position, see the corresponding truth regarding his terrestrial home, as sketched by Dr. Whewell in his most convincing essay, where he proves, " The Earth is really the domestic hearth of this solar system, adjusted between the hot and fiery haze on one side, the cold and watery vapor on the other." Of the Plurality of Worlds, p. 320

Line 625. *Wrapt in impervious mists,* &c.

Geology seems to have established (1) that the earth has existed for vast periods of time before the creation of man; (2) that each period terminated with an epoch of convulsion; (8) that each period was an advance on the condition of the one preceding it; (4) that the last great convulsion, by which the mountain chains of the Alps and Andes were thrust from below, occurred probably not more than ten thousand years ago. Now such a convulsion must have reduced our planet to the state described in the words "The earth was (or rather 'had become') without form and void, and darkness was upon the face of the deep" (Gen. i. 2). I believe, therefore, in common with many, that the first verse of Holy Scripture narrates the original creation of the heavens and earth; that the second verse describes the state of confusion to which our globe had been reduced by the last great terrestrial convulsion which preceded the history of our species; and that the narrative which follows is an optical description of six literal days' creative work (each day probably corresponding to some vast geological period) during which our world, as it now is, was fashioned by God in the sight of the angelic hosts. See Hitchcock's Geology; Birks' Bible and Modern Thought; McCaul's Essay in Aids to Faith; McCausland's Sermons in Stones.

Lines 648—652.

See Hugh Miller's "Vision of Creation," Testimony of the Rocks.

Line 949. *God of the world and guardian of mankind.*

The titles ascribed to Satan and his angels appear to me too explicit to be understood of merely usurped dominion, "the prince of this world" (John xii. 31, &c.), "the god of this world" (2 Cor. iv. 4), "the prince of the power of the air" (Eph. ii. 2), "the rulers of the darkness of this world" (Eph. vi. 12), &c. The devil probably veiled a falsehood under a garb of truth, when he said to our Lord, "All this power will I give Thee, and the glory of them: for that is delivered unto me; and to whomsoever I will I give it" (Luke iv. 6).

Line 967. *The Bridegroom's friend.*
See John iii. 29.

BOOK V.

Line 23. *Nor odds appear'd,* &c.
See Birks' Difficulties of Belief, pp. 91, 92.

Line 61. *Unfallen had Lucifer received his charge.*

When our Lord says, " He (the devil) was a murderer from the beginning, and abode not in the truth " (John viii. 44), the word rendered " murderer " (ἀνθρωποκτόνος), strictly " manslayer," indicates
that no time anterior to the creation of man is intended, and seems to
prove not only that the devil was the first sinner, but that the murder of our first parents' innocence was his first overt act of successful
rebellion. Compare 1 John iii. 8.

Line 67. *Earth had not kept her circling birthday yet.*

This seems probable from the birth of Cain being subsequent to
the expulsion of Adam and Eve from paradise.

Line 177. *Another image of Omnipotence.*

" Ita fornicatur anima, cùm avertitur abs te, et quærit extra te ea
quæ pura et liquida non invenit, nisi cùm redit ad te. Perversè te imi-
tantur omnes qui longè se à te faciunt, et extollunt se adversùm te.
Sed etiam sic te imitando indicant creatorem te esse omnis naturæ;
et ideo non esse quò à te omni modo recedatur. Quid ergo in illo
furto ego dilexi: et in quo Dominum meum vel vitiosè atque perversè
imitatus sum? An libuit facere contra legem saltem fallaciâ, quia
potentatu non poteram, ut mancam libertatem captivus imitarer faci-
endo impunè quod non liceret, TENEBROSA OMNIPOTENTIÆ SIMILI-
TUDINE. Ecce est ille servus fugiens Dominum suum, et consecutus
umbram. O putredo, O monstrum vitæ, et mortis profunditas.
Potuitne libere quod non licebat, non ob aliud, nisi quia non licebat."
S. Augus. Confes. liber ii. 14.

Line 235. *Who, if prolific as foretold, shall fill, &c.*
Gen. iii. 15. Matt. iii. 7. John viii. 44. 1 John iii. 8.

Lines 354—356.
See Paradise Lost, Book iv., lines 323, 324.

Line 438. *Then first I saw, then spake I.*

See Paradise Lost, Book ix., lines 549—732. Whether Milton
was the first to suggest that the serpent ascribed its own power of
speech to the virtue of the fruit of the forbidden tree, I know not.
But when once suggested, the thought appears so natural and necessary that any other method of approach would seem constrained
and unlikely.

Lines 506—525.
See Paradise Lost, Book ix., lines 900—916.

Lines 538—547.
See Paradise Lost, Book ix., lines 163—171.

Line 601. *First altar, and first holocausts.*
"It is extremely probable that some beasts, sacrificed by Divine appointment, furnished the skins with which Adam and Eve were clothed." Scott.

Line 626. *The mercy-seat.*
The cherubim are always represented in Holy Writ as in immediate attendance on the Divine Majesty when God stoops to communion with his creatures, or succors them in their hour of need. Thus the flaming sword appears symbolic of the Divine justice, and the cherubim of the Divine mercy. See this subject ably discussed in Duns' Biblical Natural Science, who states in confirmation of his own view, "The most eminent expositions left in the world, which are the two Jewish Targums, paraphrase the verse thus, 'And He thrust out the man, and caused the glory of His presence to dwell of old, at the East of the garden of Eden, above the two cherubim.'" Vol. i., p. 146.

Line 651. *Myriads have fall'n : myriads twice told are firm.*
"And his (the dragon's) tail drew a third part of the stars of heaven, and did cast them to the earth." Rev. xii. 4. This Scripture, though as I believe describing events subsequent to our Lord's ascension, may afford some clew to the relative numbers of the elect and fallen angels. Compare Paradise Lost, Book v., line 710.

Lines 682—694.
Compare Job ii. 3.

Line 707. *Patient because Eternal.*
Æternus est, tardat, longanimis est. S. Aug. in Ps. xcl. 6.

Lines 719—730.
Compare Dan. x. 13. 20. 2 Pet. ii. 11. Jude 9.

Line 781. *Clasp'd as the promised Seed.*
"Some render the words I have gotten a man from the LORD (Gen. iv. 1), I have gotten a man, the LORD." This sense is grammatically the most natural one. Eve may have supposed that the promise (Gen. iii. 15) was now fulfilled." Wordsworth.

Lines 790—797.
Compare Gen. v. 24 with Jude 14, 15.

Lines 807—817. *Uziel and Samchasai his mate.*

These were the traditional names of the angels who fell and inter-married with the daughters of men (Targum Jonathan). See Gen. vi. 1—4. The judgment of the Jewish Church and of the most an-cient fathers was express, that by "the sons of God," there named, angels were intended. Thus Josephus writes, "For many angels of God accompanied with women, and begat sons that proved unjust, and despisers of all that was good, on account of the confidence they had in their own strength." To which statement Whiston appends the note, "This notion, that the fallen angels were in some sense the fathers of the old giants, was the constant opinion of antiquity." And such, as Wordsworth, who is not himself of this opinion, says, was the view of Justin Martyr, Tertullian, Irenæus, Athenagoras, Cyprian, and others. Since their time the current of interpretation has set in the opposite direction, and these "sons of God" have been held to be the godly descendants of Seth. But of these judgments, I am persuaded the old was better.

In the first place, sons of God was then a distinctive name for angels. See Job i. 6; ii. 1; xxxviii. 7. The last is most emphatic, for it states that at the creation, when men were not, "All the sons of God shouted for joy." Secondly, in the passage itself the contrast is marked and express betwixt the spiritual nature of the sons of God and the complex nature of those with whom they mingled in unholy wedlock. Thirdly, it is to this lapse of angels that in all probability both St. Peter and St. Jude refer. The former writes, "God spared not angels (ἀγγέλων, there is no article) that sinned, but having cast them into hell, delivered them to chains of darkness, reserved unto judgment" (2 Pet. ii. 4). The latter, "And angels (again there is no article, — angels, not men only), those who kept not their own prin-cipality (ἀρχήν), but left their proper habitation, He hath kept under darkness with everlasting chains unto the judgment of the great day" (Jude 6).

Other Scriptures, which speak of evil angels as having still free range over our fallen world (Job i. 7. 1 Kings xxii. 21. Zech. iii. 1. Matt. iv. 8. Mark v. 9. Eph. ii. 2; vi. 12. Rev. xii. 9—12), pre-clude our referring the words of St. Peter and St. Jude, quoted above, to all the angels who have fallen from their allegiance. And it seems most probable that the allusion is to Gen. vi. 1—4; for St. Jude pro-ceeds to refer to Sodom and Gomorrah. Of which cities he says that they "in like manner to these (τούτοις, i.e. these angels) having given themselves over to fornication, and having gone after strange flesh, undergo the vengeance of eternal fire." The angels that fell debased their high original by commingling with the daughters of men: the inhabitants of Sodom not only lived in unnatural crimes (Rom. i. 27), but burned in their lust towards the celestial visitants who came under the shadow of Lot's roof. The rebel angels were cast down to Tartarus. The cities of the plain were overwhelmed with fire and brimstone, an awful type of the doom of their inhabitants. Thus like sin was visited with like indignation.

Faber, in his Many Mansions, speaks very contemptuously of this view, as "sundry strange incongruous fables," and says, "such idle tales the masculine mind of Milton rejected as forming no meet sub-ject for poetry to any one who reverenced the Scriptures: he (Milton) rightly views the Mosaic *sons of God* as *men*, the once grave and holy posterity of Seth. See Paradise Lost, xi. 556—627." Be it so: but what were Milton's later and more matured thoughts, as expressed in Paradise Regained (Book ii., lines 178—181)?

> " Before the flood, thou [Belial] and thy lusty crew,
> False titled sons of God, roaming the earth,
> Cast wanton eyes on the daughters of men,
> And coupled with them, and begot a race," &c.

Milton's masculine mind, therefore, veered to the view here advo-cated, which can however only be decided by the general analogy of Scripture, and this seems to me decisive in its favor. See Birks' Difficulties of Belief, p. 95; and the question argued under "Giants." Smith's Dictionary of the Bible.

Line 886. *Grieved within His heart*, &c.

See Gen. vi. 6.

Lines 900—920.

See note on Book i., line 671: to which I would only add a few words from Wordsworth's Commentary, who writes on Gen. vii. 21, "We may well believe that, as the flood increased very gradually, many may have repented who were not able to reach the ark; and the Holy Scriptures reveal to us that the death of Christ and His descent into the place of departed spirits were not without benefit to them." And again on 1 Pet. iii. 20, "St. Peter says that the rest disobeyed while the ark was preparing. He uses the aorist tense, ἀπειθήσασι. He does not say that when the ark *had been prepared*, and when the ark was *shut*, and when the flood came, and it was too late for them to reach it, they all remained impenitent. Perhaps some were penitent at the eleventh hour, like the thief on the cross."

BOOK VI.

Gen. iv. 26.   Line 45. *Some obscure suppliants.*

Lines 96—118, and 160—179. *Baalim* and *Ashtaroth.*
" Ashtoreth was the principal female deity of the Phœnicians, as Baal was the principal male deity. It is a peculiarity of both names that they frequently occur in the plural, and are associated together in this form (Judg. x. 6. 1 Sam. vii. 4; xii. 10). Gesenius maintained that by these plurals were to be understood statues of Baal and Astarte; but the more correct view seems to be that of Movers, that the plurals are used to indicate different modifications of the divinities themselves. In the earlier books of the Old Testament only the plural Ashtaroth occurs, and it is not till the time of Solomon, who introduced the worship of the Sidonian Astarte, and only in reference to that particular goddess Ashtoreth of the Sidonians that the singular is found in the Old Testament (1 Kings xi. 5. 33. 2 Kings xxiii. 13)." Smith's Dictionary of the Bible, under Ashtoreth. My suggestion explains the plural form as in the parallel case of the holy cherubim and seraphim, described indifferently in the singular or plural number (Ps. xviii. 10; lxxx. 1. Ezek. x. 15, 20,) — whose association, however, is not represented as precluding distinct and separate action (Isa. vi. 6. Rev. xv. 7).

Lines 100—106.
See Herschel's Outlines of Astronomy, Sec. 833—851.

Lines 119—139.
See Gen. xi. 1—9.

Line 141. *Apollyon.*
See Rev. ix. 11.

Line 151. *Ourselves o'er them presiding.*
Dan. x. 13. 20.

Line 171. *Mylitta call'd.*
" Among the groups of winged figures was a curious representation of the Assyrian Venus, Mylitta or Astarte, in an indecent posture, which indicated the peculiar nature of her worship." Layard's Nineveh, Vol., ii. p. 7.

Lines 215—219.
See Prov. vii. 26. 27.

Lines 233—263.

See Paradise Lost, Book i., lines 678—688.

Line 265. *Moloch.*

This fire-god was the tutelary deity of the children of Ammon: see 1 Kings xi. 7. And it is of this god Moses writes " Thou shalt not let any of thy seed pass through the fire to Molech " (Lev. xviii. 21).

Line 381. *O subtle Sammael.*

Sammael (*blindness*, or *ignorance of God*), the angel of death (Targum Jonathan).

Lines 420—424.

See Ps. ii. 4; xxxvii. 13. Prov. i. 26.

Lines 464—474.

In symbol of the great leviathan,
The dragon, &c.

Compare the words of the prophet, " O arm of the Lord, awake, as in the ancient days, in the generations of old. Art thou not it that hath cut Rahab (Egypt), and wounded the dragon? Art thou not it which hath dried the sea, the waters of the great deep; that hath made the depths of the sea a way for the ransomed to pass over? " (Isa. li. 9, 10) with the earlier prediction of a still future triumph, " In that day the Lord with His sore and great and strong sword shall punish leviathan, the piercing serpent, even leviathan, that crooked serpent; and He shall slay the dragon that is in the sea " (Isa. xxvii. 1); and with the description of leviathan, " He beholdeth all high things: he is a king over all the children of pride " (Job xli. 34).

Line 483. *Twice ten thousand chariots.*
Ps. lxviii. 17.

Line 502. *Moloch's shrine and Remphan's star.*
Acts vii. 43.

Line 521. *Gaunt altars rose, &c.*
1 Kings xi. 7.

Line 562. *And slept.*

This may be inferred from " the secret being revealed in a night vision " (Dan. ii. 19).

Line 608. *Chaldea's monarch, brooding o'er his dream.*

It seems probable that the image of gold which Nebuchadnezzar set up in the plain of Dura was a perversion of his dream; and possible that the furnace, into which the three children were cast, was that in which the metal had been fused for the gigantic idol.

Line 640. *Descending with the speed of seraphim.*

" Whiles I was speaking in prayer, the man Gabriel, . . . being caused to fly swiftly, touched me," &c. (Dan. ix. 21.) These words appear to prove that intervals of space, however swiftly traversed, are not annihilated for angels.

Lines 644—650.

See Dan. x. xi. xii.

BOOK VII.

Line 23. *Of Jacob's dream.*
Gen. xxviii. 10—22.

Line 25. *Funereal rites on Pisgah's brow.*
Compare Deut. xxxiv. 6 with Jude 9.

Line 27. *Of that Arch-fiend,* &c.
Job. i. 6, and ii. 1.

Line 32. *Of David moved by him,* &c.
1 Chron. xxi. 1.

Line 33. *Of the strife on Carmel,* &c.
1 Kings xviii. 19—40.

Line 36. *Of the car, that fiery car,* &c.
2 Kings ii. 11.

Line 40. *Of that false emissary,* &c.
1 Kings xxii. 21.

Line 42. *Of Joshua, son of Josedech,* &c.
Zech. iii. 1.

Line 62. *Watchman, what of the night ?*
Isa. xxi. 11.

Line 94. *Finding the rigid interdict relax'd,* &c.

" That whole period was the hour and power of darkness, of a darkness, which then immediately before the dawn of a new day was the thickest. . . . . It was exactly the period for such soul-maladies as these [demoniacal possessions], in which the spiritual and the bodily should be thus strangely interlinked, and it is nothing wonderful that they should have abounded then: for the predominance of certain spiritual maladies at certain epochs of the world's history, which were especially fitted for their generation, with their gradual decline and disappearance in others less congenial to them, is a fact itself admitting no manner of question." Trench on Miracles, p 162.

Line 113. *A heavenly cohort arm'd,* &c.

" And suddenly there was with the angel a multitude of the heavenly host " (στρατιᾶς, "army ") (Luke ii. 13). In the word "army " we may discern an intimation that this hour was not without peril from the hosts of darkness, who we know crowded in their malignity round the death of the Saviour (Luke xxii. 53), and would doubtless have gladly disturbed His birth.

Line 133. *Took of the lamps,* &c.

The words of St. Matthew, " And lo, the star which they saw in the East went before them till it came and stood over where the young child was " (Matt. ii. 9.), seem to decide that this miraculous appearance was some luminous meteor, like a star, which was not so distant, but that it seemed to move, and thus beckon the wise men to follow its leading. If so, it was probably through angelic agency.

Line 150. *Mary kept her secret close.*
Luke ii. 19.

Line 153. *His brethren, for they err,* &c.

In Matt. xiii. 55, 56 we read, " Is not this the carpenter's son? is not His mother called Mary? and His brethren, James, and Joses, and Simon, and Judas? and His sisters, are not they all with us?" Many have sought to prove that by the brethren and sisters here named *cousins* are intended: but the simplest and fairest interpretation is, that they were the younger brothers and sisters of our Lord, the children of Mary and Joseph after the birth of Christ. They are mentioned after the marriage in Cana as going down with *His mother* to Capernaum (John ii. 12). They came *with His mother* to speak with Him (Matt. xii. 46. Mark iii. 31. Luke viii. 19). The only place in the Gospels where they are spoken of without Mary, is John vii. 3—10; but there it is added, " they did not believe on Him," which could not be said of her. And, when next we read of them, it is again with His mother (Acts i. 14). Such is the witness of the New Testament; and there is a verse in the Old Testament (Ps. lxix. 8) which is strongly corroborative of this view. It is eminently a Messianic Psalm. And here we find not only " I am become a stranger unto *my brethren,*" which might admit of a wider interpre-

27

tation, but also, "and an alien unto *my mother's children*," which
allows of but one meaning. The virginity of Mary before the birth
of Christ is a great truth taught us by God Himself: her perpetual
virginity afterwards is, I believe, a fiction of man, without any war-
rant of Holy Scripture. See Alford's note on Matt. xiii. 55.

Line 177. *Their father sank.*

It seems almost certain from Joseph appearing in no incident of
our Lord's public ministry, that he had died previously.

Line 264. *Eastward towards the wilds of Araby.*

That the scene of the temptation was not the region between Jerusalem and Jericho, but the wilderness of Arabia, appears probable
from the incident mentioned by St. Mark, that our Lord " was with
the wild beasts;" and from the typical histories of Israel, Moses, and
Elijah. See Wordsworth's note on Mark i. 13.

Line 345. *For on these very rocks, &c.*
Deut. viii. 8.

Line 352. *The dizzy porch, &c.*

"The most probable opinion is that 'the pinnacle of the temple '
was the topmost ridge of the στοὰ βασιλική, on the south side of the
temple." Ellicott.

Line 413. *To me committed, &c.*
See note on Book iv., line 949.

Line 534. *The crest of snowy Hermon.*

" Standing amid the ruins of Cæsarea, one does not need to ask
where the Mount of Transfiguration is. Hermon, the grandest and
most beautiful of all the mountains of Palestine, has established its
claim to the title of THE HOLY MOUNT." (The Giant Cities of
Bashan, p. 103.) Hermon's perennial snows may have suggested the
words of the Evangelist, " His raiment became shining, exceeding
white as snow " (Mark ix. 3). The traditional mountain, Tabor,
was at that time probably crowned with a castle, and therefore
almost certainly not the site.

Line 543. *Brought them, one bodiless, embodied one.*
See note on Book ii., line 1002.

Lines 574—590.
Luke x. 17—20.

Line 592. *The lonely Ephraim.*
John xi. 54.

Line 595. *Whose disembodied spirit we sometime kept.*

The words "Christ is risen from the dead, the firstfruits of them that slept" (1 Cor. xv. 20), seem to indicate that although others had been raised from the dead before the resurrection of our Lord (1 Kings xvii. 22. 2 Kings iv. 35; xiii. 21. Matt. ix. 25. Luke vii. 15. John xi. 44), His human spirit was the first which repassed the gates of Death, and re-ascended from Hades to earth. Hitherto *vestigia nulla retrorsum.*

Line 606. *The ride of lowly triumph,* &c.
Luke xix. 28—44.

Line 612. *The lonely curse.*
Matt. xxi. 19.

Lines 619—628.
John xii. 20—33.

Line 630. *He made the widow's heart,* &c.
Mark xii. 41—44, and xiii. 1.

Line 631. *As once Ezekiel saw,* &c.
Ezek. x. 4. 19, and xi. 23.

Lines 650—659.
John xiii. 1—17.

Line 674. *Now readily assumed the ready throne.*
Luke xxii. 3. John xiii. 2. 27.

Lines 678—692.
John xvii. 1—26.

Lines 822—837.

"Having spoiled (ἀπεκδυσάμενος, *having stripped away from Himself*) the (hostile) principalities and powers, He made a show of them with boldness, having triumphed over them in it (i.e. in the cross)" (Col. ii. 15). "The expression *having stripped away from Himself* most probably implies that our Lord by His death stripped away from Himself all the opposing hostile powers of evil that sought, in the nature which He had condescended to assume, to win for themselves a victory." Ellicott.

Lines 838—859.

See note on Book i., line 671. (1) That our Lord in His disembodied human spirit descended to the Hades of departed souls seems demonstrable from the words of David, "Thou wilt not leave my soul in hell" (Ps. xvi. 10), as expounded of Christ by St. Peter (Acts

ii. 27. 31). See Pearson on the Creed. (2) That He visited the deep, not Gehenna, but that region of Hades, on the nether side of the great gulf (Luke xvi. 23), in which the lost await the judgment of the great day, appears most probable from such Scriptures as the following: " Let not the waterflood overwhelm me, neither let the deep swallow me up, and let not the pit shut her mouth upon me " (Ps. lxix. 15): and again, " Free among the dead, ... they are cut off from Thy hand: Thou hast laid me in the lowest pit, in darkness and in the deeps " (Ps. lxxxviii. 4—7): see also Ps. xviii. 5— 15, quoted below: and from the significant type of Jonah, who was cast into the deep before he was swallowed by the great fish. (3) That he gained the region of the Blessed Dead in Hades, betwixt the ninth hour, when He yielded up the Ghost, and the close of that Jewish day three hours after, may be regarded as certain from His words to the dying thief, " To-day shalt thou be with Me in Paradise " (Luke xxiii. 43). Thus while His atoning sacrifice was completed for ever on Calvary, it appears that His self-abasement was not ended on the cross, nor indeed until His resurrection.

Lines 860—901.

The Eighteenth Psalm seems expressed in language too majestic and august to bear the burden of a less mystery than that of the death and resurrection of David's Son and David's Lord. The close of the Psalm is quoted by St. Paul (Rom. xv. 9), as fulfilled in Christ: and this appears to justify a similar application of the magnificent proem.

Line 914. *He came not to the dead,* &c.

All the Scriptures which bear upon our Lord's going down to Hades, such as Ps. xvi. 9—11. Eph. iv. 9. 1 Pet. iii. 18, 19, represent it as an unprecedented act of Redeeming love and condescension. Nor are there wanting intimations in the Word of God that the accomplishment of Christ's work on earth was a mighty promotion in the bliss of those saints who had already fallen asleep in Him. Then and not till then, are they called " the spirits of just men made perfect " (Heb. xii. 23). See Alford on Heb. xi. 40, who comparing the two verses says, " The writer seems to testify that the advent and work of Christ have changed the estate of the Old Testament fathers and saints into greater and perfect bliss, an inference which is forced on us by many other passages in Scripture." Indeed it could hardly be otherwise, when we remember that the mystical body of Christ is one whole family in heaven and earth (Eph. iii. 15).

Lines 929—937.

See notes on Book i., line 671, and Book v., lines 900—920.

Lines 1066—1086.

Ps. xxiv.

Line 1097. *Advancing with His precious blood.*

Heb. ix. 12.

Lines 1099—1105.

See Eph. i. 20, 21.

Line 1111. *Cleansed with the virtue of His blood those courts,* &c.

Compare "It pleased the Father that in Him should all fulness dwell and, having made peace by the blood of His cross, by Him to reconcile all things unto Himself; by Him, I say, whether they be things in earth, or THINGS IN HEAVEN (Col. i. 19, 20), with "It was necessary that the patterns of things in the heavens should be purified with these; but THE HEAVENLY THINGS THEMSELVES with better sacrifices than these " (Heb. ix. 23). On these passages I venture to refer the reader to my Commentary on the New Testament.

BOOK VIII.

Line 49. *Jehovah is a man of war.*

Exod. xv. 3.

Line 54. *The Sevenfold Spirit.*

Rev. iv. 5.

Line 80. *Scatter'd for a week of years.*

See note on Book vii. 822—837. The discomfiture of the hosts of darkness by the death and resurrection of Christ, synchronizing with the Pentecostal effusion of the Spirit, may afford another clew to the marvellous triumphs of the Gospel betwixt the ascension of our Lord, and the martyrdom of St. Stephen (Acts ii. 46, 47, and vi. 7).

Line 108. *As foreshadow'd,* &c.

See John xii. 32.

Line 163. *The Great High Priest of God.*

Can this sacerdotal office explain why our Lord is here represented as *standing* at God's right hand? (Acts vii. 55.)

Line 172. *For nine long months of years.*
See below, note on lines 270—287.

Lines 185—202.

For the historical interpretation of these symbolic horses, I must refer the reader to Elliott's Horæ Apocalypticæ, of which I have given a brief resumé in my Commentary. I here only add my opening words : —

" As the four successive empires of Babylon, Persia, Greece, and Rome were prefigured in vision to the prophet Daniel by the emblems of a lion, a bear, a leopard, and a fourth beast, dreadful and strong exceedingly, and as in another vision the kingdoms of Persia and of Greece had been respectively foretold by the symbols of a ram and a goat, so here the Roman empire is depicted under the emblem of a war-horse, an animal sacred to Mars, the reputed father of their nation, and as such emblazoned on their coins and standards. The compound symbol of the horse and its rider signifies the empire and its imperial government. This was the great antagonistic power to Christ and His kingdom in the apostle's days. And as in this prophecy we have two cities set before us in vivid contrast — Babylon and Jerusalem; two women — one the mother of harlots, the other the Bride, the Lamb's wife; two armies — those of hell and of heaven; two thrones — that of Satan and that of God, so at the close we read of another white horse and its rider, the true King of kings and Lord of lords. But here, as is evident, whatever this composite emblem signifies under the first seal, it must signify under the second, third, and fourth."

Line 226. *Perpetua.*

See Milner's Church History, Vol. i., pp. 304—309.

Lines 253—259.

The historical fulfilment of the fifth seal (Rev. vi. 9–11) is doubtless to be found in those fierce and sanguinary persecutions of the Church of Christ, which, breaking out from time to time during the first three centuries, reached their terrible climax in the reign of Diocletian. It was the last convulsive effort of heathendom to crush Christianity. For ten dreadful years the waves of fiery trial rolled successively over the provinces of the Roman empire. Every province yielded its contingent to the noble army of witnesses for the truth. And this period is distinguished in history as " the era of martyrs."

Lines 260—269.

The sixth seal (Rev. vi. 12—17) prefigures, as I believe, the overthrow of Paganism throughout the Roman Empire at the time of Constantine. That the figurative language employed is not too strong to foreshadow that mighty revolution, will appear from comparing with it the emblematic prefigurements in Scripture of other national catastrophes. See Isa. xiii. 9—13　Jer. iv. 23.　Ezek. xxxii. 7

Lines 270—287.

On the significance of the mystic Bride, and of the dragon (Rev xii. 1—6), I venture to make the following extracts from my Commentary: —

"*And there appeared a great wonder in heaven* — the Roman firmament of political power and ascendancy — *a woman clothed with the sun, &c.* This woman, who is spoken of as the mother of ' those who keep the commandments of God' (ver. 17), is without doubt the true visible Church of Christ on earth. Her clothing with the sun imports her investiture with imperial favor; the moon, which, as the faithful witness in heaven (Ps. lxxxix. 37), reflects the light of the sun, being under her feet, signifies her ecclesiastical supremacy in a Christian empire: her coronal of twelve stars may well represent her glory as upholding a faithful pastorate, the pastorate of those who cleave to the doctrine of the twelve apostles; and her pregnancy and travail denote a period of oppression and agony before a crisis of deliverance, and fruitfulness, and joy. So it is said of Jerusalem, 'Before she travailed she brought forth; before her pain came she was delivered of a man child. . . . Shall a nation be born at once?' (Isa. lxvi. 7, 8. Cf. Mic. v. 3.)

"Such was the state of the Church when the Emperor Constantine first embraced the faith of Christ, and threw over her the mantle of his imperial protection. Purified in the furnace of the Diocletian persecution, 'she looked forth as the morning, fair as the moon, clear as the sun, and terrible as an army with banners' (Song vi. 10). Moreover, it has been observed that 'as the time of gestation from the conception to the birth in women with child is known to be forty weeks, or two hundred and eighty days, so, from the first rise of our Saviour's kingdom, at His resurrection and ascension, A.D. 33, till the famous edict for the universal liberty and advancement of Christianity by Constantine and Licinius, A.D. 313, which put an end to the pangs of birth in the heaviest persecution that ever was then known, was exactly two hundred and eighty years.' Whiston.

"*And there appeared another wonder in heaven* — i.e., as before, in the firmament of the Roman empire — *and behold a great dragon, fiery red, &c.* The great dragon is the devil (see ver. 9), the god of this world. In the Old Testament the power of Egypt, as the enemy

of God and of His Church, is thus described (Isa. xxvii. 1; li. 9.
Ezek. xxix. 8). But here the devil is represented as animating the
pagan empire of Rome; for the seven heads of the dragon signify
the seven hills on which Rome was built, and the seven forms of
government which successively prevailed there. (See Rev. xvii.
9—18.) The ten horns denote the ten kingdoms into which the
western empire was at length divided (Dan. vii. 23—27), which had
as yet received no sovereignty."

In the rapture of the woman's new-born child to God and His
throne, we may not only trace the political ascendancy of Christianity, but, followed as it is by her own flight into the wilderness for
1260 years, we are reminded that during the time of the Church's
warfare, her kingdom is not of this world.

Lines 292—594.

The following extract will show the terrestrial meaning I attach to
the celestial warfare described Rev. xii. 7—12. One thing only I
would add, that if, as I humbly conceive, there has been a real counterpart to the conflicts of the Church militant here on earth in the
heavenly places themselves, such war, I am persuaded, took place,
not as our great poet describes it, before the creation of man, but after
the ascension of our Lord.

"*And there was war in heaven, &c.* This war in the firmament of
the Roman empire seems to embrace all the conflicts between heathenism and Christianity for political ascendancy, A.D. 311—363, from
Constantine's first avowal of the faith of Christ to the death of Julian
the apostate. How far the hosts of darkness and the angels of light
intermingled in these conflicts is one of those deep mysteries upon
which the light of Scripture shines but dimly. We know that St.
Paul, describing the daily warfare of the saints, says, 'We wrestle
not against flesh and blood, but against principalities, against powers, against the rulers of the darkness of this world, against spiritual
wickedness in the heavenly places' (Eph. vi. 12). We know that
when Elisha was in danger, 'the mountain was full of horses and
chariots of fire round about him' (2 Kings vi. 17). Nor, if such are
the foes and such the guardian spirits of every servant of God, is it
unlikely that the eventful contest on the Roman earth had its counterpart in a yet more terrible struggle betwixt the armies of the
archangel Michael and the legions of the prince of the power of
the air (Eph. ii 2). This is confirmed by Dan. x. 13. 21; xii. 1, and
Jude 9. But, deeply interesting as are these glimpses into the world
of spirits, the terrestrial conflict betwixt Paganism and Christianity

seems mainly prefigured in this symbolic language. The warfare was long and sharp, but it ended in the total defeat of heathenism, and in the deposing of idolaters from all rule and authority. They never regained their supremacy. The saints of God thought indeed that the predicted triumph of Messiah's kingdom had arrived. The end was not yet. But it was in itself a true and glorious victory, and the pæans of the Church on earth were re-echoed by the loftier halle-lujahs of exulting angels and of the spirits of the just made perfect in heaven. They saw therein a pledge of the final dethronement of Satan. They rejoiced that he could no longer prefer his ceaseless and bitter accusations, as of old. They ascribed all the victory to the blood of the Lamb, and to the word of the martyrs' testimony. They called on all the inhabitants of heaven to swell the tide of gratitude and joy. While a deeper note of warning, perhaps issuing from the throne of God, predicted the yet bitterer and more deadly wrath of the ejected spirit of evil, during the short time of his permitted devas-tations. The time might seem long to the weary and waiting Church, but it was short as recorded in the annals of heaven, and in prospect of the eternity to come."

Line 597. *A strange refrain of woe.*
See Rev. xii. 12.

Line 659. *First let us loose, &c.*
Rev. xii. 15.

Line 670. *Now let us counterfeit Himself, Triune.*

Such a threefold conspiracy, the master-piece of hell, is described in the Apocalypse, where St. John says, "I saw a wild beast rising up out of the sea, having seven heads and ten horns, . . . and upon his heads the name of blasphemy: . . . and the dragon gave him his power, and his throne, and great authority. . . . And I saw another wild beast coming up out of the earth, and he had two horns like a lamb, and he spake as a dragon, and he exerciseth all the power of the first beast in his presence (ἐνώπιον αὐτοῦ), and causeth the earth and them that dwell therein to worship the first beast" (Rev. xiii. 1, 2. 11, 12). Here the dragon, as appears from ch. xii. 3, represents Pagan Rome; the first wild beast, Rome Papal; the second wild beast, who is described as "the false prophet who wrought miracles in the beast's presence" (ch. xix. 20), the Papal hierarchy. The Paganism of ancient Rome was merged in the great Antichristian apostasy, and this was supported to the utmost by the hierarchy of that corrupt Church.

But not only did the dragon represent the persecuting power of

Pagan Rome, but we are expressly told that the dragon is "that old serpent, called the devil and Satan " (Rev. xii. 9). There was a spiritual agent animating Paganism, none other than the prince of hell. Hence by analogy we may infer there was another spiritual agent animating Papal Rome, to whom the dragon tendered his power, and yet a third spiritual agent animating the Papal hierarchy. Such an hypothesis is strongly confirmed by the intense personality which breathes in the words " These both (the beast and the false prophet) were cast alive into a lake of fire burning with brimstone " (Rev. xix. 20; and see xx. 10). Such an association of evil spirits is not without parallel, as appears from the words of our Lord (Matt. xii. 43—45), and might be well anticipated from the malignity of the powers of darkness in their last conspiracies against the truth.

Line 712. *His well-beloved, by us betray'd, debauch'd.*

For proof that the woman upon whose forehead was a name written " MYSTERY, BABYLON THE GREAT, THE MOTHER OF HARLOTS AND ABOMINATIONS OF THE EARTH " (Rev. xvii. 5) is none other than the Papal Church, I would refer the reader to Archdeacon Wordsworth's masterly essay " Is not the Church of Rome the Babylon of the Apocalypse? " an essay which is in my view altogether unanswerable.

Line 743. *The bride is hidden in the wilderness.*
Rev. xii. 6 and 14.

Lines 751—793.

See Rev. vi. and vii.; which I believe embrace the history of the fourth, fifth, and sixth centuries.

Line 797. *Baalim, heal'd of his wound,* &c.

See Rev. xiii. 1, and xvii. 8, where we read, " The beast that thou sawest was and is not; and shall ascend out of the bottomless pit, and shall go into perdition: and they that dwell on the earth shall wonder, whose names are not written in the book of life from the foundation of the world, when they behold the beast that was, and is not, and yet is." The beast as an imperial Pagan power was slain by the sword of Constantine, but yet ascends out of the abyss, as popery, born of hell, ascended to reanimate the sinking empire of Rome, and shall go into perdition when its destined reign of 1260 years is finished. This is an infernal counterfeit of the resurrection of the Lord of life.

Lines 830—852.

See Rev. ix., which by a marvellous consensus of interpreters is allowed to describe the rise and progress of Mohammedanism. Almost simultaneously at the beginning of the seventh century, Popery in the West, and the religion of the false prophet in the East, arose to try to the uttermost the faith of God's elect.

Line 889. *Lo, from the heavens descended One,* &c.
See Rev. x. 1—7, which describes the blessed Reformation.

Line 914. *According to His word.*
Matt. x. 23.

Lines 933—954.

Rev. xv. and xvi., which I believe delineate those preparative judgments of the last and present century, that usher in the Advent of the Prince of Peace.

Line 979. *As he had open'd things unknown by me,* &c.
See Paradise Lost, Book viii. 203—205.

Line 1019. *The first portends our tryst.*
See Num. x. 1—10.

BOOK IX.

Line 67. *Not spouse, but what is symbolized by spouse*
The words of our Lord are express, " The children of this world marry and are given in marriage; but they which shall be accounted worthy to obtain that world, and the resurrection from the dead, neither marry nor are given in marriage; neither can they die any more; for they are equal unto the angels, and are the children of God, being the children of the resurrection " (Luke xx. 34—36), and for ever close the door against any theories of a Mohammedan Paradise.

Line 71. *A reflex glory' and image of myself.*
1 Cor. xi. 7.

Lines 120—148.

There are many intimations in Holy Scripture that the latest conflicts of the Church will be the worst, her last birth-pangs the most severe. (Isa. lix. 19, 20. Dan. xii. 1. Luke xviii. 8. Rom. viii. 19—22.)

Lines 156—205.

If the Paradise of the Blessed Dead is *below* (see note on Book i., line 671), it follows that there must be an ascent of the disembodied saints to earth before, at the voice of God, they are raised from the grave, and before their spirits, reunited to their glorified bodies, rise to meet the Lord in the air.

Lines 216—246.

See Ezek. i. 1—28. These lines are transferred, with some modifications, from my Seatonian Prize Poem "Ezekiel." The prophet's sublime vision of the chariot of Deity is the alone source from which any writer could venture to draw. See Milton's admirable paraphrase, Paradise Lost, Book vi., lines 746—766.

Line 298. *The Lord Himself descended with a shout.* See 1 Thess. iv. 16, 17.

Line 306. *The incandescent sky from East to West.* Matt. xxiv. 27.

Line 312. *Save on the hills of Zion,* &c. Compare Dan. x. 7, and Acts ix. 7.

Lines 367—391.

It appears that the fall of Babylon (Rev. xiv. 8; xvi. 19; xviii. 1— 24) takes place at the Advent of our Lord, when He comes *for His saints,* but that the destruction of the Papal Antichrist and the binding of Satan do not occur, however short the interval may be, until He returns, after the marriage supper, *with His saints.* See Rev. xix. 19—21; xx. 1, 2.

Lines 392—414.

See Zech. xii. 10—14; xiii. 1. Mal. iv. 5, 6. Although John Baptist came in the spirit and power of Elijah, our Lord's words are express that Elijah himself "shall come and restore all things" (Matt xvii. 11).

Lines 440—462.

Ezek. xvi. 1—14.

Line 472. *My love, my dove,* &c. Song of Solomon i. 15; ii. 16; iv. 7; v. 2.

Line 572. *The marriage supper of the Lamb.* Rev. xix. 9, and Luke xxii. 30.

Line 621. *Half a week of years.* There are many who think that the duration of Israel's last fiery trial will be for three years and a half, from Dan. ix. 27 and other Scriptures.

Lines 634—685.

Rev. xix. 11—16, and Ps. xlv. 2—17.

BOOK X.

Line 43. *There remains a Sabbath, &c.*

"There remaineth, therefore, a rest (σαββατισμός, " a sabbath rest ") for the people of God " (Heb. iv. 9).

Line 45. *But not, as many thought.*

So Cowper in his exquisite lines —

" Six thousand years of sorrow have well nigh
Fulfill'd their tardy and disastrous course
Over a sinful world; and what remains
Of this tempestuous state of human things
Is merely as the working of a sea
Before a calm, that rocks itself to rest."

Winter Walk at Noon.

Lines 59—108.

See Ezek. xxxviii. 1—16. Dan. xii. 1. Zech. xiv. 1—8.

Lines 106—110.

The last form of the abomination of desolation (Matt. xxiv. 15): the last usurpation of the Papal Antichrist who " exalteth himself above all that is called God, or that is worshipped; so that he as God sitteth in the temple of God, showing himself that he is God" (2 Thess. ii. 4): the last development of the mystery of iniquity, the triple conspiracy of hell (Rev. xix. 19). See note on Book viii., line 670.

Lines 121—133.

The solemn words of our Lord, " How can Satan cast out Satan? And if a kingdom be divided against itself, that kingdom cannot stand. And if a house be divided against itself, that house cannot stand. And if Satan rise up against himself, and be divided, he cannot stand, but hath an end " (Mark iii. 23—26), suggest that at the time of the end there will be such a dissolution of the conspiracy of hell, such a rupture in the empire of darkness, such a suicidal strife amid the principalities of evil.

Line 161. *Behind Elijah's mantle.*
See note, Book ix., lines 892—414.

Lines 163—182.
See Ps. l. 8. The last clause of Zech. xiv. 5. 2 Thess. i. 7—9 Rev. i. 7.

Lines 187—201.
" These both (the beast and the false prophet) were cast alive into a lake of fire burning with brimstone " (Rev. xix. 20).

Lines 201—215.
Rev. xx. 1—8.

Lines 219—247.
" For behold the Lord will come with fire and with His chariots like a whirlwind, to render His anger with fury, and His rebuke with flames of fire: for by fire and by His sword will the Lord plead with all flesh, and the slain of the Lord shall be many " (Isa. lxvi. 15, 16). This is parallel with Rev. xix. 21. On the discriminative character of this fiery judgment, see an earlier prophecy in the Apocalypse (Rev. xiv. 9—11).

Lines 248—259.
See Isa. xiv. 9—20.

Line 284. *His feet rested on Olivet.*
Zech. xiv. 4.

Lines 288—298.
Compare " When thou passest through the fire thou shalt not be burned, neither shall the flame kindle upon thee " (Isa. xliii. 2), with the remarkable words, "I have covered thee in the shadow of Mine hand, that I may plant the heavens, and lay the foundations of the earth, and say unto Zion, Thou art My people " (Isa. li. 16).

Line 307. *The mountain of the Lord had risen sublime.*
Isa. ii. 2. Micah iv. 1.

Line 308. *Olivet was cleft.*
Zech. xiv. 4.

Line 319. *A river of perennial waters flow'd.*
Ezek. xlvii. 1—12. Zech. xiv. 8.

Isa. lx. 1.
Line 336. Zion rose.

Line 338. Entering His temple courts.
Compare Ezek. xliii. 1—5.

Line 368. Words of grateful praise.
" And then shall every man have praise of God " (1 Cor. iv. 5)

Line 415. For full fruition of the light of God.
That the beatific vision of the face of the Eternal Father is possible
for created beings, if unfallen, appears from the words of our Lord
respecting the angelic guardians of the little ones who believe in
Him, " In heaven their angels do always behold the face of My Father
which is in heaven " (Matt. xviii. 10): but that this loftiest privilege
is not vouchsafed to the Church Universal until after the Millennium
and after the final judgment, may be perhaps inferred from the
reservation till then of this glorious promise in the Apocalypse,
" They shall see His face; and His name shall be in their foreheads "
(Rev. xxii. 4). If so, the Millennial Sabbath, as we might have surmised, will be in this respect also an education for that which is to
come.

Lines 418—438.
Ps. lxvii. 1, 2.   Isa. xxxii. 15; lii. 7.   Matt. xi. 11.

Lines 439—464.
Isa. xxxv. 1—10; xli. 18—20; lv. 12, 13.

Lines 465—489.
Isa. xi. 6—9; lxv. 25.

Lines 490—505.
Joel ii. 21—27.   Isa. xxx. 26.

Isa. ii. 4.
Line 505. War was unknown, &c.

Line 510. Babel's confusion was unlearn'd, &c.
Not only " In that day shall there be one Lord," but it is added
' And His name one " (Zech. xiv. 9). " Tongues shall cease " (1
Cor. xiii. 8).   One song arises from every creature on the earth
(Rev. v. 13).

See Ps. lxxii.   Isa. lx.
Line 514. No labor now was lost, &c.

Ezek. xxxvii. 25.
Line 520. David, vicegerent, &c.

Line 522. *The Twelve, &c.*
Matt. xix. 28.

Line 527. *A royalty of priests.*
Isa. lxi. 6.

Line 546. *Evil lurk'd unseen, &c.*
This appears from the remarkable prophecy which, describing the
Millennial state, says, "The child shall die an hundred years old,
but the sinner being an hundred years old shall be accursed" (Isa.
lxv. 20). Here we read of sin and curse and death; whereas, after
the Millennium and the judgment, death shall be destroyed, and there
shall be no more curse (Rev. xxi. 4 and xxii. 3).

Line 556. *Nor prophecy was mute.*
Rev. xx. 7.

Line 567. *Nor wounds though rare, &c.*
Ezek. xlvii. 12.

Line 585. *And angels up and down those radiant stairs, &c.*
Compare John i. 51 with Gen. xxviii. 12.

BOOK XI.

Lines 1—11.
"The Son of man shall send forth His angels, and they shall gather
out of His kingdom all things that offend and them which do iniquity,
and shall cast them into a furnace of fire: there shall be wailing and
gnashing of teeth" (Matt. xiii. 41, 42).

Line 19. *Oppressive silence, &c.*
"The wicked shall be silent in darkness" (1 Sam. ii. 9).

Line 25. *Silence but no sleep, &c.*
Isa. lvii. 21.   Rev. xiv. 11.

Line 41. *The Lord is righteous.*
Exod. ix. 27.

Line 80. *Shall we humbly sue, &c.*
See Paradise Lost, Book iv., lines 80—104.

Lines 148—157.
"That he should deceive the nations no more till the thousand

years should be fulfilled: and after that he must be loosed a little season " (Rev. xx. 3).

Lines 191—195.

" And when the thousand years are expired, Satan shall be loosed out of his prison, and shall go out to deceive the nations which are in the four quarters of the earth, Gog and Magog, to gather them together to battle: the r umber of whom is as the sand of the sea " (Rev. xx. 7, 8).

Lines 198, 199.

See Paradise Lost, Book x., lines 410—414.

Lines 206—215.

See Paradise Lost, Book ix., lines 58—68.

Line 220. *The sparse and rare remains of ill.*

See note, Book x., line 546.

Line 283. *Penuel.*

See Book iv., lines 456—469.

Lines 334—344.

See Isa. lxvi. 23, and Zech. xiv. 16.

Lines 432—458.

" And they went up on the breadth of the earth, and compassed the camp of the saints about, and the beloved city " (Rev. xx. 9).

Line 460. *Which shook the first fell council of the damn'd.*

See Book vi., lines 420—424.

Line 469. *The dreadful storm of fire, &c.*

" And fire came down from God out of heaven, and devoured them " (Rev. xx. 9).

Line 474. *A whisper ran, &c.*

See Exod. xiv. 25.

Lines 492—518.

" And Death and Hades delivered up the dead that were in them " (Rev. xx. 13). " All that are in the graves shall hear His voice, and shall come forth, they that have done good unto the resurrection of life, and they that have done evil unto the resurrection of damnation " (John v. 28, 29). From Rev. xx. 4, 5, we learn that a thousand years intervene betwixt the resurrection of the just and that of the unjust, although in the perspective of prophecy they are often presented simultaneously to our view.

28

Lines 519—539.

" And Death and Hades were cast into the lake of fire " (Rev. xx. 14). It is only of the Hades of the lost St. John is here speaking.

Lines 540—558.

See 2 Pet. iii. 7—10. That the camp of the saints and the beloved city will be exempted from this final fire, having been already purified at the beginning of the Millennium, seems clear from Rev. xx. 9 and Isa. li. 16.

Lines 559—594.

"And I saw a great white throne, and Him that sate on it, from whose face the earth and the heaven fled away, and there was found no place for them. And I saw the dead, small and great, stand before God: and the books were opened: and another book was opened, which is the book of life " (Rev. xx. 11, 12). And compare Dan. vii. 9, 10.

Lines 595—623.

Matt. xxv. 31—33. Rom. xiv. 10—12. 1 Cor. iv. 5. See also Matt. x. 42. 2 Cor. ix. 6. 2 Tim. iv. 8. Rev. xxii. 12.

Lines 637—645.

Matt. xxv. 34.

Lines 646—672.

" Do ye not know that the saints shall judge the world? " (1 Cor. vi. 2.)

Lines 673—705.

" Reserved unto judgment " (2 Pet. ii. 4). "Know ye not that we shall judge angels? " (1 Cor. vi. 3.)

Lines 706—745.

"It shall bruise thy head " (Gen. iii. 15). "And the devil that deceived them was cast into the lake of fire and brimstone, where the beast and the false prophet are " (Rev. xx. 10).

Lines 787—794.

Matt. xxvi. 24.

Lines 800—806.

See Book viii., lines 226—252.

Lines 832—840.

" They watch for your souls as they that must give account, that they may do it with joy, and not with grief: for that is unprofitable for you " (Heb. xiii. 17).

Lines 855—867.

Matt. xxv. 41. Rev. ii. 26, 27.

Lines 868—880.

"And these shall go away into everlasting punishment" (Matt. xxv. 46).

Line 881. *All shook except the Throne of Judgment.*

See Paradise Lost, Book vi., lines 831—834.

Line 890. *He was in tears.*

Compare Gen. vi. 6. Ezek. xviii. 32. Luke xix. 41—44.

Line 901. *And judgment is His strange and dreadful work.*

"That He may do His work, His strange work; and bring to pass His act, His strange act" (Isa. xxviii. 21).

Lines 909—919.

Rev. xiv. 10, 11, and xix. 3.

Lines 919—927.

Heb. x. 31; xii. 29.

Lines 928—957.

See note, Book iii., line 875. On this most solemn and awful theme, I would only add that Holy Scripture supplies us with the most express assurances that the powers of evil shall be for ever subjugated under the feet of the Son of God. His enemies shall be made His footstool (Ps. cx. 1). "He must reign till He hath put all enemies under His feet" (1 Cor. xv. 25). "For this purpose the Son of God was manifested, that He might destroy (λύσῃ) the works of the devil" (1 John iii. 8). These Scriptures stand inflexibly opposed to that mediæval tradition, which pictures devils tormenting men, and men blaspheming God for ever, and assure us of the eternal repression of every act of evil, and of the eternal silencing of every word of rebellion.

Lines 970—1020.

Nor is the repression of evil the only result of the Divine judgment which the Word of God reveals. It also declares that even the lost shall confess that Jesus Christ is Lord, to the glory of God the Father (Phil. ii. 9—11. Rev. v. 13). So of Pharaoh, the most signal example of obduracy which earth has seen, God says, "I will at this time send all My plagues upon thine heart . . . that thou mayest know that there is none like Me" (Exod. ix. 14): for a time Pharaoh did know and confess, "The Lord is righteous, and I and my people are wicked" (Exod. ix. 27): but the judgment being relaxed, he re-

belled again and again. In that future world of woe, the punishment
is ETERNAL (Matt. xxv. 46. 2 Thess. i. 9), and the enforced submission and confession will be eternal likewise. And then shall the
marvellous words of the Psalmist be acknowledged by all, "God
hath spoken once, twice have I heard this; that power belongeth
unto God: also unto Thee, O Lord, belongeth MERCY; for Thou
renderest to every man according to his work" (Ps. lxii. 11, 12)

BOOK XII.

Line 47. *The earth, emerging from her flood of fire*, &c

St. John says, " I saw a new heaven and a new earth; for the first
heaven and the first earth were passed away " (Rev. xxi. 1). Our first
impression from these words, which introduce the glories of the eternal
ages beyond the millennium, might be that the present heavens and
earth would be utterly brought to nought. Other scriptures, however, prove that not the annihilation, but the renovation of our world,
is here foretold. Thus the land of promise was given to Abraham
and his seed for an "everlasting possession" (Gen. xvii. 8). Zion,
we read, shall be "an eternal excellency" (Isa. lx. 15). Jesus
Christ "upon the throne of His father, David, will reign over the
house of Jacob for ever; and of His kingdom there shall be no end "
(Luke i. 33). God will " not un-create," but " re-create " that which
He has made for His glory. That the terms here used do not compel
us to interpret them as signifying " annihilation," appears from a
comparison of the language used by St. Peter in describing the deluge, "the world that then was perished " (2 Pet. iii. 6. 13), and from
the yet more striking parallel of the new birth of the soul to God
"If any man be in Christ, he is a new creature: old things are passed
away; behold all things are become new" (2 Cor. v. 17). The
world, though it "perished " in the deluge, was not annihilated; and
the soul, that is born of God, though renewed, does not lose its iden-
tity with its former self. This will be the perfected "regeneration,"
of which our Lord spoke (Matt. xix. 28). The renewal, which com-
mences at the second advent, and continues during the millennium,
will be consummated after the final judgment. The millennial
heavens and earth will be *new*, compared with those which are now
(see Isa. lxv. 17—25); but this renovation will only be completed in
those which are to last for ever and can never be shaken or removed.

Line 60. *Her late apparel was not found.*
Ps. cii. 25, 26.

Lines 65—75.
See Rev. xix. 8.

Lines 91—102.
See Isa. liv. 1—10. .

Lines 103—127.
" God is gone up with a shout, the LORD with the sound of a trumpet " (Ps. xlvii. 5).   See the whole of this exultant Psalm.

Line 128. *Before us now it rose, builded aloft, &c.*

The question has been keenly controverted whether the new Jerusalem (Rev. xxi. xxii.) is actually the abode of the heavenly citizens,
or only a representation of the Church Triumphant under the emblem
of a city.   The advocates of a purely symbolical meaning maintain,
" The bride is a city, and the city is a bride: both expressions are
therefore figures to describe the glorious community of ransomed
souls, the mystical body of Christ, and blessed company of all faithful
people."   But to this it may be sufficient to reply that, in the con-
trasted case of Babylon (Rev. xvii. 1—3, 18), the woman is a city,
and the city is a woman.   Both expressions are figures to denote the
apostate Papal Church.   But this does not prevent the existence of
the actual city of Rome, a material structure, which shall be consumed
with material fire.   The site and the buildings are, indeed, of very
secondary importance to the character of the harlot Church who
occupies them; for it is her faithlessness which gives them all their
disastrous significance.   But there they are, seven hills crowned with
edifices on the banks of the Tiber.   So of the new Jerusalem: the city,
it is true, is a type of a spiritual building compacted of living stones,
which is growing an holy temple unto the Lord (Eph. ii. 21).   But
this does not preclude the possibility of an actual fabric, composed of
heavenly material, which shall never be destroyed.   Here, too, the
site and the structure are of inferior moment to the virgin bride who
shall dwell therein; for it is her saintliness which gives all its significance to her palace home.   That home, however, exists, a glorious
reality, an abiding city yet to come — a city which hath foundations,
whose designer and builder is God. (See Heb. xi. 10. 16; xiii. 14,
which Scriptures strongly confirm this view.)   We are thus irresistibly led to the conclusion that the heavenly Jerusalem here described
is both real and typical — an actual city, of which every part typifies
the spiritual temple of living stones.   For as the glorified body will

be the worthy habitation of the perfectly regenerate spirit — a building of God, an house not made with hands, eternal in the heavens (2
Cor. v. 1) — so the celestial city will be the meet dwelling-place of
the saints for ever, and their spiritual characteristics will each and all
find a counterpart in that marvellous structure prepared for them by
their God. Hence it is by no means easy, nor perhaps is it always
desirable, to interpret the various details here given. They awaken
conceptions of delight which we cannot always define or describe.
But let us suffer those images of glory to float through our mind, and
to rest in our heart, until we exclaim —

> "Jerusalem! Jerusalem! would God I were in thee!
> When shall my labors have an end, thy joys when shall I see?"

And perchance this unveiling of the glories to come has accomplished
its chief intent: it has weaned us from earth; it has drawn us to
heaven.

Line 144. *The agate once Chalcedon's peerless boast.*
The chalcedony was a striped agate found at Chalcedon.

Lines 160—164.
See Heb. viii. 5; ix. 23, and the important words regarding Solomon's temple, which are often forgotten when those regarding the
Mosaic tabernacle are remembered, 1 Chron. xxviii. 11, 12. 19. Regarding the temple likewise we are there assured "the pattern of all
was BY THE SPIRIT," and was, we cannot doubt, only a more elab-
orate revelation of the heavenly sanctuary.

Line 166. *Some high watch among the lasting hills.*
Rev. xxi. 10.

Lines 168—189.
See Rev. iv. 1—11, and note on Book iv., lines 295—801.

Lines 194—236.
See note, Book x., line 415, and compare Col. i. 22 with Jude 24.

Lines 237—252.
Matt. xi. 27. Heb. i. 8. Rev. xix. 12.

Lines 253—269.
Ps. xcvii. 7, as unfolded Heb. i. 6. Eph. i. 20—22. Phil. ii.
9—11.

Lines 270—292.
In these lines I have attempted to express thoughts contained in
the following notes from my commentary on 1 Cor. xv. 24—28 —

"And then, when the whole creation is thus subjected to the Son, who is the Creator and Heir of all things, then shall the Son also Himself be manifestly subordinate, by His own willing and holy self-presentation of Himself and the ransomed universe to the Eternal Father. And so God will be all in all — not the Father without the Son, nor the Father and the Son without the co-eternal Spirit but Father, Son, and Spirit in the unity of the Godhead, being worshipped and adored by things in heaven, and things in earth, and things under the earth.

"Of this profound mystery, when in the future glory the clouds of sin and sorrow shall be for ever swept away, perhaps the experience of saints in their access to, and communion with, God on earth, may afford some faint adumbration. When in prayer they are most conscious of the struggle with unbelief and sin, how vividly they realize the mediatorship of the man Christ Jesus! they seem to come first to Jesus, and, through Him, they have access by One Spirit unto the Father. But when God in Christ lifts up the light of His countenance in clearest effulgence upon them, as they kneel at the footstool of the throne of grace, then it is often rather the Unity of Essence in the Godhead than the Trinity of Persons which fills and absorbs their souls; they are in the presence of Him who is Love; they dwell in God, and God in them. And at such an hour God to them is 'all in all.'"

Line 827. *His priestly abode within the House of God.*

Such appears to be the primary meaning of the words of our Lord, "In My Father's house are many mansions" (John xiv. 2); for He had already consecrated this name "My Father's house" to describe the temple at Jerusalem (John ii. 16). Heaven is thus revealed under the similitude of a temple, containing mansions for all the members of the royal priesthood.

Lines 858—868.

See Eph. iii. 10.

Lines 869—893.

"That in the ages to come He may show the exceeding riches of His grace in His kindness towards us through Christ Jesus" (Eph. ii. 7).

Lines 393—410.

St. Paul's words (1 Cor. xiii. 13) are express, "*And now*" (νυνὶ δέ, not referring to *time*, but to *reality*, "as the case really is,") "*abideth faith, hope, love.*" These three Divine graces are not like our imperfect knowledge, and imperfect utterance, which will vanish away.

These are imperishable and eternal. These abide for evermore. It is true that those things, which are now objects of faith and hope, will be objects of sight and of blessed fruition then; but to a finite being, however wide the expanse which is his own, there must ever be an infinite unknown beyond, and all that lies beyond the limit of his intuition will exercise faith and hope. These graces then *abide*. But love will ever have a supremacy over faith and hope, for it is the immediate reflection of Him who is love.

Lines 411—454.

Compare the prophetic Psalm, "I will declare Thy name unto My brethren: in the midst of the congregation will I praise Thee" (interpreted of our Lord, Heb. ii. 12): also His own words, "The time cometh when I shall no more speak unto you in parables; but I shall show you plainly of the Father" (John xvi. 25): and the apocalyptic vision of the white-robed multitudes whom no man could number, "who are before the throne of God, and serve Him day and night in His temple" (Rev. vii. 15).

Lines 455—482.

See Rev. xxi. 2.

Lines 482—490.

If the earthly Zion is "an eternal excellency" (Isa. lx. 14, 15), and the holy land of promise is "an everlasting possession" secured by an everlasting covenant to Abraham and his seed (Gen. xvii. 7, 8), may we not humbly from analogy infer that other terrestrial localities likewise will be recognized?

Lines 491—500.

See Isa. xlix. 19, 20.

Lines 501—513.

"The earth shall be filled with the knowledge of the glory of the Lord, as the waters cover the sea" (Hab. ii. 14).

Lines 514—525.

See Rev. xxi. 3.

Lines 526—545.

"And the nations" ["of them which are saved," these words are omitted in the best MSS.] "shall walk in the light of it" (Rev. xxi. 24).

Lines 546—569.

Compare Isa. lxvi. 24 with the solemn revelations of the end of the ungodly introduced once and again amid the glories of the eternal kingdom (Rev. xxi. 8. 27; xxii. 15).

Lines 570—598.

"Ye shall know that I have not done without cause all that I have done in it, saith the Lord God" (Ezek. xiv. 23).

Lines 599—633.

For the proof from Holy Scripture that the human family, when sin and death are for ever overcome, shall go on multiplying its blessed generations without end, these notes are too limited to afford space. I must refer to the abundant evidence collated, in Birks' "*Daniel*," Vol. i., ch. xvi., and in his "Outlines of Unfulfilled Prophecy," ch. xv.; and also to a most thoughtful and suggestive work, recently published, Shepheard's Tree of Life. This we may well believe, that whereas it is recorded "God formed the earth and made it, He created it not in vain, He formed it to be inhabited" (Isa. xlv. 18), the same untiring Goodness will in His own time people with intelligent worshippers the countless orbs of the heavens. Of the whole ransomed Church we are assured it is but "a kind of firstfruits of His creature" (James i. 18). The illimitable harvest is yet to be gathered in. May our hearts only be in unison with the inspired doxology (Eph. iii. 20, 21), "Now unto Him that is able to do exceeding abundantly above all that we can ask or think, according to the power that worketh in us, unto Him be glory in the Church by Christ Jesus unto all the generations of the age of the ages! Amen."

Cambridge: Press of John Wilson and Son.

530, BROADWAY, NEW YORK,
May 1, 1870.

ROBERT CARTER & BROTHERS'

NEW BOOKS.

Now Complete,

DR. HANNA'S LIFE OF CHRIST.

I. EARLIER YEARS.	V. THE LAST DAY OF OUR
II. MINISTRY IN GALILEE.	LORD'S PASSION.
III. CLOSE OF THE MINISTRY.	VI. FORTY DAYS AFTER THE
IV. PASSION WEEK.	RESURRECTION.

6 vols. 12mo, uniform.   Price $1.50 per volume.

" They are fine instances of restrained imagination. They keep within historical bounds and the limits of critical interpretation, and yet make the persons and events real and life-like. They never overstep the exactness of critical scholarship, nor the reverence of true faith. Nothing of importance is omitted: the finer and more obscure traits are caught, and yet nothing doubtful or exaggerated is imparted." — *Baptist Monthly.*

" The exceeding grace of the style will charm the reader, while the thoroughly Evangelical spirit will commend it to all Christian readers." — *American Presbyterian Review.*

KITTO'S BIBLE ILLUSTRATIONS.

At half price.   The 8 vols. in 4.   Cloth, $7.00; half calf, $12.00.

" The work is almost indispensable to a minister or Sabbath-school teacher. It covers the whole Bible ground, from Eden to Patmos, and paints in a grand panorama of beauty the majesty and wonders of the Word. It is a treasury of illustration on all Scripture themes."

DR. McCOSH'S LOGIC.

12mo. $1.50.

" Although a compend of dry logic, it is by no means a dry book. It is full of thoughtful analysis. Its illustrations are drawn from every branch of study." — *Scottish American.*

*** *Any of these books sent by mail, postage prepaid, on receipt of the price.*

MEMOIR OF THE REV. WM. C. BURNS. By
the Rev. ISLAY BURNS, D.D. Crown 8vo, gilt top. $2.50.

" The most apostolic ministry, in our judgment, that the church has seen since the apostolic days, was the ministry of the Rev. Wm. C. Burns. He crossed oceans, learned strange languages, lived a solitary life, endured hardness as a good soldier of Jesus Christ, and made full proof of his ministry. Such characters and lives are rare, but they are needful for the instruction of the Church." — *Presbyterian.*

LIFE OF JAMES HAMILTON, D.D. By the Rev.
Dr. ARNOT. Crown 8vo, gilt top. $2.50.

" Of Arnot's biography it is enough to say, in one word, it is *exquisitely done.* There is not a syllable of needless eulogy, and no lumber-pile of gossiping epistles about nothing to mere nobodies. The book paints Hamilton ' to the life,' from his early childhood in Strathblane to the close of his remarkable career of study and toil in London." — *Rev. T. L. Cuyler, in the Evangelist.*

YESTERDAY, TO-DAY, AND FOREVER. A
Poem in Twelve Books. By Rev. E. H. BICKERSTETH. 12mo. $2.00.

" The most simple, the richest, and the most perfect sacred poem which recent days have produced." — *London Morning Advertiser.*

THE SPIRIT OF LIFE; OR, SCRIPTURE TESTI-
MONY TO THE DIVINE PERSON AND WORK OF THE HOLY GHOST. By Rev. E. H. BICKERSTETH. $1.25.

" This is an able and exhaustive work, bearing the marks of scholarship and genius." — *Herald and Presbyterian.*

D'AUBIGNÉ'S HISTORIES. 10 vols.
I. THE HISTORY OF THE REFORMATION IN THE SIXTEENTH CENTURY. By J. H. MERLE D'AUBIGNÉ, D.D. 5 vols. 12mo. $6.00.
II. HISTORY OF THE REFORMATION IN THE TIME OF CAL-VIN. Being a Sequel to the first work. 5 vols. $10.

" Dr. Merle's great work enchains the attention of the reader by its graphic and life-like style and its dramatic representations of actors and events. The historical romances of Walter Scott are hardly more absorbing in interest than are these volumes of D'Aubigné; while the latter, unlike the former, are conscientiously faithful chronicles of events, the influence of which is daily felt throughout the modern civilized world."– *Rev. Dr. Ray Palmer.*

RYLE'S NOTES ON JOHN. Vol. II. $1.50.

" In these brief and familiar comments we find combined with the fruits of the author's critical study of the Scriptures, that fervent piety, earnest love for souls, and directness of address to the heart and conscience, which have rendered his writings so deservedly popular." — *Presbyterian.*

THE DAY DAWN AND THE RAIN, AND OTHER
SERMONS. By the Rev. JOHN KER. $2.00.

" We have not seen a volume of sermons for many a day which will so thoroughly repay both purchase and perusal and reperusal. And not the least merit of these sermons is, that they are very suggestive." — *Contemporary Review.*

** Any of these books sent by mail, postage prepaid, on receipt of the price.

REMOVING MOUNTAINS: Life Lessons from the Gospels. By Prof. J. S. Hart. $1.25.

"The author, who is an accomplished writer, here gives us some of the ripe fruits of his thoughtful study of the sacred narrative. It is a book that Christian readers will highly prize, and from which they will derive much spiritual nourishment." — *Christian Intelligencer.*

SORROW. By the Rev. John Reid. 12mo. $2.00

"Many who have tasted grief—and who has not?—will find in these eloquent pages much that will soothe and strengthen their hearts." — *Watchman and Reflector.*

TALES FROM ALSACE. 16mo. $1.50.

"We have read nothing finer in the line of literature to which it belongs. The pictures of Christian faith, patience, and heroism are exquisitely drawn. The style is clear, animated, and singularly captivating." — *Dr. Palmer.*

BONAR'S BIBLE THOUGHTS AND THEMES.

Old Testament . . . $2.00	Acts, &c. $2.00
Gospels 2.00	

"This is a collection of condensed riches of Bible truth. The author has walked in the fields of the Old and New Testaments and gathered a harvest of ripe fruits, which he spreads invitingly for the Christian reader. The volumes are beautifully printed on toned paper."

GOD IS LOVE; or, Glimpses of the Father's Infinite Affection for His People. 16mo. $1.25.

"One of the most prolific and vigorous public writers of the day." — *British Standard.*

KRUMMACHER'S AUTOBIOGRAPHY. 8vo. $3.00.

"The style of the work is animated, fresh, and familiar. The picture of his early domestic life is homely, and yet strikingly beautiful." — *American Presbyterian.*

WORDS OF COMFORT for Parents Bereaved of Little Children. By William Logan. $1.25.

"Never before, at least in this country, has love intertwined so lovely and so sweet a wreath—a true *Immortelle*—to lay on the grave of departed childhood." — *Evangelical Repository.*

THE EMPTY CRIB. A Book of Consolation. By the Rev. T. L. Cuyler. $1.00.

"This beautiful volume will find a welcome in many a household in which loved ones, touched by 'God's finger,' have fallen asleep." — *Independent.*
"A real gem; the outpouring of a stricken parent's sorrows into the very bosom of the Saviour." — *Christian Advocate.*

BIBLE WONDERS. By Rev. Dr. Newton. $1.25.

BUSY BEES in Margaret Russel's School. 1.25.

A BRAID OF CORDS. A Tale. By A. L. O. E. 18mo. 90 cents.

** *Any of these books sent by mail, postage prepaid, on receipt of the price.*

THE BESSIE BOOKS. 6 vols. in a box. $7.50.
The vols. are also sold separately at $1.25 each.

I. SEASIDE.
II. IN THE CITY.
III. FRIENDS.

IV. MOUNTAINS.
V. AT SCHOOL.
VI. TRAVELS.

"Most decidedly *juvenile*, and yet so true to nature, so lively, winsome, and insrtuctive, that both old and young will be charmed with their simplicity, and richly rewarded by their lessons. Really, it makes the heart younger, warmer, better, to bathe it afresh in such familiar, natural scenes, where benevolence of most practical and blessed utility is seen developing itself, from first to last, in such delightful symmetry and completeness as may, and we hope will, secure many imitators." — *Watchman and Reflector.*

LILY'S LESSON. By JOANNA H. MATHEWS, author
of the "Bessie Books." 75 cents.

THE GOLDEN CAP. By J. DE LIEFDE. 9 illustrations. $1.25.

"Taking the illustrations and the stories together, this is one of the best books for youth that has been issued for a long time. Our young folks have literally devoured its contents."

LITTLE EFFIE'S HOME. By the author of "Bertie Lee," "Donald Fraser," &c. 4 illustrations. $1.25.

"Little Effie loses her parents by the foundering of the ship in which they were passengers, but is herself washed ashore, and is found and tenderly cared for by a family who live near the coast. They are simple, God-fearing people, who adopt her as a daughter, and the account of their efforts to do good among their neighbors, and the success which they meet, fills a large portion of the book." — *American Literary Gazette.*

"This story is very gracefully told." — *Presbyterian.*

BUTTERFLY'S FLIGHTS. By the author of the "Win and Wear" Series. 6 vols. in a box. $4.50. The volumes are *not* sold separately.

I. MOUNT MANSFIELD.
II. SARATOGA.
III. NIAGARA.

IV. MONTREAL.
V. SEA SIDE.
IV. PHILADELPHIA.

"These six volumes, put up in a neat box, bound in uniform style, and giving the experiences of a bright, buoyant, restless, inquisitive, radiant, and chattering little lady of ten years, with a great deal about other people, and the interesting things at the various places visited, will be found full of zest and overflowing with animal spirits. There is no hope that people who demand dull, solemn, straight-laced books can be made to approve these breezy, bubbling volumes; and whoever is afraid of having the little people become too interested in books to be willing to break off in the middle of a cnapter and go to bed at eight o'clock had better keep this box of books out of the house. But they who wish to combine wholesome lessons of life with the pleasantest sort of literary entertainment for the children, may be sure of finding what they are looking for in 'Butterfly's Flights.'" — *Morning Star.*

OUR FATHER IN HEAVEN. By the Rev. J. H.
WILSON. Illustrated. $1.25.

⁎⁎ *Any of these books sent by mail, postage prepaid, on receipt of the price.*

CPSIA information can be obtained
at www.ICGtesting.com
Printed in the USA
LVHW100017181022
730905LV00003B/175